THE MOON ROCK

By

ARTHUR J. REES

Double 9
BOOKS

The Moon Rock

by Arthur J. Rees

Copyright © 2024

ISBN: 978-93-58595-25-3

Published by

DOUBLE 9 BOOKS

2/13-B, Ansari Road, Daryaganj
New Delhi – 110002
info@double9books.com
www.double9books.com
Tel. 011-40042856

ABOUT THE AUTHOR

Australian mystery author Arthur John Rees (1872-1942) was born in Australia. He was a Melbourne native who briefly worked for the Melbourne Age before switching to the New Zealand Herald. He most likely traveled to England in his early 20s. In the preface to Great Short fiction of Detection, Mystery, and Horror, 1928, Dorothy Sayers attests to his skill as a writer of crime-mystery fiction. Two of his pieces were included in a detective story anthology published in the United States. His writings have been translated into German and French, respectively. He most likely visited Europe in his early 20s and spent some time living in England. His books frequently take place in English locales.

CONTENTS

Chapter I..7

Chapter II 10

Chapter III...15

Chapter IV..24

Chapter V 31

Chapter VI..36

Chapter VII 39

Chapter VIII...44

Chapter IX..48

Chapter X 55

Chapter XI..62

Chapter XII 69

Chapter XIII...79

Chapter XIV...86

Chapter XV 92

Chapter XVI..102

Chapter XVII 109

Chapter XVIII 118

Chapter XIX..125

Chapter XX 131

Chapter XXI..139

Chapter XXII 148

Chapter XXIII 158

Chapter XXIV...165

Chapter XXV 175

Chapter XXVI...184

Chapter XXVII..194

Chapter XXVIII 204

Chapter XXIX...217

Chapter XXX 225

Chapter XXXI...232

Chapter XXXII..245

Chapter XXXIII 250

Chapter XXXIV 255

Chapter I

The voice of the clergyman intoned the last sad hope of humanity, the final prayer was said, and the mourners turned away, leaving Mrs. Turold to take her rest in a bleak Cornish churchyard among strangers, far from the place of her birth and kindred.

The fact would not have troubled her if she had known. In life she had been a nonentity; in death she was not less. At least she could now mix with her betters without reproach, free (in the all-enveloping silence) from the fear of betraying her humble origin. Debrett's Peerage was unimportant in the grave; breaches of social etiquette passed unnoticed there; the wagging of malicious tongues was stopped by dust.

Her husband lingered at the grave-side after the others had departed. As he stood staring into the open grave, regardless of a lurking grave-digger waiting to fill it, he looked like a man whose part in the drama of life was Care. There was no hint of happiness in his long narrow face, dull sunken eyes, and bloodless compressed lips. His expression was not that of one unable to tear himself away from the last glimpse of a loved wife fallen from his arms into the clutch of Death. It was the gaze of one immersed in anxious thought.

The mourners, who had just left the churchyard, awaited him by a rude stone cross near the entrance to the church. There were six—four men, a woman, and a girl. In the road close by stood the motor-car which had brought them to the churchyard in the wake of the hearse, glistening incongruously in the grey Cornish setting of moorland and sea.

The girl stood a little apart from the others. She was the daughter of the dead woman, but her head was turned away from the churchyard, and her sorrowful glance dwelt on the distant sea. The contour of her small face was perfect as a flower or gem, and colourless except for vivid scarlet lips and dark eyes gleaming beneath delicate dark brows. She was very young—not more than twenty—but in the soft lines of her beauty there was a suggestion of character beyond her years. Her face was dreamy and wayward, and almost gipsy in type. There was something rather disconcerting in the contrast between her air of inexperienced youth and the sombre intensity of her dark eyes, which seemed mature and disillusioned, like those of an older person. The slim lines of her figure had the lissome development of a girl who spent her days out of doors.

She stood there motionless, apparently lost in meditation, indifferent to the bitter wind which was driving across the moors with insistent force.

"Put this on, Sisily."

Sisily turned with a start. Her aunt, a large stout woman muffled in heavy furs, was standing behind her, holding a wrap in her hand.

"You'll catch your death of cold, child, standing here in this thin dress," the elder lady continued. "Why didn't you wear your coat? You'd be warmer sitting in the car. It's really very selfish of Robert, keeping us all waiting in this dreadful wind!" She shivered, and drew her furs closer. "Why doesn't he come away? As if it could do any good!"

As she spoke the tall form of Robert Turold was seen approaching through the rank grass and mouldering tombstones with a quick stride. He emerged from the churchyard gate with a stern and moody face.

"Let us get home," he said, and his words were more of a command than request.

He walked across the road to the car with his sister and daughter. The men by the cross followed. They were his brother, his brother's son, his sister's husband, and the local doctor, whose name was Ravenshaw. With a clang and a hoot the car started on the return journey. The winding cobbled street of the churchtown was soon left behind for a road which struck across the lonely moors to the sea. Through the moors and stony hills the car sped until it drew near a solitary house perched on the edge of the dark cliffs high above the tumbling waters of the yeasty sea which foamed at their base.

The car stopped by the gate where the moor road ended. The mourners alighted and entered the gate. Their approach was observed from within, for as they neared the house the front door was opened by an elderly man-servant with a brown and hawk-beaked face.

Walking rapidly ahead Robert Turold led the way into a front sitting-room lighted by a window overlooking the sea. There was an air of purpose in his movements, but an appearance of strain in his careworn face and twitching lips. He glanced at the others in a preoccupied way, but started perceptibly as his eye fell upon his daughter.

"There is no need for you to remain, Sisily," he said in a harsh dry voice.

Sisily turned away without speaking. Her cousin Charles jumped up to open the door, and the two exchanged a glance as she went out. The young man then returned to his seat near the window. Robert Turold was speaking emphatically to Dr. Ravenshaw, answering some objection which the doctor had raised.

"... No, no, Ravenshaw—I want you to be present. You will oblige me by remaining. I will go upstairs and get the documents. I shall not keep you long. Thalassa, serve refreshments."

He left the room quickly, as though to avoid further argument. The elderly serving-man busied himself by setting out decanters and glasses, then went out like one who considered his duty done, leaving the company to wait on themselves.

Chapter II

The group in the room sat in silence with an air of stiff expectation. The members of the family knew they were not assembled to pay respect to the memory of the woman who had just been buried. Her husband had regarded her as a drag upon him, and did not consider her removal an occasion for the display of hypocritical grief. Rather was it to be regarded as an act of timely intervention on the part of Death, who for once had not acted as marplot in human affairs.

They were there to listen to the story of the triumph of the head of the family, Robert Turold. Most families have some common source of interest and pride. It may be a famous son, a renowned ancestor, a faded heirloom, even a musical daughter. The pride of the Turold family rested on the belief that they were of noble blood—the lineal inheritors of a great English title which had fallen into abeyance hundreds of years before.

Robert Turold had not been content to boast of his nobility and die a commoner like his father and grandfather before him. His intense pride demanded more than that. As a boy he had pored over the crabbed parchments in the family deed-box which indicated but did not record the family descent, and he had vowed to devote his life to prove the descent and restore the ancient title of Turrald of Missenden to the Turolds of which he was the head.

There was not much to go upon when he commenced the labour of thirty years—merely a few old documents, a family tradition, and the similarity of name. And the Turolds were poor. Money, and a great deal of it, was needed for the search, in the first instance, of the unbroken line of descent, and for the maintenance of the title afterwards if the claim was completely established. But Robert Turold was not to be deterred by obstacles, however great. He was a man with a single idea, and such men are hard to baulk in the long run.

He left England in early manhood and remained away for some years. His family understood that he had gone to seek a fortune in the wilds of the earth. He reappeared—a saturnine silent man—as suddenly as he had gone away. In his wanderings he had gained a fortune but partly lost the use of one eye. The partial loss of an eye did not matter much in a country like England, where most people have two eyes and very little money, and therefore pay more respect to wealth than vision.

Robert Turold invested his money, and then set to work upon his great ambition with the fierce restlessness which characterized all his proceedings in life. He married shortly after his return. He soon came to the conclusion that his marriage was a great mistake—the greatest mistake of his life. His wife had borne him two girls. The first died in infancy, and some years later Sisily was born. His regrets increased with the birth of a second daughter. He wanted a son to succeed him in the title—when he gained it. Time passed, and he became enraged. His anger crushed the timid woman who shared his strange lot. His dominating temperament and moody pride were too much for her gentle soul. She became desperately afraid of him and his stern ways, of that monomania which kept them wandering through the country searching for links in a [pedigree] which had to be traced back for hundreds of years before Robert Turold could grasp his heart's desire.

When She died in the house on the cliffs where they had come six months before, Robert Turold had accomplished the task to which his life had been devoted. Some weeks before he had summoned his brother from London to disclose his future plans. The brothers had not met for many years, but Austin was quick to obey when he learnt that a fortune and a title were at stake. The sister and her husband, Mr. and Mrs. Pendleton, had reached Cornwall two days before the funeral. They were to take Sisily back to London with them. It was Robert Turold's intention to part with his daughter and place her in his sister's charge. For a reason he had not yet divulged, Sisily was to have no place in his brilliant future. He disliked his daughter. Her sex was a fatal bar to his regard. He had heaped so many reproaches on her mother for bringing another girl into the world that the poor woman had descended to the grave with a confused idea that she was to blame.

Sisily had a strange nature, reticent, yet tender. She had loved her mother passionately, and feared and hated her father because he had treated his wife so harshly. She had been the witness of it all—from her earliest childhood to the moment when the unhappy woman had died with her eyes fixed on her husband's implacable face, but holding fast to her daughter's hand, as though she wanted to carry the pressure of those loving fingers into the grave.

A clock on the mantel-piece ticked loudly. But it was the only sound which disturbed the quietness of the room. The representatives of the family eyed one another with guarded indifference. Circumstances had kept them apart for many years, and they now met almost as strangers.

Mrs. Pendleton sat on a sofa with her husband. She was a notable outline of a woman, large and massive, with a shrewd capable face and a middle-class mind. She lived, when at home, in the rarefied atmosphere of Golders Green, in a red house with a red-tiled roof, one of a streetful similarly afflicted, where she kept two maids and had a weekly reception day. She was childless, but she disdained to carry a pet dog as compensation for barrenness. Her husband was a meagre shrimp of a stockbroker under his wife's control, who golfed on Sundays and played auction bridge at his club twice a week with cyclic regularity. He and his wife had little in common except the habit of living together, which had made them acquainted with each other's ways.

Mrs. Pendleton had not seen either of her brothers for a long time. Robert had been too engrossed in digging into the past for the skeletons of his ancestors to do more than write intermittent letters to the living members of his family, acquainting them with the progress of his search. Austin Turold, Robert's younger brother, had spent a portion of his life in India and had but recently returned. He had gone there more than twenty years before to fill a Government post, taking with him his young wife, but leaving his son at school in England for some years. His wife had languished and died beneath an Indian sun, but her husband had become acclimatized, and remained until his time was up and he was free to return to England with a pension. His sister and he met on the previous day for the first time since he had left England for India, and Mrs. Pendleton had some difficulty in identifying the elderly and testy Anglo-Indian with the handsome young brother who had bade her farewell so many years before. And, she had even more difficulty in recognizing the fair-haired little boy of that time in the good-looking but rather moody-faced young man who at the present moment was seated near the window, staring out of it.

The fifth member of the party was Dr. Ravenshaw, who practised in the churchtown where Mrs. Turold had been buried, and had attended her in her illness.

But he had not been asked to share in the family council on that account. His presence was due to his intimacy with Robert Turold, which had commenced soon after the latter's arrival in Cornwall. The claimant for a title had found in the churchtown doctor an antiquarian after his own heart, whose wide knowledge of Cornish antiquities had assisted in the discovery of the last piece of evidence necessary to establish his claim.

Dr. Ravenshaw sat a little apart from the other, a thickset grey figure of a man, with eyes reddened as though by excessive reading, and usually protected by glasses, which just then he had removed in order to polish them with his handkerchief. In age he was sixty or more. His thick grey beard was mingled with white, and the heavy moustache which drooped over his mouth was quite white. He presented a common-place figure in his rough worn tweeds and heavy boots, but he was a man of intelligence in spite of his unassuming exterior. He lived alone, cared for by a single servant, and he covered on foot a scattered practice among the fishing population of that part of the coast. His knowledge of Cornish antiquities and heraldic lore had won him the confidence of Robert Turold, and his kindness to Mrs. Turold in her illness had gained him the gratitude of her daughter Sisily.

It was Austin Turold who caused a diversion in this group of lay figures by walking to the table and helping himself to a whisky-and-soda. Austin bore very little resemblance to his grim and dominant elder brother. He had a slight frail figure, very carefully dressed, and one of those thin-lipped faces which seem, to wear a perpetual sneer of superiority over commoner humanity. The movements of his white hands, the inflection of his voice, the double eyeglass which dangled from his vest by a ribbon of black silk, revealed the type of human being which considers itself something rarer and finer than its fellows. The thin face, narrow white forehead, and high-bridged nose might have belonged to an Oxford don or fashionable preacher, but, apart from these features, Austin Turold had nothing in common with such earnest souls. By temperament he was a dilettante and cynic, who affected not to take life seriously. His axiom of faith was that a good liver was the one thing in life worth having, and a far more potent factor in human affairs than conscience. He had at one time regarded his brother Robert as a fool and visionary, but had seen fit to change that opinion latterly.

He paused in the act of raising his glass to his lips, and looked over the silent company as though seeking a convivial companion. His son was still staring out of the window. The little stockbroker, seated on the sofa beside his large wife, made a deprecating movement of his eyebrows, as though entreating not to be asked. Austin's cold glance roved to Dr. Ravenshaw.

"Doctor," he said, "let me give you a whisky-and-soda."

Doctor Ravenshaw shook his head. "I have a patient to visit before dark," he said, "a lady. I do not care to carry the smell of spirits into a sick-room."

"But this is a special occasion, Ravenshaw," persisted the other. "We do not restore a title every day."

"Austin!" The voice of Mrs. Pendleton sounded from the sofa in shocked protest.

"What's the matter?" said Austin, pausing in the act of pouring some whisky into a glass.

"It would be exceedingly improper to drink a toast at such a moment."

"What's the matter with the moment?"

"The day, then. Just when we have buried poor Alice." Mrs. Pendleton had not seen her brother's wife for ten years before her death, but she had no difficulty in bringing tears to her eyes at the recollection of her. She dried her eyes with her handkerchief, and added in a different tone: "I fancy Robert is coming."

A heavy step was heard descending the stairs. Austin drained his glass, and Dr. Ravenshaw adjusted his spectacles as Robert Turold entered the room.

Chapter III

With parchments and papers deep on the table before him, Robert Turold plunged into the history of his life's task. The long hand of the mantelpiece clock slipped with a stealthy movement past the twelve as he commenced, as though determined not to be taken by surprise, but to keep abreast of him.

An hour passed, but Robert Turold kept steadily on. His hearers displayed symptoms of boredom like people detained in church beyond the usual time. Humanity is interested in achievement, but not in the manner of its accomplishment. And Robert's brother and sister knew much of his story by heart. It had formed the sole theme of his letters to them for many years past. Mrs. Pendleton's thoughts wandered to afternoon tea. Her husband nodded with closed eyes, and recovered himself with convulsive starts. Austin Turold fixed his glance on the ceiling, where a solitary fly was cleaning its wings with its legs. From the window Charles Turold presented an immobile profile. Only Dr. Ravenshaw seemed to listen with an interest which never flagged.

Yet it was a story well worth hearing, that record of indomitable pertinacity which had refused to be baulked by years or rebuffs. Men have acquired titles more easily. That was apparent as Robert Turold related the history of his long and patient investigation; of scents which had led nowhere; of threads which had broken in his hand; of fruitless burrowings into the graves of past generations. These disappointments had lengthened the search, but they had never baffled the searcher nor broken his faith.

The story began in the fourteenth century, when the second Edward had summoned his trusty retainer Robert Turrald from his quiet home in leafy Buckinghamshire to sit in Parliament as a baron, and by that act of kingly grace ennobled him and his heirs forever. Successive holders of the title were summoned to Parliament in their turn until the reign of the seventh Henry, when one succeeded whose wife brought him three daughters, but no sons. At his death the title went into abeyance among this plurality of girls. In peerage law they were his coheirs, and the inheritance could not descend because not one of them had an exclusive right to it. The daughters entered a convent and followed their parents to the grave within a few years, the Crown resumed the estate, and the title had remained in abeyance ever since.

But the last Lord Turrald had a brother Simon, a roystering blade and lawless adventurer, who disappeared some years before his elder brother's death. Little was known of him except that he was supposed to have closed a brawling career on the field of Bosworth, when Richard the Crookback was killed and the short-lived dynasty of York ended.

The Turolds' family deed-box told a different story. There was a manuscript in monkish hand, setting forth, "in the name of God, Amen," the secret history of Simon, as divulged by him on his deathbed for the information of his two sons. In this confession he claimed kinship with the last Lord Turrald of Great Missenden. But he had not dared to claim the title and rich estates on his brother's death, because he was a proscribed man. He had been a Yorkist, and had fought for Richard. That might have been forgiven him if he had not unhorsed his future king at Bosworth and almost succeeded in slaughtering him with his own reckless hands. So he had fled, and had remained in obscurity and a safe hiding-place after his brother's death, preferring his head without a title to a title without a head.

On this document, unsigned and undated, with nothing to indicate the place of its origin, the Turold family based its claim of descent from the baronial Turralds of Great Missenden. But the Turold history was a chequered one. Their branch was nomadic, without territorial ties or wealth, without continuance of chronology. They could not trace their own genealogy back for two hundred years. There was a great gap of missing generations which had never been filled in. It was not even known how the document had come into their possession. Simon's two sons and their descendants had vanished into unknown graves, leaving no trace. But the family clung fast to their belief that they were the lineal descendants of the Turralds of Buckinghamshire.

It had remained for Robert Turold to prove it. His father and grandfather had bragged of it, had fabricated family trees over their cups, and glowed with pride over their noble blood, but had let it go at that. Robert was a man of different mould. In his hands, the slender supposition had been turned into certainty. By immense labour and research he built a bridge from the first Turold of whom any record existed, backwards across the dark gap of the past. He traced the wanderings of his ancestors through different generations and different counties to Robert Turold, who established himself in Suffolk forty years after the last Lord Turrald was laid to rest in his family vault in the village church of Great Missenden.

The construction of this portion of his family tree occupied Robert Turold for ten years. There were scattered records to be collected, forgotten wills to be sought in county offices, parochial registers to be searched for births and deaths. A nomadic family has no traditions; Robert Turold had to trace his back to the darkness of the Middle Ages. It was a notable feat to trace the wanderings of an obscure family back so far as he did, but even then he seemed as far away from the attainment of his desire as ever. There remained a gap of forty years. To establish his claim to the title he had to prove that the Turolds sprang from the younger brother of the last Lord Turrald, who had allowed the title to lapse for fear of losing his head if he came forward to claim it.

It did not seem a great gap to bridge after following a wandering scent through four centuries, but the paltry forty years almost beat Robert Turold, and cost him five years additional search. It was a lucky chance, no more, which finally led him to Cornwall, but it was the hand of Providence (he said so) which directed his footsteps to the churchtown in which Dr. Ravenshaw lived. It was there he discovered the connecting link in the signature of a single witness on a noble charter which granted to the monks of St. Nicholas "all wreck of sea which might happen in the Scilly Isles except whales." To the eye of Robert Turold's faith the illegible scrawl on this faded scroll formed the magic name of Simon Turrald.

For once, faith was justified by its works. The signature was indeed Simon Turrald's; not the younger brother of the last Lord Turrald, but Simon's son.

Bit by bit, Robert Turold succeeded in fitting together the last pieces of the puzzle which had eluded him for so long. Simon Turrald, the brother, had fled to Cornwall, where he had married a Cornishwoman who had brought him two sons. The elder, Simon, had taken religious vows, and established a priory at St. Fair, a branch of the great priory of St. Germain. The holy fathers of the order had long since vanished from this earth to reap the reward of their goodness (it is to be hoped) in another world, but the remains of the priory still stood on a barren headland near Cape Cornwall. And there was a tomb in St. Fair church, behind the altar, marked by a blue slab, with an indent formerly filled by a recumbent figure. On the blue slab was a partly obliterated inscription in monkish Latin, which yielded its secret to him, and divulged that the remains beneath were those of Father Simon of St. Fair.

With this important discovery to help him, Robert Turold had very little difficulty in completing the particulars of the family genealogy. Further search of the churchtown records brought to light that Simon's other son, Robert, left Cornwall as a young man, and after some years of wandering had settled in Suffolk. Father Simon, of course, died without family, but Robert married, the family name came to be spelt "Turold," and thus was founded that branch of the family of which the last Robert Turold was now the head. The family tree was complete.

Such was the substance of Robert Turold's life quest, and the story had occupied two hours in telling.

"I have petitioned the King's most excellent majesty to terminate the abeyance in my favour and declare that I am entitled to the peerage," he concluded. "I have no doubt that my claim will be admitted. I have set out the facts with great care, and in considerable detail. I have traced a clear line of descent back to Simon Turrald, younger brother of the last baron, and there are no coheirs in existence. Ours is the last surviving branch, or it would, perhaps, be better if I said that Austin and myself, and Austin's son, are the only male members of the family. It is a difficult matter to give effectual proof of a long pedigree, but my lawyer has not the least doubt that the House of Lords will admit the validity of my claim, and will terminate the abeyance in my favour. The Attorney General has inspected my proofs, and I am to appear before the Committee for Privileges next week. In a few weeks at the outside, allowing for the worst of law's delays, I shall be Lord Turrald."

Robert Turold's whole bearing was transfigured as he made this announcement. His sound eye gleamed, his shrunken form seemed to expand and fill, and his harsh sallow features took on an expression which was almost ecstatic. It was his great moment, the moment for which he had lived for twenty years, and it compensated him for all his worry, delayed expectation, fruitless labour, and the bitter taste of the waters of despair.

"I shall be Turrald of Great Missenden," he said, and again the expression of his face showed what the words meant to him.

"Bob! So you've actually succeeded after all!" Mrs. Pendleton stepped quickly across to her brother as he sat regarding his audience from behind his pile of documents. It was like a sister, at that moment, to slip back to the juvenile name and kiss his elderly face with tears in her eyes. Robert Turold received the caress unmoved, and she went back to the sofa.

"Lord Turrald! It sounds well," murmured her husband, whose ideas were sufficiently democratic to give him a sneaking admiration for a title. He gazed at his brother-in-law with a new respect, discerning unsuspected indications of noble blood in his grim visage.

"How do you account for the two forms of spelling your family name?" observed Dr. Ravenshaw. "The House of Lords will require proof on that point, will they not?"

"I shall be able to satisfy them," returned Robert Turold. "The first Robert Turold reverted to the Norman spelling when he settled in Suffolk. Turrald is the corrupted form, doubtless due to early Saxon difficulties with Norman names. The Saxons were never very glib at Norman-French, and there was no standardized spelling of family names at that period."

"It would be interesting to know how the name of Simon came to be bestowed upon the Simon Turrald who fled to Cornwall after Bosworth. The name is Biblical—not Norman. The Normans were pagan, worshipping Woden and Thor, though supposed to be Christianized after Charles the Simple ceded Neustria to Rollo."

"Simon was a good mediaeval name in France and was fairly common in England from the twelfth century until after the Reformation. It was Norman, as being that of an apostle, and was never popular among the Puritans."

"It seems a pity that you cannot claim the Turrald estates," put in Austin. "They must have been immensely wealthy."

"It is quite out of the question," replied Robert decisively. "They have been alienated for centuries. But it has been part of my life's work to provide for the upkeep of the title when I gained it. I shall be able to ensure my heirs an income of nearly eight thousand pounds a year."

It was Mrs. Pendleton's first intimation of the amount of the fortune her brother had gained abroad. "Eight thousand a year!" she exclaimed. "Oh, Robert, it is wealth."

"One could live very comfortably on eight thousand a year," remarked her husband, "very comfortably indeed."

"It's not much to support a title, after the tax-gatherers have taken their pound of flesh in income tax and super-tax," said Austin. "Robert, with his iron frame, will probably outlive a weakling like myself, but if he doesn't I'm sure I shall find it difficult to keep up the title on the money."

"One word!" said Dr. Ravenshaw, with a quick glance at Robert Turold. "This is a barony by writ that you are claiming. Does not your daughter succeed you if you gain it, and not your brother?"

"No," replied Robert Turold. "The next holder of the title, after me, will be my brother, and his son will succeed him."

Little Mr. Pendleton looked questioningly at his brother-in-law.

"A similar question was on my lips," he said hesitatingly. "I know very little of such matters, but in view of our family's probable entry into the ranks of the old nobility I have deemed it my duty to make myself acquainted, to some extent, with the history of the Turrald title and peerage law. It seems a very complicated business—peerage law, I mean—in the case of baronies by writ, but I certainly gathered the impression that a sole daughter can succeed, although several daughters are regarded as coheirs."

"My daughter cannot succeed to the Turrald title," rejoined Robert Turold. The words seemed to be wrung out of him reluctantly.

"It is not for me to question your knowledge—your great knowledge—of English peerage law, Robert," pursued Mr. Pendleton with a kind of timid persistence. "But I brought a book down with me in the train in which I remember reading that the right of a single daughter to succeed to a barony by writ had been well established by the Clifton case and several others. I am not precisely aware what the Clifton case is, but I've no doubt that you are well versed in the particulars of it. As you have no son your daughter has priority of claim over your brother and his son. From what you say I can see that I must be quite wrong, but I'd be glad if you would explain to me."

"You have stated the law accurately enough," said Robert Turold, "but my daughter does not succeed to the title."

"Why not?"

Embarrassment, perceptible as a cloud, deepened on Robert Turold's face. He regained his self-control with an effort.

"There was an informality in my marriage," said he at last. "My daughter's birth was irregular."

"Do you mean that she is illegitimate?" asked Dr. Ravenshaw.

Robert Turold inclined his head. "Yes," he said.

At this admission his sister bounced from the sofa with a startled cry. "So that was why there was no name plate on the coffin," she exclaimed. "Oh, Robert, what a terrible thing—what a disgrace!"

"Spare me your protests until you have heard the explanation," Robert coldly rejoined. "She"—he pointed a hand in the direction of the churchyard—"was married before she met me. She kept the fact from me. It was apparently a secret passage in her life. During our long association together she gave no hint of it. She confessed the truth on her deathbed. In justice to her memory let me say that she believed her husband dead."

Robert Turold told this with unmoved face in barest outline—etched in dry-point, as it were—leaving his hearers to fill in the picture of the unhappy woman who had gone through life tormented by the twin demons of conscience and fear, which had overtaken her and brought her down before she could reach the safe shelter of the grave.

Mrs. Pendleton, whose robust mind had scant patience with the policy of cowardice which dictates death-bed confessions, regretted that Alice, having remained silent so long, had not kept silence altogether.

"You do not intend to make this scandal public, Robert?" she said anxiously.

"I am compelled to do so," was the gloomy response.

"Is it necessary?" she pleaded. "Cannot the story be kept quiet—if not for Alice's sake, at least for Sisily's? You must consider her above all things. She is your daughter, your only child."

"I agree with Aunt," said Charles Turold. He rose from the window-seat and approached the table. "Sisily must be your first consideration," he said, looking at Robert Turold.

"This has nothing to do with you, Charles," interposed Austin hastily.

"I think it has," said his son. "You told me nothing about this, you know."

"I was not aware of it myself," replied his father.

"Now that I know, I shall have nothing further to do with this," continued the young man. "I'm not going to help you wrong Sisily."

"I hardly expected such lofty moral sentiments from you," said Austin, with a dark glance.

His son flushed as though there was a hidden sting behind the jibe. He appeared to be about to say something more, but checked himself, and went back to his seat by the window.

"Is there no way of keeping this matter quiet, Robert?" said his sister imploringly.

"I see none," was the rejoinder. "It is a very painful disclosure, but I think it is inevitable. Do you not agree with me, Austin?"

"Do not ask my opinion," his brother coldly replied. "It is for you to decide."

Robert Turold paused irresolutely. "What do you say, Ravenshaw?" he said, glancing round at the silent figure of the doctor. "I asked you to be present this afternoon to have the benefit of your advice. I owe much to you, so I beg you to speak freely."

"Since you have asked my advice," said Dr. Ravenshaw gravely, "I say that I entirely agree with Mrs. Pendleton. Your first duty is to Sisily. She should out-weigh all other considerations. If you make her illegitimacy public you may live to be sorry for having done so."

Mrs. Pendleton cast a moist, grateful glance at the speaker, but Austin Turold turned on him a look of cold hostility.

Robert Turold sat brooding for a few moments in silence. He had asked advice, but his own mind was made up. The humane views of his sister and Dr. Ravenshaw were powerless to affect his decision. The monstrous growth of his single purpose had long since strangled such transient plants as human affection and feeling in his heart and mind.

"The facts must be made public," he said inexorably. "The honour of a noble family is in my hands, and I must do my duty. It would be an insult to my Sovereign and my peers, and a grievous wrong to our family, if I concealed any portion of the truth. I shall make adequate provision for Sisily. You will not refuse to take charge of her, Constance, because of this disclosure?"

"You ought to know me better than that, Robert. She'll need somebody to take care of her, poor child! But who is to tell her the truth? For I suppose she must be told?"

"I want you to tell her," said Robert Turold. "Choose your time. There is no immediate hurry, but she must be in no false hopes about the future. She had better be told before the Investigations Committee meets."

"Bother the Investigations Committee!" exclaimed Mrs. Pendleton. "Really, Robert—"

Mrs. Pendleton broke off abruptly, in something like dismay. She had a fleeting impression of a pair of eyes encountering her own through a crack in the doorway, and as swiftly withdrawn. She walked quickly to the door and flung it open. There was nobody outside, and the passage was empty.

"We have been talking family secrets with the door open," she said, returning to her seat. "I thought I saw one of the servants eavesdropping."

"My servants would not listen at doors," said Robert Turold coldly. "You must have imagined it."

Mrs. Pendleton made no rejoinder. She had a strong belief that someone had been watching and listening, but she could not be sure.

"We must really be going," she announced, with a glance at the clock. "Joseph" —such was her husband's name—"you had better go and see if the car is ready, and I will go for Sisily. Is she upstairs in her room, Robert?"

"I believe so," said Robert Turold, bending abstractedly over his papers. "But you had better ask Thalassa. He'll tell you. Thalassa will know."

Mrs. Pendleton looked angrily at him, but was wise enough to forbear from further speech. She instinctively realized that her brother was beyond argument or reproof.

She went upstairs to look for her niece, but she was not in her room. She came downstairs again and proceeded to the kitchen. Through the half-open door she saw the elderly male servant, and she entered briskly.

"Can you tell me where Miss Sisily is, Thalassa?" she asked.

"Miss Sisily is out on the cliffs." Thalassa, busy chopping suet with a knife, made answer without looking up. There was something absurdly incongruous between the mild domestic occupation and the grim warrior face bent over it.

"When did she go out?" asked Mrs. Pendleton, struck by a sudden thought.

Thalassa threw a swift sidelong glance at her. "It might be an hour ago," he said.

"Do you know where I am likely to find her?"

Thalassa pointed vaguely through an open window.

"Somewhere along there," he said. "Miss Sisily is fond of the cliffs. If you're going to look for her you'd best not go round by the back of the house, or you'll fall over, like as not. It's a savage spot, only fit for savages—or madmen." He turned his back and bent over his chopping board again.

Mrs. Pendleton turned away in perplexity, and walked up the passage to the front door. There her eye fell on the figure of Charles Turold, lounging moodily over the gate, smoking a cigarette.

She walked down the flinty path and touched his arm. "Would you mind going and looking for Sisily?" she said. "She is out on the cliffs, Thalassa says." She pointed a hand in the direction she supposed the girl to be.

The young man's moodiness vanished in eager alacrity. "Certainly," he replied. "I'll go with pleasure." He tossed away his cigarette and disappeared around the side of the house.

Chapter IV

Sisily first opened her eyes on a grey day by a grim coast, and life had always been grim and grey to her. Her memory was a blurred record of wanderings from place to place in pursuit of something which was never to be found. Her earliest recollection was of a bleak eastern coast, where Robert Turold had spent long years in a losing game of patience with the sea. He had gone there in the belief that some of his ancestors were buried in a forgotten churchyard on the cliffs, and he spent his time attempting to decipher inscriptions which had been obliterated almost as effectually as the dead whose remains they extolled.

The old churchyard had been called "The Garden of Rest" by some sentimental versifier, but there was no rest for the dead who tried to sleep within its broken walls. The sea kept undermining the crumbling cliffs upon which it stood, carrying away earth, and tombstones, and bones. Nor was it a garden. Nothing grew in the dank air but crawling things which were horrible to the eye. There were great rank growths of toadstools, yellow, blue, livid white, or spotted like adders, which squirmed and squelched underfoot to send up a sickly odour of decay. The only green thing was some ivy, a parasitic vampire which drew its lifeblood from the mouldering corpse of an old church.

It was in this desolate place that the girl conceived her first impression of her father as a stern and silent man who burrowed among old graves like a mole. Robert Turold had fought a stout battle for the secret contained in those forgotten graves on a bleak headland, but the sea had beaten him in the long run, carrying off the stones piecemeal until only one remained, a sturdy pillar of granite which marked the bones of one who, some hundred and fifty years before had been "An English Gentleman and a Christian" — so much of the epitaph remained. Robert Turold hoped that it was an ancestor, but he was not destined to know. One night the stone was carried off with a great splash which was heard far, and left a ragged gap in the cliffside, like a tooth plucked from a giant's mouth.

When Sisily first saw the cliffs of Cornwall she was reminded of those early days, with the difference that the Cornish granite rocks stood firm, as though saying to the sea, "Here rises England."

The house Robert Turold had taken looked down on the sea from the summit. It was a strange place to build a house, on the brink of a broken Cornish cliffline, above the grey surges of the Atlantic, among a wilderness of dark rocks, facing black moors, which rolled away from the cliffs as lonely and desolate as eternity. The place had been built by a London artist, long since dead, who had lived there and painted seascapes from an upstairs studio which overlooked the sea.

The house had remained empty for years until Robert Turold had taken it six months before. It was too isolated and lonely to gain a permanent tenant, and it stood in the teeth of Atlantic gales. The few scattered houses and farms of the moors cringed from the wind in sheltered depressions, but Flint House faced its everlasting fury on the top of the cliffs, a rugged edifice of grey stone, a landmark visible for many miles.

The house suited Robert Turold well enough, because it was near the churchtown in which he was conducting his final investigations. It never occurred to him to consider whether it suited his wife and daughter. It was a house, and it was furnished; what more was necessary? It was nothing to him if his wife and daughter were unhappy. It was nothing to him if the sea roared and the house shook as he sat poring at nights over his parchments in the dead artist's studio. He had other things to occupy his mind than Nature's brutality or the feelings of womanhood.

Sisily had climbed down to the foot of the rocks. She was sitting in her favourite spot, a spur of rock overhanging a green nook in the broken ugliness of the cliffs, sheltered from the sea by an encircling arm of rock, and reached by a steep path down the cliff. Around her towered an amphitheatre of vast cliffs in which the sea sang loud music to the spirit of solitude. In the moaning waters in front of the cove a jagged rock rose from the incomparable green, tilted backward and fantastically shaped, like a great grave face watching the house on the summit of the cliff.

The rock had fascinated the girl from the first moment she had seen it. In the summer months, tourists came from afar to gaze on its fancied resemblance to one of the illustrious dead. But to Sisily there was a secret brooding consciousness in the dark mask. It seemed to her to be watching and waiting for something. For what? Its glance seemed to follow her like the eyes of a picture. And it conveyed a menace by its mere proximity, even when she could not see it. When she looked out of her window at night, and saw only the shadow of the rock with the face veiled in darkness, she seemed to hear the whisper of its words: "I am here. Do not think to escape. I will have you yet."

Among the fisher-folk of that part of the coast it was known as the Moon Rock. The old Cornish women had a tradition that when a fishing-boat failed to return to that bay of storms, the spirit of the drowned man would rise to the surface and answer his wife if she hailed him from the shore. It was a rite and solemn ceremony, now fallen into decay. There was a story of one young wife who, getting no answer, left her desolate cottage at midnight and swam out to the Moon Rock at high tide. She had scrambled up its slippery sides and called her husband from the summit. She had called and called his name until he came. In the morning they were found — the wife, and the husband who had been called from the depth of the sea, floating together in one of the sea caverns at the base of the Moon Rock, their white faces tangled in the red seaweed which streaked the green surging water like blood.

Sisily knew this story, and believed it to be true. Sometimes, when the moon lingered on the black glistening surface of the Moon Rock, she fancied she could see a misty fluttering figure on the rock, and hear it calling … calling. She would sit motionless at her window, straining her ears for the reply. After a time the response would come faintly from the sea, at first far out, then sounding louder and clearer as the spirit of the husband guided his drowned body back to his wife's arms. When it sounded close to the rock the evanescent figure on the summit would vanish to join the spirit of her husband in the churning waters at the base. Then the face of the Moon Rock seemed to smile, and the smile was so cruel that Sisily would turn from the window with a shudder, covering her face with her hands.

Her strange upbringing may have contributed to such morbid fancies. In his monstrous preoccupation with a single idea Robert Turold had neglected his duty to his daughter. She counted for nothing in his scheme of life, and there were periods when he seemed to be unconscious of her existence. She had been allowed to grow up with very little education or training. She had passed her childhood and girlhood in remote parts of England, without companions, and nobody to talk to except her mother and Thalassa, who accompanied the family everywhere. She loved her mother, but her love was embittered by her helplessness to mitigate her mother's unhappy lot. Thalassa was a savage old pagan whose habitual watchful secretiveness relaxed into roaring melody in his occasional cups; in neither aspect could he be considered a suitable companion for the budding mind of a girl, but he loomed in her thoughts as a figure of greater import than her father or mother. Her father was a gloomy recluse, her mother was crushed and broken in spirit. Thalassa had been the practical head of the house ever since Sisily could remember anything, an autocrat who managed the domestic economy of their strange household in his own way, and brooked no interference. "Ask Thalassa—Thalassa will know," was Robert Turold's unvarying formula when anybody attempted to fix upon him his responsibility as head of the house. Sometimes Sisily was under the impression that her father for some reason or other, feared Thalassa. She could recall a chance collision, witnessed unseen, through a half-open door. There had been loud voices, and she had seen a fiery threatening eye—Thalassa's—and her; father's moody averted face.

From a child she had developed in her own way, as wild and wayward as the gulls which swooped around the rocks where she was sitting. Nature revealed her heart to her in long solitary walks by sea and fen. But of the world of men and women Sisily knew nothing whatever. The secrets of the huddle of civilization are not to be gathered from books or solitude. Sisily was completely unsophisticated in the ways of the world, and her deep passionate temperament was full of latent capacity for good or evil, for her soul's salvation or shipwreck. Because of her upbringing and temperament she was not the girl to count the cost in anything she did. She was a being of impulse who had never learnt restraint, who would act first and think afterwards.

Her dislike of her father was instinctive, almost impersonal, being based, indeed, on his treatment of her mother rather than on any resentment of his neglect of herself. But Robert Turold had never been able to intimidate his daughter or tame her fearless spirit. She had inherited too much of his own nature for that.

At that moment she was sitting motionless, immersed in thought, her chin on her hand, looking across the water to the horizon, where the Scilly Islands shimmered and disappeared in a grey, melting mist. She did not hear the sound of Charles Turold's footsteps, descending the cliff path in search of her.

The young man stood still for a moment admiring her exquisite features in their soft contour and delicate colouring. He pictured her to himself as a white wildflower in a grey wilderness. He could not see himself as an exotic growth in that rugged setting—a rather dandified young man in a well-cut suit, with an expression at once restless and bored on his good-looking face.

He scrambled down the last few slippery yards of the path and had almost reached her side before she saw him.

"I have been sent for you," he explained. "I knew I should find you here."

She got up immediately from the rock where she had been sitting, and they stood for a moment in silence. She thought by his look that he had something to say to her, but as he did not speak she commenced the ascent of the stiff cliff path. He started after her, but the climb took all his attention, and she was soon far ahead. When he reached the top she was standing near the edge looking around her.

"This is my last look," she said as he reached her side. Her hand indicated the line of savage cliffs, the tossing sea, the screaming birds, the moors beyond the rocks.

"Perhaps you will come back here again some day," he replied.

She made no answer. He drew closer, so close that she shrank back and turned away.

"I must go now," she hurriedly said.

"Stay, Sisily," he said. "I want to speak to you. It may be the final opportunity—the last time we shall be alone together here."

She hesitated, walking with slower steps and then stopping. As he did not speak she broke the silence in a low tone—

"What do you wish to say to me?"

"Are you sorry you are leaving Cornwall?" he hesitatingly began.

She made a slight indifferent gesture. "Yes, but it does not matter. Mother is dead, and my father does not care for me." She flushed a deep red and hastily added, "No one will miss me. I am so alone."

"You are not alone!" he impetuously exclaimed—"I love you, Sisily— that is what I wished to say. I came here to tell you."

He caught a swift fleeting glance from her dark eyes, immediately veiled.

"Do you really mean what you say?" she replied, a little unsteadily.

"Yes, Sisily. I have loved you ever since I first met you," he replied. "And, since then, I have loved you more and more."

"Oh, why have you told me this now?" she exclaimed. "You think I am lonely, and you are sorry for me. I cannot stay longer. Aunt will be waiting for me."

He sprang before her in the narrow path.

"You must hear what I have to say before you go," he said curtly. "We are not likely to meet again for some time if we part now. I intend to leave England."

She looked at him at those words, but he was at a loss to divine the meaning of the look.

"You are leaving England?" A quick ear would have caught a strange note in her soft voice. "Oh, but you cannot—you have responsibilities."

"Are you thinking of the title, and your father's money?" he observed, glancing at her curiously. "What do you know about it, Sisily?"

"I have heard of nothing but the title ever since I can remember," she replied.

"I learnt for the first time this afternoon that I was brought down here to rob you," he said gloomily.

"I am glad for your sake if you are to have it—the money," she simply replied.

He answered with a bitter, almost vengeful aspect.

"I would not take the money or the title, if they ever came to me. They should be yours. I will show them. I will let them know that they cannot do what they like with me." He brought out this obscure threat in a savage voice. "If I had only known—if I had guessed that your father—" He ceased abruptly, with a covert glance, like one fearing he had said too much.

She kept her eyes fixed on the lengthening shadows around the rocks.

"Do not take it so much to heart," she timidly counselled. "It is nothing to me—the title or the money. They made my mother's life a misery. My father was always cruel to her because of them, I do not know why. It is in his nature to be cruel, I think. He has a heart of granite, like these rocks. I hate him!" She brought out the last words in a sudden burst of passion which startled him.

"What nonsense it all is!" he exclaimed, suddenly changing his tone. "All this talk about a title which may never be revived. Let them have it between them, and the money too. Sisily, I love you, dear, love you better than all the titles and money in the world. I am not worthy of you, but I will try to be. Let us go Sway and start life ... just our two selves."

"I cannot." She stood in front of him with downcast gaze, and then raised her eyes to his.

Had he been as experienced in the ways of her sex as he believed himself to be, he would have read more in her elusive glance than her words.

"You may be sorry if you do not," he said, with a sudden access of male brutality. "There are reasons—reasons I cannot explain to you—"

"Even if there are I cannot do what you ask," she replied. Her face was still averted, but her voice was steady.

"Then do you want to go with Aunt to London?" he persisted, trying to catch a glimpse of her hidden face.

She shook her head.

"Or to stay with your father?"

"No!" There was a strange intense note in the brief word.

"Then come with me, Sisily. I love you more than all the world. We have nobody to please except our two selves."

"You have your duty to your father to consider."

"Let us leave him out of the question," said the young man hurriedly. "He is as selfish and heartless as—his brother. I tell you again, I'll have nothing to do with this title or your father's money. I will make my own way with you by my side. I have a friend in London who would be only too glad to receive you until we could be married. You are leaving your home to-night, and you are as free as air to choose. Will you come?"

"Of course," he began again, in a different tone, as she still kept silent, "it may be that I have misunderstood. I thought that you had learnt to care for me. But if you dislike me—"

"Do not say that," she replied, turning a deeply wounded face towards him. "It is not that—do not think so. You have been kind and good to me, and I—I shall never forget you. But I—I have a contempt for myself."

"I have a contempt for myself also after this afternoon," he retorted. "Come, Sisily—"

"No, it is impossible. Hark, what was that?" The girl spoke with a sudden uplifting of her head. Above them, from the direction of the house, the sound of a voice was heard.

"It is Aunt calling me," she said, "I must go. Good-bye."

"Is it good-bye, then?"

"It must be. But I shall often think of you."

He had the unforgettable sensation of two soft burning lips touching the hand which hung at his side, and turned swiftly—but too late. She was speeding along the rocky pathway which led to the house.

"Wait, Sisily!" he cried.

A seabird's mournful cry was the only answer. He glanced irresolutely towards the path, and then retraced his steps towards the edge of the cliffs.

A cold sun dipped suddenly, as though pulled down by a stealthy invisible hand. The twilight deepened, and in the lengthening shadows the rocks assumed crouching menacing shapes which seemed to watch the solitary figure standing near the edge, lost in thought.

Chapter V

Through the flowers on the hotel dining-table Mrs. Pendleton was able to watch her niece unnoticed, because the flowers occupied such an unreasonably large space on the little round table set for three. Besides, Sisily had been engrossed in her own thoughts throughout the meal. Mrs. Pendleton was disturbed by her quietness. There was something unnatural about it—something not girlish. She had not spoken once during the drive from Flint House to Penzance, and she sat through dinner with a still white face, silent, and hardly eating anything.

Mrs. Pendleton supposed Sisily was fretting over her mother, but she did not understand a girl whose grief took the form of silence and stillness. She would have preferred a niece who would have sobbed out her grief on her shoulder, been reasonably comforted, and eaten a good dinner afterwards. But Sisily was not that kind of girl. She was strange and unapproachable. There was something almost repellent in her reserve, something in her dark preoccupied gaze which made Mrs. Pendleton feel quite nervous, and unfeignedly relieved when Sisily had asked to be allowed to go to her room immediately the meal was concluded.

As she sat at the table, reviewing the events of the afternoon, after the girl had taken her departure, Mrs. Pendleton regretted that she had consented to take charge of Sisily. She flattered herself that she was sufficiently modern not to care a row of pins for the stigma on the girl's birth, but there were awkward circumstances, and not the least of them was her own rash promise to break the news to Sisily that she was illegitimate. That disclosure was not likely to help their future relations together. Mrs. Pendleton reflected that she knew very little about her niece, whom she had not seen since she was a small girl, but the recollection of her set face and tragic eyes at the dinner table impelled prompt recognition of the fact that she was going to be difficult to manage.

But there was more than that. With a feeling of dismay Mrs. Pendleton's mind awoke to a belated realization of the scandal which would fasten on Sisily and her birth if Robert succeeded in establishing his claim to the title. A peer of the realm with an illegitimate, disinherited daughter! The story would be pounced upon by a sensational press, avid for precisely such topics. In imagination Mrs. Pendleton saw the flaming headlines, the photographs, and the highly spiced reports in which every detail of her brother's private life was laid bare for a million curious eyes.

Such an exposure was too terrible to be faced. Mrs. Pendleton saw her own comfortable life affected by it; saw her position in her small social circle shaken and overwhelmed by the clamour of notoriety. She saw herself the focus of the malicious tea-table gossip of all her friends. Decidedly, it would not do.

She did her brother the justice to realize that he had overlooked the public effect of the disclosure of his painful domestic secret as completely as she had. He had forgotten that his accession to the peerage would make him, as it were, a public figure, and the glamour which the newspapers would throw over his lifelong quest would invest every act of his life with a publicity from which he could not hope to escape. If he had foreseen this, he would have made some other arrangement for his daughter's future, not for the girl's sake, but for the honour of the famous old name of which he was so fanatically proud.

The question remained, what was to be done? Robert would have to be told, of course. Mrs. Pendleton's first impulse was to retract her promise to take charge of Sisily, and wash her hands of the whole affair. Then she thought of the money, and wavered. Robert had made her a generous offer, and the money would have helped so much! She had already planned the spending of the cheque he had given her that afternoon. She had thought of a new suite of drawing-room furniture, and bedroom carpets. She had a vision of a small motor-car, later on.

As she pondered over the situation she thought she saw a way out—a way so simple and practical that she was astonished that it had not occurred to her before.

Mrs. Pendleton was a woman of decision and prompt of action when she made up her mind. Her mind was made up now. She glanced across the table at her husband. "Joseph!" she said.

Mr. Pendleton, hidden behind the sheets of a newspaper just arrived from London, had the temerity not to hear. He was in a grumpy mood, arising, in the first instance, from having been dragged away from his business and his club to Cornwall. It was nothing to him that he was in the Land of Lyonesse. His brief impression of the Duchy was that it was all rocks, and that Penzance was a dull town without a proper seafront, swarming with rascally shopkeepers who tried to sell serpentine match-boxes at the price of gold ones, and provided with hotels where dull tourists submitted to a daily diet of Cornish pasties and pollock under the delusion that they were taking in local colour in the process. Mr. Pendleton's stomach resented his own rash deglutition of these dainties, and in consequence he was suffering too much with acute indigestion to think of the compensation he would gain at next year's Academy by standing with a bragging knowing air before pictures of the Cornish coast, expatiating to his bored acquaintances (who had never been to Cornwall) on their lack of merit compared with the real thing. Like most husbands, Mr. Pendleton had been able to reach the conclusion that the real cause of his bodily and mental discomfort was his wife, so he maintained a sulky silence behind the pages of his newspaper.

With that lack of ceremony which the familiarity of marriage engenders in the female breast, his wife leant across the table and plucked the paper from his hand.

"Listen to me, Joseph," she said, "I want to talk to you."

Lacking the newspaper screen, Mr. Pendleton's rebellious tendencies instantly evaporated beneath his wife's searching eye.

"Yes, my dear," he replied meekly. "What about?"

"About Sisily. Did you notice that she did not speak a word during dinner?"

"Perhaps she was overcome with grief, my dear."

"Nonsense! Grief does not make a woman speechless. She's one of the dumb sort of girls. I always mistrust a girl who hasn't plenty to say for herself."

"Well, you know, my dear, she has had a strange sort of life. She hasn't had the educational advantages of other young women" — Mr. Pendleton was going to add "in her station of life," but a timely recollection of the afternoon's disclosures caused him to substitute: "with wealthy fathers."

"Robert has neglected his duty to her shamefully. I've been thinking it all over, and I'm half sorry now that I consented to take charge of her."

"Then why do it?" said her husband placidly.

"It's the scandal I fear," rejoined his wife, pursuing her own thought. "There's bound to be a lot of talk and newspaper publicity when Robert comes into the title. It would be much better to keep this quiet, after all these years. There is really no occasion for it, if Robert will only listen to reason. Robert wishes to avoid future trouble and complications about the succession. That could be arranged by getting Sisily to sign some agreement renouncing all claim on the title."

"I doubt if such a document would be legal, my dear," said her husband dubiously.

"That wouldn't matter in the least," replied Mrs. Pendleton, with a woman's contempt for the law. "It would be purely a family arrangement. Sisily could be assured by somebody in whom she has reliance—not her father, of course—that there was some legal reason why she could not succeed. I do not think there would be any trouble with her. She does not look the kind of girl to delight in a title and a lot of money. Robert would have to settle a handsome allowance on the poor child—indeed, it is the very least he can do! If Robert agreed to this course there would be no need to blurt out the brutal truth, and I would take Sisily under my charge."

Mr. Pendleton saw several objections to his wife's plan, but he had long learnt the futility of domestic argument—on the husband's side at least. "How much do you consider your brother ought to allow Sisily?" he asked.

"Two thousand a year. Robert can well afford it."

"Do you think your brother Austin would agree?"

"Of course he wouldn't. Austin is horribly selfish. He wouldn't give Sisily a penny if he had his way, now that he knows the truth. But I don't intend to consult Austin in the matter. I thought of asking Dr. Ravenshaw to go with me and try and influence Robert. Robert trusts him implicitly, and he seems to have a great deal of influence with him. I feel sure he would do his utmost to bring Robert to listen to reason. Do you not think my plan a good one?"

In the secret depth of his heart Mr. Pendleton did not, but with the moral cowardice of a husband he forebore from saying so. "It might be tried," he feebly muttered.

"Very well, we will try it, then," said his wife, rising from her seat as she spoke. "Go and order that motor-car we had this afternoon while I get ready."

Mr. Pendleton was accustomed to his wife's energetic way of doing things on the spur of the moment, but he had never become used to it. "Do you intend to go and see your brother to-night?" he said, with an air of surprise.

"Why not?"

Mr. Pendleton sought for a reason, but could find none. "It's rather late, isn't it?" he suggested.

"Nonsense!" Mrs. Pendleton glanced at her wrist watch. "It's not much past eight."

"Why not leave it until the morning?" said her husband, with a lingering glance at the cheery glow of the log-fire in the lounge. "It's a beast of a night to be out. Hark to the wind!"

"If it is to be settled, it must be settled to-night," said Mrs. Pendleton decisively. "There'll be no time in the morning for anything, if we are to catch the ten o'clock train for London. Beside, Austin would see us if we went there in daylight, and I do not want him to know anything about it— he would only try and put obstacles in our way."

"What about Sisily?"

"She will be quite all right in her room. She looked tired out, and needs a good night's rest. You had better see about the car at once."

Mr. Pendleton said no more, and his wife bustled away to put on her outdoor things. When she descended from her room her husband was awaiting her in the lounge, and the head-light of the hired motor-car gleamed in the darkness outside.

They set out through the narrow uneven streets, which smelt strongly of mackerel and pitch. In a few minutes the car was clear of the town, and running at an increased pace through the gusty darkness of the moors.

Chapter VI

With a face grimly immobile as the carved head of a heathen god, Thalassa stood at the front door watching the departure of Sisily and her aunt until the car was lost to sight in a dip of the moors. Then with a glance at the leaping water at the foot of the cliffs, grey and mysterious in the gloaming, he turned and went inside the house.

It was his evening duty to prepare the lamps which lighted up the old house on the cliffs. Sisily generally helped him in that tedious duty, but she was gone, and for the future he must do it alone.

The lamps were kept in a little lowbrowed room off the stone kitchen. There Thalassa betook himself. Robert Turold disliked the dark, and a great array of lamps awaited him: large ones for the rooms, small ones for the passages and staircase. Thalassa set to work with a will, filling them with oil, trimming the wicks, and polishing the glasses with a piece of chamois leather.

As he filled and trimmed and polished he sang to himself an old sea song:

"The devil and me, we went away to sea,
In the old brig 'Lizbeth-Jane' — "

His voice was gruff and harsh, and the melody, such as it was, did nothing to relax his expression, which remained grim and secret as ever.

Each lamp he lit as he finished it, and their gathered strength gushed in a flood of yellow light on his crafty brown face and deep-set eyes. He placed several of the lamps on a tray, carefully lowered the wicks, and carried them to their allotted places, returning for others until only half a dozen small lamps remained. These he gathered on the tray and took upstairs.

Night had fallen; the wind was rising without, and seemed to rustle and whistle in the draughty passages of the old house. Thalassa placed one lamp at the head of the stairs, and others in the niches of the passage, where they flickered feebly and diffused a feeble light. Halfway down the passage he paused before a closed door. It was the room in which Sisily's mother had died. With an expressionless face he went in and left the last lamp burning dimly on the mantelpiece, like a votary candle on an altar of the dead. Issuing forth again he cast a look around him and walked to Robert Turold's study at the end of the passage. The door was closed, but he opened it and entered.

Robert Turold was busily engaged writing at a large table by the light of a swinging lamp. He looked up from his papers as Thalassa entered, and thoughtfully watched him as he trimmed the lamp and tended the fire. With these duties completed Thalassa still lingered, as though he expected his master to speak.

"What's the glass like to-night, Thalassa?" remarked Robert Turold absently.

The allusion was to a weather glass which hung in the hall downstairs. As a topic of conversation it was as useful to master and servant as the weather is to most English people. That is to say, it helped them when they were wordbound.

"Going down fast," replied Thalassa.

"Then I suppose we are in for another rough night."

"The glass is always going down in Cornwall, and we are always in for another rough night," responded the servitor curtly. "Are you going to stay much longer in the forsaken hole?"

"Not much longer," replied his master in a mild tone.

"It is, perhaps, a dreary spot to you, but not to me—no, never to me. The last link in my long search has been found here—hidden away in this little out-of-the-way Cornish place. Think of that, Thalassa! I shall be Lord Turrald."

"I don't see what good it will do you," retorted the man austerely. "You've spent a mint of money over it. I suppose that's your own affair, though. But what's to come next? That's what I want to know."

"When I leave Cornwall—"

"You mean we, don't you?" Thalassa interrupted.

"Of course I mean you as well as myself," Robert Turold replied almost humbly. "I should be sorry to part with you, Thalassa, you must be well aware of that. It is my intention to purchase a portion of the family estate at Great Missenden, which is at present in the market, and spend the remainder of my life in the place which once belonged to my ancestors. That has been the dream of my life, and I shall soon be able to carry it out."

A silence fell between them upon this statement, and Robert Turold's eyes turned towards his papers again. But Thalassa stood watching him, as though he had something on his mind still. He brought it out abruptly—

"And what about your daughter?"

"My daughter is going to London with my sister for a prolonged visit," said Robert Turold hurriedly. "She needs womanly training and other advantages which I, in my preoccupations, have been unable to bestow upon her. It is greatly to her advantage to go."

Robert Turold gave this explanation with averted face, in a tone which sounded almost apologetic. The relative positions between them seemed curiously reversed. It was as though Thalassa were the master, and the other the man.

"Oh, that's it, is it?" Thalassa turned a cautious yet penetrating eye upon his master. "Well, she's your own daughter, so I suppose you know what's the best for her." He spoke indifferently, but there was an odd note in his voice. He picked up his tray, and carelessly added: "For my part I shall be glad to get out of Cornwall. It's a savage place, only fit for savages and seagulls. There's the wind rising again."

A violent gust shook the house, and rattled the window-panes of the room. It was the eyrie in which the deceased artist had painted his pictures, with two large windows which looked over the cliff. Again the gale sprang at the house, and smote the windows with spectral blows. Downstairs, a door slammed sharply.

"Damn the wind!" exclaimed Thalassa peevishly. "There's no keeping it out. I'm going downstairs to lock up now. You'll have your supper up here, I suppose?"

"Yes. I have a lot of work to do before I go to bed."

Thalassa left the room without further speech, and Robert Turold began rummaging among his papers with a hand which trembled slightly. The table was littered with parchments, old books, and some sheets of newly written foolscap. He picked up his pen and plunged it into a brass inkstand, then paused in thought. His face was perturbed and uneasy. It may be that he was reviewing the events of the day, wondering, perhaps, whether he had paid too high a price for the attainment of his ambition. For it he had sacrificed his daughter and the woman who now slept in the churchyard near by, indifferent to it all. Nothing could restore to him the secret he had divulged that afternoon.

A shade of apprehension deepened on his downcast face. Then he frowned impatiently, and plunged into his writing again.

Chapter VII

On leaving his master's room Thalassa went swiftly downstairs and disappeared into some remote back region of the lonely old house. He had other duties to perform before his day's work was finished. There was wood to be chopped, coal to be brought in, water to be drawn. Nearly an hour elapsed before he reappeared, candle in hand, and entered the kitchen.

A little woman with a furtive face, sharp nose, and blinking eyes was seated at one end of the kitchen table with playing-cards spread out in front of her. She looked up at the sound of the opening door, and fear crept into her eyes. She was Thalassa's wife, but the relationship was so completely ignored by Thalassa that other people were apt to forget its existence. The couple did the work of Flint House between them, but apart from that common interest Thalassa gave his wife very little of his attention, leading a solitary morose life, eating and sleeping alone, and holding no converse with her apart from what was necessary for the management of the house.

How he had ever come to bend his neck to the matrimonial yoke was one of those mysteries which must be accounted a triumph for the pursuing sex—a tribute to the fearlessness of woman in the ardour of the chase. On no other hypothesis was it possible to understand how such a feeble specimen of womanhood had been able to bring down such an untoward specimen of the masculine brute. Outwardly, Thalassa had more kinship with a pirate than a husband. There was that in his swart eagle visage and moody eyes which suggested lawless cruises, untrammelled adventure, and the fierce wooing of brown women by tropic seas rather than the dull routine of married life. As a husband he was an anomaly like a caged macaw in a spinster's drawing-room.

Mrs. Thalassa's victory had ended with bringing him down, and she soon had cause to regret her temerity in marrying him. Thalassa repaid the indignity of capture by a course of treatment which had long since subdued his wife to a state of perpetual fear of him—a fear which deepened into speechless shaking horror when he stormed out at her in one of his black rages. Some women would have taken to drink, others to religion. Mrs. Thalassa sought consolation in two packs of diminutive and dog-eared cards. Her shattered spirit found something inexpressibly soothing in the intricacies of patience: in the patchwork of colour, the array of sequences, the sudden discovery of an overlooked move, the dear triumph of a hard-won game.

It was thus she was occupied now, shuffling, cutting, and laying out her rows with quick nervous movements of her worn little hands. She glanced once more at her husband as he entered, and then bent over her cards again.

The night had descended blackly, and the wind moaned eerily round the old house. Thalassa sat in a straight-backed wooden chair listening to the wind and rain raging outside, and occasionally glancing at his wife, who remained absorbed in her patience. Half an hour passed in silence, broken only by the rattling of rain on the window, and the loud ticking of the clock on the mantelpiece. Suddenly the bell of Robert Turold's room rang loudly in its place behind the kitchen door.

It was one of the old wired bells, and it sprang backwards and forwards so violently under the impulse of the unseen pull that the other bells ranged alongside responded to the vibration by oscillating in sympathy.

Thalassa watched them moodily until the sound ceased. He then left the kitchen with deliberate tread, and stalked upstairs.

The door of his master's study was closed. He opened it without troubling to knock, but started back in astonishment at the sight which met his eyes. Robert Turold was crouching by the table like a beaten dog, whimpering and shaking with fear. He sprang to his feet as Thalassa entered, and advanced towards him.

"Thank God you've come, Thalassa," he cried.

"What's the matter with you?" said Thalassa sternly.

"He's come back, Thalassa—he's come back."

"He? Who?"

"You know whom I mean well enough. It was—" His voice sank suddenly, and he whispered a name in the man's ear.

Thalassa's brown cheek paled slightly, but he answered quickly and roughly—

"What nonsense are you talking now? How can he have come back? How often must I tell you that he is dead?"

"You mean that you thought he was dead, Thalassa. But he is alive."

"How do you know?"

"I heard him."

"Heard him! What do you mean?"

"I heard his footsteps pattering around the house, as clear and distinct as that night on that hellish island. Shall I ever forget the sound of his footsteps then, as he raced over the rocks, looking back at us with his wild eyes, and the blood streaming down his face—running and running until he stumbled and fell? The sound of his running footsteps as he clattered over the rocks have haunted me day and night ever since. I heard them again to-night."

"I tell you again that he is dead. What! Do you think that you could hear footsteps on a night like this?" The man stepped quickly across to the nearest window and flung it open. The room was filled with rushing wind, and the window curtains flapped noisily. "And where would he be running to? Do you suppose he could climb up here from outside?"

"It might have been his spirit," murmured the other.

"Spirits don't cross the ocean, and their footsteps don't clatter," responded Thalassa coldly. "The house is all locked up, and there is no other house near by. Come, what are you afraid of? You are worrying and upsetting yourself over nothing. I'll bring you up your supper, and some whisky with it. And the sooner you leave this cursed hole of a place, the better it will be."

He crossed over to the fireplace and poked the coal into a red glow, and then turned to leave the room. It was plain that his words had some effect on Robert Turold, and he made an effort to restore his dignity before the witness of his humiliation left him.

"No doubt you are right, Thalassa," he said in his usual tone. "My nerves are a little overstrung, I fancy. You said the house was locked up for the night, I think?"

"Everything bolted and barred," said Thalassa, and left the room.

He returned downstairs to the kitchen, where he wandered restlessly about, occasionally pausing to look out of the window into the darkness of the night. The rain had ceased, but the wind blew fiercely, and the sea thundered at the foot of the cliffs. The gloom outside was thinning, and as Thalassa glanced out his eye lighted on a strange shape among the rocks. To his imagination it appeared to have something of the semblance of a man's form standing motionless, watching the house.

Thalassa remained near the window staring out at the object. While he stood thus, a faint sound reached him in the stillness. It was the muffled yet insistent tap of somebody apparently anxious to attract attention without making too much noise, and coming, as it seemed, from the front door. Thalassa glanced at his wife, but she appeared to have heard nothing, and her grey head was bent over her cards. He walked noiselessly out of the kitchen, closing the door gently behind him.

His wife remained at the table, unconscious of everything but the lay of her cards; shuffling, dealing, setting them out afresh in perpendicular rows, muttering at the obstinacy of the kings and queens as though their painted faces were alive and sensitive to her reproof. The old house creaked and groaned in the wind, then became suddenly silent, like a man overtaken by sleep in the midst of stretching and yawning. Time sped on. Thalassa did not return, but she did not notice his absence. More rain fell, beating against the window importunately, as if begging admission, then ceased all at once, as at a hidden command, and again there was a profound silence.

A piece of coal jumped from the fire with a hissing noise, and fell at Mrs. Thalassa's feet. She got up to replace it, and observed that she was alone.

She thought she heard her husband's footsteps in the passage, and opened the door. But there was nobody there. The lower part of the house was gloomy and dark, but she could see the lamp glimmering on the hall stand. She was about to return to her seat when the hall lamp suddenly mooned up, cast monstrous shadows, and went black out.

This fantastic trick of the lamp frightened her. What had made it flare up like that and go out? And whose footsteps had she heard? With a chill feeling of fear she shut the door and turned again to her game. But for once the charm of the cards failed her. Where was Jasper, and why did he not return? Silence held oppressive empire; her fears plucked at her like ghostly hands. The lamp and the footstep—what did they mean? Had she really heard a footstep?

She thought she saw something white in the uncurtained space of the window. She buried her face in her hands, lacking the courage to cross the room and pull down the blind.

Mysterious noises overhead, like somebody creeping on all-fours, drew her eyes back to the door opening into the passage. With dismay she saw it was not properly shut. She wondered if she dared go and lock it. Suppose it was her husband, after all? And the noises? Were they real, or had she imagined them?

There came to her ear an unmistakable sound like the slamming of a door above her. A sudden accession in the quality of her fear sent her flying to the passage door to lock it. Before she could get there the door flew open violently, as though hit by a giant's hand, and then the wind blew coldly on her face. The lamp on the kitchen table sent up a straight tongue of flame in the draught, and also went out. As she stood there with straining eyes a cry rang out overhead, followed in a space immeasurable to the listener in the gulf of blackness, by a shattering sound which seemed to shake the house to its foundations. Then the external blackness entered her own soul, shrouding her consciousness like the sudden swift fall of a curtain.

Chapter VIII

It seemed a long wild journey in the dark, but actually only half an hour passed before the car emerged from the wind and rain of the moors into the dimly-lighted stone street of the churchtown. A few minutes later the car stopped, and the driver informed Mr. and Mrs. Pendleton in a Cornish drawl that they had reached Dr. Ravenshaw's.

Husband and wife emerged from the car and discerned a square stone house lying back from the road behind a white fence. They walked up the path from the gate and rang the bell.

A rugged and freckled servant lass answered the ring, and stared hard at the visitors from a pair of Cornish brown eyes. On learning their names she conducted them into a small room off the hall and departed to inform the doctor of their arrival.

Dr. Ravenshaw came in immediately. The quick glance he bestowed upon his visitors expressed surprise, but he merely invited them to be seated and waited for them to explain the object of their late visit. The room into which they had been shown was his consulting room, furnished in the simplest fashion—almost shabbily. There were chairs and table and a couch, a small stand for a pile of magazines, a bookcase containing some medical works, and a sprawling hare's-foot fern in a large flowerpot by the window. Mr. Pendleton seated himself near the fern, examining it as though it was a botanical rarity, and left his wife to undertake the conversation. Mrs. Pendleton was accustomed to take the lead, and immediately commenced—

"I have taken the liberty of coming to ask your advice about my niece, doctor. You heard what my brother said this afternoon?"

Dr. Ravenshaw inclined his head without speaking, and waited for her to continue.

"As you are a friend of my brother's—"

"Hardly a friend," he interrupted, with a gesture of dissent. "Our acquaintance is really too short to warrant that term."

There was a professional formality about his tone which pulled her up short. Like all impulsive people she was chilled by a lack of responsiveness.

Her impulse in visiting him had hoped for an interest equalling her own. She reflected now that she should have remembered that nobody liked being bothered with other people's affairs. She recovered her feminine assurance and went on, with a winning smile.

"But you are in my brother's confidence, doctor—you were present at our family gathering this afternoon. It is because of that I have come to see you again, at this late hour. My husband and I are returning to London in the morning, and there would be no other opportunity. I have been thinking over all my brother said this afternoon, and I am very much distressed about my niece."

He gave a short comprehending nod which encouraged her to proceed.

"I am extremely desirous of preventing this scandal of my brother's marriage coming to light after all these years," she earnestly pursued. "It seems to me that Robert has decided to let the truth be known without first considering all the circumstances. He has forgotten that if he succeeds in restoring the title he will come prominently into the public eye. As the holder of a famous name his affairs will have a public interest, and details will be published in the newspapers and eagerly read. That is why this story about Sisily's mother would be so terrible for all of us, and especially for Sisily."

"I should think your brother had foreseen all this." said Dr. Ravenshaw, after a short pause.

"I do not think Robert has realized it," Mrs. Pendleton eagerly rejoined. "He is a most unworldly man, and lives in a world of his own. His whole life has been devoted to the idea of restoring the title. He has thought of nothing else since he was a boy. He is quite incapable of understanding what a sensation this story of an earlier marriage will cause if it is made public. Indeed, I did not realize it myself until afterwards. Then I decided to come and see you, and ask your help."

"I quite agree with you that it would be better if the story could remain unknown, after all these years. But how can I help you?"

She had anticipated that question, and proceeded to unfold her plan.

"It might be kept quiet, I think," she said meditatively. "It is Robert's duty to keep it secret for Sisily's sake. I am chiefly concerned about her. Girls are difficult, so different from boys! It wouldn't be so bad if she were a boy. A boy could change his name and emigrate, go on a ranch and forget all about it. But it is different for a girl. Leaving the shock out of the question, this thing would spoil Sisily's life and ruin her chances of a good marriage if it was allowed to come out. People will talk. It is inevitable that they should, in the circumstances. I fancy the matter could be arranged in a way to satisfy Robert—so as not to interfere with his plans about the title."

"What do you suggest?"

"Sisily could be told that there is some obstacle which prevents her succeeding to the title. Robert has not brought her up as an heiress with expectations. He has never treated her fairly, poor girl. It was his dream to have a son to succeed him. Not that it would have made any difference if Sisily had been a son, after what's come to light! Sisily would never question anything that was told her about this wretched title, for I'm quite sure that the idea of inheriting it has never entered her head. It certainly never entered mine. I thought titles descended in the male line. I don't know, really, but that has always been my idea."

"It depends on the terms of the original creation. The Turrald barony originally went into abeyance among several daughters. One daughter could have succeeded. There is nothing in the wording of the original writ to prevent it—no limitation to male heirs. It is now well established by precedent that a daughter can inherit a barony by writ. But for the unhappy obstacle revealed by your brother's story, his daughter would undoubtedly have succeeded to the restored title on his death."

"I'm sure it's very good of you to explain it to me," murmured Mrs. Pendleton, in some confusion of mind. "It sounds quite reasonable, too. A woman can inherit the throne of England, so why not a title? But it never occurred to me before. Sisily, of course, cannot succeed to my brother's title because of her birth. But is there any need for this to be known? Could she not sign a paper renouncing her rights in return for a share of my brother's fortune?"

"I doubt if the law would approve of the arrangement if it became known."

"The law should realize that it was done from the best of motives to keep from an innocent girl a secret which would darken her life," responded Mrs. Pendleton with decision.

"I wasn't looking at it altogether in that light," replied Dr. Ravenshaw with a slow shake of the head. "But it might have been tried—oh yes, it might have been tried." He rose from his chair, and paced thoughtfully up and down the room.

"Is it too late to try it now?" she asked.

He looked at her thoughtfully.

"In what way?"

"By trying to persuade my brother to change his mind."

"He is not likely to change his mind."

"That," responded Mrs. Pendleton, "remains to be put to the test. I intend to see him to-night, before it is too late. I beg you for Sisily's sake to come with me and try and persuade him."

"Such a request as you propose to make should come only from a member of the family," replied Dr. Ravenshaw. "It is a matter in which I would rather not be involved. If you wish support, I would remind you that there are two other members of your own family—your other brother and his son—staying temporarily in this churchtown, not far from here. Why not go to them?"

With a charmingly feminine gesture Mrs. Pendleton washed her hands of the other members of the family. "I would not dream of going to Austin," she said in decided tones. "He would not approve of my plan, nor, indeed, would Robert listen to him if he did. But he would listen to you, I feel sure. That is my reason for coming to you." She rose from her seat, and sought to shepherd him into compliance by approaching him with a propitiatory smile. "Do come, doctor. I have trespassed too much on your kindness already, but oblige me further in this."

"It's rather late for a visit," he replied.

"It's only half-past nine," she said, with a glance at her wrist watch. "My brother sits up till all hours over his papers and books. I will take all responsibility upon myself for the visit. I will tell Robert that I literally had to drag you with me, and he will understand that we simply had to see him to-night, as he knows we are going home to London first thing in the morning. Do come, Dr. Ravenshaw. The car is waiting."

He consulted his own watch.

"Very well, Mrs. Pendleton," he assented. "I will accompany you. Please excuse me while I get my coat."

He rejoined them in a moment or two, and they proceeded outside to the waiting car.

Chapter IX

A few minutes later the car stopped in the gloom outside the old house on the cliffs. The storm had passed, but the sea still raged white beneath an inky sky. A faint gleam from a shuttered front window pointed a finger of light to the gravel path which led to the front door.

Mrs. Pendleton knocked, and an answer came quickly. The door was partly opened, and Thalassa's voice from within parleyed: "Who's there?"

"Mrs. Pendleton—your master's sister," was the reply. "Let us in, Thalassa."

The door was at once opened wide, and Thalassa stood back for them to enter. By the light of the lamp he carried they saw that he was dressed and coated for a journey, with his hat on.

"I'm glad you've come," he said to Dr. Ravenshaw. "It's you I was just going out to fetch."

There was something strange in his manner, and the doctor looked at him quickly. "What's the matter with you, man? Is there anything wrong?"

"That's what I don't know. But I'm afeered, yes, by God, I'm afeered."

His voice broke hoarsely, and he stood before them with his eyes averted from the three wondering faces regarding him. Mrs. Pendleton stepped quickly forward, and grasped his arm.

"What is it, Thalassa? Has anything happened to my brother?"

"There's been a great noise in his room, like as if something heavy had crashed down, then silence like the grave. I went up and called—an' tried to open the door, but I couldn't."

"Why didn't you try to break in the door?" said Dr. Ravenshaw.

"Tweren't my place," was the dogged retort. "I know my place. I was just going to St. Fair for you and his brother."

"How long is it since this happened—since you heard the crash, I mean."

"Not many minutes agone. Just before you came to the door."

"Light us upstairs at once, Thalassa," said Mrs. Pendleton sharply.

"Mrs. Pendleton, will you wait downstairs while we investigate?" suggested Dr. Ravenshaw.

"No," she resolutely answered. "I will come with you, doctor. Robert may need me. Do not let us waste any more time."

She slipped past him to Thalassa, who was mounting the stairs. Dr. Ravenshaw hurried after her. Mr. Pendleton, with an obvious call on his courage, followed last. The lamp in Thalassa's hand burnt unsteadily, first flaming angrily, then flickering to a glimmer which brought them to a pause, one above the other on the stairs, listening intently, and looking into the darkness above.

"His bedroom is open and empty," said Thalassa when they had reached the end of the passage above. "See!" He pointed to the gaping door, and then turned to the closed one opposite. "He's in here." His voice sank to a whisper. "It was from here the noise came."

He placed the lamp on the floor, and knocked hesitatingly on the dark panel of the closed door, then again more loudly, but there was no reply. Far beneath them they could hear the solemn roar of the sea dashing against the cliffs, but there was no sound in the closed chamber. Its stillness and hush seemed intensified by the clamour of the sea, as though calamity were brooding in the darkness within.

"Robert, Robert!" The high pitch of Mrs. Pendleton's voice shattered the quietude like the startling clang of an unexpected bell. "Knock again, Thalassa, more loudly, very loudly," she cried, in the shrill accents of tightened nerves.

Thalassa approached the door again, but recoiled swiftly. "God A'mighty!" he hoarsely exclaimed, pointing, "what's that?"

They followed the direction of his finger to the floor, and saw a sluggish thin dark trickle making its way underneath the door. Mr. Pendleton stooped and examined it, but rose immediately.

"There's been trouble in there," he said, with a pale face.

"How could anybody get in?" said Thalassa sullenly. "The door is locked from the inside, and it's two hundred feet from the windows to the bottom of the cliffs."

"Oh, for pity's sake stop talking and do something," cried Mrs. Pendleton hysterically. "My poor brother may be dying." She rattled the door-handle. "Robert, Robert, what is the matter? Let me in. It is I—Constance."

"We must break in the door," said Dr. Ravenshaw. "Stand away, Mrs. Pendleton, please. Now, Thalassa, both together."

The doctor and the servant put their shoulders to the door. Mr. Pendleton watched them with a white face, but did not go to their assistance. At the fourth effort there was a sound of splintering wood, the lock gave, and the door swung back.

They peered in. At first they could see nothing. The light of the swinging-lamp had been lowered, and the interior of the room was veiled in shadow. Then their eyes detected a dark outline on the floor between the table and the window—the figure of a man, lying athwart the carpet with arms outstretched, face downwards, the spread finger-tips clutching at some heavy dark object between the head and the arms.

Thalassa stepped across the threshold, and with shaking hand turned up the lowered wick of the swinging lamp. The light revealed the stark form of Robert Turold. At this sight Mrs. Pendleton broke into a loud cry and essayed to cross the room to her brother's side.

"Keep back, Mrs. Pendleton!" cried Dr. Ravenshaw, interposing himself in front of her. "I begged of you not to come upstairs. Mr. Pendleton, take your wife away at once."

But Mr. Pendleton's timorous and inferior mind was incapable of translating the command into action. He could only stare dumbly before him.

"No, no! Let me stay, I will be calm," Mrs. Pendleton pleaded. "Is—is he dead, doctor?"

Dr. Ravenshaw crossed to the centre of the room and bent over the body, feeling the heart. Husband and wife watched him, huddled together, their white faces framed in the shadow of the doorway. In a moment he was on his feet again, advancing towards them. "We can do no good here, Mrs. Pendleton," he said gently. "Your brother is dead."

"Dead? Robert dead!" Her startled eye sought his averted face, and her feminine intuition gathered that which he was seeking to withhold. "Do you mean that he has been killed?" she whimpered.

"I fear that there has been—an accident," he replied evasively. He stood in front of them in a way which obscured their view of the prone figure, and a small shining thing lying alongside, which he alone had seen. "Come," he said, in a professional manner, taking her by the arm. "Let me take you downstairs." He got her away from the threshold, and pulled the broken door to, shutting out the spectacle within.

"Are you going to leave him there—like that?" whispered Mrs. Pendleton.

"It is necessary, till the police have seen him," he assured her. "We had better send Thalassa in the car to the churchtown. Go for Sergeant Pengowan, Thalassa, and tell him to come at once. And afterwards you had better call at Mr. Austin Turold's lodgings and tell him and his son. Hurry away with you, my man. Don't lose a moment!"

Thalassa hastened along the passage as though glad to get away. His heavy boots clattered down the staircase and along the empty hall. Then the front door banged with a crash.

The others followed more slowly, stepping gently in the presence of Death, past the little lamps, hardly bigger than fireflies, which flickered feebly in their alcoves. They went into the front room, where a table lamp gave forth a subdued light. Mrs. Pendleton turned up the wick and sank into a chair, covering her face with her hands.

It was the room where only that afternoon Robert Turold had unfolded the history of his life's quest: a large gloomy room with heavy old furniture, faded prints of the Cornish coast, and a whitefaced clock on the mantel-piece with a loud clucking tick. Dr. Ravenshaw knew the room well, but Robert Turold's sister had seen it for the first time that day, and the recollection of what had taken place there was so fresh in her memory that it brought a flood of tears.

"Poor Bob!" she sobbed. "He denied himself all his life for the sake of the title, and what's the good of it all—now?"

That was the only light in which she was able to see the tragedy in the first moment of the shock. Other thoughts and revelations about her brother's strange death were to come later, when her mind recovered its bearings. For the moment she was incapable of thinking coherently. She was conscious only of the fact that her brother had been cut off in the very moment of success—before it, indeed; ere he had actually tasted the sweets of the ambition he had given all his years to gain.

Silence fell between them, broken only by the clucking of the whitefaced clock and the dreary sound of the wind outside, crying round the old house like a frightened woman in the dark. Nearly an hour passed before they heard the sound of a guarded knock at the front door. Dr. Ravenshaw went and opened it. Austin Turold was standing on the threshold.

"This is bad news, doctor," he said, stepping quickly inside. "I came ahead of the others—walked over. Thalassa is waiting at the churchtown for the sergeant, who is away on some official business, but expected back shortly. They may be here at any minute."

He spoke a little breathlessly, as though with running, and seemed anxious to talk. He went on—.

"How did it happen? Tell me everything. I could get nothing out of Thalassa. He was detained at the police station for a considerable time, waiting for Pengowan, before he came to me with the news. He gave a great knock at the door of my lodgings like the thunder of doom, and when I got downstairs he blurted out that my brother was killed—shot—but not another word of explanation could I get out of him. What does it all mean?"

"I cannot say. Your sister and I reached the house just as Thalassa was about to leave it to seek my assistance. Your sister is in the sitting-room."

Austin Turold brushed past the doctor and opened the door of the lighted room. At his entrance Mrs. Pendleton sprang from her seat to greet him. Grief and horror were in her look, but surprise contended with other emotions in Austin's face. She kissed him with clinging hands on his shoulders.

"Oh, Austin," she cried, "Robert is dead—killed!"

"The news has shocked me to the last degree," responded her brother. "What has happened? Did somebody send for you? Is that what brought you here?"

Mrs. Pendleton shook her head, embarrassed in her grief. She remembered that she wished to keep the object of her visit secret from her younger brother, and she could not very well disclose the truth then.

"Not exactly," she replied, a trifle incoherently. "I wanted to see Robert again before I returned to London in the morning. So we motored over after dinner, and found him—dead." Fresh tears broke from her.

Austin Turold wandered around the room quickly and nervously, then drew Dr. Ravenshaw to the door with a glance. "I should like to go upstairs before the police come," he whispered.

Dr. Ravenshaw nodded, and they went upstairs together. The shattered door creaked open to their touch, revealing the lighted interior and the dead man prone on the floor. Austin approached his brother's corpse, eyed it shudderingly, and turned away. Then he stooped to look at the small revolver lying alongside, but did not touch it. Again he bent over the corpse, this time with more composure in his glance.

The object on which the outstretched arms rested was an old Dutch hood clock, which had fallen or been dragged from a niche in the wall, and lay face uppermost, the glass case open and smashed, the hands: stopped at the hour of half-past nine. It was a clock of the seventeenth century, of a design still to be found occasionally in old English houses. A landscape scene was painted in the arch above the dial, showing the moon above a wood, in a sky crowded with stars. The moon was depicted as a human face, with eyes which moved in response to the swing of the pendulum. But the pendulum was motionless, and the goggle eyes of the mechanism stared up almost reproachfully, as though calling upon the two men to rescue it from such an undignified position. At the bottom of the dial appeared the name of Jan Fromantel, the famous Dutch clockmaker, and underneath was an inscription in German lettering—

"Every tick that I do give
Cuts short the time you have to live.
Praise thy Maker, mend thy ways,
Till Death, the thief, shall steal thy days."

"Look at the blood!" said Austin Turold, pointing to a streak of blood on the large white dial. "How did it happen?"

"I know very little more than yourself. Your sister called at my house about an hour ago and asked me to accompany her here. She wished to see your brother on some private business, and she was very anxious that I should accompany her. Thalassa let us in, and said he was afraid that there was something wrong with his master. We came upstairs immediately, burst in the door, and found—this."

"Did Thalassa hear the shot?"

"He says not, only the crash."

"That would be the clock, of course. Was my brother quite dead when you found him?"

"Just dead. The body was quite warm."

"The door was locked from inside, I think you said."

"We found it locked."

"Then it must have been locked from inside," returned the other, who appeared to be pursuing some hidden train of thought. "But where's the key? I do not see it in the door. Oh, here it is!" He stooped swiftly and picked up a key from the floor. "Robert must have taken it out after locking the door."

"Perhaps it fell out when we were breaking in the door," observed the doctor.

"Of course. I forgot that. I notice that the clock is stopped at half-past nine." He bent down to examine it. "My brother kept private papers in the clock-case," he added. "Yes—it is as I thought. Here are some private documents, including his will. I had better take charge of them."

"Yes; I should if I were you," counselled his companion.

Austin rose to his feet and placed the papers in his pocket.

"It is plain to me—now—how it happened," he said. "Poor Robert must have shot himself, then tried to get his will from the clock-case when he fell, bringing down the clock with him."

"Is that what you think?" said Dr. Ravenshaw.

"I see no other way of looking at it," returned Austin rapidly. "The door was locked on the inside, and the room couldn't be reached from the window. This house stands almost on the edge of the cliff, which is nearly two hundred feet high. My feeling is that after my poor brother shot himself he remembered in his dying moments that his will was hidden in the clock-case and might not be found. He made a desperate effort to reach it and dragged it down as he fell."

The doctor listened attentively to this imaginary picture of Robert Turold's last moments.

"But why should he destroy himself?" he queried.

"Grief and remorse. Do you remember the disclosure he made to us this afternoon? It is a matter which might well have preyed upon his mind."

"I see," said the other thoughtfully. "Yes, perhaps you may be right."

Their conversation was interrupted by the sound of a loud knocking downstairs.

"That must be the police," observed Dr. Ravenshaw. "Let us go down."

Chapter X

"Why should Robert commit suicide?"

That was the burden of Mrs. Pendleton's cry, then and afterwards. There was an angry scene in the old cliff house between brother and sister before the events of that night were concluded. She utterly refused to accept Austin's theory that their brother, with his own hand, had discharged the revolver bullet which had put an end to his life and ambitions. Sitting bolt upright in indignant amazement, she rejected the idea in the sharpest scorn. It was nothing to her that the police sergeant from the churchtown shared her brother's view, and that Dr. Ravenshaw was passively acquiescent. She brushed aside the plausible web of circumstances with the impatient hand of an angry woman. They might talk till Doomsday, but they wouldn't convince her that Robert, of all men, had done anything so disgraceful as take his own life. Arguments and events, the locked door and the inaccessible windows — pathetically masculine insistence on mere details — were wasted on her. The marshalled array of facts made not the slightest impression on her firm belief that Robert had not shot himself.

Shaking a large finger of angry import at Austin, and addressing herself to him alone, she had said —

"Robert has been murdered, Austin, I feel sure. I don't care what you say, but if there's law in England I'll have his murderer discovered."

And with that conclusion she had indignantly left the house with her husband, leaving her brother to walk back to his lodgings at the churchtown in moody solitude across the rainy darkness of the moors.

For herself, she returned to her hotel to pass a sleepless night, tossing by the side of her placidly unconscious husband as she passed the tragic events of the night in review and vainly sought for some clue to the mystery. The dreadful logic of the circumstances which pointed to suicide, hammered at her consciousness with deadening persistence, but she resolutely refused to give it entry. Why should Robert commit suicide? Why indeed? It was the question which had sprung to her lips when she first heard Austin's belief, and it was to that she now clung in the midst of her agonizing doubts, as though the mere wordless insistence in her mind made it an argument of negation which gathered force and cogency by frequent repetition.

But in the mass of teeming thoughts which crowded her brain in the silence of the small hours, she long and vainly sought for any other theory which would account for her brother's death. If he had been murdered, as in the first flush of her indignation she had declared, who had killed him? Who had gone to the lonely old house in the darkness of the night, and struck him down?

It was not until the first faint glimmering of dawn was pushing its grey way through the closed shutters that there came to her the recollection of an incident of the previous day which had left a deep mark upon her mind at the time, but had since been covered over by the throng of later tremendous events. It was the memory of that momentary glance of a pair of eyes through the slit of the door while her brother was telling of his daughter's illegitimacy and her mother's shame. In the light of Robert's subsequent death that incident appeared in a new sinister shape as a clue to the commission of the deed itself. With the recollection of that glance there sprang almost simultaneously before her mental vision the grim and forbidding features of her brother's servant, Thalassa.

If she had been asked, Mrs. Pendleton could not have given a satisfactory reason for linking Thalassa with the incident of the eyes, but she was a woman, and not concerned about reasons. The two impressions had scurried swiftfooted, into her mind together, and there they remained. She was now convinced that she had all along believed it was Thalassa she had seen watching through the door, watching and listening for some fell purpose of his own. She knew nothing about Thalassa, but she had taken an instant dislike to him when she first saw him. That vague dislike now assumed the form of active suspicion against him. She determined, with the impulsiveness which was part of her temperament, to bring her suspicion before the police at the earliest possible moment.

She was essentially a woman of action, and in spite of her sleepless night she was up and dressed before her husband was awake. He came down to breakfast to find his wife had already finished hers, and was dressed ready to go out.

"Where is Sisily?" he asked, with a glance at the girl's vacant place.

"I've ordered her breakfast to be taken to her room, and sent word to her to rest in bed until I go to her," his wife replied. "I have a painful ordeal before me in breaking the news of Robert's death to her. It's all over the hotel already, unfortunately. Sisily is out of the way of gossip in her room. After I've seen her I shall leave her in your charge, Joseph. I shall have plenty on my hands to-day."

Mr. Pendleton received this mandate with a blank face, and momentarily regretted that the arrangements for their departure by the morning's train had been cancelled. Then his better nature asserted itself, and he meekly replied that he would do what he could. "What do you suggest?" he asked.

"Take her for a walk," responded his wife. "Try and keep her interested and her mind occupied."

With these words she left the breakfast table and proceeded upstairs to Sisily's room before going out. On the way there she again regretted having undertaken the responsibility of her niece's future. She had not disturbed Sisily on the previous night. She had tried her door on her way to her own room, but it was locked, so she had let the girl sleep on, and deferred breaking the tragic news until the morning.

She now paused outside the door reluctantly. But she was not the woman to shrink from a duty because it was unpleasant, and womanly sympathy for her unhappy niece banished her diffidence. She knocked lightly and entered.

Sisily was seated by the window reading. A breakfast tray, still untouched, stood on a small table beside her. She put down her book as her aunt entered, and rose to greet her.

Mrs. Pendleton bent over the girl and kissed her, and took her hand. As she did so she observed that Sisily looked worn and fatigued, with black rings under her eyes, as though she, too, had passed a sleepless night. But she was wonderfully pretty, the elder woman thought, and nothing could rob her of the fresh charm of youth and beauty.

"Sit down, Sisily," she said, leading her back to her chair, and taking another one beside her. "I have sad news for you, dear, and you must be a brave girl. Something has happened to your father."

"What has happened?" asked Sisily quickly. Then, as if taking in the import of her aunt's tone, rather than her words, she added: "Do you mean that he is ... dead?"

Mrs. Pendleton inclined her head with tears in her eyes. "It is worse even than that," she went on, her voice drooping to a whisper. "He ... he has been killed. We found him last night. Listen, dear, I will tell you all."

She gave the cold fingers a comforting pressure as she spoke, but the hand was immediately withdrawn, and Sisily sprang away from her, then turned and regarded her with blazing eyes and a white face.

"Tell me about it!" she said.

Mrs. Pendleton imparted as much of the facts as she felt called upon to relate. There was something about the girl's reception of the news which puzzled her, and her own look fell before the sombre intensity of her gaze. Sisily heard the story in silence, and when it was finished, merely said—

"I think I would like to be left alone for a little while, if you don't mind."

"Oh, you mustn't sit here moping, my dear," said Mrs. Pendleton, with an attempt at cheerfulness which she felt to be clumsy and ill-timed, but Sisily's manner had momentarily disconcerted her. "You had better put on your hat and coat and go out with your uncle. He is waiting downstairs for you. It is very sad, very terrible, but you must let us help you bear it. You must not stay here alone."

"You are very kind"—the girl's lips quivered slightly, though her face remained calm—"but I would rather not go out. I should prefer to be left alone."

There was in her expression a despairing yet calm detachment and resolve which forced Mrs. Pendleton in spite of herself to yield to her wish with a meekness which was almost timidity.

"Very well, dear," she said. "If you feel like a walk later on, you will find your uncle downstairs."

As she left the room she heard the door shut behind her.

But Mrs. Pendleton had other things to think about that morning than the strangeness of her niece's disposition and the manner in which she had received the news of her father's death. The horror of that event filled her own thoughts to the exclusion of everything else, and she was determined to remain in Cornwall until the mystery was explained.

She glanced at her watch as she reached the bottom of the stairs. She had breakfasted early, and it still wanted a few minutes to ten o'clock. The lobby of the hotel was deserted, and through the glass doors leading to the breakfast-room she could see a few guests still at their morning meal. A porter was sweeping the front entrance, and of him she enquired the way to the police station, and set out for it.

It was chill and grey after the storm, with a sky obscured by scudding clouds, but a gleam of truant sunshine was sporting wantonly on the hoary castled summit of St. Michael's Mount, and promised to visit the town later on. Mrs. Pendleton walked briskly, and soon arrived at the police station.

A young constable in the office came forward as she entered and enquired her business. She disclosed her name, and her relationship with the inmate of Flint House, deeming that would be sufficient to gain her an interview with somebody in authority. In that expectation she was not disappointed. The constable favoured her with a good hard stare, went into another room, and reappeared to say that Inspector Dawfield would see her at once.

She followed him into the inner room, where a slight man of middle age was seated at a leather-covered table opening his morning correspondence. He looked up and bowed as he saw his visitor, but waited until the constable had retired before he spoke.

"Good morning," he said. "What can I do for you?"

His eye regarded her with a thoughtful glance. His professional interest had been aroused by the strange death of the occupant of Flint House, whose object in visiting Cornwall had been common gossip in the district for some time past.

"It is about my brother's death that I wished to see you." Mrs. Pendleton spoke earnestly, drawing her chair closer with the feeling that the man before her had sufficient intelligence to give her a sympathetic hearing.

"So I gathered from your card. It seems a very sad case. Sergeant Pengowan's report has just reached me. Anything I can do for you—" Inspector Dawfield pretended to occupy himself in cutting open an official envelope with scrupulous care.

"Sergeant Pengowan regards it as a case of suicide, does he not?" asked Mrs. Pendleton rigidly.

"Well, yes, I believe he does," replied Inspector Dawfield. "There is no doubt on that point, is there? Your brother's revolver was lying near him, and the door was locked on the inside."

"There is the greatest doubt in my mind," returned Mrs. Pendleton vehemently. "I do not—I cannot believe that my brother has taken his own life. In fact, I am sure he did not."

On hearing these words Inspector Dawfield looked at his visitor again, with something more than surprise in his eyes, then he pulled a document from a pigeonhole and hastily scanned it.

"Pengowan's report states quite definitely that it is suicide," he said as he replaced it. "In the face of that, do you think—"

"I think my brother has been murdered," she said in a decided voice.

"This is a very grave statement to make, Mrs. Pendleton. Have you anything to support it? Anything which has not been brought to light, I mean?"

Mrs. Pendleton proceeded to give her reasons. She had thought over what she was going to say as she came along, and she spoke with growing conviction, intensified by the sight of the earnest attentive face before her.

The incident of the person she had detected looking through the door took on a new significance as she related it. By her constant association of the eyes with the disliked face of her brother's servant, she had unconsciously reached the conclusion that she had all along recognized the eavesdropper as Thalassa.

"You say your brother was talking about some family matters at the time?" asked Inspector Dawfield, as she related that part of her story.

"Yes," responded Mrs. Pendleton. She had repressed all mention of her brother's announcement of his daughter's illegitimacy, but afterwards she tried to persuade herself that it slipped her memory at the time.

"It's common enough for servants to listen at doors," remarked Inspector Dawfield. "In this case it may seem to have a sinister interpretation because of what happened afterwards. How long has this man been in your brother's employ?"

"A number of years, I believe," replied Mrs. Pendleton. "But he has a wicked face," she added hastily, as though that fact cancelled a record of lengthy service. "I took a dislike to him as soon as I saw him."

Inspector Dawfield veiled a slight smile with a sheet of foolscap. "Have you any other reason for suspecting him?"

"Oh, I wouldn't like to say that I suspect Thalassa, or anybody else." Mrs. Pendleton was prompt with this assurance. "But there are certain things which seem to me to need further investigation. There's the question of the door being locked on the inside. It seems to me that the door might have been locked on the outside, and the key dropped in there afterwards. The door had to be smashed before we could get in, and the key wasn't in the door then, you know."

Dawfield nodded thoughtfully. "Who has charge of the keys in your brother's house? This servant with the strange name—Thalassa, is it?"

"Yes, and he was upstairs in my brother's room last night, after we came down. And when we got there he was ready to go out, with his hat and coat on. It all seems very strange."

Again the courteous inspector hid a slight smile. His lady visitor might disclaim suspecting anybody, but her inferences carried her to the same point.

"What do you wish me to do?" he asked.

"I feel there should be further inquiries. Sergeant Pengowan does not strike me as the kind of man capable of bringing to light any mystery which may be hidden behind my brother's supposed suicide. He does not look at all intelligent. I thought of sending a telegram to Scotland Yard, but I decided to see you first."

The hint was not lost on Inspector Dawfield, but it was unnecessary. It was his duty to look into her complaint and make further inquiries into the case.

"Your statement shall certainly be investigated," he said emphatically. "I am rather short of men just now, but I'll see if I can get Bodmin to send over a man. I will inquire immediately, if you will excuse me."

He retired into a curtained recess in a corner of the room, where Mrs. Pendleton could see him holding a colloquy over the telephone. After rather a lengthy conversation he returned to announce that a detective was coming over by the next train to investigate the case.

"The Bodmin office is sending over Detective Barrant, of Scotland Yard," he explained. "He happens to be in Cornwall on another case, and was just on the point of returning to London. I was able to speak to him personally and relate the facts of your brother's death. He decided to telephone to Scotland Yard, and come over here at once. He will arrive soon after lunch. I will take him to Flint House myself. He may wish to see you later on. Will you be at your hotel?"

"If not, I will leave word where I can be found," replied Mrs. Pendleton, rising as she spoke. "Good morning, and thank you."

She left the police station feeling that she had accomplished an excellent morning's work, and hurried back to the hotel with visions of letters to be written and telegrams to be sent before lunch. But she was destined to do neither. As she entered the lounge, her eye fell upon its solitary occupant, a male figure in a grey lounge suit sitting in her favourite corner by the window. It was her brother Austin.

Chapter XI

He rose from his seat as he saw her, but waited for her to approach. Her eyes, dwelling on his face, noted that it was not so angry as she had last seen it, but smoothed into the semblance of sorrow and regret, with, however, something of the characteristic glance of irony which habitually distinguished him, though that may have been partly due to the pince-nez which glittered over his keen eyes. There was something of an art in Austin Turold's manner of wearing glasses; they tilted, superiorly, at the world in general at an acute angle on the high bridge of a supercilious nose, the eyes glancing through them downwards, as though from a great height, at a remote procession of humanity crawling far beneath.

At that moment, however, there was nothing superior in his bearing. It was so unwontedly subdued, so insistently meek, that it was to be understood that his mission was both conciliatory and propitiatory. That, at least, was the impression Mrs. Pendleton gathered as her brother informed her that he had been waiting nearly an hour to see her.

She reflected that he must have arrived shortly after she left the hotel to go to the police station, and she wondered what had induced her brother to rise at an hour so uncommonly early for him, in order to pay her a morning visit.

"I was up betimes," said Austin, as though reading her thought. "Sleep, of course, was impossible. Poor Robert!"

Mrs. Pendleton waited impatiently for him to disclose the real reason of an appearance which had more behind it, she felt sure, than to express condolences about their common bereavement. Of Robert she had always stood a little in awe, but she understood her younger brother better. As a boy she had seen through him and his pretensions, and he did not seem to her much changed since those days.

"I have been upset by our difference last night, Constance," he pursued. "It seems deplorable for us to have quarrelled—yes, actually quarrelled— over our poor brother's death."

His sister's face hardened instantly. "That wasn't my fault," she said distantly.

"You'll excuse me for saying that I think it was. You took an altogether wrong view of his — his death; a view which I hope you've seen fit to change after a night's reflection."

"You mean about Robert committing suicide?"

Austin inclined his head.

"I haven't changed my opinion in the slightest degree," she retorted. "I am still quite convinced that Robert did not commit suicide."

Austin darted an angry glance at her, but controlled himself with a visible effort. "Have you reflected what that implies?" he asked in a low tone.

"What does it imply?"

"Murder." He breathed the word with a hurried glance around him, as though apprehensive of being overheard, but the lounge was empty, and they were quite alone.

"I am aware of that."

"Then is it still your intention to go to the police with this terrible suspicion?" he asked, in a voice that trembled with agitation.

It was on the tip of Mrs. Pendleton's tongue to reply that she had already been to the police, but she decided to withhold that piece of information until she had heard all that her brother had to say.

"Certainly," she replied.

"Then you must be mad," was his indignant rejoinder. "Have you considered the scandal this will entail upon us all?"

"Not half such a scandal as that Robert should be murdered and his family permit the crime to go unpunished."

"I do not think that you have given this matter sufficient consideration. It is for that reason I have come to see you this morning — before you take action which you may have reason to regret later on. I want you to think it over carefully, apart from a mere feminine prejudice against the possibility of a member of the family destroying himself. If you will listen to me I think that I shall be able to convince you that Robert, deplorable though it may seem, did actually commit suicide."

"What's the use of going through all this again?" said Mrs. Pendleton wearily. "Robert would not commit suicide."

"Suicide is always difficult to explain. Nobody can say what impels a man to it."

"Robert had no reason to put an end to his life. He had everything to live for — everything in front of him."

"You cannot say that a man bordering on sixty has everything in front of him. I know it's considered middle-aged in this misguided country, where people will never face the facts of life, but in simple truth Robert had finished with life to all intents and purposes."

"You won't say that when you come to sixty yourself, Austin. Robert was a great strong man, with years of activity before him. Besides, people don't kill themselves because they are growing old."

"I never suggested it. I was merely pointing out that Robert hadn't everything in front of him, to use your own phrase."

"In any case he would not have killed himself," replied Mrs. Pendleton sharply. "Such a disgrace! He was the proudest of men, he would never have done it."

"You always hark back to that." There was faint irritation in Austin's tone.

"I really cannot get away from it, Austin. Can you conceive of any reason?"

"There was a reason in Robert's case. I did not mention it to you last night in the presence of the police sergeant, but I told Dr. Ravenshaw, and he is inclined to agree with me. Since then I have thought it over carefully, and I am convinced that I am right."

"What is the reason?"

"You recall the disclosure Robert made to us yesterday afternoon?"

"About his marriage and Sisily?"

"Yes. It must have been very painful to Robert, more painful than we imagine. It would come home to him later with stunning force—all that it implied, I mean. At the time Robert did not foresee all the consequences likely to ensue from it. It was likely to affect his claim for the title, because he was bound to make it known. When he came to think it over he must have realized that it would greatly prejudice his claim. A body like the House of Lords would do their utmost to avoid bestowing an ancient name on a man, who, by his own showing, lived with a married woman for twenty-five years, and had an illegitimate daughter by her. These are painful things to speak of, but they were bound to come out. My own feeling is that Robert had a bitter awakening to these facts when it was too late—when he had made the disclosure. And he may have felt remorse—"

"Remorse for what?"

"Remorse for giving the secret away and branding his daughter as illegitimate on the day that her mother was buried. It has an ugly look, Constance, there's no getting away from that."

He lapsed into silence, and awaited the effect of his words. Mrs. Pendleton pondered over them for some moments in manifest perturbation. There was sufficient resemblance between Austin's conclusions and the thoughts which had impelled her nocturnal visit to Flint House, to sway her mind like a pendulum towards Austin's view. But that only lasted for a moment. Then she thrust the thought desperately from her.

"No, no; I cannot—I will not believe it!" she cried in an agitated voice. "All this must have been in Robert's mind beforehand. His letters to me about Sisily indicated that there were reasons why he wished me to take charge of her. Robert had weighed the consequences of this disclosure, Austin—I feel sure of that. He was a man who knew his own mind. How carefully he outlined his plans to us yesterday! He was to appear before the Investigations Committee next week to give evidence in support of his claim to the title. And he told me that he was purchasing a portion of the family estate at Great Missenden, and intended to live there. Is it logical to suppose that he would terminate all these plans and ambitions by destroying himself? I, for one, will never believe it. I have my own thoughts and suspicions—"

He turned a sudden searching glance on her. "Suspicions of whom?"

"I took a dislike to that terrible man-servant of Robert's from the moment I saw him," said Mrs. Pendleton, setting her chin firmly.

This feminine flight was too swift for Austin Turold to follow.

"What has that to do with what we are talking about?" he demanded.

"When we reached the door last night it was Thalassa who let us in, with his hat and coat on, ready to go out. There was something strange and furtive about his manner, too, for I never took my eyes off him, and I'm sure he had something on his mind. I'm quite convinced it was he who was listening at the door yesterday afternoon. And he's got a wicked and crafty face."

"Good God!" ejaculated Austin Turold, as the full force of his sister's impressions reached his mind. "Do you mean to say that because you took a dislike to this unfortunate man's face, you think he has murdered Robert?

And yet there are some feminists who want to draw our judges from your sex! My dear Constance, you cannot make haphazard accusations of murder in this reckless fashion."

"I am not accusing Thalassa of murder," said Mrs. Pendleton, with a fine air of generosity. "And there's more than my dislike of his face in it, too. He was looking through the door in the afternoon—"

"You only think that," interrupted her brother.

"I feel sure it was he. It was also strange to see him with his hat and coat on when he answered our knock. He told Dr. Ravenshaw that he was going to the churchtown for him."

"That reminds me that I haven't yet heard what took you up to Flint House last night, Constance," said her brother, looking at her fixedly. "What were you doing there at that late hour, and why was Ravenshaw with you?"

Mrs. Pendleton told him, and he listened coldly. "I think you might have consulted me first before Dr. Ravenshaw," he observed.

"I didn't because I thought you would have put obstacles in my way," she replied with frankness.

"I most certainly should. Of course the whole position may be altered now, with Robert's death. Have you told Sisily?"

"Yes. She took it almost passively. She is the strangest girl, but after last night I look upon her as a sacred charge—Robert's last wish."

"It will be best for you to take charge of her, I think," said Austin absently. "I expect she is provided for in Robert's will. I found that in the old clock case last night, and I've handed it to the local lawyer who drew it up. But this is beside the point, Constance. I have come over here this morning to beg of you to let this terrible business rest where it is. There is not the slightest doubt in my mind that our unhappy brother has ended his own life—all the facts point to it only too clearly—and I particularly desire, for all our sakes, that you do nothing to put your ill-informed suspicions into action. Let the thing drop."

"It is too late," said Mrs. Pendleton decidedly. "I have already been to the police. There is a detective from Scotland Yard on his way over from Bodmin."

"You might have told me this before and saved my time," said Austin, rising with cold anger. "In my opinion you have acted most ill-advisedly.

However, it's too late to talk of that. No, there is no need to rise. I can find my way out."

Austin Turold left the hotel, and made his way up the crooked street to the centre of the town. His way lay towards Market Jew Street, where he intended to hire one of the waiting cabs to drive him back to St. Fair. As he neared the top of the street which led to the square, his eye was caught by the flutter of a woman's dress in one of the narrow old passages which spindled crookedly off it. The wearer of the dress was his niece Sisily. She was walking swiftly. A turn of the passage took her in the direction of the Morrab Gardens, and he saw her no more.

Her appearance in that secluded spot was unexpected, but at the moment Austin Turold did not give it more than a passing thought. He hurried across Market Jew Street and engaged a cabman to drive him home.

The ancient vehicle jolted over the moor road in crawling ascent, and in due time reached the spot where the straggling churchtown squatted among boulders in the desolation of the moors, wanting but cave men to start up from behind the great stones to complete the likeness to a village of the stone age. The cab drifted along between the granite houses of a wide street, like a ship which had lost its bearings, but cast anchor before one where a few stunted garden growths bloomed in an ineffectual effort to lessen the general aspect of appalling stoniness. Austin Turold paid the cabman and walked into this house. He opened the door with his latchkey, and ascended rapidly to the first floor.

Lunch was set for two in the room which he entered, and Charles Turold was seated at the table, turning over the pages of a book. He glanced up expectantly, and his lips formed one word —

"Well?"

"It is not well," was the testy response. "My charming sister has called in the assistance of Scotland Yard. You'll have to stay. We've got to face this thing out."

His son received this piece of news with a pale face. "You should have foreseen this last night," he said.

"I saw Sisily in Penzance — near the gardens."

"Where was she going?" asked Charles, flushing slightly.

"I really cannot say. You should be better acquainted with her movements than I," was the ironical response. "You do not suppose I have been altogether blind to your infatuation, do you? If you choose to go walking and flirting with a girl on Cornish moors you must expect to be observed. As a matter of fact I thought it rather a good move on your part, until I learnt the secret of Sisily's birth."

"I tell you I won't stand this," exclaimed Charles, springing up from the table.

"Won't?" said his father. "You carry things with a high hand—Jonathan." His look dwelt coldly on his son. "Do not be a fool. Sit down and let us have lunch, and we'll discuss afterwards what's best to be done."

Chapter XII

With a slightly incredulous air Inspector Dawfield placed his London colleague in possession of his own knowledge of the facts of the case, based on the statements made to him by Mrs. Pendleton that morning and the facts as set forth in Sergeant Pengowan's report.

Detective Barrant listened attentively, with the air of a man smiling to himself. He was not actually doing so, but that was the impression conveyed by his keen bright eyes. He was a Londoner, with an assured manner, and the conviction that his intelligence was equal to any call which might be made upon it. By temperament he was restless, but his work had given him a philosophical outlook which in some measure counterpoised that defect by causing him to realize that life was a tricky and deceptive business in which intelligence counted for more than action in the long run. He had a wider outlook and more shrewdness than the average detective, and he already felt a keen interest in the case he had been called in to investigate.

When the inspector had finished his story he picked up the blue foolscap on which was inscribed the sprawling report of the churchtown sergeant. With a severe effort he mastered the matter contained under the flowing curves and flourishes.

"The local man seems certain that it is suicide," he said, "but the sister's statement certainly calls for further investigation. How far away is this place?"

"Flint House? About five miles across the moors. I've hired a motor-car to drive you up. Nothing has been disturbed so far. As soon as I learnt you were coming I telephoned to Pengowan to leave things as they were until you arrived."

Barrant nodded approval. "Let us go," he said.

The car was waiting outside. The way lay through the town and then across the moors in undulating ascent until at the highest point a rough track crossed the road at a spot where four parishes met. On one side of these cross-roads was a Druidical stone circle, and on the other was a wayside cross to the memory of an Irish female saint who had crossed to Cornwall as a missionary in the tenth century, after first recording a holy vow that she would not change her shift until she had redeemed the whole of the Cornish natives from idolatry.

From the cross-roads the way again inclined downward to the sea in increasing savageness of desolation. Stones littered the purple surface of the moors, or rose in insecure heaps on the steep slopes, as though piled there by the hands of the giants supposed to have once roved these gloomy wilds. Solitude held sway, but there was more than solitude in that lonely aspect: something prehistoric and unknown, unearthly, incomprehensible. Cairn Brea and the Hill of Fires brooded in the distance; the remains of a Druid's altar showed darkly on the summit of a nearer hill. No sound broke the stillness except the faint and distant sobbing of the sea.

St. Fair lay almost hidden in a bend or fold of the moors about a mile before them, and beyond it Dawfield pointed out to his companion Flint House, standing in gaunt outline on a tongue of coast thrust defiantly into the restless waters of the Atlantic.

"A lonely weird place," said Barrant, eyeing his surroundings attentively. "An ideal setting for a mysterious crime."

They drove on in silence until they reached the churchtown. Inspector Dawfield steered the car to the modest dwelling of Sergeant Pengowan, whom they found at his gate awaiting their arrival—a shaggy figure of a rural policeman of the Cornish Celtic variety, with no trace of Spanish or Italian ancestry in his florid face, inquisitively Irish blue-grey eyes, reddish whiskers, and burly frame.

Inspector Dawfield bade him good-day, and added the information that his companion was Detective Barrant, of Scotland Yard. Pengowan greeted Barrant with the respect due to the name of Scotland Yard, and took a humble seat at the back of the car.

They went on again, and in a few minutes the car stopped at the end of the rough moor track, close to where the black cliffs dropped to the grey sea.

Flint House rose solitary before them, perched with an air of bravado upon the granite ledge, as though defying the west wind which blustered around it. The unfastened gate which led to the little path banged noisily in the breeze, but the house seemed steeped in desolation. A face peeped furtively at them from a front window as they approached. They heard a shuffling footstep and the drawing of a bolt, and the door was opened by a withered little woman who looked at them with silent inquiry.

"Where's your husband?" asked Sergeant Pengowan.

She glanced timidly up the stairs behind her, and they saw Thalassa descending as though in answer to the question. He scanned the police officers with a cautious eye. Barrant returned the look with a keen observation which took in the externals of the man who was the object of Mrs. Pendleton's suspicions.

"You are the late Mr. Turold's servant?" he said.

"Put it that way if you like," was the response. "Who might you be?"

Barrant did not deign to reply to this inquiry. "Take us upstairs," he said.

"Pengowan wants us to look at the outside first," said Dawfield, but Barrant was already mounting the stairs.

"You do so," he called back, over his shoulder. "I'll go up."

At the top of the staircase he waited until Thalassa reached him. "Where are Mr. Turold's rooms?" he asked.

Thalassa pointed with a long arm into the dim vagueness of the passage. "Down there," he said, "at the end. The study on the right, the bedroom opposite."

"Very well. You need not come any further."

The old man's eyes travelled slowly upward to the detective's face, but he kept his ground.

"Did you hear me?" Barrant asked sharply. "You can go downstairs again."

Again the other's eyes sought his face with a brooding contemplative look. Then he turned sullenly away with moving lips, as though muttering inarticulate words, leaving Barrant standing on the landing, watching his slow descent.

When he was quite sure that he was gone, Barrant turned down the passage-way. He had his reasons for wishing to be alone. The value of a vivid first impression, the effect of concentration necessary to reproduce the scene to the eyes of imagination, the mental arrangement of the facts in their proper order and conformity — these were things which were liable to be broken into by the disturbing presence of others, by the vexatious interruption of loudly proffered explanations.

He knew all the facts that Inspector Dawfield and Sergeant Pengowan could impart. He knew of Robert Turold's long quest for the lost title, the object of his visit to Cornwall, his near attainment to success, his summons to his family to receive the news. In short, he was aware of the whole sequence of events preceding Robert Turold's violent and mysterious death, with the exception of the revelation of his life's secret, which Mrs. Pendleton had withheld from Inspector Dawfield. Barrant had heard all he wanted to know at second hand at that stage of his investigations, and he now preferred to be guided by his own impressions and observations.

His professional interest in the case had been greatly quickened by his first sight of Flint House. Never had he seen anything so weird and wild. The isolation of the place, perched insecurely on the edge of the rude cliffs, among the desolation of the rocks and moors, breathed of mystery and hinted at hidden things. But who would find the way to such a lonely spot to commit murder, if murder had been committed?

Reaching the end of the long passage, he first turned towards the study on the right. The smashed door swung creakingly back to his push, revealing the interior of the room where Robert Turold had met his death. Barrant entered, and closed the broken door behind him. It was here, if anywhere, that he might chance to find some clue which would throw light on the cause.

The profusion of papers which met his eye, piled on the table and filling the presses and shelves which lined the musty room, seemed, at the outset, to give ground for the hope that such an expectation might be realized. But they merely formed, in their mass, a revelation of Robert Turold's industry in gathering material for his claim. There were genealogical tables without number, a philology of the two names Turold and Turrald, extracts of parish registers and corporation records, copies from inscriptions from tombstones and mural monuments, copied pedigrees from the British Museum and the great English collections, a host of old deeds and wills, and other mildewed records of perished hands. But they all seemed to have some bearing on the quest to which Robert Turold had sacrificed the years of his manhood.

He had died as he lived, engrossed in the labour of his life. A copy of Burke's "Vicissitudes of Families" was lying open on the table, and beside it were two sheets of foolscap, covered with notes in thin irregular handwriting. The first of these depicted the arms of the Turrald family, as originally selected at the first institution of heraldry, and the quarterings of the heiresses who had married into the family at a later date.

The second sheet was headed "Devonian and Cornwall branch of the Turolds," and contained notes of Robert Turold's ancestral discoveries in that spot. The notes were not finished, but ended abruptly in the middle of a sentence: "It is necessary to make it clea—"

Those were the last words the dead man had written. He had dropped the pen, which lay beside the paper, without finishing the word "clear."

The sight of this unfinished sheet kindled Barrant's imagination, and he stood thoughtful, considering the meaning of it. Was it the attitude of a man who had committed suicide? Was it conceivable that Robert Turold would break off in the middle of a sentence, in the middle of a word, and shoot himself? It seemed a strange thing to do, but Barrant's experience told him that there were no safe deductions where suicides were concerned. They acted with the utmost precipitation or the utmost deliberation. Some wound up their worldly affairs with businesslike precision before embarking on their timeless voyage, others jumped into the black gulf without, apparently, any premeditated intention, as if at the beckoning summons of some grisly invisible hand which they dared not disobey. Barrant recalled the strange case of a wealthy merchant who had cut his throat on a Bank holiday and confessed before death that he had felt the same impulse on that day for years past. He had whispered that the day marked to him such a pause in life's dull round that it seemed to him a pity to start again. He had resisted the impulse for years, but it had waxed stronger with each recurring anniversary, and had overcome him at last.

Every suicide was a law unto himself. Barrant willingly conceded that, but he could not so easily concede that a man like Robert Turold would put an end to his life just when he was about to attain the summit of that life's ambition. It was a Schopenhauerian doctrine that all men had suicidal tendencies in them, in the sense that every man wished at times for the cessation of the purposeless energy called life, and it was only the violence of the actual act which prevented its more frequent commission. But Barrant reflected that in his experience suicides were generally people who had been broken by life or were bored with it. Men of action or intellect rarely committed suicide, not because they valued life highly, but because they had so much to do in their brief span that they hadn't time to think about putting an end to it. Death usually overtook them in the midst of their schemes.

Robert Turold was not a man of intellect or action, but he belonged to a type which, as a rule, cling to life: the type from which zealots and bigots spring—men with a single idea. Such men shrink from the idea of destroying the vital engine by which their idea is driven forward. Their ego is too pronounced for that.

It was true that Robert Turold believed he had realized the aim for which he had lived, and therefore, in a sense, had nothing more to live for. But that point of view was too coldly logical for human nature. Its presumption was only applicable to a higher order of beings. No man had ever committed suicide upon achieving the summit of an ambition. There were always fresh vistas opening before the human mind.

Barrant left the study for the opposite room where the body of Robert Turold had been taken. It was his bedroom, and he had been laid upon the bed.

Death had not come to him easily. His harsh features were set in a stern upward frown, and the lower lip was slightly caught between the teeth, as though bitten in the final rending of the spirit. But Barrant had seen too much of violent death to be repelled by any death mask, however repellent.

He eyed the corpse closely, and then proceeded to examine the death wound. In doing so he had to move the body, and a portion of the sleeve fell back, exposing the left arm to the elbow. Barrant was about to replace it when his eye lighted upon a livid mark on the arm. He rolled back the garment until the arm lay bare to the shoulder. The disclosure revealed four faint livid marks running parallel across the arm, just above the elbow.

The arms had been straightened to the body to the elbows, and then crossed decorously on the breast. Barrant walked round to the other side of the bed, knelt down by the edge of it, and examined the underneath part of the arm. A single livid mark was imprinted upon it.

The inference was unmistakable. The four upper marks were fingerprints, and the lower one a thumb mark. Somebody had caught the dead man's arm in such a strenuous grip that the livid impression had remained after death.

The discovery was significant enough, but Barrant was not at that moment prepared to say how much it portended. It seemed certain that the marks had not been made by Robert Turold himself. Their position suggested a left-hand clutch, though only a finger-print expert could definitely determine that point. Even if they were not, it was too far-fetched a supposition to imagine a man gripping his own arm hard enough to bruise it.

The relative weight of this discovery was, in Barrant's mind, weakened by the fact that the marks might have been caused by the persons who had carried the body from the next room. Nevertheless, the marks must be regarded as infirmative testimony, however slight, of the fallibility of the circumstantial deductions which had been made from the discovery of the body in a locked room, with windows which could not be reached from the outside.

The presumption of suicide rested on the theory that the circumstances excluded any other hypothesis. But Barrant reflected that he did not know enough about the case to accept that assumption as warranted by the facts. The one certainty was that the study could not have been reached from the outside. Barrant had noted the back windows before entering the house; his subsequent interior examination had strengthened his conviction that they were inaccessible. Underneath the study windows there was only the narrowest ledge of rock between that side of the house and the edge of the cliffs. A descent from the windows with a rope was hazardously possible, but ascent and entrance by that means was out of the question.

On the other hand, the theory of interior inaccessibility had a flaw in it, due to the presence of five different people in the room before the police arrived. Their actions and motives would have to be most carefully weighed and sifted before the implication of the discovery of the finger-marks could be determined.

The rather breathless entrance of Inspector Dawfield put an end to Barrant's reflections. He explained that Sergeant Pengowan, in his anxiety to maintain the correctness of his official report, had taken him to various breakneck positions at the back of the house and along the cliffs in order to demonstrate the impossibility of anybody entering Robert Turold's rooms from outside. The sergeant was at that moment engaged in a room downstairs drawing up his reasons for that belief. "A kind of confirmatory report," Dawfield explained. "He fears that his reputation is at stake."

"He can save himself the trouble," said Barrant. "The solution of Robert Turold's death lies in these two rooms, if anywhere."

Something in his companion's tone caused Inspector Dawfield to direct an interrogative glance at him. "Have you discovered something?" he asked.

"Finger-marks on the left arm, a left-hand impression, I should say."

He drew back the loose sleeve of the dead man, and Dawfield examined the marks attentively. "This is strange," he said. "It looks suspicious."

"Strange enough, and certainly suspicious. The point is, is it suspicious enough to upset the theory of suicide? The marks are too faint to enable us to determine whether they are of recent origin. But I think that we must assume that they are. It has occurred to me that they may have been caused when the body was picked up from the floor of the other room and carried in here."

"In that case the marks would have been underneath the arm. In lifting a heavy weight like a corpse it would be natural to place the hands under the shoulders, for greater lifting power."

"There's something in that, but it's by no means certain. It would depend on the position of the body. According to Pengowan's report, Robert Turold was found lying face downward. The body would have to be turned over before it was lifted, and the grip might have been made in pulling it over. We must find that out."

"It's a point which can be settled at once by questioning Thalassa. He helped Pengowan carry the body into this room."

"That is the very thing I do not wish to do," rejoined Barrant quickly. "We have to remember that Thalassa is, for the time being, suspect. Mrs. Pendleton's suspicions of him may be based on the slightest foundation, but we are bound to keep them in mind."

"Do you not intend to question him at all?"

"Not at present. His attitude when he brought me upstairs was that of a man on his guard, expecting to be questioned. I saw that at once, and decided to say nothing to him. I will take him by surprise later on, when he is off his guard, and if he is keeping anything back I may be able to get it out of him. But we must not be too quick in drawing the conclusion that those marks were made by him."

"What makes you say so?" asked Inspector Dawfield.

"Thalassa has a long bony hand, with fingers thickened by rough work. I noticed it when he was pointing to these rooms from the passage. This grip looks as if it might have been made by a smaller hand, with slim fingers. Look how close together the marks are! Unfortunately, that's about all we're likely to deduce from them, and I doubt if a finger-print expert will be able to help us. Observe, there are no finger-prints—merely faint marks of the middle of the fingers, and a kind of blur for the thumb. But the thing is suspicious, undoubtedly suspicious."

"Still, the door was locked from inside," said Dawfield. "We mustn't lose sight of that fact."

"And the key was found in the room. We must also remember that there were several people in the room after the door was burst open, including the dead man's brother. It seems that it was he who first propounded the suicide theory to Dr. Ravenshaw, and subsequently to Pengowan. Do you know anything about the brother?"

"I know nothing personally. Pengowan tells me that Robert Turold secured lodgings for his brother and his son in an artist's house at the churchtown about six weeks ago. They arrived next day, and are still there. I understand that the brothers have been in pretty close intimacy, meeting each other practically every day, either at the churchtown or in this house."

"Do you know what took place at the family gathering which was held in this house yesterday afternoon, after the funeral?"

"All I know is that Robert Turold informed his family that he was likely to succeed in his claim for the title. Mrs. Pendleton was rather vague about the details, but she did say that her brother had placed his daughter in her charge, and had made a long statement to them about his future plans."

"She did not indicate what those plans were?"

"Only in the vaguest way. I remember her saying that her brother was a wealthy man: the one wealthy member of the family, was the way she put it. Her principal preoccupation was her suspicion of the man-servant, based on seeing him listening at the door. She was very voluble and excited—so much so that I did not attach much importance to what she said, and did not ask her many questions."

"It is of the utmost importance that we should find out all we can about this family council yesterday. It is possible that it may throw some light on Robert Turold's death. I am not prepared at present to say whether it is suicide or not, but apart from any suspicious circumstances, I feel that there is some justification for Mrs. Pendleton's belief that a wealthy and successful man like her brother was not likely to take his own life, unless there was some hidden reason for him to do so. If we knew more of what happened downstairs yesterday we might be in a better position to judge of that. The case strikes me as a very peculiar one—indeed, it has some remarkable features. My first task will be to interview all the persons who were present at yesterday's gathering. Can you tell me if the brothers were on good terms?"

"I believe so."

"Is Austin Turold a poor man?"

"I know nothing about him. But what has that got to do with it?"

"It may have much to do with it. He may have stood to inherit a fortune from Robert."

"You surely do not suspect the brother?"

"I suspect no one, at present," returned Barrant. "I am merely glancing at the scanty facts within our knowledge and seeing what can be gathered from them. Robert Turold is found dead in his study, with his hands on an old clock, where he kept important papers, including his will. We are indebted to Austin Turold for that knowledge. But how did Austin Turold come to know that his brother kept his will in the clock-case? Did Robert tell him, or did he find it out? Was Austin aware of the contents of the will? Why did Robert go to the clock? Was his idea to destroy the will? And was that after or before he was shot, or shot himself?

"These are questions we cannot answer without further knowledge, but they seem to point to the existence of some family secret of which we know nothing. We must find out what it is. I shall first interview Austin Turold, and then call on Dr. Ravenshaw, if time permits. You'd better drop me at the churchtown on your way back to Penzance. There's really nothing to detain you any longer."

They returned to the churchtown in the motor-car, and Pengowan from the back seat directed the way to Austin Turold's lodgings.

Chapter XIII

"Oh yes, I'm modern enough," said Austin Turold, balancing his cigarette in his white fingers, and glancing at Barrant with a reflective air — "that is to say, I believe in America and the League of Nations, but not in God. It's not the fashion to believe in God or have a conscience nowadays. They both went out with the war. After all, what's a conscience to a liver? But here I am, chattering on to distract my sad thoughts, although I can see in your eye that you have it in you to ask me some questions. Well, go ahead and ask them, and I will answer them — if I can."

"I do wish to ask you some questions," said Barrant — "questions connected with your brother's death."

"I know very little about it. It was a most terrible shock to me, I assure you, and is likely to detain me in this barbarous place longer than I intended — greatly against my will."

"I understand you came to Cornwall at your brother's request?"

"Yes. My brother sent for me and my son more than a month ago, so we came at once. I'll forestall the further inquiry I see on your lips, and tell you why I came so promptly. My brother Robert was the wealthy member of the family, and I was the poor one — a poor devil of an Anglo-Indian with nothing on this side of the grave but a niggardly Civil Service pension!

"When we arrived I found that Robert had already taken these lodgings for us, which was as near as he could get accommodation to his own house. I did not object to that arrangement, because I do not like hotels nowadays — not since the newly-rich started to patronize them. So here I've been rusticating ever since, conferring daily with my poor brother, and eating the four meals a day which are provided with the lodgings by the estimable people of this house. My landlord is an artist. That is to say, he's forever daubing pictures which nobody buys. I've come to the conclusion that most people dislike Cornwall because of the number of bad pictures which are painted here. You see some samples of my host's brush on these walls. They are actually too bad to be admitted to the Academy. My poor host and hostess, being unable to make ends meet, were obliged to take in lodgers. The fact, however, is not unduly obtruded. We discuss Art at night, and not the scandalously high price of food. I get on very well, but then I can adapt myself to any society. I pride myself on being a philosopher. But my son is not so facile. My worthy entertainers regard him as a Philistine, and bestow very little of their attention upon him. He spends his time in taking long walks through the wilds. He is out walking at present. I am sorry he is not here."

The conversation was suspended by the entrance of an elderly maid servant with a long and melancholy white face, thickly braided hair, strongly marked black eyebrows, wearing a black dress with white apron, and a white bow in her hair, who came to ask if Mr. Turold required any more tea. On learning that he did not she withdrew as noiselessly as she had entered.

"I see you are looking at our parlour-maid," said Austin Turold, following the direction of his visitor's glance.

"She's a strange sort of parlour-maid," admitted the detective. "She reminds me of — of — "

"A study in black and white," suggested his host. "Her face is her fortune. She's sitting to Brierly — that's my host — for his latest effort. He's painting her as the Madonna or Britannia — I really forget which. A new type, you know. The servants in this house are engaged for their faces. They had a villainous scoundrel of a man-servant — a returned soldier — engaged as Judas Iscariot, who bolted last week with the silver spoons. But all this is beside the point, Mr. Barrant, and I must not waste your time. You have come here for a specific purpose — to turn me inside out. What can I tell you?"

"I want to know all that you can tell me about your brother's death," said the other, with emphasis.

"But what can I tell you that you do not already know?" exclaimed Austin, raising his eyebrows with a helpless look. "Ask me what questions you like, and I'll endeavour to answer them. When the famous Detective Barrant — for I understand from the newspapers that you are famous — takes an interview in hand I expect him to handle the situation in a masterly fashion, as befits his reputation. So ask your questions, my dear fellow, and I'll do my utmost to respond." Austin Turold took off his glasses, and posed himself in an attitude of expectation, with his eyes fixed upon the detective's face.

Barrant eyed the elder man with a puzzled curiosity which was tolerably masked by official impassivity. Barrant had his own methods of investigation and inquiry. He brought an alert intelligence, a seeing eye, and a false geniality to bear in his work. Unversed in elaborate deduction, he flattered himself that he knew enough about human nature to strike the balance of probabilities in almost any case. His cardinal article of faith was that there was nothing like getting on good terms with those he was interviewing in order to find out things. Most people were on their guard against detectives, who too often took advantage of their position to assume offensive airs of intimidation, whereas the great thing was to disarm suspicion by a friendly manner. Barrant had cultivated pleasantness with considerable success. Some who were not good judges of physiognomy were apt to overlook the watchful eyes in his smiling affable presence, and talk freely—sometimes too freely, as they later on discovered to their cost. A chance word, a significant phrase, was sufficient to set him burrowing underground with the activity of a mole, to burst into the open later on with all his clues complete, to the confusion of the trusting person with an unguarded tongue.

He had put these tactics into execution with Austin Turold. Austin, taking tea when he called, in a bright blue room hung with pictures, had received his visitor with a charming cordiality, insisted on his taking tea with him, and then let loose a flood of small-talk, as though he were delighted with his visitor. His welcome was so perfect, his manners so gracefully unforced, that Barrant had an uneasy suspicion that he was being beaten at his own game, and was slightly out of countenance in consequence. Up to that moment he could not, for the life of him, decide whether Austin Turold's polished self-assurance was a mask or not. It seemed too natural to be assumed.

"Your own opinion is that your brother committed suicide?" he asked again.

"No other conclusion is possible, in my mind."

"But did he have any reason, that you know of, to commit suicide?"

Austin shrugged his shoulders. "Suicide is not usually associated with reason," he observed. "But in Robert's case there is a reason, or so it seems to me. I have not seen him for many years, but during my recent close association with him I was struck by two things: the solitary aloofness of his mind, and his overwhelming pride—pride in the family name. These two traits in his character coloured all his actions. In the first place, he disliked opening his mind to anybody, but the stronger influence, his family pride, overcame his habitual secretiveness when he thought it necessary and desirable to do so in furtherance of his darling ambition—the restoration of this title. Men who lead a solitary, self-contained life, like my brother, become introspective and ultra-sensitive, and face any intimate personal revelation with the utmost reluctance. They will nerve themselves to it when the occasion absolutely requires, but the after effects—the mental self-probings, the agonized self torture that a self-conscious proud man can inflict on himself when he comes to analyze the effects of his disclosure on other minds, are sometimes unendurable."

Austin put forward this analysis of his brother's state of mind with a gravity which was in complete contrast with the light airiness of his tea-table gossip, and Barrant felt that he was speaking with sincerity.

"Yes, I can understand that," he said with a thoughtful nod.

"I think that is what happened in my brother's case, when he felt called upon to reveal, as he did yesterday, a shameful family secret which hurt him in his strongest point—his family pride."

"Stop a minute," interrupted Barrant, in a surprised voice. "I really do not follow you here. What is this shameful secret to which you refer?"

Austin Turold looked surprised in his turn. "It had to do with his marriage and his daughter's legitimacy," he slowly replied. "Surely my sister imparted this to the Penzance police inspector, when she besought his assistance?"

"I know nothing about it," replied Barrant quickly and emphatically. "I shall be glad if you will tell me."

"Certainly."

Austin Turold related the story of his brother's. Again he spoke in careful grave words, and with a manner completely divested of any trace of his habitual flippancy.

"It appears to me that this revelation must have had a very painful effect on Robert's mind," he added. "You must remember that he was an abnormal type. An ordinary man would not have made such a disclosure on the day of the funeral of the woman who was supposed to be his wife. But all Robert's acts hinged on his one great obsession. He allowed nothing to come between him and his one ambition—not even his wife (let us call her so) and child. But it would come home to him afterwards—I mean the normal point of view—the way the world would regard such a disclosure— and I have no doubt that his belated mental anguish and morbid thoughts impelled him to take his life. Understand me, Mr. Barrant, I do not mean that he did this through remorse, but through the blow to his pride. He couldn't face the racket—the gossip, the notoriety and all the rest of it."

"But according to your story, your brother had nothing to blame himself for," said Barrant. "You say that he was ignorant of this earlier marriage until recently?"

"Public sentiment will not look at it that way. People will say he sacrificed a dead woman and his daughter to his own selfish ends—threw them over when he had attained his ambition. That's what came home to him, in my opinion."

"I see." Barrant was silent for a while, turning this over in all its bearings. "Yes. There may be something in that point of view. But did not your brother confide this story to you before yesterday?"

"When we were alone together during the last few days he frequently seemed on the point of telling me something. I could see that by his manner. But he never got beyond a certain portentousness, as it were. It's my belief now that he wanted to tell me, but couldn't quite bring himself to it. I am very sorry that he didn't."

"Do you know how long your brother has been aware of this earlier marriage?"

"Quite recently, I believe. He gave us to understand yesterday that it was a death-bed confession."

"Are there any proofs of the earlier marriage?"

"I am afraid I cannot enlighten you on that point either."

"This is very strange," said Barrant. "The proofs are very important. This disclosure vitally affected your brother's ambitions, and was therefore likely to influence his views regarding the disposition of his property."

He shot a keen glance at his companion. Austin laid aside his glasses and bent earnestly across the table.

"I will be frank with you," he said, "quite frank. My brother told me a little more than a week ago that he had made a new will, and that I was his heir."

"Where is this will?"

"I found it in the clock-case at Flint House last night, and I have since handed it to the lawyer who drafted it."

"Your brother gave you no indication of this before?"

"No. He told me when I came that he had summoned me to Cornwall because of the great change in the family fortunes. As I was his only brother he desired my presence in the investigation of the final proofs and the preparation of his claim for the House of Lords. Nothing was said about the succession then. Robert was very excited, and talked only of his own future. I feel sure that he was not then thinking of who was to succeed to the title after his death. He looked forward to enjoying it himself. I certainly did not give it a thought, either. Who could have foreseen this tragic event?"

"Do you know anything about this peerage?"

"Not till latterly. I never took it seriously, like Robert. I looked upon it as a family fiction. I understand that the Turrald barony was a barony by writ—whatever that may be. The point is that if my brother had lived to restore it, the title, on his death, would have descended to his only daughter, if she had been born in wedlock. As she is illegitimate, the title would have descended to me, and after me to my son."

"You were here last night when they brought you the news of your brother's death, I understand?" remarked Barrant, in a casual sort of way.

"Yes; I did not go out again after I returned from the funeral."

"Was your son home with you?"

"Most of the time. He came in later than I, and then went out for a walk when the storm cleared away. I did not see him again until this morning. Thalassa came for me with the news of my brother's death, and I did not get back from Flint House until very late."

"I suppose you are aware your sister does not share your view that your brother committed suicide?"

"I understand she has some absurd suspicion about Thalassa, my brother's servant."

"Why do you call her suspicion absurd?" asked Barrant cautiously.

"It is more than absurd," replied Austin warmly. "I am ashamed to think that my sister should have given utterance to such a dreadful thought against a faithful old servant who has been with Robert for half a lifetime, and was devoted to him."

"Mrs. Pendleton saw him looking through the door."

"She only thought so. She went to the door immediately to find out who it was, but there was nobody there."

"Do you think she imagined it?"

"No; I think somebody was there, but it is by no means certain that it was Thalassa. It might have been Thalassa's wife. It might even have been Robert's daughter."

"Was not Miss Turold present at the family gathering?"

"No; my brother naturally did not wish her to be present, and she went upstairs. She went out while we were in the room. The door was slightly open, and she may have glanced in as she passed."

"But this person was listening."

Austin Turold shrugged his shoulders.

"Was your brother talking about his marriage at the time?"

"Yes."

"Could Miss Turold have heard what he was saying?"

"Anybody could. The door was partly open."

"There is some mystery here."

Barrant spoke with the thoughtful air of one viewing a new vista opening in the distance. These surmises about the listener at the door, by their manifest though perhaps unintended implication, pointed to a deeper and more terrible mystery than he had imagined.

Austin Turold did not speak. Darkness had long since fallen, and a lamp, which had been brought in by the maid who was also the model, stood on the table between the two men, and threw its shaded beams on their faces. A clock on the mantel-piece chimed eight, and aroused Barrant to the flight of time.

"I must get back," he said. "I intended to see Dr. Ravenshaw, but I shall leave that until later. Can I get a conveyance back to Penzance?"

"There is a public wagonette. I am not sure when it goes, but it starts from 'The Three Jolly Wreckers' at the other end of the churchtown."

"'The Three Jolly Wreckers!' That's rather a cynical name for a Cornish inn, isn't it?"

"Oh, the Cornish people are not ashamed of the old wrecking days, I assure you."

He accompanied Barrant to the door with the lamp, which he held above his head to light him down the garden path. Barrant, glancing back, saw him looking after him, his face outlined in the darkness by the yellow rays of the lamp.

Chapter XIV

Barrant found the inn at the dark end of a stone alley, with the sound of tipsy singing and shuffling feet coming through the half-open door. He made his way up three granite steps into a side-entrance, catching a glimpse through a glass partition of shaggy red faces and pint pots floating in a fog of tobacco smoke. A stout landlord leaned behind the bar watching his customers with the tolerant smile of a man who was making a living out of their merriment. He straightened himself as he caught sight of Barrant, and opened the sliding window. The detective inquired about the wagonette, and learnt that it had not yet arrived.

"The roouds is rough, and old Garge Crows takes his time," said the landlord, eyeing Barrant with a heavy stare. "'Tain't as thow 'e had a passel of passergers to be teeren rownd after."

"Can you give me some supper while I'm waiting?"

"Sooper?" The innkeeper scratched his chin doubtfully. "'Tis late in the ebenin' to be getting sooper. There's nawthing greut in the howse. You could 'ave some tay—p'raps an egg."

"That will do."

The innkeeper roared forth a summons, which was answered by a rugged Cornish lass from the kitchen. She cast a doubtful glance on the young man when she learnt what was required, and took him into a small sitting-room, where she left him to gaze at his leisure upon a framed portrait of Cecil Rhodes, a stuffed gannet in a large glass case, and a stuffed badger in a companion case on the other side of the wall. In about twenty minutes she returned with a tray, and placed before the detective a couple of eggs, some bread and butter, saffron cake, and a pot of tea. The eggs were of peculiar mottled exterior, and when tasted had such a strong fish-like flavour as to suggest that they might have been laid by the gannet in its lifetime, and stowed away by a careful Cornish housewife until some stranger chanced to visit that remote spot. Barrant was hungry enough to gulp them down, though with a wry face. He had just finished a second cup of very strong tea when he heard the clatter of a vehicle outside, and the girl thrust a tousled dark head through the door to announce the arrival of Mr. Crows and his wagonette.

Barrant paid for his food and went out. An ancient hooded vehicle filled the narrow way, drawn by a large shaggy horse which turned a gleaming eye on the detective as he emerged, and snorted loudly, as though resenting the prospect of having to drag his additional weight back to the town. The driver sat motionless on the box, watching the caperings of the tipsy tin-miners through the half-open door: a melancholy death'shead of a man, with a preternaturally long white face, and a figure shrouded in a dark cloak, looking as though he might be Death itself, waiting for the carousers to drop dead of apoplexy before carrying them off in his funereal equipage. In reply to Barrant's question he informed him that the vehicle was destined for Penzance, and immediately the detective entered the dark interior he drove off with disconcerting suddenness, as though he had been waiting for him only, and was determined to make sure of him before he had time to escape.

The shaggy horse lumbered forward at an unwilling trot, like an animal disillusioned with life. Soon they cleared the churchtown and entered the darkness of the moors. A long and tiring day disposed Barrant to slumber. He had begun to nod sleepily when the wagonette stopped with a jerk which shook him into wakefulness. He was able to make out that they had reached the highest elevation of the moors—the cross-roads from where Inspector Dawfield had shown him Flint House in the distance that afternoon. He could just discern the outlines of the wayside cross and the old Druidical monolith, both pointing to the silent heavens in unwonted religious amity.

"Good ebenen', Garge." A lusty voice hailed out of the darkness, and then Barrant was aware of somebody entering the wagonette, a large male body which plumped heavily on his knees as it started again.

"Bed pardin, I'm sure. Aw dedn't knaw Crows had another passenger to-night." A husky voice spoke unseen. "'Taint often it 'appens." There was the splutter of a match, and as it flared up Barrant saw a pair of twinkling grey eyes regarding him from a brown and rugged face. "Old Garge never reckons on haavin' passengers back by th' laast wagonette, so 'e never lights up inside. I'll make a light now, then we'll be more comfortable." He struck another match and lit the candle in the wagonette lamp, and was revealed to Barrant's eyes as a stout and pleasant-faced man of fifty or so, with something seamanlike, or at least boatmanlike, in his appearance. He gave the detective a smile and a nod, and added, "Old Crows is fullish mean about candles."

"It's a wonder he drives the wagonette at all, if there is no demand for it," remarked Barrant.

"Aw, there's a'plenty demand for it—always lots of passergers except by this one," rejoined the man in the blue suit. "You'd be surprised how people gets about in these paarts." He was studying the detective's face with interest. "You be a Londoner," he said quickly. "What braught you down here?"

"How do you know that I'm a Londoner?" said Barrant, parrying the latter part of the question.

"I can tell a Londoner at once," returned the other.

"'Twould be straange if I couldn't. I'm Peter Portgartha. P'raps you haven't heard of me, but I'm well known hereabouts, and if you want to see any of the sights, you'd best coome to me, and I'll show you round."

"A guide, eh?"

"There be guides and guides. I'll say nathin' about th' others, but there's nobody knaws this part of Cornwall like me. I was born and bred and knaw every inch of it. Before the waar I've had London ladies say to me: "Ave you ever seen the Bay of Naples, or the Canaries? Oh, you should see them, Mr. Portgartha, they're ever so much more grand than Cornwall.' Well, while the war was on I did see the Canaries and Bay of Naples at Government's expense on a minesweeper, and they're not a patch on the Cornwall coast. There's nathin' to beat it in the world."

"It's good, is it?" said Barrant, with his accustomed affability to strangers. "If I want to see any of it I'll get you to show me round."

"Just came along to th' Mousehole and ask for Peter Portgartha. There's a great cave at the Mouse's Hole—that's what we call it hereabouts, that ain't to be beaten in the whole world. If your good lady's here, bring her with you to see it. There ain't nobody else can show it to her like I can. The London ladies don't like goin' down the Mousehole cave as a rule, because it's a stiffish bit of a climb, and in the holiday season there's always a lot of raffish young fellows hangin' round to see the ladies go down—to see what they can see, you knaw. But I never 'ave no accidents like that. No bold-eyed young chap ever saw the leg of any lady in my charge—not so much as the top of a boot, because I knaw how to taake them down. I'm well known to some of the 'ighest ladies in the land because I 'ev been aable to take care of their legs when they were goin' down. I've had letters from them thaankin' me. You've no idea how grateful they be."

This startling instance of the stern morality of aristocratic womanhood was unfortunately wasted on Barrant, whose thoughts had reverted to the principal preoccupation of his mind. Mr. Portgartha rambled on.

"Aw, but it's strange to be meetin' you like this, in old Garge's wagonette. For twelve months I've been goin' acrass the moors to see a sister of mine, who's lonely, poor saul, havin' lost her man in the war—drawned in a drifter 'e was—and catchin' this wagonette back every night, with never a saul to speak to, until last night. Last night there was a passerger, and to-night there's you. Tes strange, come to think of it." He looked hard at Barrant as if for some confirmatory expression of surprise at this remarkable accession to the wagonette's fares. He waited so long that Barrant felt called upon to say something.

"Who was your fellow passenger last night?"

"Now you're asking me a question which takes a bit of answerin'," replied Mr. Portgartha. "'Twas like this. I was waitin' at the crass-roads for old Garge to come along, when a young womon came up out of th' darkness and stood not far from me—just by the ol' crass. I tried to maake out who she was, but it was too daark. So I just says to her, 'Good ebenin', miss, are you waitin' for the wagonette too?' She never answered a word, and before I could think of anything else to say old Garge came along, and we both got in. She sat in a corner, silent as a ghooste. Well, then, I went to light th' lamp, same as I have to-night, but as luck would 'ave it, I hadn't a match. I knaw it was no use askin' old Garge, 'cos he'd pretend not to hear, so I turned to the young womon sittin' opposite, and asked her if she had a match in her pocket. And do you knaw, I declare to gudeness she never said nawthen, not so much as a word!"

"Perhaps she was dumb?" Barrant suggested.

"Aw, iss, doomb enough then," retorted Mr. Portgartha. "I tried her two or three times more, but couldn't get a word out of her. Well, at last I began to get narvous, thinkin' she might be a sperit. So I leant across to her an' says, 'Caan't you say a word, miss? It's only Peter Portgartha speaking, he's well known for his respect for your sect. No young womon need be frightened of speakin' to Peter Portgartha.' And with that she spaaks at last, with a quick little gasp like a sob—I'm thinking I can hear it at this minute—'Aw,' she says, 'why caan't you leave me alone?' 'Never be afraaid,' I says, for I have my pride like other folk, 'I'll say no more. Peter Portgartha has no need to foorce his conversation where it ain't welcome.'"

"A strange girl!" said Barrant, beginning to feel an interest in the story. "Have you no idea who she was?"

"Wait a bit," continued Mr. Portgartha, evidently objecting to any intrusion on his right, as narrator, to a delayed climax. "Well, there we sat, like two ghoostes, till we got to Penzance, but all the time I was thinkin' to mysel' that I'd find out who she was. I sed to myself I'd ride on to the station, instid of gettin' out a piece this side of it so as to make a short cut across to the Mouse's Hole, as I usually do. But that stupid old fule Garge pulled up as usual and bawls through the window, 'Are you going to keep me here all night, Peter?' Before I could say a word the young womon says: 'I'll get out here.' With that she puts the fare into his hand through the open window, and slips out afore I knew what she was going to do. If it hadn't been for my rhoomatics, which I got in the war, I'd 'a followed her. As it was, I couldn't."

"So you didn't see her face, after all?" asked Barrant quickly.

"I didn't, in a manner of speakin'. But I did get a glimpse of her as she passed near the lamp-post—just a half-sight of two big dark eyes in a white face as she went past. I wouldn't 'a thought no more of it," added Mr. Portgartha, laying an impressive hand on his companion's knee, "but for what happened at Flint House last night."

"What's that got to do with it?" In his quickened interest Barrant vainly strove to make his voice appear calm.

"Because the young womon must have coome from Flint House."

Barrant scrutinized his companion sharply in the dim light. "Why do you think so?" he asked.

"For'n thing, the wayside crass where she picked up the wagonette is not far from Flint House by acrass the moors—closer'n goin' from the house on the cliffs t' the churchtown, which is a good slant to the north of it. From Flint House to the crass-roads it's straight as a dart, if you know yer way, with only one house twixt it till you come arver to it—old Farmer Bardsley, who ain't got no wemmenfolk, so it's sartin she didn't come from theer. She wasn't a maa'iden from any of the farms of the moors, for I know them all. But it weren't till this marning that I got a kind of notion who she was. I dropped into the *Tolpen Arms* to have a drop of something for a cawld I've got, and some of the fishermen were talkin' about th' old gentleman of Flint House blowing his head off last night with a gun. It made me feel queery-like when I heerd aboot it. 'Why,' I says, 'that'll be about the time I saw the strange young womon in ol' Crows' wagonette. She must 'ave come from Flint House, now I coome to think of it.' 'What young woman was that?' asked 'Enery Waitts. So I told them what had happened to me, just like I've told it to you. Mrs. Keegan, the land-lady, who was list'ning, says, 'I shouldn't be surprised if it was Mr. Turold's daughter that you saw. I heard yesterday that his sister was staying at Penzance, so p'raps she was going to her, after it happened. So if it was her it's not surprisin' she didn't want to speak to you in her grief.'"

"Did you ever see Miss Turold?"

"I've never see any one of the Flint House folk, though I've heerd of them, often enough."

"Did you notice in which direction this girl went?"

"No. She passed the lamp-post as if she were maakin' up Market Jew Street, but I suppose she ced 'ave turned off anywhere to the right or left."

"What time was it when the wagonette reached the cross-roads on the moor, where she got in?"

"About the same time as to-night, getting on for ten, mebbe."

"She was quite alone?"

"As lonely as any she ghooste, standin' theer by the old crass. 'Twaas because I thought she'd feel feersome that I spoke to her."

Barrant relapsed into a thoughtful silence which lasted until the wagonette pulled up and his fellow-traveller prepared to alight. Then he turned to him and said—

"Good-night. I may see you again."

He fumbled at the interior window as he spoke, opened it, and touched the driver on the shoulder. "Drive me to the Central Hotel," he said. "Go as fast as you can, and I'll give you ten shillings!"

Mr. Crows nodded a cold acquiescence, and they rattled off down the silent street, leaving on Barrant's mind a receding impression of a startled red face staring after them from the footpath. The wagonette jolted round a corner, and ten minutes later stopped at the entrance of the hotel where Mrs. Pendleton was staying.

Chapter XV

When Barrant learnt from the trembling lips of Mrs. Pendleton that she had not seen her niece since that morning, his first step was to get Sisily's full description, and call up Dawfield on the hotel telephone with instructions to have all the railway stations between Penzance and London warned to look out for her. That was a necessary precaution, but it did not need Dawfield's hesitating information about time tables to convince him that it was almost futile. The later of the two trains by which Sisily might have fled from Cornwall had reached London and discharged its passengers somewhere about the time that Mr. Peter Portgartha, in the depth of the rumbling wagonette, was paying his tribute to shrinking female modesty as exhibited on Mousehole rocks.

After doing this Barrant returned to the empty lounge, where Mrs. Pendleton sat in partial darkness with tearful face. All the other guests had retired, and a lurking porter yawned longingly in the passage, waiting for an opportunity to put out the last of the lights and get to bed.

In the first shock of Barrant's violent apparition and angry questions, Mrs. Pendleton had tried, in a bewildered way, to insist that her niece had not left her room on the previous night. But now, in her troubled consideration of the new strange turn of events surrounding her brother's death, she saw that she might have been deceived on this point. Barrant, for his part, had not the slightest doubt of it when he heard that her belief rested on no stronger foundation than Sisily's early withdrawal from the dining-room on the plea of fatigue, and the fact that her bedroom door was locked when Mrs. Pendleton returned from her own visit to Flint House. Sisily's subsequent flight eliminated any uncertainty about that, and established beyond reasonable doubt her identity with the silent girl who had entered the returning wagonette at the cross-roads. The coincidence of those two facts had a terrible significance. Barrant had no doubt that Sisily had gone to her own room early in order to find an opportunity to pay a secret visit to her home, for a purpose which now seemed to stand sinisterly revealed by her disappearance. He also thought he saw the motive—that vital factor in murder—looming behind her nocturnal expedition. But that was a question he was not inclined to analyze too closely at that moment. He wanted to know how she had been able to disappear that day without the knowledge of her aunt.

Mrs. Pendleton had a ready explanation of that. She said that after returning from her visit to the police station that morning she had been engaged with her brother Austin until nearly lunch-time, and when she went up to Sisily's room she found it empty. She concluded that her niece had gone out somewhere to be alone with her grief—she was the type of girl that liked to be alone. After lunch Mrs. Pendleton had letters to write, and then she had gone to her bedroom and fallen sound asleep till dinner-time, worn out by the shock of her brother's death, and the sleepless night which had followed it. When Sisily did not appear at dinner she began to grow uneasy, but sought to convince herself that Sisily might have gone on a *char-à-banc* trip to Falmouth which had been advertised for that day. The incongruity of a sad solitary girl like Sisily nursing her grief in a public vehicle packed with curious chattering trippers did not seem to have occurred to her. But as time passed she grew seriously alarmed, and sent her husband out to make enquiries.

She had sat in the lounge listening with strained ears for the girl's footsteps until Barrant arrived.

"Has your niece any friends in Cornwall or London, or anywhere, for that matter, who would receive her?" Barrant abruptly demanded.

"I really do not know," said Mrs. Pendleton.

She wiped the tears from her eyes with a large white handkerchief. She was overwhelmed by the shock of her niece's disappearance, and the terrible interpretation Barrant evidently placed upon it. But Barrant was in no mood to allow for her confused state of mind.

"You had better try and remember," he said irritably. "It seems to me that I've been kept in the dark. You went to the police to demand an investigation into your brother's death, but you did not say anything of the disclosure he made to you yesterday of his daughter's illegitimacy. Instead of doing so, you only directed suspicion to his man-servant. Meanwhile your niece, who was placed in your care, disappears to heaven knows where, and you took no steps to inform the police. You have acted very indiscreetly, Mrs. Pendleton, to say the least."

"I did not know—I did not think," gasped Mrs. Pendleton. She endeavoured to commence a flurried explanation of the mixed motives and impulses which had swayed her since her brother's death, but Barrant cut it short with an impatient wave of the hand.

"Never mind that now," he said. "I have lost too much time already. Have you no idea where your niece is likely to have sought refuge?"

Mrs. Pendleton shook her head. "Robert had no friends," she said, "and Sisily led a very lonely life. Robert told me that yesterday. That was the reason he wanted me to take charge of her—so as to give her the opportunity of making some girl friends of her own age."

She paused, embarrassed by the recollection that her brother's real intention in placing Sisily in her charge was altogether different. Barrant noted her hesitation, and interpreted it aright.

"No," he said. "The real reason of your brother parting with his daughter provides the motive for her return to his house last night. What happened between them is a matter for conjecture, at present. Apparently she was the last person who saw him alive before he was shot, and now she is not to be found."

There was something so portentously solemn in his manner of speaking these last words that his listener quaked in terror, and gazed at him with widened eyes. Barrant turned abruptly to another phase.

"Are you quite sure that it was the man-servant you saw looking through the door yesterday afternoon?"

It was proof of the fallibility of human testimony that Mrs. Pendleton had sincerely convinced herself that she was quite sure. "Yes," she said.

Barrant looked doubtful. By reason of his calling he was well aware of the human tendency to unintentional mistake in identity. With women especially, the jump from an impression to a conclusion was sometimes as rapid as the thought itself.

"Did you see his face?" he asked.

"Only the eyes. But I am sure that they were Thalassa's eyes."

Barrant did not press the point. He did not doubt the honesty of her belief, but the words in which it was conveyed suggested hasty impression rather than conviction. Such proofs of identity were not to be relied upon.

"Had your brother's servant any reason, so far as you know, to be listening at the door?" he asked.

"All servants are curious," murmured Mrs. Pendleton. She shook her head wisely, as one intimating a wide knowledge of their class.

"All curious servants are not murderers," returned Barrant. "This man has been in your brother's service for a long time, has he not?"

"For a great number of years. Almost ever since Robert returned to England, I think."

"So Mr. Austin Turold informed me. Had he any grudge against his master?"

"Thalassa? I really couldn't tell you, because I do not know. But he has a most truculent and overbearing manner — not at all the kind of manner you expect in a servant, and he seemed to do just what he liked. I disliked him as soon as I saw him. I'm sure he looks more like some dreadful old sea pirate than a gentleman's servant. I would not have him in my household." Mrs. Pendleton set her lips firmly. "No, not for a single moment. But I suppose poor Robert was attached to him from long association."

Barrant nodded in an understanding way. "Then this man Thalassa must have known your niece from childhood," he said in a casual tone. "Was he attached to her, do you think?"

"I know nothing of that."

"That's rather a pity," he said with a gentle shake of the head. He looked at her knowingly. "I do not understand you," she faltered.

"You had grounds for your suspicions of Thalassa — reasonable grounds. He must have admitted your niece into the house last night, you know. I must get it out of him."

She gave a start, for she saw now where his drift of questions was taking them. With a sickening sense of horror she realized that her slight suspicions were being used by him to help fashion a case against her own flesh and blood.

"What are you suggesting?" she breathed, with a nervous look.

"Nothing at present," he said, with a quick realization of the fact that he was in danger of talking too much. "Can you tell me if your niece is provided with money?"

"My brother gave her twenty-five pounds in bank notes yesterday — he told me."

"That is enough to keep her for some weeks. You are quite sure you cannot form any idea where she has gone?"

"No," said Mrs. Pendleton coldly, with a belated inward resolve not to be so ready in volunteering information to the police in future.

"I should like to see the room your niece occupied last night," he said.

That was a search which brought nothing to light. Barrant left the hotel just as little Mr. Pendleton returned to it with an alarmed face and a feeling of personal guilt at his failure to find Sisily.

Barrant passed him with a side glance, his mind full of the problem of the girl's disappearance. He left the hotel in a state of thoughtfulness, fully realizing the difficulties of the task which lay before him in tracing Sisily's movements on the previous night, and discovering where she had flown. The deeper questions of motive and the inconsequence of some of her actions he preferred to leave till later. Action, and not mental analysis, was the need of the moment. Barrant prided himself on being a man of action, and he was also a detective. The thrill of pursuit stirred in his blood.

His later activities that night and the following day brought to light many things, but not all that he wanted to know. He convinced himself, in the first place, that it was possible for the girl to have left her room and returned to it on the night of her father's death without any of the inmates of the hotel being aware of her absence. That lessened the complexity of the case by absolving Mrs. Pendleton from the suspicion of pretended ignorance. Barrant was also convinced the aunt believed her niece to be in bed and asleep during the time of her own visit to her brother's house. Sisily had to pass the office of the hotel in going out and returning, but she could easily have done so unobserved. There were few guests at that season of the year, and the proprietor's daughter, who looked after the office, was in the dining-room having her dinner at half-past seven. She went to bed shortly after ten, leaving the front entrance in charge of the porter, who had duties to perform in various parts of the house. And it was possible to descend the stairs and leave the hotel without being seen from the lounge or smoking-room.

There was a wagonette to St. Fair from the railway station at half-past-seven. The hotel dinner was at a quarter to seven for the convenience of some permanent guests, and Sisily, who left the table before the meal was concluded—about a quarter-past seven, according to Mrs. Pendleton—had time to catch the wagonette. On the assumption that even a Cornish wagonette would cover the journey of five miles across the moors in less than an hour, Sisily had probably reached her father's house at half-past eight or a little earlier. The stopped clock in the study indicated that he met his death at half-past nine. If so, Sisily must have left Flint House shortly before her aunt's arrival to catch the returning wagonette at the cross-roads where the young woman was seen waiting by Peter Portgartha.

But that plausibly conceived itinerary of events needed the support of proof, and there Barrant found himself in difficulty.

The morning's enquiries made it manifest that Sisily had left Penzance by the mid-day train on the previous day. After leaving Mrs. Pendleton, Barrant had gone to the station. The sour and elderly ticket-clerk on duty could give him no information, but let it be understood that there was another clerk selling tickets for the mid-day train, which was unusually crowded by farmers going to Redruth. The other clerk, seen in the morning, had no difficulty in recalling the young lady of Barrant's description. She was pretty and slight and dark, with a pale clear complexion, and she carried a small handbag. She asked for a ticket to London. The clerk understood her to ask for a return ticket, but as she picked it up with the change for the five pound note with which she paid for it, she said that she thought she had asked for a single ticket. He assured her that she had not, but offered to change it. At that moment the departure of the train was signalled, and she ran through the barrier without waiting to change the ticket. The incident caused him to observe her, and his description tallied so completely with Mrs. Pendleton's description that Barrant had not the least doubt that it was Sisily.

On the strength of this information Barrant applied to a local magistrate for a warrant for the girl's arrest. He was well aware that he had not yet gathered sufficient evidence to satisfy the law that she had murdered her father, but his action was justified by her flight and the presumption of her secret visit to her father's house when she was supposed to be in bed and asleep at the hotel.

These things fulfilled, Barrant then applied his mind to the question of Thalassa's complicity. If Sisily's actions on the night of her father's death, and her subsequent flight, simplified matters to the extent of deepening the assumption of murder into a practical certainty, they added to the complexity of the case by giving it the appearance of a carefully planned crime in which Thalassa seemed to be deeply involved.

The insistent necessity of motive which should explain the events of that night with apt presumptions, threw Barrant back on the suggestion, made by Austin Turold, that it was really Sisily whom Mrs. Pendleton had detected looking through the door of the downstairs room when the other members of the family were assembled within listening to Robert Turold. Barrant told himself that Mrs. Pendleton's suspicion of Thalassa rested on nothing more substantial than feminine prejudice, an unreasoning impulse of dislike which would leave few men alive if it always carried capital punishment in its train.

The substitution of Sisily for Thalassa provided a convincing motive for murder. The overheard revelation of her mother's shame and her own precarious condition in the world when she might reasonably have been counting on becoming an heiress of note, were sufficient to account for the nocturnal return and an effort to entreat justice or compel silence – the alternatives depended on the type of girl. From what Mrs. Pendleton had told him of Sisily and her love for her mother – poor Mrs. Pendleton had insisted, all unwittingly, very strongly on that – Barrant had pictured her as a brooding yet passionate type of girl who might have committed the murder in a sudden frenzy of determination to prevent her father making public the unhappy secret of her mother's life. That was an act by no means inconsistent with the temperament of a strongwilled and lonely girl, whose stormy passions had been wrought to the breaking-point by disclosures made on the very day that her loved mother had been buried in a nameless grave. There was, additionally, the motive of self-interest, awakened to the lamentable fact that she had no claim on her father beyond what generosity might dictate. In short, Barrant believed the motive for the murder to be a mixed one, as human motives generally are. At that stage of his reasoning he did not ask himself whether worldly greed was likely to enter into the composition of a girl like Sisily.

This reconstruction of the crime pointed to an accomplice, and that accomplice must have been the man-servant. Nobody but Thalassa could have let the girl into the house; and he could have dropped the key in the room after the door was broken open. That theory not only presupposed strong devotion on Thalassa's part for a girl he had known from childhood, which was a theory reasonable of belief, but it also suggested that he bore a deep grudge against his master on his own account, sufficient to cause him to refrain from doing anything to prevent the accomplishment of the murder, and to risk his own skin afterwards to shield the girl from the consequences. This aspect of the case struck Barrant as very strange and deep, because it failed to account for Sisily's subsequent flight. If Thalassa had jeopardized himself by keeping silence about her visit, and had returned the key to her father's room in order to create the idea of suicide, why had she dispelled the illusion by running away, bringing both her accomplice and herself into danger? Had she been, seized with terror, perhaps due to Mrs. Pendleton's insistence on her belief of murder, or had Thalassa conveyed some warning to her that inquiries were likely to be put afoot?

These were questions to which Barrant felt he could find no answer until he had seen Thalassa and attempted to wrest the truth from him.

He postponed his visit to Flint House until the evening. He wanted to make the journey as Sisily had made it on the previous night, in order to find out, as nearly as possible, the exact moment she had arrived at her father's house. He was not even in a position to prove that she had gone by the wagonette until he had questioned the driver.

He took his way to the station that evening with the feeling that it would be difficult to get anything out of Thalassa, whatever the reasons for his silence. He instinctively recognized that the authority of the law, which strikes such terror into craven hearts, would not help him with this old man whose glance had the lawless fearlessness of an eagle. But he had confidence in his ability to extract the truth, and Thalassa, moreover, was at the disadvantage of having something to hide. It would be strange if he did not succeed in getting the facts out of him.

The St. Fair wagonette was pulled up outside the station. Mr. Crows, master of his destiny and time-tables, reclined in front, regarding with a glazed eye his drooping horse. Inside, some stout women with bundles waited patiently until it suited the autocrat on the box seat to start on his homeward way. Mr. Crows showed no indication of being in a hurry. His head nodded drowsily, and a little saliva trickled down his nether lip. He straightened himself with a sudden jerk as Barrant climbed up beside him.

"What be yewer doin' yare?" he demanded.

"I'm going to St. Fair," said Barrant.

"I doan't allow no passergers to sit alongside o' me."

"You'll have to put up with it for once," returned Barrant curtly, in no way softened by the odour of Mr. Crows' breath.

As this was a reply which no resident of St. Fair would have dared to make, Mr. Crows bent a muddled glance on his fare, and by a concentrated effort recalled the face of the man who had given him ten shillings on the previous night. He decided to pocket the present indignity in the hope of another tip.

"Aw right," he said, with unwonted amiability, "yewer can stay where yew are—for wance."

He applied himself to driving the wagonette. Sobriety was not an essential of the feat. The horse knew the way, drew clear of the town without accident, and jogged into the long winding road which stretched across the moors. The shadows deepened into night, and Mr. Crows lighted a solitary lamp in the front of his vehicle.

"Aren't you going to light up inside?" asked Barrant, when the lamp was flickering faintly.

"No," replied Mr. Crows shortly. "It don't pay. Let 'em set in the dark."

"Not enough passengers, eh?"

"Moren enough fat old wommen on the out journey," declared Mr. Crows passionately. "That's because it's all up-hill. But they walk in downhill to save a shellen. *I* know them." He brooded darkly. "It's all part of the plan," he went on. Then, as though feeling that this latter statement, in itself, erred on the side of vagueness, he added—"to worrit a man."

"How many passengers did you have on your last journey in, last night?"

"Two on 'em." Mr. Crows, with forefinger and thumb, snuffed his nose as he had previously snuffed the candle in the lamp. "There was Peter Portgartha and a young woman. I happen to know it was a young 'un because she went away at such a rate when she got out. When wommen begins to get up in years they go in the legs, same as harses."

"Would you know her again if you saw her?" asked Barrant eagerly.

"Not if you was to sware me on the Howly Trinity."

"Did this young woman travel up with you by this wagonette last night?"

Mr. Crows couldn't say for that. There were six insides, that was all *he* knew. He disremembered anything about them.

"Surely you notice the passengers you carry?"

Mr. Crows, with the air of one propounding an insoluble riddle, asked his fare why should he take notice of his passengers? He weren't paid for that—no, not he. What's more, the night was a dark one. He knew there was six insides because six fares was put through the winder, but whether they was put through by men or ma'adens or widder wommen was moren he cud say.

He again called on the Trinity to attest his ignorance.

"Their shellens is nuthin' to me"—the reference was to the passengers. "They wouldn't pay for the harse's feed. I work for the Duchy, I do, which is almost the same as being in Guvverment, ain't it? I remember yew, thow—because yew gave me ten shellens for driving yew to the Central hotel last night." Mr. Crows cast a quick glance at his fare to see how he took this artful reminder of his munificence. "But as for their bobs—" He spat into the night in order to express his contempt for the insignificance of such small sums.

There was a tap at the window behind him. He unfastened the pane, and a spectral hand came through with a coin. Mr. Crows took it, the hand disappeared, to be replaced by another, more dirty than spectral, with a coin in the outstretched palm, like its predecessor.

"You see," said Mr. Crows, when he had collected six shillings in this manner. "What's the need for to look at them? I've learnt them to hand in their fares this way. Saves time and talk for nothing. Why should I look at a lot of fat old wommen? I ain't paid for that. It's quite enough to let them set in my cab, wearing out my cushions with their great fat bodies, without looking at them." He eyed Barrant with some sternness.

"But this was not a fat old woman," said Barrant. "She was a pretty young girl."

"Ma'ad or widder, it's all the same to me," returned the misogynist. "Some holds with the sex and finds them soothing, but I was never took up with them myself. I prefers beer. Every man to his taste."

"Did any of the passengers alight at the crossroads?"

They were nearing the cross-roads as he spoke, and the rude outline of the wayside cross loomed out of the shadows directly ahead.

"I couldn't tell you that, neither. I always stop at the cross-roads, in and out. It's one of my regular stopping-places. Come to think of it, though, somebody did get out at the cross-roads last night."

"A man or woman?" asked Barrant with eagerness.

"A woman. She went off acrass the moors that way." Mr. Crows pointed an indifferent whip into the blackness which rested like a pall between the white road and the distant roaring sea. "She was a wunner to go, too—out of sight in a moment, she was."

"Thank you. I'll get down here, too."

As the wagonette stopped at the cross-roads Barrant jumped down from his seat and disappeared in the indicated direction before Mr. Crows could summon his slow wits to determine the value of the coin which the detective had pressed into his passively expectant palm.

Chapter XVI

The twilight had deepened into darkness when Barrant reached Flint House. A faint ray of light flickered from the kitchen window on the giant cliffs, like a taper from a doll's house. He approached the window by a line of rocks which guarded it like sentinels, and looked in.

Within, Mrs. Thalassa sat alone by the table in a drooping attitude of dejection or stupor. Her head was bent over her crossed hands, which rested on the table, and her grey hair, escaping from the back comb which fastened it, fell on both sides of her face. An oil lamp smoked on the table beside her, sending forth a cloud of black vapour like an unbottled genie, but she did not heed it. There was something uncanny in her complete detachment from the restless activity of life. The dead man lying upstairs was not more still.

Had Barrant known her better he would have had matter for surprise and conjecture in the fact that her patience cards stood untouched in their shabby leather case, but knowing nothing of that he fell to wondering what her husband had seen in such a queer little creature to marry her. The consideration of that question led him to the conclusion that perhaps Thalassa had been impelled to his choice by the realization that she was as good-looking a wife as he could afford. Barrant reflected that women resembled horses in value. The mettlesome showy ones were bred to display their paces for rich men only. Serviceable hacks, warranted to work a lifetime, could not be expected to be ornamental as well as useful. So long as they pulled their burdens without jibbing overmuch, one had to be content.

He began to wonder where Thalassa was, and moved closer to the shadow of one of the rocks in case he happened to be prowling around the house. In the silence of the night he listened for the sound of footsteps on the rocks, but could hear nothing except the moan of the sea and the whimper of a rising wind. His eye, glancing upwards, fell upon a chink of shuttered light in the back of the house which looked down on the sea. The light came from the dead man's study, and had not been there a few moments before.

Barrant walked to the kitchen door and tapped lightly. There was no answer, but somewhere within the house a dog howled dismally. The door handle yielded to his touch when he tried it, and he walked in.

The little old woman at the table made a sudden movement at his appearance, but he gave her a reassuring smile and nod. She sat quite still, with a look of fear in her eyes. Above his head he heard someone moving in the study.

"Your husband is upstairs?" he asked in a voice which was little more than a whisper. "I want to see him—I am going up to him."

He did not wait for her to reply, and she watched him out of the room with staring eyes. Stealthily he directed his steps to the staircase, and with infinite precautions for silence commenced to ascend. But midway he stumbled in the dark, and the stair creaked loudly. Above his head a door opened sharply, and when he reached the landing he saw the figure of Thalassa framed in the lighted doorway at the far end of the long passage, listening.

"Who's there?" he cried; then his eye fell on Barrant, advancing swiftly from the darkness towards the light. "What do you want?" he said. "How did you get in?"

Barrant looked past him into the room. There was a litter of papers on the table and shelves, as he had last seen it, but it did not seem to him that anything had been disturbed. The door of the death chamber opposite was closed.

"What are you doing up here?" he said sternly.

Thalassa did not deign to parley. "What do you want?" he repeated, looking steadily at the detective.

"Did you hear what I said to you?" angrily demanded Barrant. "Were you not told not to interfere with these rooms in any way? You have no right up here."

"More right than you have to come into a house like a thief," retorted Thalassa coldly. "I have my work to do. The place must be looked after, whether I'm spied on or not."

"I advise you not to take that tone with me," replied the detective. "As you are here, you had better come into this room again, and shut the door behind you. I have some questions I want to put to you."

Thalassa followed Barrant into the room and stood by the table, the rays of the swinging-lamp throwing his brown face into sharp outline. "What do you want to know?" he asked.

"I want you to tell me everything that happened in this house on the night your master was found dead."

"There's not much to tell," began Thalassa slowly. "When it happened I was down in the cellar, breaking some coal. I heerd my wife call out to me from the kitchen. I went up from the cellar, and she was standing at the kitchen door, shaking like a leaf with fright. She said there'd been a terrible crash right over her head in Mr. Turold's study. I took a lamp and went upstairs, and knocked at the door, but I got no reply. I knocked three times as loud as I could, but there wasn't a sound. At that I gets afeered myself, so I put on my hat and coat to go across to the churchtown to fetch Dr. Ravenshaw. Then a knock come to the front door, and when I opened the door there was the doctor and Mr. and Mrs. Pendleton."

"How long was that after the crash upstairs?"

"No longer than it took me to go upstairs, knock at the door, and getting no answer, go downstairs to put on my coat and hat. I was just winding a comforter round my throat when I heered the knock."

"It did not occur to you to break in the door of your master's room when you got no answer and found it locked?"

"No it never, and you wouldn't have done it in my place."

"You heard no sound of a shot?"

"Not down in the cellar. I fancy I heered the sound of the clock falling. It came to me all muffled like, though it frightened her rarely." He pointed downward to the kitchen. "And it frightened the dog, too, started it barking."

"Is that the dog I heard whining downstairs?"

"Maybe it is. I've got it shut up in the cellar."

"Whose dog is it?"

"His." Thalassa's eyes travelled towards Robert Turold's bedroom.

"Is it howling through grief?"

"More like from fright. Dogs are like people, frightened of their own shadows, sometimes. I shut it up because it kept trying to get upstairs to his room. It's a queer surly sort of brute, but fond enough of him. He used to take it out for long walks."

"What kind of dog is it?"

"A retriever."

"So that's all that happened that night, is it?" said Barrant, in a meditative voice. "You have told me all?"

Thalassa nodded. His brown face remained expressionless, but his little dark eyes glittered warily, like a snake's.

"Think again, Thalassa," urged Barrant, in a voice of the softest insistence. "It may be that you have forgotten something—overlooked an incident which may be important."

"I've overlooked nothing," was the sullen response.

"There's just an odd chance that you have," said Barrant, searching the other's face from raised contemplative eyebrows. "The best of memories plays tricks at times. It's always better not to be too sure. Think again, Thalassa, if you haven't something more to tell me."

"I've told you everything," Thalassa commenced, then straightened his long bony frame in a sudden access of anger, and brought his hand sharply down on the table. "What are you trying to badger me for, like this? You'll get nothing more out of me if you question me till Doomsday."

"But why should you keep anything back?" asked Barrant softly.

Thalassa looked at him with a startled air, then recovered himself quickly. "I'm not keeping anything back," he said. "Why should you say that?"

"I did not say it. You said I'd get no more out of you."

"Because there is nothing more to be got. Is that plain enough?"

"Quite. Well then, let us go over the events of this night once more. Perhaps that will help you to recall something which you have forgotten."

"That's not likely."

"Nevertheless, we will try. You were busy in the coal cellar at the time, I think you said?"

"At what time?" said Thalassa with a quick glance.

"At the time the crash happened upstairs."

"Yes."

"What time was that?"

"How should I know? Do you suppose there's a clock in the coal cellar? It must have been about half-past nine."

"According to the clock upstairs. Did you think I had overlooked that? Then you heard your wife call, and went to the kitchen. Next, you went upstairs, tried your master's door, found it locked, and decided to go for assistance. But before you could do so Mr. and Mrs. Pendleton and Dr. Ravenshaw arrived. Have I got it right?"

"That be right."

"All except one thing, Thalassa."

Thalassa met Barrant's look steadily, with no sense of guilt in his face. "Well?" he said.

"I see that you do not intend to be frank. Let me help your memory a little. Did you have no other visitors—before Mr. and Mrs. Pendleton and Dr. Ravenshaw arrived?"

"Visitors?" There was scorn now in his straight glance, but nothing more. "Is this a place where there's likely to be visitors?"

"Not in the ordinary course of events"—Barrant was still smilingly affable—"but the night your master met his death was not an ordinary night. Somebody may have come to the house."

He paused, again searching for some sign of guilty consciousness in the face revealed in such clear outline near him, but saw none. Again, Thalassa met him with answering look, but remained mute.

"Thalassa"—Barrant's voice remained persuasive, but to an ear attuned to shades, there was a note of menace underlying its softness—"you know there was somebody else here that night."

"Somebody? Who?"

"Your master's daughter—Miss Sisily Turold." Barrant brought it out sharply and angrily.

Thalassa turned a cold glance on him. "If you know that why do you ask me?" he said.

"Because you let her in!"

Thalassa surveyed him with the shadow of a smile on his motionless face. "Do you take me for a fool?" he said. "I let nobody in."

"Thalassa," said the detective earnestly, "let me advise you, for your own sake, to tell the truth now. You may be keeping silence through some mistaken idea of loyalty to your master's daughter, but that will do her no good, nor you either. I know more than you think. If you persist in keeping silent you will put yourself in an awkward position, and it may be the worse for you. You were seen listening at the door of the room downstairs on the day of your master's death."

"So that's it, is it? You think you'll fit a rope round my neck? I'm to say what you want to save it? To hell with you and your policeman's tricks! I don't care that for them." He snapped his long brown fingers in Barrant's face.

"You've a bold tongue, you scoundrel," said Barrant, flushing angrily. "Take care where it leads you. Once more, will you tell me the truth?"

"I've told you all I know."

"Do you mean to tell me that you did not see your master's daughter, or let her into the house?"

"I did not."

"Could anybody have got into the house without your knowledge?"

"Maybe."

"Did you hear anybody?"

"How could I hear anybody when I was down in the coal cellar?"

The open sneer on Thalassa's face suggested that he was not to be caught by verbal traps. Barrant perceived, with a smouldering anger, that the man was too clever to be tricked, and too stout of heart to be frightened. By accident or design he had a ready story which was difficult to demolish without further knowledge of the events of that night. Barrant decided that it would be useless, at that moment, to apply himself to the effort of worming anything out of Thalassa. He had shown his own hand too freely, and placed him on his guard. There was also the bare possibility that he had told the truth, so far as he knew it. One last shot he essayed.

"You are acting very foolishly, but I shall not arrest you—yet," he said impressively. "I shall tell the local police to keep an eye on you."

"Is it the Cornish savage from the churchtown—him with the straw helmit?" said Thalassa, with a harsh laugh.

The last shot had missed fire badly. The lawless spirit of the man was not to be intimidated by a threat of arrest—a threat which the detective had reason for not putting into effect just then. Barrant moved towards the door with the best dignity he could command.

"Light me downstairs to the kitchen," he said. "I want to see your wife."

Thalassa seemed about to say something at that, then thought the better of it, and walked out of the room. Outside in the passage he picked up a small lamp glimmering in a niche of the wall, and led the way downstairs. They reached the kitchen in silence, and went in.

The little grey woman at the table was seated in the same posture as Barrant had last seen her, her hands crossed in front of her, her head bent. She glanced up listlessly as they entered. Barrant crossed the room, and touched her arm. She shook in a pitiful little flurry of fear, then became motionless again.

"Mrs. Thalassa, I want to speak to you," said Barrant, raising his voice, as though to a deaf person. "Is this where you were sitting the night before last, when you heard the crash in your master's room upstairs?"

"Put the knave on the rubbish heap," she muttered without looking up.

"Listen to me, Mrs. Thalassa"—he spoke still louder. "Did you hear the shot before the crash?"

The loud tone seemed to reach the remote consciousness of her being, and she started up in another flurry. ... "Coming, coming, sir. Jasper, where's the tray?..." she stood thus for a moment, then dropped back into her chair, her eyes fixed on the opposite wall.

"What's the matter with her?" said Barrant, turning to her husband.

"She's been like it ever since it happened," said Thalassa, in a low tone. "That's how I found her when I came from the cellar."

"Did she hear the shot — or see anything?"

"That's more than I can tell you. When I came from the cellar she seemed mazed with fright, and kept pointing to the ceiling. All I could make out from her was that there'd been a great crash upstairs. When I came down again after trying the door she was lying on the floor in a faint, and I carried her in to her bed. It's floored her wits."

"She's had a very bad shock," said Barrant gravely. He regarded her attentively, her vacant eyes, mouthing lips, trembling hands, her uncanny fixed glance which seemed to behold something unseen. Strange suspicions flowed through his brain as he watched her. What terrible experience had befallen her? What did she know of the mysterious events that had happened in that silent house? He endeavoured to follow the direction of her gaze, but it seemed to be fixed on the row of bells behind the kitchen door. Then, like a half-awakened sleeper released from the horror of a nightmare, she sank back in her previous listless attitude, and fell to muttering again.

As Barrant watched her, Thalassa watched them both with an anxiety which would have aroused Barrant's suspicions if he had seen it. But Thalassa's face was again closely guarded when he did look up.

"You'll get neither rhyme nor reason out of her," said Thalassa, as their glances met.

"I'll try once more," murmured Barrant, almost to himself. He turned to her again, but this time he did not lay his hand on her arm. "Mrs. Thalassa" — he spoke more gently — "will you try and understand me?"

"Red on black ... black on red." Her hands moved restlessly.

In a sudden recognition of the futility of trying to gather anything from that clouded brain, Barrant turned abruptly away without another word. And the black gaze of Thalassa followed him through the door and out into the darkness of the night.

Chapter XVII

The bell in the darkened chambers rang with the insistent clamour of mechanism responding with blind obedience to a human hand, but Mr. Anthony Brimsdown suffered it to pass unnoticed. As an elderly bachelor, living alone, he was sufficiently master of his own affairs to disregard the arrival of the last post, leaving the letters as they were tumbled through the slit in the door downstairs until he felt inclined to go and get them.

He was standing in the centre of the room examining an unusual trinket—a gold hoop like a bracelet, with numbers and the zodiac signs engraved on the inner surface. Mr. Brimsdown had discovered it in a Kingsway curiosity shop a week before. It was a portable sun-dial of the sixteenth century. A slide, pushed back a certain distance in accordance with the zodiac signs, permitted the sun to fall through a slit on the figures of the hours within—a dainty timekeeper for mediaeval lovers. Mr. Brimsdown was no gallant, nor had he sufficient imagination to prompt him to wonder what dead girl's dainty fingers had once held up the bright fragile circle to the sun to see if Love's tryst was to be kept. His joy in the sun-dial was the pride of the collector in the possession of a rare thing.

But that night it failed to interest him. He put it down with a sigh, and resumed his restless pacing of the room.

It was his office, but he preferred it to his chambers at the end of the passage. He said the air was better, but it is doubtful whether that was the reason. Perhaps Mr. Brimsdown felt less lonely among his legal documents, meditating over battles he had won for dead legatees. As a solicitor he was "strong on the Chancery side" and had gained some famous judgments for notorious litigants—men who had loved the law so well that their souls might well have been found—knowing no higher heaven—in the office where the records of their forgotten lawsuits were buried. And in death, as in life, they would have been glad to confide their affairs to the man whose lot it had been to add "Deceased" to so many of the names on the black steel deed-boxes which lined the shelves.

Mr. Brimsdown lived for the law. As a family lawyer he was the soul of discretion, an excellent fighter, wary and reticent, deep as the grave, but far safer. The grave sometimes opens and divulges a ghastly secret from its narrow depths. There was no chance of getting anything out of Mr. Brimsdown, dead or alive. He had no wife to extract bedroom confidences from him, no relations to visit in expansive moments, he trusted nothing to paper or diary, and he did not play golf. He was a solitary man, of an habitual secretiveness deepened by years of living alone.

His lips moved now, and he spoke aloud. His voice sounded sharply in the heavy silence.

"A calamity—nothing less. How did it happen? Was it grief for his wife?"

His face showed unusual agitation—distress even. It was well his clients could not see him at that moment. To them he was a remote enigmatic figure of conveyances and legal deeds; one deeply versed in human follies and foibles, but impervious to human feeling, independent of human companionship. The reserved glance of his cold grey eye betokened that he guarded his own secrets as closely as he guarded the secrets entrusted to him professionally. But there was human nature in him—deep down. It was not much—a lock of hair in a sealed packet in his pocket-book. The giver was dead and gone to dust, sleeping in an old churchyard near the Strand, forgotten by all who had ever known her—except one. Sometimes in the twilight a tall figure would stand musing beside that forgotten grave for awhile, then turn away and walk swiftly up the narrow river street, across the Strand, and through the archway to Grey's Inn.

"Thirty years!" he murmured. Then his mind seemed to hark back to his previous thought, after the fashion of a man who thinks aloud—"No, no; not his wife. He did not care enough for her for that. Thirty years—wasted. My heart bleeds when I think of it. Ought I to go down? Did he wish for me? I wonder—"

His distress as he paced the room was more apparent than ever. Again, his clients would have been astonished if they had witnessed it. In their opinion he was hard as nails and a stranger to the softer feelings of the heart. They would as soon thought of attributing sentiment to one of the japanned deed-boxes. But they would have accepted the surprising revelation with well-bred English tolerance for eccentricity, not allowing it to affect their judgment that Mr. Brimsdown was one of the soundest and safest lawyers in England.

His agitation arose from the death of Robert Turold—his client. He had gathered that piece of news from an evening newspaper in the restaurant where he had dined. Mr. Brimsdown had reached an age when the most poignant events of human life seem little more than trifles. It was in the nature of things for men to die. As a lawyer he had prepared many last wills and testaments—had helped men into their graves, as it were— unmoved. But that unexpected announcement of Robert Turold's death had come to him as an over-whelming shock. He had left his meal unfinished, and returned to his chambers to seek consolation, not in prayer, but in his collection of old clocks and watches. In the dusk he had set out his greatest treasures—the gold sun-dial, a lamp clock, an early French watch in blue enamel, and a bed repeating clock in a velvet case. But the solace had failed him for once. Even the magic name of Dan Quare on the jewelled face of the repeater failed to stir his collector's heart.

His regard for Robert Turold was deep and sincere. His dead client had been his ideal of a strong man. Strong and unyielding—like a rock. That was the impression Robert Turold had conveyed at their first interview many years before, and his patience and tenacity in pursuit of his purpose had deepened the feeling since. The object of his search had the lawyer's sympathy. Mr. Brimsdown had a reverence for titles—inherited titles, not mere knighthoods, or Orders of the British Empire. For those he felt nothing but contempt. He drew the sharpest distinction between such titled vulgarians and those who were born into the world with the blood running blue in their veins. He regarded Robert Turold as belonging to this latter class. It was nothing to him that he was a commoner in the eyes of the world, with no more claim to distinction than a golf-playing city merchant. He had believed in his story from the first, and had helped him in that belief. Turrald of Missenden! It was a great old name. Mr. Brimsdown rolled it round his tongue as though it were a vintage port—pronounced it lingeringly, rolling the "rr's" sonorously, and hissing the "ss's" with a caressing sibilant sound.

Turrald of Missenden! Robert Turold was the lineal descendant of the name, and worthy of the title. Mr. Brimsdown had always felt that, from the very first. There was something noble and dominating in his presence. Blood told; there could be no doubt of that.

What stronger proof of it could be found than the dogged strength with which the dead man had persisted for thirty years in his effort to claim as his rightful due a baronial title which had been in abeyance for four hundred years?

And he would have succeeded—was on the verge of success—but for this unlucky stroke of Death's.

With a sigh for the frailty of human hopes, Mr. Brimsdown put an end to his reflections and went downstairs for the post.

By the dim light of the lowered hall gas he saw an envelope lying on the floor—a thick grey envelope addressed to himself in a thin irregular hand. The sight of that superscription startled him like a glimpse of the unseen. For it was the handwriting of the subject of his thoughts—Robert Turold.

With the stiff movement of an ageing man he picked up the letter and went upstairs again. In some subtle way the room seemed changed. He had a sudden inexplicable sensation of nervousness and depression. Shaking it off with an effort, he opened the envelope in his hand with an odd reluctance—the feeling that he was prying into something which was no concern of his. He drew out the single grey sheet and unfolded it. The letter was dated from Flint House on the previous day. There was but a few lines, but the lawyer was pulled up at the beginning by the unusual familiarity of the address. "My dear Brimsdown" was unusual in one so formal as Robert Turold. But the handwriting was his—undoubtedly. Mr. Brimsdown had seen it too often to be mistaken. With the growing idea that the whole thing was confounding to sober sense and reason, he read on—

> "Can you postpone all your other engagements and come to
> Cornwall on receipt of this? If you will telegraph the train you
> travel by I will have a conveyance to meet you at Penzance
> and bring you to Flint House. This is a matter of importance."

A postscript followed in the strangest contrast to the formal note—a postscript hasty and blotted, which had evidently been added in extreme agitation of mind—

> "For God's sake lose no time. Come at once."

The tremulous urgent words stared out from the surface of the grey paper in all the piteous futility of an appeal made too late. Glancing up, Mr. Brimsdown's eye rested on the shelf where the deed box of Robert Turold reposed, and he mechanically reflected that it would be necessary to have the word "Deceased" added to the white-lettered inscription on the black surface. Mr. Brimsdown sighed. Then, shaking off the quiescence of mind which his brooding had engendered, he applied his faculties to the consideration of a situation which at first sight seemed fantastic as a nightmare.

The letter was not more remarkable than its despatch after the writer's death, but the summons to Cornwall was not in itself surprising. He recalled a similar visit to Norfolk some years before, and the recent correspondence between them made it clear that the claim had reached a stage which required careful legal handling. Robert Turold had forwarded copies of the final proofs of the family descent discovered in Cornwall, and Mr. Brimsdown had prepared the claim for the termination of abeyance which was to be heard by the House of Lords. Mr. Brimsdown was also aware of the summoning of the other members of the family to Cornwall to impart the news to them. A very natural and proper proceeding on Robert Turold's part, he had deemed it.

He believed he knew every intimate detail of the ambition on which Robert Turold had immutably set his heart. Had they not been discussed between them, again and again, in that room—his bitterness that he had no son, his fear that the regained title might be extinguished again in female descent, his grievance that the succession could not be altered. It was his dream to found a new line of Turralds, and be remembered as the head of it. "If you could only get the descent taken outside the limits of the original creation, Brimsdown—" The harsh voice, uttering these words, seemed to reach Mr. Brimsdown in the muffled silence at that moment. He had told him, again and again, that the thing was impossible. If the Turrald barony was called out of abeyance it was an act of Royal grace and favour. They had no rights—he insisted on that—and any attempt to influence the Crown about the line of succession might endanger the claim.

And now Robert Turold was dead in the midst of his plans—dead when he had almost gained the peak of his dreams.

It seemed incredible, almost impossible. Death at such a moment assumed an unexpected reality as an actual and tangible mocker of human ambitions. And this letter with its postscript—what was the meaning of it? The lawyer knew nothing of Robert Turold's announcement to his family on the previous day. If he had, it would have intensified his feeling that the letter hinted at some terrible secret hidden behind the thick curtain of his client's strange and sudden death. The hasty postscript suggested a quickened sense of a growing danger which Robert Turold had seen too late to avert.

What danger? Mr. Brimsdown could form no idea. He reflected that he really knew very little of Robert Turold's private life in spite of the long association between them. He must have had other interests at one time or other beside the eternal question of the title. Mr. Brimsdown had vaguely understood that the money he had invested for Robert Turold had been gained abroad—in the wilds of the earth—in his client's early life, but his client had never confided to him the manner of the gathering. That was a page in the dead man's life of which his trusted legal adviser knew nothing whatever. It was unsafe to assume that the page, if revealed, would throw any light on his tragic death, but there was a possibility that it might.

The evening newspaper he had brought home lay on the carpet at his feet exposing the headline—"A Cornish Mystery"—which had caught his eye at the restaurant. Mr. Brimsdown picked up the sheet and read the report again. There was nothing in it to help him. It was only a brief notification of the facts—of a death which, in the words of the newspaper's local correspondent, "pointed to suicide."

Suicide! The letter on which the ink was still bluish and fresh, seemed to convey Robert Turold's denial of the suggestion that he had taken his life. It was the cry of a man who had looked into the dark place of fear and seen Death lurking within. Only mortal terror could have called forth that passionate frantic appeal. And that appeal accomplished its purpose, although it came too late. Robert Turold was dead, but the call for elucidation rang loudly from his coffin. The dead man's hand beckoned him, and he dared not disobey. He determined to go to Cornwall.

Outside in the darkness a clock chimed, and one of his own treasures repeated the hour with a soft mellifluous note. Eleven! He had an idea that there was—or used to be—a midnight train to Cornwall. He crossed to his bureau and consulted a time-table. Yes—to Penzance from Paddington. He decided to catch it.

His preparations for departure were quickly made. The writing of a note to his clerk and the packing of a bag were matters soon accomplished. In a quarter of an hour he had picked up a taxicab at the Holborn stand near his chambers and was on his way to the station.

There was plenty of light and stir at Paddington, which appeared like a great and glowing cavern in the cold darkness of the night. There were engines shunting, cabs arriving, porters and passengers rushing about with luggage, throngs of people. It happened that the midnight train from Cornwall was overdue, and fluttered women waiting for friends were importuning bored officials about the delay. Sleepy children stared with wondering eyes at pictorial efforts to beguile the tedium of waiting for trains. There were geographical posters comparing Cornwall favourably to Italy; posters of girls in bathing costume beckoning to "the Cornish Riviera;" posters of frolicsome puppies in baskets ticketed "Lucky Dogs, They're Off to Penzance."

The passengers waiting for the midnight train to that resort did not do equal justice to this flattering assumption of its delights. They seemed, on the whole, rather to regard themselves as unlucky dogs (if the term could be applied to parties of women), and were huddled together on the station seats in attitudes suggestive of despair. Men flirting with barmaids in the bars may have considered themselves lucky dogs, but whisky played an important part in their exhilaration.

The belated train came rushing in with an effusion of steam, like a late arrival puffing out apologies, bringing a large number of passengers back to London from Penzance. They scrambled on to the platform with the dishevelled appearance of people who had been cooped up for hours. First-class passengers eased their pent-up energy by shouting for luggage porters and bundling their women into taxicabs. The third-class passengers, whose minor importance in the scheme of things did not warrant such displays of self-importance, made meekly and wearily for the exits.

They were dammed back at the barriers by two ticket collectors, whose adroit manipulation of the gates prevented more than one person trickling through at a time, and turned the choked stream of humanity within into a whirlpool of floating faces and struggling forms. As Mr. Brimsdown stood regarding this distracting spectacle from the outside, he saw one of the ticket collectors grasp the arm of a girl who was just emerging, at the same time shutting the gate on a stout woman following, thus effectually blocking the egress of those behind.

The girl turned quickly at the touch of the detaining hand, and there was fear in her face.

"What do you want?" she said, framing the words with an obvious effort.

The ticket collector was a man whose natural choleric temperament was accentuated by the harassing nature of his employment. He tore in two portions the ticket which the girl had just given him, and thrust half into her hand.

"Here's your return half. Why don't you look what yer doin' when givin' up yer ticket? You women are the limit. Now, mother, for God's sake don't be all night getting through that there barrier. There's others want to get 'ome, if you don't."

Having by this adroit remonstrance spiked the wrath, as it were, of the stout and angry woman he had jammed in the gate, he permitted the resumption of the trickle of impatient passengers.

Mr. Brimsdown followed with his eye the pretty girl who had been forgetful enough to give up a return ticket instead of a half one. She had stopped outside the barrier, gazing round with a troubled face at the immensity of the station and the throngs of hurrying people.

The lawyer looked at her hard, from a little distance. "Where have I seen that face before?" he murmured to himself.

Her beauty was of a sufficiently rare type to attract attention anywhere, except, perhaps, at a London railway station at midnight. She was unused to her surroundings and she was not a city product. So much was obvious, though her clear pale face and slim young figure did not suggest rusticity. Her dark eyes glanced quickly and nervously around her, and then she started to walk slowly towards one of the main entrances.

A luggage porter hurried towards her, intent on tips. The broad back of a policeman was outlined in the entrance. The girl looked wistfully from the policeman to the porter, then appeared to make up her mind. She extracted a silver coin from her purse, and proffered it timidly to the porter. The porter showed no timidity in accepting it.

"Luggage, miss, in the van?" he asked. "Just you wait 'ere."

"I have no luggage," Mr. Brimsdown heard her say. Her eyes wandered downward to the little handbag she carried. "I wanted to ask you—I am a stranger to London. Can you tell me a place where I could stay; for the night—somewhere quiet and respectable?"

Mr. Brimsdown found himself listening anxiously for the porter's reply. By all the laws of Romance he should have had an old mother in a clean and humble home who would have been delighted to give the girl shelter for the sight of her pretty face. But pretty girls are plentiful in London, and kind-hearted old women are rare. The porter seemed surprised at the inquiry. He pushed his blue cap back from a shock of red hair, and pondered the question deeply. Then he made a valiant feint of earning his shilling by throwing out suggestions of temperance hotels in Russell Square and the Euston Road. He warmed to the subject and depicted the attractions of these places. Quiet and cheap, and nothing respectabler in the 'ole city of London. They was open at all hours. His own sister stayed in one when she come to town.

"Would you give me the address?" the girl wistfully asked.

The porter shook his head cautiously. He had evidently no intention of pawning his sister's reputation for a shilling given him by a strange girl who might have designs on the spoons of temperance hotels.

"How do I get to Euston Road?" asked the girl with a quick realization of the fact that she had obtained London value for her shilling.

"By the Metropolitan." He pointed to a blazing subterranean archway which at that late hour was still vomiting forth a mass of people. "Book at the first winder."

Mr. Brimsdown watched the girl until she disappeared out of sight down the steps. He then turned away to seek his own train, the insistent feeling still haunting him that he had seen her pretty wistful face before. He taxed his memory to recall where, but memory made no response. It seemed a long time ago — like a glimpse from the face of the dead. Mr. Brimsdown strove to put the idea from him as a trick of the imagination.

He beckoned to a porter, who took his bag to a first-class carriage in the Penzance train. Mr. Brimsdown settled himself comfortably in a corner seat. A few minutes later the train moved out on the long night journey to Penzance.

Chapter XVIII

The clock in Dr. Ravenshaw's study ticked loudly in the perfect stillness and then struck ten with a note of metallic derision as though rejoicing in the theft of an hour from a man who prided himself on knowing the value of time. Startled to find that it was so late, Barrant sprang to his feet and rang the bell. A sleepy Cornish maid appeared in answer, and Barrant informed her that he could not wait any longer.

"The doctor may be in at any time now, sir," the girl eagerly assured him, as though she were in league with the clock to steal more of his time.

"I will call again," said Barrant curtly.

"Any message, sir? Oh, here's the doctor now. A gentleman to see you, sir."

Dr. Ravenshaw advanced into the room. He looked tired and weary, as if he had spent a long vigil by a patient. He dismissed the girl with a nod, and turned inquiringly to his visitor.

"I am Detective Barrant, doctor; I have waited to see you on my way back from Flint House. I am investigating the case."

"Yes?" said the doctor inquiringly. "Please be seated."

"It is a strange case, you know," began the detective. "And one of the strange things about it is that the dead man's relatives differ whether it is murder or suicide. That's what brings me to you. You are a medical man, and you knew Robert Turold intimately. Would you consider him a man of suicidal tendencies?"

"Many men have tendencies towards suicide at odd moments," replied the doctor, "particularly men of Robert Turold's temperament."

"Was there anything in Robert Turold's demeanour which suggested to you recently that he valued his life lightly, or was likely to take it?"

"I would rather not give a definite opinion on that point. I have to give evidence at the inquest, you know."

Barrant nodded. He realized the force of the doctor's objection to the expression of a view which might be proved erroneous later. So he turned to another phase of the case.

"You saw Robert Turold's body soon after you arrived at Flint House?"

"Within a few minutes."

"How long had he been dead?"

"About ten minutes, I should say."

"What was the cause of death?"

"He was shot through the main blood vessel of the left lung. It was possible to arrive at that conclusion from the very severe haemorrhage. The blood was still flowing freely when we broke into the room. That would cause death from heart failure, following the haemorrhage, within two or three minutes, in all probability."

"He was quite dead when you entered the study?"

"Quite."

"How long after was the body carried into the bedroom?"

"An hour or more. It was some time before Pengowan arrived, and Thalassa and he removed the body a little later."

Barrant looked disappointed at his reply. "Would it be possible to make marks on a corpse after that length of time?" he asked.

"What sort of marks?" asked the doctor.

"There was a mark of five fingers on the left arm, made by a left hand."

"Then you have finger-prints to help you?"

"Unfortunately no. It's a grip—a clutch—which, will not reveal print marks in the impressions. I thought they might have been caused during the removal of the body."

"It is not possible to make such marks on a corpse. Reaction sets in at the moment of death. Sometimes blue spots appear on a dead body, and such appearances have been occasionally mistaken for bruises."

"Did you observe any marks when you examined the body?" asked Barrant as he rose to his feet.

"No, but my examination was confined to ascertaining if life was extinct."

Barrant thanked him and said good night. The doctor rose also, and escorted him to the door.

Outside, a wild west wind sprang at him. Barrant pulled his hat over his eyes and hurried away.

The following morning he sought out Inspector Dawfield at his office in Penzance and disclosed to him his conclusions about the case.

"I intend to go to London by this morning's train, Dawfield," he announced. "We must find Robert Turold's daughter."

"You think she has gone to London?"

"I feel sure of it, and I do not think it will be difficult to trace her. I shall try first at Paddington. I will get the warrant for her arrest backed at Bow Street, and put a couple of good men on the search before returning here. You had better have the inquest adjourned until I come back. This is no suicide, Dawfield, but a deep and skilfully planned murder."

"I should think the flight of the girl makes that pretty clear," said Dawfield, as he made a note on his office pad.

Barrant shook his head. "It's too strange a case for us to have any feeling of certainty about it yet," he said. "There is some very deep mystery behind the facts. Every step of my investigation convinces me of that. The disappearance of Miss Turold does not explain everything."

"She was up at Flint House on that night, and now she is not to be found. Surely that is enough?"

"This is not a straightforward case. It's going to prove a very complicated one. But I have come to the conclusion that the quickest way to get at the truth is to find Sisily Turold. Her flight suggests that she is implicated in the crime in some way, and it may even mean that she is guilty."

"Do not the circumstances point to her guilt?"

"Circumstances can lie with the facility of humanity, at times. Moreover, we do not know all the circumstances yet. But let us examine the facts we have discovered. We believe that the girl visited her father's house on the night of his death, and has since disappeared. We must assume that it was she who was seen listening at the door during the afternoon by Mrs. Pendleton, because that assumption provides strong motive for the murder by giving the key of interpretation to Miss Turold's subsequent actions. We must picture the effect of that overheard conversation on the girl's mind. She had been kept in ignorance about the secret of her birth, and she suddenly discovers that instead of being a prospective peeress and heiress, she is only an illegitimate daughter, a nameless thing, a reproach in a world governed by moral conventions. Her prospects, her future, and her life are shattered by her father's act. The effect might well be overwhelming. She broods over the wrong done to her, and decides to go to Flint House that night and see her father, though not, I think, with the premeditated idea of murder. Her idea was to plead and remonstrate with him."

"Why do you think that?" asked Dawfield.

"She could not have foreseen that her absence from the hotel would pass unnoticed. That was pure luck, due to Mrs. Pendleton's chance visit to Flint House. It was just chance that the girl did not encounter her aunt there. She must have got away from Flint House shortly before Mrs. Pendleton arrived. But the strongest proof that there was no premeditation is to be found in the fact that Miss Turold made the journey openly, in a public conveyance."

"And returned the same way," put in Dawfield.

"I confess that her action in taking that risk after the murder strikes me as remarkable," observed Barrant thoughtfully. "But she would be anxious to return as speedily as possible, and perhaps she was aware that the last wagonette from St. Fair to Penzance is generally empty. But we can only speculate about that. She must have reached Flint House not later than half-past eight or perhaps a few minutes earlier, if she walked quickly across the moors. I ascertained that by taking the same wagonette last night, and walking across the moors from the cross-roads, as she did. The murder was not committed until half-past nine, according to the stopped clock, which is another point suggesting lack of premeditation. Let us assume that up to the time she arrived at Flint House she had no intention of murdering her father. She knocked, and was perhaps admitted by Thalassa, and went up to her father's room. What happened during that interview? We do not know, but we are told that Robert Turold was a man of harsh, unyielding disposition, the slave of his single idea, which was the acquisition of a lost title. Such a man was not likely to be moved by pleading or threats. We must imagine a long and angry scene, culminating in the daughter snatching up her father's revolver and shooting him."

"Thalassa told Pengowan that Robert Turold kept the revolver in the drawer of his writing table," Dawfield remarked.

"I have read Pengowan's report," returned Barrant impatiently, "and I am assuming that Robert Turold's daughter knew where it was kept. This is a purely constructive theory of her guilt, and we have to assume many things. We must further assume that when she left the room she locked the door behind her and brought away the key in order to suggest suicide. When she got downstairs she told Thalassa the truth, and begged him to shield her. He promised to do so, and when the door of the study was broken open he took an opportunity to drop the key on the floor, in order to suggest the idea that Robert Turold had locked himself in his room before shooting himself, and that the key was jolted out of the lock when the door was burst in. It was an infernally clever thing to do. That's the case against the girl, Dawfield. What do you think of it?"

"It sounds convincing enough."

"It would sound more convincing to me if it was entirely consistent with the other facts of the case. Have you those sheets of unfinished writing which were found in Robert Turold's study?"

Dawfield produced two sheets of foolscap from his desk. Barrant laid them on the table, and examined them with a magnifying glass.

"It is certain that Robert Turold did not put down his pen voluntarily," he said. "He stopped involuntarily, in the midst of a word. That suggests great surprise or sudden shock. The letter 'e' in the word 'clear' terminates in a sprawling dash and a jab from the nib which has almost pierced the paper. Could the unexpected appearance of his daughter have startled him in that fashion? It rather suggests that somebody sprang on him unawares, surprising him so much that he almost stuck the pen through the paper."

"Might not that have been his daughter?"

"Women scratch like cats when they use violence, but they do not spring like tigers. I have been examining those marks on Robert Turold's arm again, and I have come to the conclusion that they were made by somebody in a violent passion."

"I have the photographs here," said Dawfield, rummaging in a drawer. "They do not help us at all. There are no finger-prints — nothing but blurs."

Barrant glanced at the photographs and pushed them aside.

"I have been thinking a lot about those marks," he said. "They strike me as a very important clue. I have been examining them very closely, and discovered the faint impression of finger-nails in the marks left by the first and second fingers. That suggests that the owner of the hand was in a state of ferocity and tightened nerves."

"I do not see that."

"Allow me to experiment on your arm. When I grip you firmly, as I do now, you can feel my fingers pressing their whole length on your flesh, can you not?"

"I can indeed," said Dawfield, wincing. "You've a pretty powerful grip. I shall be black and blue."

"The grip on Robert Turold's arm is quite a different thing," pursued Barrant earnestly. "Do not be afraid, I am not going to demonstrate again.

It was more in the nature of a pounce—a sort of tiger-spring hold, made by somebody in a state of great mental excitement, with tightened muscles which caused a tense clutch with the finger-tips, the nails digging into the skin, the fingers bent and wide apart. My opinion is that it is a man's grip."

"Thalassa?"

"That I cannot say. He's a cunning and wary devil, and I could get nothing out of him last night. He says he was in the coal cellar when his master met his death. That's where he showed his cleverness in protecting himself as well as shielding the girl, because if he was actually down in the coal cellar she might have gained entrance to the house and left it again without Thalassa knowing anything about it. He says that he admitted nobody, and heard nobody."

"Perhaps he helped in the murder, and sprang on his master."

"That is possible. But why should Thalassa spring on his master in maniacal excitement? To secure the revolver to shoot him? I can see no other reason. What happened afterwards? Robert Turold wasn't shot immediately. Some seconds, perhaps minutes, elapsed. What took place in that brief yet vital space of time? Did Thalassa hold his master in a grim clutch while the girl took the revolver out of the drawer and shot him? What took Robert Turold to the clock in his dying moments? These are questions we cannot answer at present. But it is certain that whoever committed the murder left the room immediately after firing the shot, and the door was locked on the outside and the key removed. If the daughter committed the murder it was probably Thalassa who replaced the key in the room afterwards."

"Have you any doubt on that point?"

"The probabilities point to Thalassa, but it was Austin Turold who actually picked up the key. It is as well not to lose sight of that fact."

Inspector Dawfield looked up quickly, but his colleague's face revealed nothing of his thoughts.

"Hadn't you some idea that the marks on the arm might have been caused by the removal of the body into the next room?" he hazarded.

"Not now," Barrant replied. "That theory was only tenable on the supposition that life was not completely extinct when the body was removed. But I interviewed Dr. Ravenshaw on that point last night, and what he told me disposes of that theory."

"I heard something from one of my men this morning which may have some bearing on the case," remarked Dawfield. "There has been a lot of local gossip about it. Robert Turold was generally regarded as very eccentric. When he crossed the moors from the churchtown to Flint House it was his custom to go almost at a run, glancing over his shoulder as he went, as if afraid."

"I have heard nothing of this," commented Barrant. "Is the story to be believed, do you think?"

"A fisherman of the churchtown told my man in a graphic sort of way. He says that Robert Turold had a dog which he used to take with him on these walks, and he says that the master used to cover the ground with such great strides that the dog had to run after him panting, with lolling tongue."

"That sounds stretched," said Barrant. "Most fishermen exaggerate. However, I'll look up this man when I return, and question him. It never does to throw away a chance." He glanced at his watch and rose to his feet. "I'll be off now to catch the train. If anything important occurs during my absence you'd better send me a wire to Scotland Yard."

Chapter XIX

It was from Mrs. Pendleton that Mr. Brimsdown gained his first real knowledge of the drama of strange events surrounding Robert Turold's death. In response to his call at the hotel she came down from her room fingering his card nervously, her eyes reddened with weeping, and an air of tremulous bewilderment about her which sat ill on her massive personality.

The lawyer greeted her with formal courtesy. He was newly shaved and bathed, his linen was spotless, and his elderly grey eyes looked out with alert watchfulness on a world of trickery.

"As your late brother's legal adviser for many years, I felt it incumbent upon me to come down," he said, fixing a grave glance on the distracted lady before him. "It seemed to me that I might be of some use, perhaps, assistance. That is the object of my call."

The fact that she had not seen Mr. Brimsdown before did not lessen the hysterical gratitude with which Mrs. Pendleton received this piece of information. The events of the last forty-eight hours had shaken her badly. Her brother's tragic death, and the terrible suspicion which enveloped Sisily, had stripped her of her strength, and left her with a feminine longing to cast her burden on a man's shoulders. She had discovered to her dismay that a husband who has been snubbed and kept under for twenty years is apt to prove a thing of straw when a woman likes to feel that the male sex was devised by Providence to take the wheel from female hands if the barque of life drifts on the breakers. But Mr. Pendleton had revealed no latent capacity to play the part of the strong man at the helm in the crisis. He had shown himself a craven and kept out of the way, leaving his wife to her own resources. The appearance of Mr. Brimsdown was as timely to her as the arrival of a heaven-sent pilot in a storm.

"Thank you," she murmured incoherently. "Such a dreadful end. Poor dear Robert." She sobbed into her handkerchief.

"A deplorable loss to his family — and England," assented the lawyer. "I am glad to see you. They ascertained your address for me at the hotel where I am staying. I have been resting after travelling all night, and I shall go and see the police in the morning. So far I have only read the reports in the

London evening papers, and there may be intimate particulars which were not disclosed to the press. If such exist, perhaps you will impart them to me. You need not hesitate to disclose to me all you know. Your late brother honoured me with his confidence for nearly thirty years." Mr. Brimsdown coughed discreetly.

His tone invited confidences which Mrs. Pendleton, in her perplexity of spirit, was only too anxious to impart to a sympathetic ear. Mr. Brimsdown, sitting stiffly upright, his eyes fixed on a portrait of Royalty glimmering inanely down at them through a dirty glass frame on the opposite wall, listened with unmoved front. Yet the story had its surprises, even for him. Not the least of them was the fact that Mrs. Pendleton's description of her niece tallied with the appearance of the girl whose identity he had tried to recall at Paddington. He was chagrined to think he had failed to recognize his late client's daughter, but he recalled that it was ten years since he had seen Sisily, who was then a dark-eyed little girl. At Norfolk. Oh, yes! he remembered her readily enough now, playing innocently about some forgotten tombstones in a deserted graveyard on a wild grey coast, while her father wrested savagely with the dead for his heritage. Strange that he should have met her again at the moment of her flight, when he was setting out for Cornwall in response to her dead father's letter! Life had such ironical mischances.

He said nothing of this chance encounter, or of Robert Turold's letter, to the dead man's sister who was now pouring out her fears and suspicions to him. He was a receptacle into which confidences might be emptied, but he gave nothing in return. Mrs. Pendleton did not need that. Her state of mind compelled her to speak, and her impulsiveness hurried her along on the high tide of a flood of words. The story she had to tell oppressed her listener with the sense of some great unknown horror. It was like trying to see a dark place by lightning. The flashes of her revelations revealed a distorted surface, but not the hidden depths. Mrs. Pendleton's agitated mind, doubling in and out a maze of conjectures like a distracted hare, turned again and again to the question of Sisily's complicity in her father's death.

"I can hardly believe it even now," she said with a shudder. "Such a sweet pretty girl! And yet — there was something strange in her manner. I remarked it to Joseph — my husband — before this happened." She pressed her handkerchief to her eyes.

The lawyer, with a sideways glance at the Royal portrait opposite, which seemed in the act of smiling blandly at his companion's grief, reflected, soberly enough, that sweet and pretty girls were as human as the rest of creation, if it came to that.

"Charlie Turold—my nephew, you know—will have it that she is innocent."

"In spite of her disappearance?"

"Yes. He came this morning, before I was up, to see if I knew where Sisily had gone. After tea he came again in a terrible state, raving against the detective for taking out a warrant for her arrest. He said it was madness on his part to imagine that a girl like Sisily would kill her father. I told him that as Sisily had disappeared he could hardly blame the police for looking for her. He turned on me when I said that, and used such violent language that I was quite frightened of him. But I make allowances, of course."

"Why?" the lawyer asked, looking at her.

"I think Charlie is very fond of Sisily," murmured Mrs. Pendleton with womanly intuition.

"Do you mean that they love each other?" said the lawyer, regarding her attentively.

"I cannot say about Sisily. And I never guessed it of Charlie until this morning. I'm sure poor Robert had no idea of it. He would never have agreed—after what he told us on the day of the funeral, I mean."

Mr. Brimsdown gave a tacit unspoken assent to that. Some men might have welcomed such a solution of an ugly family scandal, but not Robert Turold, with his fierce pride for the honour of the title which he had sought to gain.

"Is your nephew's belief in Miss Turold's innocence based on anything stronger than assertion? Does he suspect any one else?"

"He did not say so. He was very excited, and talked on and on, without listening to me in the least. He seems very impulsive and headstrong. I noticed that on the day of the funeral. When Robert told us about his marriage, Charles said to him that his first duty was to his daughter. Robert looked so angry."

"I can well believe it," murmured the lawyer. "The young man must have courage."

"Oh yes, he served with distinction in the war," Mrs. Pendleton innocently rejoined. "In temperament he takes after me, I think, more than after his father. Austin and I never did think alike. We even disagreed over poor Robert's terrible death. Austin thought he had … destroyed himself." Her voice dropped to a shocked whisper.

"On what grounds did he base that belief?" Mr. Brimsdown cautiously asked.

"He thought the circumstances pointed to it," she rejoined. "But I knew better—I knew Robert would never do anything so dreadful. Besides, had I not seen that horrible old man-servant glaring through the door? That is why I went to the police."

As Mrs. Pendleton showed a tendency to repeat herself, Mr. Brimsdown rose to terminate the interview. Mrs. Pendleton rose, too, but she had not yet reached the end of her surprises for him.

"And then there's Robert's will—so strange! Really—"

"The will! What will?" interrupted the lawyer testily. "Did your brother make his will down here?"

"Yes. A will drawn up by a local lawyer—a man with the extraordinary name of Bunkom—a most terrible little creature. Bunkom, indeed!" continued Mrs. Pendleton, shaking her head with a feeble assumption of sprightliness. "Everything is left to my brother Austin. I do not mind in the least about myself. After all, Robert and I met almost as strangers after many years, and I want nothing from him. But his treatment of this unfortunate girl, his daughter, is really too dreadful. I do not wish to speak ill of the dead, but I must say that much, whether Sisily had anything to do with Robert's death or not, for, of course, Robert couldn't have known about that at the time—when he made his will, I mean," concluded Mrs. Pendleton, in some confusion of mind.

"It is strange that your brother did not consult me before drawing up this will," said Mr. Brimsdown.

"Perhaps he imagined you might persuade him against it," sighed Mrs. Pendleton. "It is all very strange. I do not understand it a bit."

Mr. Brimsdown thought it strange, then and afterwards. Next day, after going to the police station and handing Robert Turold's letter to Inspector Dawfield, he sought out the Penzance lawyer who had drawn up the will. Mr. Bunkom was a spidery little man who spun his legal webs in a small dark office at the top of Market Jew Street, a solicitor with a servile manner but an eye like a fox, which dwelt on his eminent confrère from London, as he perused the will, with an expression which it was just as well that Mr. Brimsdown didn't see, so sly and savage was it. The Penzance spider knew his business. The will was watertight and properly attested. The bulk of the property was bequeathed to Austin Turold unconditionally. There were only two other bequests. Robert Turold had placed Thalassa and Sisily ("my illegitimate daughter") on an equality by bequeathing to them annuities of £50 a year each. Austin Turold and Mr. Brimsdown were named as joint executors, and that was all.

Mr. Brimsdown would not have occupied such a distinguished place in the legal profession if he had not been a firm believer in the sacred English tradition that a man has the right to dispose of his own property as he thinks fit. Moreover, his legal mind realized the folly of speculating over the reasons which had prompted this hurried will when the man who had made it was beyond the reach of argument, reproof, or cross-examination.

But the lack of all mention of the title was a different matter, calling for investigation. It was remarkable that a man like Robert Turold should have gone to the grave without binding his heir to prosecute the claim for the Turrald title. To that end Robert Turold had devoted his life, and to the upkeep of the title he had proposed to devote his fortune. The absence of this precaution puzzled Mr. Brimsdown considerably at first, but as he pondered over the matter he began to see the reason. Robert Turold was so close to the summit of his ambition that he had not thought it necessary to take precautions. He was a strong man, and strong men rarely think of death. Once the title was his, it descended as a matter of course to his brother, and then to his brother's son — provided, of course, that the proofs of his daughter's illegitimacy were in existence.

That conclusion carried another in its wake. If Robert Turold had not safeguarded his dearest ambition because he hoped to carry it out himself, it followed as a matter of course that he did not take his own life. Mr. Brimsdown had never accepted that theory, but it was strange to have it so conclusively proved, as it were, by the inference of an omission. That brought the lawyer back to the position that some foreboding or warning of his murder had caused Robert Turold to summon him to Cornwall by letter. The next step of his investigations led Mr. Brimsdown to the dead man's study, where that frantic appeal had been penned.

He engaged a vehicle at the hotel and drove over to Flint House in the afternoon. The impression of that visit remained. Flint House, rising from the basalt summit of the headland like a granite vault, its windows coldly glistening down on the frothy green gloom of the Atlantic far beneath, the country trap and lean black horse at the flapping gate, the undertaker's man (dissolute parasite of austere Death) slinking out of the house, and Thalassa waiting at the open door for him to approach — all these things were engraved on Mr. Brimsdown's mind, never to be forgotten. Who was it that had staged such a crime in such a proscenium, in that vast amphitheatre of black rocks which stretched dizzily down beneath those gleaming windows?

Then came other impressions: the dead man upstairs, the disordered dusty study, the stopped clock, the litter of papers. It was in the room where Robert Turold had been murdered that Mr. Brimsdown questioned Thalassa about the letter, and heard with a feeling of dismay his declaration that he had not posted it. Where was the nearest pillar box? Nearly a mile away, at the cross-roads. Could his late master have gone there to post it that night? If he had, Thalassa hadn't heard him go out. Could anybody else have posted it? No; there was nobody else to post it.

It was like questioning a head on an old Roman coin, so expressionless was Thalassa's face as he delivered himself of these replies. But the lawyer had the feeling that Thalassa was deriving a certain grim satisfaction from his questioner's perplexity, and he dismissed him somewhat angrily. Then, when he had gone, he turned to an examination of some of the papers and documents which littered the room, but that was a search which told him nothing.

When the shades of evening warned him to relinquish that task, he told himself that he really ought to go and see Austin Turold before returning to Penzance. But he shrank, with unaccountable reluctance, from the performance of that obvious duty. He felt very old and tired, and his temples were throbbing with a bad nervous headache. He therefore decided to postpone his visit to Austin Turold until later.

Chapter XX

When the interview with Austin Turold did take place, Mr. Brimsdown learnt with a feeling which was little less than astonishment that Robert Turold had died without confiding to his brother the proofs, on which so much depended, of the statement he had made on the day of his death.

"I cannot understand it," he murmured, putting down his tea-cup as he spoke.

Austin had received him in the blue sitting-room, hung with the specimens of Mr. Brierly's ineffectual art, and had given him tea, as he had given Barrant tea some days before. But there was a subtle difference in the manner of Mr. Brimsdown's reception; the tone was pitched higher, with fine shades and inflections attuned for a more gentlemanly ear.

"It disposes of the suicide theory finally and utterly," added the lawyer thoughtfully.

"The suicide theory disappeared with Robert's daughter," said Austin, glancing at his son, who had taken no part in the conversation.

"You think her disappearance suggests guilt?" asked Mr. Brimsdown.

"It hardly suggests innocence, does it?"

"I would not like to hazard an opinion," responded Mr. Brimsdown, with a thoughtful shake of the head. "My experience of women is that they are capable of the strangest acts without weighing the consequences."

"That was before the war, when women were delightfully irrational creatures, but now they're no longer so. They've become practical and coarse, like men. They smoke, drink, and tell improper stories with demure expression and heads a little on one side like overwise sparrows."

"Was Robert Turold's daughter a girl of this sort?" asked the lawyer in surprise.

"She was not."

It was Charles Turold who made answer, with an angry glance at his father. Austin, looking at him, gave an almost imperceptible shake of the head. Slight as the warning was, it was intercepted by Mr. Brimsdown's watchful eye, and he wondered what it meant.

"I do not think any useful purpose can be gained by discussing my brother's death," Austin interposed, turning to him. "It is a very painful subject, and does no good. The police are endeavouring to unravel the mystery—let us leave it to them."

"I was merely going to say that your brother would have given you the proofs of this statement about his marriage if he had meditated self-destruction," Mr. Brimsdown observed. "The proofs must be in existence, of course, but I do not think that they are at Flint House. Did your brother confide the information to you beforehand—before his public announcement, I mean?"

"Shortly before his death he hinted to me of some very important disclosure which he intended to make at the proper time—some family matter—but he did not say what it was, nor did I ask him."

His son looked at him quickly, and the lawyer doubtfully, as he made this statement, but his own glance sustained both looks serenely and equably.

"My brother did inform me, a week ago, that I would succeed to his fortune," he added.

"That proves that your brother was aware of the illegality of his marriage at that time," said Mr. Brimsdown, with an air of conviction.

"Why so?"

"Because you could not succeed to the Turrald title if your brother's daughter was legitimate."

"That would not prevent my brother disposing of his property as he thought fit," remarked Austin coldly.

"I am aware of that," replied Mr. Brimsdown guardedly. He refrained from stating what was obvious to him, that Robert Turold had intended his fortune for the upkeep of the title when gained, and for no other purpose. "After all, it does not matter very much how long your brother was aware of the fact. The great point is—where are the proofs? I cannot understand why your brother did not send them on to me. I intend to make another and longer search among his papers at Flint House. They must be found. The House of Lords will require the most convincing proof on this head before terminating the abeyance in your favour."

"If I proceed with the claim, you mean," said Austin.

The lawyer turned on him a startled glance which had something of consternation in it. His own interest in the title, was, by force of long association with Robert Turold, so deep and intimate that it had never occurred to him to suppose that the younger brother might not share in the obsession of the elder.

"Titles are at a discount nowadays—like virtuous women," proceeded Austin. "The most extraordinary people have them. Are you aware that there were nearly four thousand names in the last Royal bestowal of Orders of the British Empire? There's kingly munificence for you! It's the same with the Masonic order. The gentleman you address as 'Right Worshipful Sir' overnight delivers poultry and rabbits at your back door next morning. Democracy has come into its own, Brimsdown. Sooner or later we shall have a king wearing a cloth cap."

"Your remarks do not apply to the old nobility," returned Mr. Brimsdown austerely. "They will never become common. It would be a pity not to prosecute your brother's claim to the Turrald title. He gave thirty years of his life to establishing the line of descent."

"My brother had the temperament of a visionary," replied Austin. "I am more practical. But I shall respect his wishes, if possible, though from what you say it would seem to be quite useless to go on with the claim if the missing proofs about his wife's previous marriage are not recovered."

"That is quite true," Mr. Brimsdown admitted. "But I feel sure that they are in existence, somewhere. Your brother Robert was not the man to make a statement of that kind without the proofs. He knew the value of documentary evidence too well for that."

"But so far the proof of his daughter's illegitimacy rests on his unsupported statement, which would be quite valueless in a court of law?"

"That is so."

"If these proofs are found, do you think that my chance of regaining the title is as good as Robert's?" Austin asked. "Are the circumstances of his death likely to tell against my succeeding? I ask you because I know nothing about peerage law."

"The House of Lords has inherent rights of its own in regard to the granting of any claim," replied the lawyer carefully, "rights as the guardian of its own privileges. I do not think, however, that your claim would be rejected. The line of descent is clear, if the proofs of your brother's statement are found. The Turrald barony is a parliamentary peerage which descends to a sole daughter. You can only succeed your brother in the line of descent if she is illegitimate."

"In any case the present claim could not be gone on with, could it?"

"No. That must be withdrawn. I will write to the Home Secretary acquainting him with your brother's death. Later on, if we find the proofs, another claim can be prepared on your behalf."

"If I decide to go on with it."

"I trust that you will," said the lawyer. "It was your brother's dream to restore the title with a male line of descent."

"His dream will be fruitless so far as I am concerned," said Charles Turold, who had been listening intently to this conversation. "I shall have nothing to do with this title." He got up, and strode abruptly from the room without another word.

Mr. Brimsdown was a little surprised at the lack of manners evinced by this precipitate departure, but arose without speaking to take his own leave. Austin did not offer to escort him downstairs. He rang the bell, which was answered by the gaunt maid who had been engaged to sit as Britannia or the Madonna, and to her he consigned his departing visitor after a soft pressure of his white hand.

The maid preceded the lawyer down the staircase with a martial step which outstripped his, and waited at the foot for him to complete the descent. As Mr. Brimsdown reached the last stair, a door immediately opposite opened, and a lady came out. Mr. Brimsdown glanced at her casually in passing, and encountered her glance in return. In that brief look he observed the dawn of swift surprise in her eyes. Her careworn face flushed, and she made an eager step forward, as though about to speak. Somewhat surprised at this action on her part, Mr. Brimsdown hesitated, then, reflecting that he had probably misinterpreted a chance movement on the part of a perfect stranger, went towards the door, which the maid was holding open for him. As he passed through he glanced back, and to his astonishment saw the woman in the passage still standing in the same spot, staring fixedly after him, apparently in a state of consternation or amazement, he could not say which.

He went out of the door with a vision of her questioning gaze following him as far as she could see him. He did not think any more of it just then. A lowering sky suggested rain, and he set off at a round pace for the inn where he had left the vehicle which had brought him to the churchtown.

But quickly as he walked, a footstep behind him was quicker still, and he turned involuntarily to see who was following. Another surprise was in store for him. The tall figure hurrying after him, with the evident intention of overtaking him, was Charles Turold. The lawyer stood still and waited for him.

"I have come after you to tell you something," Charles said abruptly, "something that you ought to know. You were questioning my father about the facts of this case—about my uncle's death. You did not learn anything from him, but I can tell you my cousin Sisily is innocent."

He brought out these words with a breathlessness which may have been the result of his haste. The calmness of the lawyer's reply was in marked contrast.

"Is this merely an assertion, Mr. Turold?"

"It is more than an assertion. I can prove it to you."

Mr. Brimsdown was startled. "What do you mean by that?" he asked.

"If you will come to Flint House I will show you."

Mr. Brimsdown stroked the cautious chin of an old man plunged into a situation which he could not fathom. "Would it not be better to consult the police first?" he temporized.

"The police are now searching the country for Sisily, and there is no time to be lost."

There was something so profoundly unhappy in his appearance that pity stirred in the lawyer's heart. "Very well," he said, with another look at the lowering sky, "let us go."

That afternoon remained with the lawyer as another unforgettable memory. It was all of a piece, sombre, yet of a sharp-edged vividness: the desolation of the moors, the sting of the rain, the clamour of the sea, the seabirds soaring slowly with harsh cries. Then they stood, the pair of them, in Robert Turold's bedroom, looking down on the dead man, swathed in his graveclothes, with a wreath of flowers from Mrs. Pendleton on his breast. Removing this symbol of human pretense against the reality of things, Charles Turold bared the arm of the corpse, and pointing to it exclaimed—

"Could those marks have been made by Sisily?"

In his examination of the marks thus revealed to him, Mr. Brimsdown had the strange feeling that their existence was, in some way, the justification of the dead man's summons to him.

"Do you know how these marks were made?" he said, turning to Charles.

"I do not. But I do know that they prove that Sisily is innocent."

Charles Turold spoke defiantly, but there was a slight note of interrogation in his voice which the lawyer chose to ignore.

"They were made by a man's hand," the young man persisted, looking earnestly at him.

"Do the police know of them?"

"That I cannot tell you."

Another question was in Mr. Brimsdown's mind, but the young man's haggard face, the mingled misery and expectation of his glance, checked the utterance of it. He had the idea that Charles's manner suggested something more—some revelation yet to come. But the young man did not speak.

"Is this all you wanted to show me?" Mr. Brimsdown hinted.

"Is it not enough?"

"I do not see that it throws any light on Miss Turold's disappearance. Can you explain that?"

"How can I explain what I do not know?" Charles was silent for a moment, then added bitterly. "It may be because of her father's inhuman conduct."

"Robert Turold is dead—do not use that tone in speaking of him," the lawyer counselled.

Charles turned on him a peculiar look. "Do you think the world is the loser by his death?" he said.

Mr. Brimsdown was moved out of himself to declare that the death of Robert Turold was a distinct loss to the world. "He was a wonderful man—a notable personality," he said emphatically.

Charles gave him a moody glance, and there fell upon them a silence so complete that the dead man in the bed seemed to share in it. The lawyer had an acute perception of the fact that he had handled the situation badly. He intuitively realized that he had put himself into the opposite camp to Charles's sympathies by the uncompromising partisanship of his last remarks. He was convinced that until that moment, Charles had been meditating the question of some further disclosure. Mr. Brimsdown regretted afterwards that he made no effort to gain his confidence. He felt that if he had done so events might have taken a different course. But it is difficult to bring youth and age together. Youth sometimes yields to impulse, but not age. The lurking devil of self-consciousness whispers caution as the safer quality. Mr. Brimsdown hearkened to the whisper, and stood there in silence, while the minutes slipped by which might have bridged the gap.

There was a quick step in the passage outside, and the door opened to admit Detective Barrant. He looked inquiringly from one to the other, and addressed himself to the lawyer.

"Are you Mr. Brimsdown?" he asked.

"That is my name," the lawyer replied.

"I am Detective Barrant of Scotland Yard. I wish to speak to you privately."

His emphasis on the last word was not lost on Charles Turold. With a slight indifferent nod to Mr. Brimsdown he went out of the room, closing the door quietly behind him.

"I have come to see you about this letter which you left with Inspector Dawfield." Barrant produced the letter and took the single sheet from the grey envelope.

"That is the reason of my presence in Cornwall," said Mr. Brimsdown.

"So I imagined. What can you tell me about it?"

"Very little, except that I received it by the last post at my chambers in Lincoln's Inn Fields the night after Robert Turold's death."

"But why did he send for you?"

"That I cannot even guess."

"You surely must have some idea."

"If I had I should be only too happy to assist the course of justice by imparting it to you."

There was a dryness in the tone of this reply which warned Barrant that he had made a blunder in allowing his irritation to get the better of him. But his private opinion was that the letter was the outcome of some secret of the dead man's which he had imparted to his lawyer. He changed his mood with supple swiftness, in order to extract the information.

"This letter suggests certain things," he said, "some secret, perhaps, in Robert Turold's life, of which you may have some inkling. If you will give me some hint as to what it was, it might be very helpful."

"Unfortunately, I am as much in the dark as yourself," returned Mr. Brimsdown, rubbing his brow thoughtfully. "I cannot make the faintest guess at the reason which called forth this letter. I know next to nothing of my late client's private life. He was a man of the utmost reticence in personal matters. My relations with him were not of that nature."

This reply was delivered with a sincerity which it was impossible to doubt. In palpable disappointment Barrant turned to a renewed scrutiny of the letter, which he held open in his hand.

"It is very strange," he muttered.

"Not the least strange part of it is that I cannot ascertain who posted it," said Mr. Brimsdown, glancing earnestly at the letter. "I asked Thalassa, but he says he knows nothing about it."

"Thalassa is probably lying to you as he has lied to me. One lie more or less would not weigh on his conscience."

"Why should he tell a lie over such a small thing as the posting of a letter?"

Barrant did not reply. He was apparently absorbed in examining the postmarks on the envelope. "Indistinguishable, of course," he muttered, returning the letter to the envelope. "Had Robert Turold any enemies?" he asked.

"I never heard him speak of any."

"How did he come by his money?" asked Barrant, struck by a sudden thought. "His sister tells me that he made his money abroad."

"That I cannot tell you."

"But you invested his fortune for him, did you not?"

"I did," the lawyer agreed.

"In what circumstances?"

"It is rather a strange story," replied Mr. Brimsdown slowly.

"I should like to hear it then. It may throw some light on this letter."

"Let us go into the other room."

Mr. Brimsdown made this suggestion with a quick glance at his departed client on the bed, as though he feared some sardonic reproof from those grey immobile lips.

Chapter XXI

Barrant had returned with a feeling of irritation against the mischances of events which had brought an important piece of evidence to light after his departure for London. He had chosen to commence inquiries into Sisily's disappearance as soon as he had reached London instead of going to Scotland Yard, where a guarded telegram from Inspector Dawfield awaited him, and although he had hastened to obey the summons back to Cornwall as soon as he received it, two valuable days had been lost. It was true that in that time he had found traces of the girl which he believed would lead to her early arrest, but the letter, with its implication that the dead man was aware of his impending doom, was a highly significant clue, and strengthened Barrant's original belief that the real mystery of Robert Turold's death lay much deeper than the plausible surface of events indicated.

He sat now, with a kind of sombre thoughtfulness, listening to Mr. Brimsdown's account of his first meeting with his dead client. That story carried with it a suggestion of adventure and mystery, but it was difficult to say whether those elements had anything to do with Robert Turold's death, thirty years later. It brought up the image of a man, rugged and dominant even in youth, winning his way into the heart of a middle-aged lawyer by the story of his determination to possess an old English title. Most men have the spirit of Romance hidden in them somewhere, and chance or good luck had sent Robert Turold, on his return to England, to the one solicitor in London to whom his story was likely to make the strongest kind of appeal. The spirit of Romance in Mr. Brimsdown's bosom was no shimmering thing of thistledown and fancy, but took the concrete shape of the peerage law of England, out of which he had fashioned an image of worship to the old nobility and the days of chivalry.

Barrant gathered so much from the lawyer's description of that first meeting. And if Robert Turold had found in the solicitor the man he most needed in his search for the missing title, it was equally clear that his own great quality of rugged strength had exercised the most extraordinary sway on the lawyer—a species of personal magnetism which had never lost its original effect. It was not until the second or third meeting—Mr. Brimsdown was not quite sure which—that the question of money was introduced. The lawyer had pointed out to his client that the search for the title was likely to be prolonged and expensive, and Robert Turold had indifferently assured him that he had money at his command for that purpose lying on deposit at a London bank. The amount, when he did mention it, was much greater than Mr. Brimsdown imagined—nearly £50,000 in fact. It was at Robert Turold's suggestion that Mr. Brimsdown undertook to invest the sum at better rates of interest, and thus, before a year had passed, the whole of Robert Turold's business affairs were in the hands of the solicitor.

On one point Mr. Brimsdown was clear. He had never heard from Robert Turold how he first came into possession of this large sum of money, and his client had never encouraged inquiry on the subject. Mr. Brimsdown had once ventured to ask him how he had made his fortune, and Robert Turold, with a freezing look, had replied that he had made it abroad. Mr. Brimsdown had never again referred to the subject, deeming it no business of his.

Barrant, listening to this with the air of a man who was not to be deceived, could not see that the narration threw any illumination on the letter or the other circumstances of Robert Turold's death. It seemed too far-fetched to suppose there was any connection between the fortune which Robert Turold had brought from abroad thirty years before and the letter he had sent to his solicitor on the night of his death. The idea did indeed cross his mind that some iniquity in that money-getting may have been responsible for a belated revenge, but he dismissed that thought as too wide for the scope of his inquiry. Abroad! That was a vague word, and thirty years was a long while back.

As he contemplated the manifold perplexities of the case, Barrant tried to shut out the more sinister inference of the letter by asking himself, if after all, the postscript was not capable of some entirely innocent interpretation. But his conscientious mind refused to permit him to evade responsibility in that way. The letter could not be dismissed with a wave of one's wishing wand. It remained stubbornly in Barrant's perspective, an unexplained factor which could be neither overlooked nor ignored.

These thoughts ran through his mind as Mr. Brimsdown talked of his dead client. At the same time, the detective's attitude towards the lawyer underwent a considerable change. His professional caution, amounting almost to suspicion, became modified by the more perceptive point of view that as the dead man had turned to Mr. Brimsdown for assistance, it would be better for him to trust the lawyer also—to look upon him as an ally, and make common cause with him in the search for Robert Turold's murderer.

This changed attitude, carrying with it a seeming friendliness, the establishment, as it were, of an understanding between them, was not lost upon Mr. Brimsdown. But it had its awkward side for him, by giving added weight to the responsibility of deciding whether he should reveal or withhold his chance encounter with Sisily at Paddington. Till then, Mr. Brimsdown had been unable to make up his mind about that. There were some nice points involved in the decision. In an effort to reach a solution he broached the subject.

"Is it still your opinion that Miss Turold is guilty — after this letter?" he asked.

"Her disappearance lays upon her the obligation of explaining her secret visit to her father on the night of the murder," was the guarded reply.

"Then you intend to arrest her?"

"Yes."

"Do you know where she is?"

A quick consideration of this question led Barrant to the conclusion that it would do no harm to let the lawyer know the scanty truth.

"She is in London. I have traced her to Paddington."

Mr. Brimsdown decided that, as the detective knew that much, it absolved him from any obligation to betray the daughter of his dead client. His feeling of relief unsealed his lips, and led him into an indiscretion.

"It seems incredible that she can be guilty." As he spoke the memory of Sisily's tender and wistful face, as he had seen it that night, came back to him.

"She had some justification, you know, if she was listening at the door that afternoon," replied Barrant thoughtfully.

"It is hardly possible that she could have inflicted those marks on the arm," Mr. Brimsdown said.

"How did you learn of them?" asked the detective quickly, in a changed tone.

Too late Mr. Brimsdown realized that in contrast to his silence with Charles Turold, he had now gone to the other extreme and said too much. He hesitated, but his hesitation was useless before the swiftness of Barrant's deduction.

"Was Charles Turold showing you the marks when I found you in the other room?" he asked with a keen glance.

Mr. Brimsdown's admission of that fact was coupled with an assurance that the young man had shown him the marks because he was convinced of Sisily's innocence.

Barrant dismissed young Turold's opinions about the case with an impatient shake of the head. "Who told him about the marks?" he said.

It was the thought which had occurred to Mr. Brimsdown at the time, but he did not say so then. "How did you discover them?" he asked.

"When I was examining the body. But Charles Turold had no reason to examine the body. Perhaps Dr. Ravenshaw told him. I must ask him."

"It is a terrible and ghastly crime," said Mr. Brimsdown, in an effort to turn the mind of his companion in another direction. "There is something about it that I do not understand—some deep mystery which has not yet been fathomed. Was it really his daughter? If so, how did she escape from the room and leave the door locked inside? Escape from these windows is plainly impossible."

He crossed to the window, and stood for a moment looking down at a grey sea tossing in futile restlessness. After an interval he said—

"Do you suspect Thalassa as well?"

The detective looked at him with a cautious air: "Why do you ask that?" he said, with some restraint in his tone.

"It might account … for certain things."

Barrant shook his head in a way which was more noncommittal than negative. He wanted to ascertain what the lawyer thought, but he was not prepared to reveal all his own thoughts in return.

"Do you think that Robert Turold invented this story about his marriage?" he asked suddenly.

"For what purpose?"

"He did not want his daughter to succeed him in the title. His announcement about the previous marriage strikes me as just a little too opportune. Where are the proofs?"

"You would not talk like that if you had known Robert Turold," said the lawyer, turning away from the window. "He was too anxious to gain the title to jeopardize the succession by concocting a story of a false marriage. He had proofs—I have not the slightest doubt of that. I believe he had them in the house when he made his statement to the family."

"Then where are they now?"

"They may have been stolen."

"For what reason?"

"By some one interested."

"The person most interested is Robert Turold's daughter," said Barrant thoughtfully. "That supposition fits in with the theory of her guilt. Robert Turold is supposed to have kept valuable papers in that old clock on the wall, which was found on the floor that night. Apparently he staggered to it during his dying moments and pulled it down on top of him. For what purpose? His daughter may have guessed that the proofs of her illegitimacy were kept there, and tried to get them. Her father sought to stop her, and she shot him."

"That theory does not account for the marks on the arm," said the lawyer.

"It does, because it is based on the belief that there was somebody else in the room at the time, or immediately afterwards."

"Thalassa?"

"Yes—Thalassa. He knows more about the events of this night than he will admit, but I shall have him yet."

"But the theory does not explain the letter," persisted the lawyer with an earnest look. "Robert Turold could not possibly have had any premonition that his daughter intended to murder him, and even if he had, it would not have led him to write that letter with its strange postscript, which suggests that he had a sudden realization of some deep and terrible danger in the very act of writing it. And if Thalassa was implicated, was he likely to go to such trouble to establish a theory of suicide, and then post a letter to me which destroyed that theory?"

"We do not know that Thalassa posted the letter—it may have been Robert Turold himself. As for premonitions—" Barrant checked himself as if struck by a sudden thought, stood up, and walked across the room to where the broken hood clock had been replaced on its bracket. He stood there regarding it, and the round eyes in the moon's face seemed to return his glance with a heavy stare.

"If that fat face in the clock could only speak as well as goggle its eyes!" he said, with a mirthless smile. "We should learn something then. What's the idea of it all—the rolling eyes, the moon, the stars, and a verse as lugubrious as a Presbyterian sermon on infant damnation. The whole thing is uncanny."

"It's a common enough device in old clocks," said the lawyer, joining him. "It is commoner, however, in long-cased clocks—the so-called grandfather clock. I have seen all sorts of moving figures and mechanisms in long-cased clocks in old English country houses. A heaving ship was a very familiar device, the movement being caused, as in this clock, by a wire from the pendulum. I have never seen a specimen with the rotating moon-dial before, though they were common enough in some parts of England at one time. This is a Dutch clock, and the earlier Dutch makers were always fond of representing their moons as human faces. It was made by a great master of his craft, as famous in his native land as old Dan Quare is in England, and its mechanism has outlived its creator by more than three hundred years."

"Would it be an accurate timekeeper, do you think?" asked Barrant, looking mistrustfully at the motionless face of the moon, as though he suspected it of covertly sneering at him.

"I should think so. These old clockmakers made their clocks to keep perfect time, and outlast Time himself! And this clock is a perfect specimen of the hood clock, which marked a period in clock-making between the old weight clocks and the long cases. Hood clocks were popular in their day in Holland, but they have always been rare in this country. It would be interesting to trace how this one came into this house. No doubt it was taken from a wreck, like so much of the furniture in old Cornish houses."

"You seem to know a lot about old clocks."

Mr. Brimsdown, astride his favourite hobby, rode it irresistibly. He discoursed of clocks and their makers, and Barrant listened in silence. The subject was not without its fascination for him, because it suggested a strange train of thought about the hood clock which was the text, as it were, of the lawyer's discourse. He looked up. Mr. Brimsdown, in front of the clock, was discoursing about dials and pendulums. Barrant broke in abruptly with the question on his mind—

"Can you, with your knowledge of old clocks, suggest any reason which would cause Robert Turold to go to it? Are the works intricate? Would such a clock require much adjustment?"

"Robert Turold was not likely to think of adjusting a clock in his dying moments," returned Mr. Brimsdown, with a glance which betokened that he perfectly understood his companion had some other reason for his question.

"There's a smear of blood on the dial," said Barrant, staring at it.

"Was that made by the right or left hand?"

"The right hand was resting on the clock-face. Why do you ask?"

Mr. Brimsdown hesitated, then said: "The thought has occurred to me that Robert Turold may have gone to the clock for a different purpose— not for papers. Perhaps his last thought was to indicate the name of the murderer on the white face of the clock."

"In his blood? Rather a melodramatic idea, that! He had writing materials before him if he wanted to do that, if he thought of it. He was shot down in the act of writing, remember."

A silence fell between them on this declaration—a silence terminated by Barrant remarking that it was really late, and he must be getting back to Penzance. Mr. Brimsdown made no suggestion to accompany him. Instead he rustled papers in Robert Turold's cabinet as though to convey the impression that the sorting and searching of them would take him some time. Barrant, from whose eyes speculation and suspicion looked out from a depth, like the remote glance of a spider which had scurried to a hole, gave a slight sign of farewell, and wheeled out of the apartment without another word.

Downstairs he went, plunged in the deepest thought. Looking downward, he saw Thalassa escorting Dr. Ravenshaw to the front door. The doctor's voice reached him.

"... She must not be left alone on any account—understand that. You ought to get somebody to look after her."

"I can't afford nobody," Thalassa made reply.

Dr. Ravenshaw was about to say something more, but the figure of the descending detective caught his eye. Barrant made a detaining gesture, and the doctor waited in the passage for him. Barrant, with a slight glance at the motionless figure of Thalassa, led the way into the front room. He closed the door before he spoke.

"Doctor," he said, "have you told anybody about those marks on Robert Turold's arm?"

"I have not," said the doctor promptly, looking up. "Why do you ask?"

His glance carried conviction, and interrogation also. But it was Barrant's province to ask questions, not to answer them. He ignored Dr. Ravenshaw's.

"There's another matter, doctor," he continued. "One of the coast fishermen has a story that when Robert Turold was out on the moors he used to hasten home with great strides, like a man who feared pursuit. Did you ever observe this peculiarity in him?"

"I have observed that he used to walk at a quick pace."

"This was more than a quick pace—it was almost a run, according to the fisherman—looking backward over his shoulder as he went."

"I did not notice that, but I should not be surprised if it were true, with a man of Robert Turold's temperament."

"He feared pursuit—some unknown danger, then?"

"I cannot say. He may have suffered from agoraphobia."

"What is that?" asked Barrant.

"The dread of open spaces."

"I have heard of claustrophobia—the dread of closed spaces—but not of this."

"It is common enough—an absurd but insurmountable aversion to open spaces. The victims are oppressed by a terrible anxiety when crossing a field. I have known a man who would be terrified at the idea of crossing Trafalgar Square."

"What is the cause of agoraphobia?" asked Barrant.

"It is a nervous disorder—one of the symptoms of advanced neurasthenia."

"Did Robert Turold suffer from neurasthenia?"

"His nervous system was in a state of irritable weakness through the monomania of a fixed idea," was the reply—"too much seclusion and concentration on one object, to the exclusion of all other human interests."

"How's your patient?" said Barrant, giving the conversation an abrupt turn.

"What patient do you mean—Mrs. Thalassa?" asked Dr. Ravenshaw in some surprise.

"Yes. I gathered from what I overheard you say to Thalassa that you have been attending her."

"I have been attending her since Mr. Turold's death."

"She is in a strange condition," observed Barrant reflectively. "I was questioning her the other night, but I could get nothing out of her. She seems almost imbecile."

"She is not a woman of strong mind, and she is now suffering from a severe shock. She should be looked after or taken away from here altogether, but her husband seems quite indifferent."

"Do you think she will recover?"

"It is impossible to say."

"How do you think the shock was caused?"

"I should not like to hazard an opinion on that point, either," replied Dr. Ravenshaw gravely. He glanced at his watch as he spoke. "I must be going," he said.

They left the house together, but branched off at the gate—Dr. Ravenshaw to visit a fisherman's dying wife, and Barrant to seek the *Three Jolly Wreckers* for supper before returning to Penzance.

From the kitchen window Thalassa watched them go: the doctor walking across the cliffs with resolute stride, the detective making for the path over the moors with bent head and slower step, as though his feet were clogged by the weight of his thoughts. Thalassa watched their dwindling forms until they disappeared, and then stood still, in a listening attitude. The sound of the lawyer stirring in the study overhead seemed to rouse him from his immobility. He closed the door, and stood looking up the staircase with the shadow of indecision on his face.

Chapter XXII

Upstairs Mr. Brimsdown made unavailing search among Robert Turold's papers for proofs of his statement about his marriage. The lawyer believed that they existed, and his failure to find them brought with it a belated realization of the fact that he, too, had been cherishing hopes of Sisily's innocence. It was the memory of her face which had inspired that secret hope. That was not sentiment (so Mr. Brimsdown thought), but the worldly wisdom of a man whose profession had trained him to read the human face. Sisily's face, as he recalled it now, had looked sad and a little fearful that night at Paddington, but there was nothing furtive or tainted in her clear glance. He felt that a judge would look with marked attention at such a face in the dock. Judges, like lawyers, and all whose business it is to trip their kind into the gins of the law, scan faces as closely as evidence in the effort to read the stories written there.

But the disappearance of certain papers which had probably been abstracted from that room weighed more in the scale of suspicion against Sisily than her look of innocence. She stood to gain most by the suppression or destruction of the proofs of her mother's earlier marriage. But Mr. Brimsdown could not see that this rather negative inference against the girl brought the actual solution of the mystery any nearer. It did nothing to explain, for instance, the marks on the dead man's arm and his posthumous letter. The letter! What was the explanation of the letter? Was it not an argument of equal weight for Sisily's innocence, suggesting the existence of some hidden avenging figure glimpsed by Robert Turold in time to give him warning of his death, but not in time to enable him to avert it?

There were other things too. What was the meaning of that sly and stealthy shake of the head which Austin Turold had given his son that afternoon. A warning obviously—but a warning for what purpose? Mr. Brimsdown could not guess, but his contemplation of the incident brought before him the image of the restless and unhappy young man, as he stood by the bedside in the next room, pointing to the marks on the dead man's arm. Even in his vehement assertions of Sisily's innocence Mr. Brimsdown had conceived the impression that he was keeping something back. What did Charles Turold know? Did his father share his secret knowledge? Mr. Brimsdown could not answer these questions, and he was greatly perturbed at the way in which they brought a host of other thoughts and doubts in their train. He reflected that the Turolds, father and son, were after all the greatest gainers by their relative's death. The father came into immediate possession of a large and unexpected fortune which he would bequeath to his son. And Austin Turold was not anxious apparently to proceed with his brother's claim for the title.

These were facts which could not be gainsaid, but where did they lead? The trouble was that no conceivable theory covered the facts of the case, so far as they were known. So far as they were known! That was the difficulty. Any line of thought stopped short of the real solution, because the facts themselves were inconclusive. There was much that was still concealed— Mr. Brimsdown felt sure of that.

As he applied his mind to the problem, the definite impression came back to him, and this time with renewed force, that the mystery surrounding Robert Turold's death was something which might not bear the light of day. He set his lips firmly as he considered that possibility. If that proved to be the case it would be his duty to cover it up again. He was an adept at such work, as many of his clients, alive and dead, could have approvingly testified. He had spent much time in safeguarding family secrets. Several old families had found him their rock of refuge in distress. If he had been a man of the people, baby lips might have been taught to call down Heaven's blessings on his discreet efforts. Those members of the secluded domain of high respectability for whom he strived showed their gratitude in a less emotional but more substantial way—generally in the mellow atmosphere of after-dinner conferences … "You had better see my man, Brimsdown. I'll give you a note to him. He'll square this business for you. Safe? None safer."

Mr. Brimsdown did not accept the axiom of a great English jurist that every man is justified in evading the law if he can, because it is the duty of lawmakers not to leave any loophole for evasion. That point of view of justice as a battle of wits, with victory to the sharpest, was a little too cynical for his acceptance. But he believed it to be his duty to safeguard the interests of his client. Robert Turold was dead, and no longer able to protect his own name. It might be that the facts of his death involved some scandalous secret of the dead man's which was better undivulged, and if so it would remain undivulged, could Mr. Brimsdown contrive it. For the time being he would pursue his investigations and keep his own counsel.

The sound of an opening door and a shadow athwart the threshold disturbed his meditations. He looked up, and was confronted by the spectacle of Thalassa advancing into the room with his eyes fixed upon him.

"Well, Thalassa," he said, "what do you want?"

"To ask you something," was the response. "It's this. It's every man for himself—now that he's gone."

He jerked his thumb in the direction of the next room. "He took this house for twelve months, and so it'll have to be paid for. Can I stop here for a bit? I suppose it's in your hands to say yes or no."

His face was hard and expressionless as ever, but there was a new note in his voice which struck the lawyer's keen ear—an accent of supplication. He looked at Thalassa thoughtfully.

"You wish to stay on here until you have made other arrangements for your future—is that so?" he asked.

"That's it," was the brief reply.

Mr. Brimsdown felt there was more than that—some deeper, secret reason. Before granting the request it occurred to him to try and get what he could in exchange. Self-interest is the strongest of human motives, and men wanting favours are in a mood to yield something in return.

"Well, Thalassa," he said, amiably enough, but watching him with the eye of a hawk, "I do not think your request is altogether unreasonable—in the circumstances. I dare say it could be arranged. I'll try to do so, but I should like you to answer me one or two questions first."

"What do you want to know?"

"Was your master's daughter here—in the house, I mean—on the night of his death?"

Thalassa's face hardened. "You, too?" he said simply. "I say again, as I said before, that she was not."

"You said so," rejoined Mr. Brimsdown softly. "The question is—are you telling the truth? If you know anything of the events of that night you may be injuring Miss Turold by your silence."

For a moment Mr. Brimsdown thought his appeal was going to succeed. He could have sworn that a flicker of hesitation—of irresolution—crossed the old man's stern countenance. But the mood passed immediately, and it was in an indifferent voice that Thalassa, turning to go, replied—

"If that's what you're reckoning on, I'd better go and pack my traps."

"Oh, I don't make that a condition," replied the lawyer, acknowledging his defeat in a sporting spirit. "You can remain here and look after the house until you decide what to do. As Robert Turold's old servant you are entitled to consideration. I will help you afterwards, if you will let me know your plans. I am sure that would have been your late master's wish."

"I want nothing from *him*," Thalassa rejoined, "a damned black scoundrel."

Mr. Brimsdown was shocked at this savage outburst, but there was something so implacable in the old man's air that the rebuke he wished to utter died unspoken. Thalassa regarded him for a moment in silence, and then went on —

"Thank'ee for letting me stop on here a bit. Now I'll tell you something — about him." Again his thumb indicated the next room. "It was the night after."

"Do you mean the night after he met his death?"

"Yes. Some one was upstairs in his room — in this room."

Mr. Brimsdown gave a startled glance around him, as though seeking a lurking form in the shadows. "Here?" he breathed.

"Here, sure enough. I woke up in my bed downstairs, staring wide awake, as though somebody had touched me on the shoulder. I was just turning over to go to sleep again, when I heered a noise up here."

"What sort of a noise?"

"Like the rustling of paper. I listened for a bit, then it stopped. I heard a board creak in the next room, where we'd carried him. Then the rustling started in the other room again, right over my head. The dog downstairs started to bark. I got up, and went upstairs as quickly as I could, but there was nobody — except *him*. The dog frightened whoever it was, I suppose. Next morning I found the front room window wide open."

"Were there any footprints outside the window?"

"A man doesn't leave footprints on rocks."

"What time was it?"

"It would be about midnight, I reckon."

"Did your wife hear the noise?"

"No. She was in bed and asleep."

"Are you sure you didn't dream this?" Mr. Brimsdown asked, with a shrewd penetrating glance.

"The open window wasn't a dream," was the dogged reply.

"You might have left it open yourself."

"No, I didn't. I close the windows every night before dark."

"And lock them?"

"Not always."

The incident did not sound convincing to Mr. Brimsdown, but his face did not reveal his scepticism as he thanked Thalassa for the information. Thalassa lingered, as if he had something still on his mind. He brought it out abruptly—

"Has anything been seen of Miss Sisily?"

"Nothing whatever, Thalassa."

On that he turned away, and went out of the room, leaving the lawyer pondering over his story of a midnight intruder. Mr. Brimsdown came to the conclusion that it was probably imagination, and so dismissed it from his mind.

He resumed his work of working over the papers, but after a few minutes discontinued his search, and walked restlessly about the room. The air seemed to have the taint of death in it, and he crossed over to one of the windows and flung it up.

The window looked out on the sea, though far above it, but the slope of the house embraced in the view a portion of the cliffs at the side. As Mr. Brimsdown stood so, breathing the sea air and looking around him, he espied a woman, closely veiled, walking rapidly across the cliffs in the direction of the house.

She vanished from the range of his vision almost immediately, but a few minutes later he heard footsteps and an opening door. He was again confronted by the presence of Thalassa on the threshold. But this time Thalassa did not linger. "Somebody to see you," he announced with gruff brevity, and turned away.

The open door now revealed the figure of the woman he had seen outside. She advanced into the room.

"Mr. Brimsdown?" she said.

"That is my name," said the lawyer, eyeing her in some surprise. He recognized her as the woman who had stared after him when he left Austin Turold's lodgings, but he could not conjecture the object of her visit.

"I see you do not remember me," she sadly remarked.

"You are Mrs. Brierly, I think."

"Yes. But I was Mary Pleasington before I was married. I remember you very well, but I suppose that I have changed."

Mr. Brimsdown recalled the name with a start of surprise. He found it difficult to recognize, in the faded woman before him, the pretty daughter of his old client, Sir Roger Pleasington, whose debts and lawsuits had been compounded by death ten years before. He remembered his daughter as a budding beauty, with the airs and graces of a pretty girl who imagines her existence to be of some importance in the world. He recollected that her marriage to an impecunious young artist had caused some sensation in Society at the time. Marriage had dealt hardly with her, and no trace of her beauty or vivacity remained.

"You are the late Mr. Turold's legal adviser?" she continued, after a pause.

Mr. Brimsdown, always chary of unnecessary words, replied with a slight bow.

"I suppose you have come to Cornwall to investigate the cause of his death?"

Mr. Brimsdown remained silent, waiting to hear more.

"I—I wish to speak to you about that." Her lips quivered with some inward agitation.

"Will you not be seated?" he said, placing a chair for her.

"Will you regard what I have to say to you in strict confidence?" she queried, sinking her voice to a whisper.

"Is it about Mr. Turold's murder?"

"It—it may be."

With the recollection of previous eavesdropping in that house, the lawyer rose and closed the door. "I cannot make a promise of that kind," he said firmly, as he returned to his seat.

"No, no—of course not," she hurriedly acquiesced. "I was wrong to ask it. I have come here to tell you. When I saw you this afternoon I realized that Providence had answered my prayers, and sent somebody in whom I could safely confide. I will tell you everything. I have come here for that purpose."

She seemed to have a difficulty in commencing. Her pale grey eyes wandered irresolutely from his, and then returned. It was with a perceptible effort that she spoke at last.

"What I am about to tell you I have known for some days, but I could not bring myself to the extreme step of going to the police. Sometimes I am inclined to think that it may be only a trifling thing, easily explained, and of no importance. But sometimes — at night — it assumes a terrible significance. I need counsel — wise counsel — about it."

She paused and looked at him wistfully. As though interpreting his nod as encouragement, she went on —.

"Mr. Austin Turold and his son have been inmates of my household for the last six weeks. Mr. Robert Turold arranged it with me beforehand. I had never done anything of the kind before, but our means — my husband's and mine — are insufficient for the stress of these times. After all, people must live."

Mr. Brimsdown's slight shake of the head seemed to imply that this last statement was by no means an incontrovertible proposition, but Mrs. Brierly was not looking at him.

"Therefore, to oblige Mr. Turold we decided to afford hospitality to his brother and son. The terms were favourable, and they were gentlefolk. These things counted, and the money helped. But if I had only known — if I could have foreseen ..."

"Mr. Turold's death?" said Mr. Brimsdown, filling in the pause.

"I mean — everything," she retorted a little wildly. "My name is well known. I was in Society once. There is my husband's reputation as an artist to be considered. I would not be talked about for worlds. I acted against my husband's advice in this matter — in taking Mr. Turold and his son. My husband said it was a degradation to take in lodgers. I pointed out that they were gentlefolk. There is a difference. I wish now that I had listened to my husband's advice."

Mr. Brimsdown listened with patient immobility. His long experience of female witnesses withheld him from any effort to hasten the flow of his companion's story.

"They were very nice and quiet — particularly Mr. Austin Turold," she went on. "The son was more silent and reserved, but we saw very little of him — he was out so much. But Mr. Turold did my husband good — his breeding and conversation were just what he needed to lift him out of himself. A man goes to seed in the country, Mr. Brimsdown, no matter how intellectual he may be. Nature is delightful, but a man needs to be near Piccadilly to keep smart. Cornwall is so very far away — so remote — and Cornish rocks are dreadfully severe on good clothes. I am not complaining, you understand. We had to come to Cornwall. It was inevitable — for us. No English artist is considered anything until he has painted a picture of the Land's End or Newquay. The Channel Islands — or Devon — is not quite the same thing. Not such a distinctive hallmark. So we came to Cornwall, and my husband went to seed. That was why I welcomed Mr. Turold's conversation for him. It did him good. My husband said so himself. He derived inspiration—artistic inspiration—from Mr. Turold's talk. He conceived a picture—'Land of Hope and Glory' it was to be called—of a massive figure of Britannia, standing on Land's End, defying the twin demons of Bolshevism and Labour Unrest with a trident. He was working at it with extraordinary rapidity—when this happened.

"On the day of his brother's death we did not see much of Mr. Austin Turold. There was Mrs. Turold's funeral in the afternoon, and when he came home I thought he would prefer to be left to himself.

"He went to his sitting-room, and stayed there. My husband and I retired early that night, but later we were awakened by a very loud knock at the front door. We heard Mr. Austin Turold, who was still up, go down and open it. Then we heard a very loud voice, outside—Mr. Robert Turold's man-servant, it appears. We heard him tell Mr. Austin that his brother had been found shot. Mr. Turold returned upstairs, and some time afterwards we heard him go down again and out.

"I was so upset that I arose and dressed myself to await Mr. Turold's return. I thought he might like a cup of coffee when he returned, so I decided to go downstairs myself and prepare it. As I passed the passage which led to Mr. Charles Turold's room, I noticed a light underneath his door. I rather wondered, as he was still up, why he had not gone with his father, but I was passing on without thinking any more about it when I happened to notice that the light beneath the door was fluctuating in the strangest way. First it was very bright, then it became quite dim, but the next moment it would be bright again.

"That alarmed me so much that I walked along the passage to see what it meant. I thought perhaps the young man had fallen asleep with the window open and left the gas flaring in the wind. I stood for a moment outside the door wondering what I ought to do. Then I heard a crackling sound, and smelt something burning. That alarmed me still more, because I knew no fire had been lit in the room that day. I wondered if the bedroom was on fire, and I knelt down and tried to see through the keyhole.

"At first I could see nothing except a bright light and the shadow of a form on the wall. Then I made out the form of Charles Turold, standing in his dressing-gown in front of the fireplace, in which a fire of kindling wood was leaping and blazing. I could not make out at first what he was doing. He seemed to be stooping over the fire, moving something about. Then I saw. He was drying his clothes—the suit he had worn that day. They must have been very wet, for the steam was rising from them.

"I must have made a noise which startled him, for I saw him turn quickly and stare at the closed door, then walk towards it. I went away as quickly and noiselessly as I could, and as I turned the corner of the passage, out of sight, his door opened, and then closed again. He had looked out and, seeing nobody, gone back into his room.

"I went downstairs to make the coffee and wait for Mr. Turold. I had to wait some time. When I did hear the sound of his key in the door, I went up the hall with a cup of coffee in my hand. Mr. Turold seemed surprised to see me. He looked at me in a questioning sort of way as he took the coffee, and stood there sipping it. As he handed me back the cup he told me in a low voice that his brother was dead. I said that was why I had waited up— because I had heard the knock and the dreadful news. Mr. Turold, in the same low voice, then said he was very much afraid his brother had taken his own life.

"He then went upstairs. I again retired shortly afterwards, but I could not sleep. I was too upset—too nervous. I could not get Mr. Robert Turold's suicide out of my head. It seemed such a dreadful thing for a wealthy man to do—so common and vulgar! Suicide sticks to a family so—it is never really forgotten. It is much easier to live down an embezzlement or misappropriation of trust funds. The thought of it put the other thing—the fire and young Mr. Turold and his wet clothes—out of my head completely, for the time.

"As I was lying there tossing and thinking I heard a light footstep pass my door. I slipped out of bed, and opening the door a little, looked out. I saw Mr. Turold, fully dressed, a light in his hand, turning down the passage which led to his son's room. Then I heard the sound of a creaking door, the murmur of a low conversation, cut short by the shutting of the door. I stood there for a few minutes, and then went back to my bed and fell asleep.

"The next day it all came back to me. I had gone into Charles Turold's room for some reason when he was out, and there, on the hearth, I could see the remains of the fire he had lit overnight to dry his clothes. He had made some clumsy man-like attempt to clean up the grate, but he left some ends of the charred kindling wood lying about."

This final revelation brought a silence between Mrs. Brierly and the lawyer; a silence broken only by the distant deep call of the sea beneath the open window. The silence lengthened into minutes before Mr. Brimsdown found his voice.

"You have said nothing to anybody else about this?" He spoke almost abstractedly, but she chose to regard this question in the light of a reproach. She hurriedly rejoined—

"I did not see the necessity—then. If young Mr. Turold got caught in the storm, and chose to dry his clothes in his room, instead of putting them out for the maid, why should I tell anybody? I did not connect it with his uncle's death. I was under the impression that Mr. Robert Turold had taken his own life. It was not until the detective called to see Mr. Austin Turold that I learnt there was a suspicion of—murder. My maid overheard the detective say something while she was in and out of the room serving tea, and she told me what she had heard. I saw things in a new light then, and I was terribly upset. But I could not see my way clear until you came to the house to-day. Then I decided to tell you."

"Can you tell me what time Charles Turold came in that night?"

"I have no idea. He and his father have separate keys of the front door."

It was evident that she had told all she knew. She rose to her feet in agitation.

"I must go. My husband will be wondering where I am. But tell me, Mr. Brimsdown, do you imagine ... Is it possible ..." Her voice dropped to the ghost of a frightened whisper.

He evaded this issue with legal caution.

"You have done quite right in coming to me," he replied, as he opened the door for her departure. He held out his hand.

She touched it with trembling fingers, and went away.

Mr. Brimsdown closed the door behind her, and wearily sat down. He had been prepared to do much to shield the name of Turold, but he had not bargained for this. He did not doubt the truth of the story he had just heard, and it gave him a feeling of nausea. What a revelation of the infamy of human nature! The stupendous depth of such villainy overwhelmed him with dismay. The extent of the criminal understanding between father and son he did not attempt to fathom. His mind was filled with the monstrous audacity by which Charles Turold, apparently at the dictate of remorse, had sought to convince him of Sisily's innocence by directing attention to the marks on the dead man's arm which he had probably made himself. Could human cynicism go farther than that? A great wave of pity swept over the lawyer as he thought of the unhappy Sisily, and all that she had been compelled to endure. But why had she fled?

Long he sat there without stirring, until the shadows deepened and the grey surface of the sea dissolved in blackness.

"The police must be told of this," he said at last, in an almost voiceless whisper.

Chapter XXIII

"And suppose the police call during your absence?" said Austin Turold, glancing sharply at his son.

"Then you had better tell the truth. I am tired of it all."

"I might ask, with Pilate, What is truth?—in your case."

"You know it already, father, whether you believe me or not."

Austin Turold looked strangely at him—a look in which anger was mingled with something deeper and more searching, as though he sought to reach some secret in the depth of his soul. Impatiently he crossed the room to the fireplace, and stood with his back to the fire, facing his son.

"I do not see that there's any more risk than there was before," said Charles gloomily.

"I say there is," returned his father sharply. "What! Do you suppose you can go off to London like this, leaving me here alone, at such a moment? Do you not see that your unexplained absence, in itself, is likely to bring suspicion upon you, indeed, upon both of us?"

"I cannot help that," returned the young man desperately. "I must go and find Sisily."

"You are not likely to find her. You do not even know that she has gone to London."

"Yes. I have found out that much. She took a ticket by the midday train on the day after—it happened."

"And why do you wish to find her?"

"Because she is deeply wronged—she is innocent."

"You should be able to speak with authority on that point," said Austin, with a cold glance, which the other did not meet. "You are acting very foolishly, rushing off to London on this quixotic mission. You won't find her. Besides, no woman is worth what you are risking in this wild-goose chase. You are jeopardizing your future by an act of the maddest folly."

"There is nothing in life for me but the shadow of things — now," returned the young man in low tones. "I want nothing except to find Sisily and prove her innocence. I'm going to look for her, whatever you say."

Austin Turold made an impatient gesture.

"Very well," he said. "If Providence has made you a fool you must fulfil Providence's decree. Only, I warn you, I think you are going the right way to bring trouble on yourself. That lawyer who was here to-day — what's his name, Brimstone, Brimsdown? — has his suspicions, unless I'm very much mistaken."

Charles turned pale. "What makes you think that?" he asked.

"By the way he watched both of us."

"That accounts for his attitude when I saw him afterwards," said Charles in a startled voice.

"Afterwards — where?"

"I went after him to tell him that Sisily was innocent."

"And what else did you tell him?"

"Nothing but that — nothing that counted, at least."

"Really, Charles, your lack of intelligence is a distinct reflection on me as a parent. Fancy a son of mine trying to make a lawyer's bowels yearn with compassion! I'm positively ashamed of you. Why are you so elementary? The situation must have contained some elements of humour, though. I should like to have witnessed it. Did you call down Heaven's vengeance on the murderer in approved fashion? How did the man of parchments take it?"

"You have no heart," said his son, flushing darkly under this sarcasm. He walked towards the door as he spoke. "I am going," he said. "There is an excursion train through to Paddington to-night, and I shall catch it."

"You are determined on it, then?"

"I should be in an unendurable position if I didn't," replied the young man, and without another word he left the room.

Austin looked after him a little wistfully, as though remembering that the other was, after all, his son. He remained motionless for a moment, then crossed over to the window and looked out. As he stood so his eye was caught by two figures beneath. One was his son, walking down the garden path. The other was Mrs. Brierly, returning to the house. She walked past Charles with downcast eyes, but Austin from the window saw her turn and cast a frightened fluttering glance at the young man's retreating figure. She had seen him, then, but did not want to recognize him. As she hurried up the garden path Austin caught a glimpse of her face, and observed that it was white and drawn.

"What's the matter with my estimable landlady?" he murmured as he withdrew from the window.

His quick intelligence, playing round this incident and seeking to pierce its meaning, grew alarmed. There seemed to be a menace in it. Did she know or guess something of the hidden events of that night, or had she played the spy since? He turned pale as he considered these possibilities. Women had an unerring instinct for a secret once their curiosity was aroused. But he had been careful, very careful. What did she suspect?

He thought over this problem until night fell, and retired to bed with it still unanswered.

But the solution flashed into his mind at breakfast next morning, suddenly, like light in a dark place. He was amazed that he had not seen it before. "If it is that …" he whispered. But he knew it was that; knew also, that it meant the worst. He got up from the table, then forced himself to sit down again and eat. An untouched breakfast tray might quicken the suspicions in the mind of that most treacherous woman downstairs, might hasten her hand. But why had she delayed so long?

He passed the morning between his chair and the window, watching, and listening for footsteps. He saw Mrs. Brierly leave the house early, and wondered if she would return with the police. Another reflection came to his mind. Charles had some inkling, and had fled in time. Perhaps that was just as well, if he got out of England. For himself there was no such retreat, nor did he wish it. He would have to face things out, if they had to be faced, and he did not yet despair of saving the situation, so far as it affected himself. What did that diabolical female know, really? He had a momentary vision of her stealing about the house, prying, watching, listening. He sank into a motionless brooding reverie.

The day passed its meridian, but he still sat there in solitude with his anxious thoughts. As the afternoon declined his hopes rose. Could it be that he was mistaken, that his fears were imaginary? Perhaps, after all—

At that sharp ring of the doorbell downstairs he walked noiselessly to the window, and shrank back with the startled look of a man who has had his first glimpse of the bared teeth of the law. He stood still, listening intently. He heard the door opened, a sharp question, then the sound of ascending footsteps. When the knock came at his own door he was in complete command of himself as he went to open it. He was well aware of the ordeal before him, but he did not show it. There was nothing but ironical self-possession in the glance which took in the figures of Detective Barrant and Inspector Dawfield, revealed on the threshold of the opening door.

Barrant lost no time in coming to the point. "I want to see your son," he said, entering and glancing quickly round the apartment.

"I am afraid that is impossible."

"Why?"

"He is not here."

"Where is he?"

"I think he has gone to London."

Barrant was plainly taken aback at this unexpected piece of news. "When did he go?" he demanded.

"Yesterday evening."

Barrant cast a look at Dawfield, which said plainly: "He's had word of this and bolted." His glance returned to Austin. "Can you tell me where he is staying in London?"

"I have not the least idea," returned Austin negligently.

"Does he not live with you?"

"As a rule—yes."

"What is your London address?"

Austin took a card from his case and laid it on the table. Barrant picked it up, glanced at it, and said: "Is your son likely to be there?"

"He may be, but he said nothing to me about going there. He has his own liberty of action, like every other young man of his age. May I ask the reason of these questions, Detective Barrant?"

Barrant did not choose to reply. He drew Inspector Dawfield to the doorway and conferred with him in an undertone. Austin saw Barrant slip the card into his colleague's hand, and Dawfield then hastened away. The inference was plain. Dawfield had been sent off to intercept the flight or start the pursuit. Austin found himself profoundly hoping that his son was by that time out of England.

He had not much leisure to think of that, for Barrant turned towards him again with an annoyance that he did not attempt to dissemble. "Why has your son gone to London—perhaps you can tell me that much?" he exclaimed.

"I gathered from him that it is his intention to look for his cousin Sisily."

"For what purpose?"

"Because he strongly believes in her innocence."

"It is strange that he should have rushed off like this."

"Without waiting for your visit, do you mean? Really, Detective Barrant, may I constrain you to give me some explanation of all this? I want to help you all I can, but your actions savour too much of a peremptory jack-in-the-box, even in these bureaucratic days. What is the object of this visit? Why did you want to see my son?"

"I wished to interview him."

"About what, may I ask?"

Barrant did not immediately reply, but Austin, scanning him furtively, sought to reach his thoughts by the varying shades of expression on his face. It was the state of mind of a man who was at once chagrined, amazed, suspicious, and wondering. The older man could picture Barrant thinking to himself: "This man before me—how far is he involved in this?" And, watching him mutely, Austin steeled himself for a sudden outburst: "You picked up the key. You declared it was suicide. What does that mean—now?"

But he under-estimated Barrant's intelligence. Barrant had no intention of doing anything so crude. The situation was sufficiently awkward as it stood without putting the father on his guard. Austin might guess that he was under suspicion as well as his son, but that did not matter so much. Barrant instinctively realized that flight was impossible for Austin Turold, though he might seek to warn his son not to go near their London home because the police were after him. But that was a warning which would be useless, for the police were ahead of him there. Barrant reflected that he gained nothing by not divulging the object of his visit when the inference of it was so transparently palpable. The disclosure might even serve a useful purpose by lessening Austin's apprehensions in his own case. With this consideration in view he brought it out frankly—

"I wished to question your son about his movements on the night of the murder."

"Is my son suspected—now?"

Barrant winced under the delicate inflection of irony which conveyed in that brief reply the inference of another blunder in his own changing suspicions. That sneer roused the official in him, and it was in a curt tone of command that he said—

"What time did your son get home on the day of the murder?"

"I am unable to say."

"He did not return with you after the funeral?"

"No, he did not."

"Where did he go?"

"These are strange questions, Detective Barrant. I really cannot tell you that either, because I do not know."

He put up his glasses to look at Barrant with an assumption of resentment, but the detective's return glance was hard and searching. "Was your son in to dinner that night?" he asked.

"We have midday dinner, in this house."

"Well, supper. Was he in to supper?"

Austin reflected rapidly. He dared not refuse to answer the question, and any attempt to mislead the questioner would only make things worse when the two women in the house knew the truth.

"Yes. He was in to supper."

"And went out afterwards?"

This was put more as a simple statement of fact than a question. Again, Austin's subtle intelligence could see no better course than truth.

"He did. My son frequently goes out walking of an evening after supper."

"What time did he return—on this evening?"

"I do not know."

"Do you mean that?" Barrant's tone was incredulous.

"I do." The impulse which had dictated his previous answer sprang from the thought that the foolish females downstairs could not contradict it, and he adhered calmly to the course now he was committed to it.

"What time did Thalassa come for you from Flint House with the news that your brother was dead?"

"I do not know the exact time. He called at the police station first."

"Had not your son returned by then?"

"I am unable to inform you. He frequently goes straight to his room when he returns from an evening walk."

"Then you do not know whether he was in or out when you left the house?"

"I assumed he was in, as it was after his usual time for returning."

"You did not go to his room, to see?"

"No. I did not wish to disturb him."

Barrant looked as though there was only one possible construction to be placed on these replies, but he still did not utter the question which

Austin feared and dreaded most. In a harsh peremptory voice he said—
"Show me your son's room."

In those words he stood revealed as one with all the resources of the
law at his back, able to issue commands which other people must obey. The
rights of liberty and freedom were in his hands. It needed not that to show
Austin Turold how near he stood to the edge of the precipice. The strain of
the interview had told on him. This was the first actual buffet of the beast's
paw. He led the way to his son's room and watched Barrant go through his
intimate belongings with the feeling that intelligence was a flimsy shield
against the brutal force of authority. The law in search of prey cared nothing
for such civilized refinements as intellect or self-respect. As well try to stop
a tiger with a sonnet.

The search revealed nothing, and Barrant went away without another
word. A moment later Austin heard him questioning the frightened women
on the floor beneath. Listening intently, he made out a fragment of the
conversation, sufficient to remove all doubts of the origin of the detective's
present visit. Austin's mind flew to the episode he had seen from his
window on the previous afternoon. Why in the name of heaven had this
Brierly woman been such a fool? Why had she not come to him with her
story, and asked for money to shut her mouth? Why was she sobbing and
snivelling downstairs now, when it was too late?

Chapter XXIV

Austin Turold was wrong in supposing that his son had left Cornwall to fly from England. Charles had stated his intention truly enough when he said he was going to London to look for Sisily, but he did not disclose to his father the real reason that led him there.

His visit to London was the pursuit of a definite plan. He was animated by the hope that he knew where Sisily was likely to have sought shelter. Ever since her disappearance this idea had lurked in his imagination and occupied his secret thoughts.

It was the fruit of one of their last talks together — a memory they shared in common. How well he remembered the occasion! They had been on the cliffs looking down at the Gurnard's Head wallowing like a monster with a broken back in the foam of a raging sea. It was the day after the death of Sisily's mother, and Sisily had clung to him as if he were the only friend she had in the world. She had spoken to him from the depth of an overburdened soul impelled to confide in another, telling him of her mother's sad life, unintentionally revealing something of the unhappiness of her own. And she told him a strange thing about her mother's last hours.

On her death bed the unhappy woman must have had her fears concerning the future of her daughter — belated uneasy premonitions arising after her dying confession to the man supposed to be her husband, perhaps causing her to doubt the wisdom of that revelation. That seemed plain enough to Charles afterwards, though not apparent at the time Sisily had confided in him, for she had died without giving the girl the slightest indication of her life's secret, as if in some inscrutable hope that the tangle might be made straight.

What she did do was to make a feeble effort to save her daughter from the consequences of her own unhappy act, or at least to help her if those results arose. She had whispered a name, the name of an old friend of her girlhood who would befriend her child if ever she needed help. At her urgent request Sisily had propped her up in bed while she wrote down the address. Having performed this feat with infinite labour, she dropped back on her pillow, clinging fast to the hand of the child she loved and whose future she had blasted at the command of conscience.

Charles recalled how Sisily had taken that pathetic little scrap of paper from her blouse, kissed it with quivering lips, and handed it to him in silence. He had deciphered the pencilled scrawl with difficulty. The name was Catherine Pursill, Charleswood, Surrey. It remained in his mind for a special reason. Sisily was afraid she might lose the paper (perhaps, like her mother, she had some prescience of the future) and he had endeavoured to divert her thoughts by making "memory pictures" of the name and address after the method of a thought reader. He had told her to picture a cat sitting on a window ledge, and that would fix the name in her mind. "Purr" — "Sill" — there it was! As for the place, it was only necessary to imagine him wandering in a wood (he slyly suggested it) — Charleswood, and there they were again!

Sisily had smiled wanly at these "memory pictures" and said she would always be able to remember the address of her mother's old friend by their means.

They were effectual enough in his own case. The grotesque association of ideas brought the address to his mind when he first thought of seeking Sisily in London. He decided to go to Charleswood as soon as he reached there. The dying woman seemed quite certain her old friend was still in Charleswood, although it was twenty years since she had heard from her. She had told Sisily that Mrs. Pursill's house was her own, and it had belonged to her parents before her. She had assumed that she was not likely to move. The possibility that Death might have moved her without consulting her convenience did not seem to have occurred to her.

It did to Charles Turold though, on his journey up from Cornwall. But he thrust the chilling thought resolutely from him, clinging to his slight clue because he had nothing else to sustain him, building such hopes upon it that by the time he reached London scarcely a doubt remained. He spent the last hour of his journey picturing his meeting with the runaway girl, holding her, kissing her, sheltering her in his arms from the world. And afterwards? He refused to contemplate what was to happen afterwards, and how he was to shield her from the unsentimental clutch of the law which was also seeking her. He declined also to allow his thoughts to dwell upon his own position, which was invidious and threatening enough in all conscience for a man setting out to be the buckler and shield of a girl in Sisily's plight. He put these obtrusive contingencies out of his mind. Time enough for those bitter reflections afterwards. The great thing was to find Sisily first, before shaping further action. So he reasoned, with the single purpose of a man mastered by love, and the desperate instinct of a reckless temperament which gambled with life, never looking beyond the next throw.

He retained sufficient caution to refrain from going to his father's house in Richmond when he reached London. His father's parting words lingered unpleasantly in his mind to serve as a warning against the folly of that course. The same unusual prudence compelled him to leap out of a taxi-cab as soon as he had leapt into it. For himself he did not care, but he had to be careful for Sisily's sake. So he clambered on top of a 'bus with his suit case. The same sobering feeling of responsibility directed his choice of an hotel when he descended from the vehicle into the seething streets. He chose a quiet small place off Charing Cross, and booked a room. After a bath and some lunch he went out to a neighbouring bookstall and bought a railway time-table. The next train to Charleswood left Charing Cross in less than half an hour. He walked across to the station, purchased a ticket, and took his seat. In a few minutes the train started.

Now that he was actually on the way of putting his idea to the test his former doubts assailed him again with renewed force, but he refused to listen to them. He told himself that a dying woman's idea was not likely to be wrong, and that he would find Sisily at Charleswood. She was sure to be there, because she had nowhere else to go. So he reasoned, or sought to reason, until the train slowed down at the station which held the solution of his hopes and fears.

It was a small wayside station at which he alighted—a mere hamlet set in the slumberous calm of English rural scenery, passed by express trains with a roar of derision by day and contemptuously winking tail-lights at night. On the dark green background of the distant heights an eruption of new red bungalows threatened to spread and destroy the beauty of Charleswood at no remote date. But at present the sylvan charm of the spot was unspoiled. Its meadows and fields seemed to lie happily unconscious of the contagion flaming on the billowy hills.

The porter who emerged from a kind of wooden kennel and clattered up to Charles to collect his ticket, stared hard when the young man asked if Mrs. Pursill lived at Charleswood. He appeared to give the matter deep thought before nodding affirmatively, and accompanied him to the station entrance to point out an old house lying behind a strip of white fence and a clump of dark-green trees half-way up a distant hill (not where the bungalows were cropping up, but in the opposite direction), with the intimation that it was the residence of the lady he was looking for. He then watched Charles down the rambling village street until he was out of sight.

It was a long walk—more than a mile—before Charles reached the white fence and the group of trees which shielded the house behind dark-green foliage. He caught a glimpse of partly shuttered windows peeping through this leafy screen, but it was not until he had passed through the trees that he had a clear view of the house.

The place was dreary and dilapidated, with a partly shuttered front. The green-stained walls and a mask of ivy gave the place a resemblance to a large ivy-grown tomb. Charles's spirits were depressed as he looked at it. There was something so wan and melancholy in its appearance that his high anticipations rapidly faded. In the face of that reality he could no longer picture a silver-haired gracious old lady welcoming Sisily with tears in her eyes for the sake of her dead mother. The human qualities of warmth and tenderness did not accord with that chilling neglected exterior.

He approached the door, his sensations painful enough in the mingled tumult of suspense, hope, and fear. There was no bell, only an old-fashioned brass knocker, which, with a kind of surly stiffness, resisted his attempt to use it. He managed to wrench one knock out of it, and left it suspended in the air.

There was a considerable pause before the knock was answered. Then the door was opened by a pretty slim servant girl. There was nothing funereal in her appearance except her black dress, and that was set off by a coquettish white apron. She looked at the young man with questioning bright eyes, as though surprised at his appearance there.

"Does Mrs. Pursill live here?" he asked.

"Yes, sir," she replied with a trace of hesitation.

The barometer of hope went up several degrees in Charles's breast. "Could I see her?" he eagerly said.

"I'll ask, sir. What name, please?"

"No name. Mrs. Pursill would not know it. But my business is very important."

The maid looked at him doubtfully, and left him standing there while she disappeared within. From the depth of the house an agitated feminine murmur reached him through the half-open door. "What's he like, Ruby?" "Quite the gentleman, miss—young and very good-looking." A pause, and the first voice rejoined: "Show him into the drawing-room, and ask him to sit down."

The maid came back with this message, and took Charles into a large sombre room. She gave him a fluttered glance of coquetry as she offered him a chair, as though she would have liked to linger with such an unusual visitor, then went out softly, closing the door behind her.

The room into which he had been ushered was furnished after some faded standard of departed elegance with tapestried chairs, and couches, painted screens, landscapes worked in black lutestring on white silk, and collections of stuffed humming-birds which gazed wanly at the intruder from glassy eyes. A massive dead Christ in Gobelin tapestry covered the whole side of one wall, and from the opposite one the threaded features of Joseph and his brethren stared gloomily down. These subjects accorded ill with several pieces of marble statuary scattered about the room—a reeling Bacchus, a nude Psyche, and an unchaste presentment of Leda drooping her head over an amorous swan. A broken statue of a pastoral shepherd had been laid on a table in the corner and partly covered with a cloth, where it looked very much like a corpse awaiting its turn in a dissecting-room.

Charles had a dreary wait in these surroundings. At first he sat still, but as the time passed he endeavoured to distract his anxious thoughts by walking round the room looking at the extraordinary collections of objects it contained. He was earnestly scrutinizing a lutestring picture depicting "The Origin of the Dimple"—a cupid poking his forefinger into the double chin of a fat languishing female—when the door opened and a woman entered.

She was tall and thin, and had reached that period of life when it costs a woman an effort to look in a mirror because of the menace of approaching age which stares back from the depth of frightened eyes. Her dress, however, suggested that she could not bring herself to believe she was yet out of the hunt, but was still trying to follow it breathlessly on the back of that broken-kneed and sorry steed, late middle-age. There was something ridiculous in the girlish attire intended to convince her fellow creatures that her day was not over; something terrible in the low blouse, short skirt, silk stockings, gauze, lace and fluttering ribbons with which she sought to delude the sneering figure of waiting Time.

Charles's first startled thought was that he had unwittingly entered one of those neglected shuttered houses of romance, where an eccentric female recluse sits with a waiting wedding breakfast in readiness for a bridegroom who has disappeared thirty years before. But the face of the woman advancing towards him suggested that she was not particular about the identity of the form emerging from the mists of time to rescue her from virginity. She looked as if she would have gladly surrendered that jewel to any freebooter in return for a passage in the ship of matrimony, and gone off flying the proud signal, "All's well."

She approached with a smile, and heaven knows what agitation in her breast at the sight of a handsome well-dressed young man in her lonely nest. "You wished to see me?" she asked.

"Mrs. Pursill?" he said interrogatively.

She made a negative sign. "I am Miss Pursill. My mother is an invalid."

"I am most anxious to see her."

"My mother keeps to her bedroom."

"I have come down from London purposely to see her," he said anxiously. "My business is very important."

"Could you not tell me?" she murmured.

"I am afraid not."

She fidgeted and came a little closer, as though she liked the nearness of his handsome presence.

"Very well, you shall see her, but you won't be able to talk to her. Come with me."

They went from the room and upstairs. Miss Pursill opened a door on the first floor and beckoned Charles to enter. It was a bedroom, furnished on the same scale of antique magnificence as the drawing-room downstairs. In a deep armchair in front of a fire sat an old woman, tucked up in an eiderdown of blue and white satin. She did not look round as they entered, but remained quite still — an immobile figure with a nodding head.

"That is Mrs. Pursill," said her daughter.

Charles glanced at the old woman in the chair and turned away. She was past anything except waiting for death, and it was impossible to speak to her or question her. She was in the last stage of senile decay. He masked his disappointment with an effort, conscious that the eyes of the younger woman were fixed on his face.

"If there is anything I can tell you —" she simpered, as she met his glance.

His face betrayed his anxiety.

"I had some reason to think that a young lady of my acquaintance, the daughter of an old friend of your mother's, might be staying with her."

"There is no young lady here," said Miss Pursill with a hard look. "I know nothing about it. What is her name?"

"I have made a mistake, I am afraid." Charles was instantly on his guard. "I am really very sorry —"

She was not altogether proof against the winning smile with which he tendered an apology, but she looked at him strangely as she accompanied him downstairs to the front door.

Charles went back to London with a dark and angry face. His anger was directed against Fate, which had arranged such a fantastic anticlimax for his cherished hopes. The blow was almost too much for him. He had deceived himself into thinking that he would find Sisily at Charleswood, and he felt that he had really lost her. He was now reduced to searching for her in the great wilderness of London, which seemed a hopeless task.

By the time the train reached Charing Cross he rallied from his fit of despondency. He refused to despair. Sisily was somewhere in London, at that moment walking alone among its countless hordes, perhaps thinking of him. He would find her—he must! Where to commence? She had reached Paddington only a few nights ago, so that was obviously the logical starting-point of any inquiries. To Paddington he went, this time in a taxi-cab.

He had an extraordinary initial piece of luck. Fortune, either regretting her previous treatment or tantalizing him in feminine fashion with the expectation of greater favours to come, threw him at the very outset of his inquiries against the red-headed luggage porter who had spoken with Sisily on her arrival from Penzance. The porter, leaning against the white enamelled walls of a Tube passage, pictured the scene with much loquacity, and a faithful recollection of his own share in the interview. Charles anxiously asked him if the young lady he had encountered was very pretty—pale and dark. The porter, with a judicial air, responded that looks in women was, after all, a matter of taste—what was one man's meat was another man's poison, as you might say—but this young lady had dark hair and eyes, and her face hadn't too much colour in it, so far as he remembered. He apologized for this vagueness of description on the plea that one girl was very like another to a man who saw them in droves every day, as he did. But one or two minute particulars of her dress which he was able to supply convinced Charles that he had seen Sisily. The man added that as far as he knew the young lady went on to Euston Square, though he couldn't say he'd actually seen her catch the train for there.

It was not until he had pocketed the half-crown Charles gave him that he added a piece of information of some importance.

"You're not the first who's been inquiring about this particular young lady," he said. "There was somebody before you—let me see—Thursday it was. He came strolling along, affable as you please, and seemed to know all about it before he started. 'That young lady who arrived by the Cornwall train on Tuesday night, porter, and asked you the way to Euston Square—what was she like?' That took me back a bit, but I told him, just as I've told you. He asked me another question or two, and then went into the station-master's office."

"What was he like?"

"Not much older than yourself, in a brown suit, tall and thin, with sharpish features and quick smiling eyes."

Barrant! Charles recognized the description with a sinking heart. He turned away with a sickening sense of the impotence of his own efforts. Scotland Yard was searching for Sisily, and no doubt had warned all the London police to look out for her. She might be arrested any minute. Outside the station he bought an evening paper from a yelling newsboy, and hastily scanned the headlines under the flare of a street lamp. There was nothing about the Cornwall murder. So far they were safe. His own departure from Cornwall had apparently caused no suspicion, and Sisily was still free—somewhere in London.

Where? To find her—that was his task. He rallied sharply from his despondency. He would pit himself against the police. A desperate man, guided by love, could do much—might even outwit the tremendous forces of Scotland Yard. He would not be worthy of Sisily if he lost heart because the odds were against him. Fortune's wheel might have a lucky turn in store for him.

He beckoned a passing taxi-cab. "Euston Square," he said as he entered. That was obviously the next point of his search.

But Fortune vouchsafed him no more favours that day. His dive into the crowded depths of Euston Square brought forth no result—no clue which would help in his search. He interviewed many keepers of the "temperance hotels" and boarding-houses which abounded in that quarter, all sorts of women, but all alike in their quick suspicious resentment of his guarded inquiries and in their pretended ignorance of past visitors to their dingy portals. He had little experience of the embittered sordid outlook of a class which earned its own bread by supplying indifferent food and shelter to London's floating population, but after his fiftieth repulse he had no difficulty in reaching the conclusion that the police were again ahead of him with their inquiries.

Nevertheless he persevered fruitlessly until a late hour before returning to his hotel to pass a sleepless night in a fever of baffled excitement. Not till then did he realize how much he had been upheld by the hope of finding Sisily at Charleswood. He was lost in a maze of conjectures, fears, and impossible plans, though his intelligence told him that no plan of search he could form was likely to be of the slightest use. Only luck could help him there, and it was part of the hopelessness of the situation that he dared not invoke the aid of any of those agencies or organizations which make it their business to find persons who have disappeared in London. His search must be a solitary one.

The morning saw him enter upon it with a feverish energy borrowed from the future and the desperate optimism of a temperament willing to gamble with Fortune against such incalculable odds. At first he attempted to divine the motives likely to actuate a girl ignorant of London in seeking a hiding-place there, and shaped his search accordingly; but he gave that up after a while, and decided to search the streets of the inner suburbs, in the hope of encountering her sooner or later. His method was to purchase a map of each district, and explore it thoroughly from one end to the other. He got his meals anywhere, and slept in the nearest hotel where he happened to find himself late at night. But his meals were often missed and his broken sleep haunted with nightmare visions of the pitfalls and snares spread for inexperienced girls in London.

So Charles passed nearly a week of interminable tramping of London streets, scanning the endless medley of faces in the hope of a chance glimpse of Sisily's wistful eyes and pale features. But it is one thing to gamble with Fortune, and another to win from her. Sometimes she flattered Charles with a chance resemblance which sent him flying across the traffic at the risk of his life, and once he sprang off a 'bus after a girl he saw vanishing into an Underground lift, but it was not Sisily. The end of the week saw him returning from uncharted areas of outer London to the more familiar thoroughfares of the city's life, for in that time his dauntless spirit had realized the colossal folly of any attempt to search London by system. He had no intention of abandoning his quest, but he now felt that it did not matter where his footsteps led him, because it was only by a piece of wonderful luck that he could ever hope to meet Sisily. He did not even know if she was in London. But he believed she was, and some indomitable inward whisper kept assuring him that he would find her sooner or later. So he kept on—and on, seeking the vision of his desires with the insatiable eagerness of a man pursuing the unreachable horizon of a hashish dream.

It was towards the end of this time that it occurred to Charles to wonder if Sisily had made her way to Charleswood since his first visit there. He was resting in a Lambeth public-house after an exhausting day's wanderings over South London when this thought came to him. He sat up, slapping his thigh with excitement, asking himself why he had not thought of that before. It was a chance—certainly a chance. He decided to run down to Charleswood again on the following afternoon.

He did, and found himself disappointed once more. The elegant Miss Pursill had gone to Brighton for change of air, but the pretty maid, who had been left behind to look after the house and the decayed old lady, assured him that there had been nobody to see Mrs. Pursill since his last visit. Miss Pursill went away the very next day after he was down, and there had been no callers or visitors.

She imparted this information at first with a sparkle of coquetry in her eye, then with a glance of compassion as she noticed how much the debonair visitor had changed for the worse since she saw him last. She looked at him solicitously, as though she would have liked to remove with womanly hands the marks of neglect from his apparel. From the door she watched him making his way back to the station. She stood there in the shade of the evening, following him with her eyes until the bend of the road hid him from view.

Chapter XXV

The train was moving out after the briefest stop at a place so unimportant, and he swung himself into one of the carriages gliding past him. At first he thought the compartment was empty, but as the train emerged from a tunnel immediately beyond the station gates he observed a man with glasses reading a newspaper in the opposite corner seat. That reminded him to buy an evening paper at the next stopping place, a town of some importance, where a number of intending passengers were waiting on the platform. Several pushed past him into the compartment. He did not heed them. He sat in a deep reverie, his paper unfolded in his hand, past scenes flowing through his brain as the train sped on towards London. The carriage and its occupants receded from his vision, and he was back again on the Cornwall cliffs with Sisily. Her face appeared before his eyes just as he had seen it in their last parting.

He came back with an effort to the world of events, and unfolded his newspaper. That was a daily ordeal from which he shrank, yet dared not evade. During the past week he had faced it in all sorts of places: street corners, public squares, obscure restaurants, the burrowed windings of Underground stations, and once in the dark interior of a cinema where he had followed a girl with a vague resemblance to Sisily. As the days went on and he read nothing to alarm him, his tension grew less. It really looked as if Scotland Yard and the newspapers had forgotten all about the Cornwall murder, or had relegated it to the list of undiscoverable mysteries.

He now glanced at the headlines listlessly enough. The editor could offer nothing better on his front page that night than Ireland and the industrial situation. Charles opened the sheet and looked inside. His listlessness vanished as his eye fell upon his own name. In the guise of fat black capitals it headed a half-column article about his uncle's death. Charles read it through, slowly and deliberately, to the end. He learnt that there had been what the writer called fresh developments in the case. The police were now looking for another suspect — himself. The detective engaged upon the case had suspicions of the murdered man's nephew for some time past, but had his reasons for reticence — reasons which had now so completely disappeared that Scotland Yard had made public a full description of the young man and the additional information that he was supposed to be in London. Charles found himself reading the description of himself with the detached, slightly wondering air with which a man might be supposed to read his own death notice. He weighed the personal details quite critically. Young and tall. Yes. Good-looking. Was he? Dark blue eyes. Were they? He had never thought about them. Of gentlemanly appearance. That read like the advertisement of a Cheapside tailor—what was a gentlemanly appearance, if he had it? He had always associated it with a cheap lounge suit and a bowler hat. Very well dressed—then followed the description of his clothes. But he couldn't be well dressed and of gentlemanly appearance at the same time!

These preoccupations floated lightly, almost playfully, on the surface of his mind, but the great fact had sunk to the depths like lead. His father's fears had been right, and his departure from Cornwall had drawn attention to his actions on that night. He was—what was the phrase?—wanted by the police. So was Sisily. He was searching for Sisily, and the police were searching for both of them.

What had the police discovered about him? His lips framed the reply. Everything. That was to say, all there was to find out. Obviously they had discovered his visit to Flint House on that night, or at least, that he was out in the storm during the time the murder was committed. His commonsense told him the reason for Barrant's reticence. He had kept quiet in the hope that he would go to his father's house at Richmond, which no doubt had been closely watched. Now that Barrant had come to the conclusion that the man he was after was too clever to walk into that trap, he had confided his suspicions to the newspapers in order to guard all avenues of escape by putting the public on the watch for him.

A feeling of helplessness crept over Charles as he contemplated the incredible ingenuity of the mesh of events in which he and Sisily were entangled. Any moment might terminate his liberty and see him placed under lock and key. Would it help Sisily if he gave himself up and told all he knew? That was a question he had asked himself before, and dismissed it because he realized that his own story might involve her more deeply still. And the loss of time since then, coupled with his own disappearance, intensified the risk which such a course would entail. There was no hope for her in that direction. Where, then, were they to look for hope?

He was recalled to his surroundings by a hand laid on his arm. He started and looked round. The man next to him, with a glance at the paper in his hand, asked him if he could tell him the winner of the second race at Lingfield. "It ought to be in the stop-press," he murmured. Charles turned the sheet to the indicated column, and the inquirer glanced at it with a satisfied smile, and the remark that it was only what he had expected, in spite of the weight. "A good horse," he remarked approvingly. "But perhaps you don't go in for racing yourself?"

Charles resisted an insane impulse to shout with laughter. Didn't go in for racing! He was going in for racing with a vengeance—a race against time and the police. What was he to do now?

He glanced round him restlessly. The swaying noisy train and the compartment packed with stolid faces jarred on his overburdened nerves. Why were those women in the next compartment laughing like hyenas? What was there in life to laugh over at any time? It was a thing to impose silence on all by its desolation, its unescapable doom. His eye was caught by an advertisement above the rack opposite him—an advertisement which depicted a smiling grotesque face, and advised him to buy the comic journal it represented in order to dissipate melancholy and gloom.

Fools—fools all!

While he was thus looking around him his eyes encountered a curious glance from the man in the opposite corner seat, who had been in the compartment when he entered the train at Charleswood. The man dropped his gaze at once, but there was something in the quality of the look which put Charles on his guard. Charles did not turn his head again, but, leaning back in his seat, kept the other under view from seemingly closed eyes. He was soon convinced that the man in the corner seat was watching him— shooting furtive glances across the carriage from behind the screen of his newspaper.

Was he a detective? Not if Barrant was a usual representative of the tribe. Yet there was something infernally quizzical in the scrutiny which reached him through those gold-rimmed glasses. Stay, though! Did detectives wear glasses? Wasn't there an eyesight test or something like that for officers of the law? He had never seen a policeman wearing glasses. If he was not a detective, why was he watching him? There was no reward offered for his arrest. Perhaps he belonged to the wretched type of beings who pride themselves on their public spirit—men who wrote letters to the newspapers and interfered in other people's business. The beast might have guessed his identity and wanted to show his public spirit by handing him over to the police. The newspaper in his hand! Of course. He had read his description there, and identified him.

Charles found himself conjecturing how the man would set about carrying out his task of public watchdog, if that was in his mind. He pictured the possibility of him appealing to the others in the compartment. He might get up and say: "There is a murderer in this compartment. I recognize him from the description in this paper, and I call upon you all as public-spirited citizens to see that he does not escape justice." The torpid passengers would start up, staring and looking foolish after the fashion of English people when asked to do something unusual. Would they help? There was a stout man opposite with the symptoms of a public spirit lurking in the creases of his fat self-satisfied face. Charles promised himself that he would give them a fight for it. He counted his chances. He was aware from his previous journey to Charleswood that the train he was in now ran through to Charing Cross without another stop. Perhaps the man in the corner seat would wait until they arrived there, and then give him in charge. That was a disconcerting possibility, but he could see no way of guarding against it unless he chose to drop from the train, now travelling at nearly forty miles an hour, taking the risk of being maimed or killed. He considered the advisability of that. It was a chance he might have taken casually enough on his own account, but he had also to think of Sisily. She would be quite friendless if he were killed. Besides, there was also the chance that he might be mistaken in interpreting the man's intentions by his own fears. At all events he seemed to have no thought of springing up and denouncing him. Charles decided to wait and trust to luck to escape in the crowd at Charing Cross if the man made any move there.

In ten minutes the train was running into Charing Cross station at slowing speed. Charles's mouth closed tightly, and his face flushed.

The man in the corner seat flattened his newspaper into a pocket, opened the carriage door, and sprang out on to the platform. Charles followed him quickly, and stood still watching him make his way towards the barrier. He saw him press through, give up his ticket, and disappear without so much as a backward glance.

There was something so ridiculous in this anticlimax to his poignant fears that the young man was for the moment actually exasperated. But his face and linen were wet with perspiration. Then a great feeling of relief swept over him like a cooling wave. He followed in the wake of the other passengers and emerged from the station into the street.

It was early enough for the shops to be still open, but the streets were thronged with pleasure-seekers going to restaurants and places of amusement. As he stood there a painted girl touched him on the arm with an enticing smile for such wares as she had to sell, and her solicitation awakened him sharply to the folly of standing in the lighted Strand at that hour in full view of every passing policeman. He walked slowly away, debating where to turn his steps. An outfitter's shop displaying overcoats gave him a bright idea. He walked inside and selected a long dark coat which reached to his heels, putting it on over the light and fashionable coat he was wearing. The shopman seemed surprised at his choice, but made no comment as he took his money and handed him his change. Charles caught a glimpse of himself as he went out, and was satisfied with his changed appearance. In that shapeless garment he was no longer likely to catch the eye of any unduly curious observer as a "well-dressed" man.

He now walked swiftly. Turning out of Chandos Street from the Strand, he avoided the brightly lit proximity of Leicester Square, and plunged into the crooked dark streets on the other side of Charing Cross Road. He reached New Oxford Street, crossed it, and continued along obscure streets, his head bent forward, in the unconscious habit of a man thinking deeply as he went.

In the first feeling of dismay at the discovery that the police were looking for him he had been overwhelmed by a sense of catastrophe. With the passing of that phase he was able to consider the situation with a cooler brain, and it now seemed to him that his position was not so precarious as he deemed it in the light of that shock. He knew London, and might be able to evade arrest indefinitely if he took precautions and avoided risks. But Sisily was in different case. He recalled her telling him that she had only been in London once, as a child with her father. Her inexperience of London was her greatest danger, because it was likely to attract attention. The only one to whom she could look for help was himself.

His determination to find her was doggedly renewed as he thought of that. He accepted the lengthened odds against him with the desperate dark courage of a spirit which had always regarded life as a gamble against unseen forces holding marked cards. The police were searching for him? Very well. He would pit his wits against theirs, and continue his own search for Sisily with a caution he had hitherto disdained to use.

Courage and caution! Those were the two qualities he must use in adroit combination. The plight of both Sisily and himself was desperate enough now without giving the enemy a chance by recklessness. He was like a man rowing a small boat in the immensity of a dark sea which threatened every moment to engulf him. Sisily was somewhere in that darkness, and she must be rescued. If his own cockleshell went down there could be no succour for her. That was a thought to make him keep afloat—to keep on rowing.

And suppose that he did find her, as he believed he would, sooner or later—given time. What was to happen then?

That thought pursued him in his walk that night, and was his constant companion in the lonely days and nights of his wanderings which followed. He had banished it before, but that course was no longer possible. The impalpable yet terribly real menace of authority overshadowing them both now made it imperative that all the facts should be faced. All the facts — but what were they? It was the question he asked himself again and again as he strove to twist out of the black fantasy of that horrible night some tangible shred of truth which might help them both. His own incredible share in it was forever being re-enacted in his mind, and haunted his dreams. In the night, at early dawn, at odd moments of his eternal quest, the curtain of his mind would rise on that unforgettable scene — the cliffs, the rocks, the darkling outline of Flint House, with a feeble beam of light slanting down from the upstairs window at the back which looked out on the sea. Then the gush of light from the open door, and her shape stealing forth into the darkness, followed by another — Thalassa's. And then, the final phase — the desolate house, the wind rushing noisily along dark passages, the dead form of Robert Turold in the room upstairs. What did these things mean, and what was to be the end?

His hope was that Sisily could reveal something which would furnish the key to the enigma of that night's events. From her lips he might learn enough to guide him to the hidden truth, and save them both. Sustained by the feeling that she existed somewhere near him, he continued his search day after day until in the abstracted intensity of his fancy London assumed the appearance of a wilderness of unending streets filled with pallid faces which flitted past his vision like ghosts. But the face he was seeking was never among them.

He searched with the wariness of one whose own liberty depended upon his watchfulness. A second glance, an indignant look, a turn of the head, a policeman's casual eye — any of these things would place him immediately on his guard and turn his footsteps in a different direction. He chose his sleeping places with care at the last minute, and left them at early morning when only a yawning night porter or a sleepy maid servant was astir. He never returned to the same place, nor did he go to the same restaurant twice. Most carefully did he read the newspapers, but nothing appeared in their columns to alarm him; merely an occasional perfunctory paragraph about the Cornwall murder. The favourite adjective in the journalistic etymological garden was culled for the heading, and it was described as an amazing case. Charles felt that the definition was correct enough. Early developments were faithfully promised — by the newspaper. Charles understood very well what was meant by that. It was hoped he would provide the development by falling into the hands of the police. He smiled a little at that, but the unintended warning increased his vigilance.

On the whole he felt tolerably safe in the crowded London streets. It was not as though there was any real hue and cry after him. The lonely Cornwall tragedy had not come into sufficient public notice for that, and now it seemed almost forgotten.

He had his hazards and chances, though in a different way. One was an encounter with a young man of good family whose acquaintance, commenced in France during the war, had continued in London afterwards. The two young men had seen a great deal of each other—dining and going to music-halls together. It was in Leicester Square that Charles saw him getting out of a taxi-cab to enter a hall where a professional billiard match was in progress. He paused midway at the sight of Charles, exclaiming: "Why, Tur—" The second syllable of the name was nipped off in mid-air, and the outstretched arm was dropped, as the patron of billiards took in the cut of his former friend's coat. He gazed at the ill-fitting garment with a kind of astonished animosity, and then his puzzled look shot upwards to the face surmounting it, no doubt with the feeling that he may have been deceived by a chance resemblance. Charles went past him without a sign of recognition, but he felt that the other was still staring after him.

Another day a street musician regarded him curiously from behind a barrel organ which he was turning with the lifeless celerity of one without interest in the sounds created by the process. His card of appeal—"Wanted in 1914; not wanted now"—helped Charles to recall him as a soldier of his old regiment. They exchanged glances across the card. The man gave no sign that he knew his former officer, but Charles had no doubt that he did. He placed a coin on top of the organ and went swiftly on.

A week of increasing strain slipped by, and another commenced. Then Fortune, with a contemptuous good-humoured spin of her wheel, did for Charles Turold what he could hardly have hoped to achieve in a year's effort without her aid.

It was late at night, and he was in a despondent mood after one of his recurring disappointments—this time a graceful slender shape which he had earlier in the evening pursued in a flock of home-going shop-girls until she turned and revealed a pert Cockney face which bore no resemblance to Sisily's. Several hours later he paid another of his visits to Euston Square, which he believed to be the starting-point of Sisily's own wanderings. He felt closer to her in that locality because of that. From Euston Square he walked on aimlessly, engrossed in impossible plans for finding Sisily by hook or crook, until the illuminated dial of a street clock, pointing to half-past ten, reminded him of the passage of time.

He paused and looked round. He was in an area of darkened suburban streets converging on a distant broader avenue, where occasional taxi-cabs slid past into the blackness of the night with the heartless velocity of years disappearing into the gulf of Time.

He turned his steps in the direction of this thoroughfare in order to find out the locality, but stopped half-way at the sight of a coffee-stall on the opposite side of the street. He was hungry and thirsty, and he had learnt to like the safety of these places in his wanderings. The food might be coarse, but there were no lengthy waits between courses; no curious glances from the other patrons. A couple of half-drunken young men were feeding at this stall, and a girl of the streets was standing near them. In the light of a swinging lamp the scene shone clearly in the surrounding darkness—the brass urn, the thick crockery, the head of the stall-keeper bent intently over a newspaper, the munching jaws of the customers, the girl in the background with splashes of crimson paint like blood on her white drawn face.

Charles was about to cross the street, but at that moment a policeman's helmet emerged slowly from the surrounding darkness as if irresistibly attracted by the concentric glow of the light. At the sight of him Charles shrank back into the friendly shadow of his own side of the road. The policeman emerged into the fulness of the light, serene in his official immobility. His slow yet seeing vision dwelt on the painted girl with a gaze as penetrating as that of Omnipotence in its profound knowledge of evil. He strolled towards her with a kind of indifferent benignity with which Providence has also been credited. He raised a hand, omnipotent with the authority of the law. "Better get away from here," Charles heard him warn her, and she disappeared from view in obedience to this command.

So did Charles, but in quite another direction. There was something about these chance manifestations of authority, so lightly exercised, so unhesitatingly obeyed, which never failed to thrill and impress him, as they would have thrilled and impressed any other man in his present position. They seemed to intensify the hopelessness of his own situation. He had a slight feeling of creepiness about the spine as he thought of the narrowness of that escape—though, of course, the policeman might not have identified him. But some day or other it was bound to come—that accidental confrontation which might mean his arrest.

He walked swiftly until he reached the avenue. It was a part of London that he did not know, and appeared quite deserted. He wondered which way he should turn to get back to that area of London where he usually sought a bed.

As he stood there glancing about him irresolutely, his eye caught a glimpse of somebody walking swiftly along—a slight girlish figure dimly visible in the dark vista of the empty street. There was something familiar in the girl's outline—something which caused his heart to give a great maddening jump. As he looked she turned into one of the converging streets.

He raced up the broad road, indifferent at that moment whether the eyes of all the policemen in London were upon him. When he reached the street which had swallowed her he could see nothing of the form which had excited him. Then, far ahead, he again saw it passing under a distant lamp-post and merge once more into the darkness. He ran quickly in pursuit.

The girl heard him coming and looked back anxiously. This time he saw her face. In a bound he was at her side.

"Sisily, Sisily!" he cried. "Oh, Sisily, I have found you!"

Chapter XXVI

He saw her white face sharply uplifted in the darkness, and caught the startled gleam of her dark eyes. Then she recognized him.

"You!" she breathed. "Oh, Charles, how did you find me?"

"It was chance, Sisily—but no, it was something deeper and stranger than chance." He spoke in a tone of passionate conviction. "I have been walking London day and night, seeking for you. I felt sure I should find you sooner or later. I had given up hope for tonight, though. It was so late—so late—" The tumult of his feelings checked his utterance.

"I dare not go out earlier," she whispered.

That was a reminder which brought him back sharply to the reality of things. He looked anxiously around him in the dark and empty street. In the vulgar expression they were both "wanted"—wanted by the police. The danger was doubled now that they were together. That was a freezing thought which had not occurred to him during his search for her. It occurred to him now.

"I wonder where we could go and talk in safety?" he murmured—"and decide what is best to do."

"We might go to where I am staying," she unexpectedly suggested. "It is at the end of this street."

"Would that be quite safe?" he hazarded doubtfully.

"I think so. Mrs. Johns told me that she would be very late to-night. She goes to spiritualistic meetings, and does not return home until early morning sometimes. We should be alone, and free to talk. There is nobody else in the house."

He was too eager to raise any doubts of the safety of the suggested harbourage. Their conversation, which had been carried on in suppressed and whispered tones, ceased as they advanced along the quiet street. Near the end Sisily turned into the small garden of an unlighted house. She unlocked the hall door, and they entered. He saw her bending over the hallstand, and guessing her intention, struck a match. She took it from him in silence, lit the hall gas, and shut the front door carefully. Then she struck another match from a box on the hallstand, and preceding him into a room on the right, lit the gas there.

It was a small sitting-room, simply and almost shabbily furnished, remarkable for some strange articles which were heaped at random on various small tables. There was a planchette, a tambourine, and other more mysterious appliances which suggested that the inmate spent much time with the trappings and rappings of spiritualism. Papers and journals devoted to spiritualism were scattered about the room, and framed "spirit photographs" hung on the walls.

Charles was not thinking of the interior of the room. His one thought was of Sisily. He had not seen her clearly in the dark street. She appeared to him now unchanged, her dear face as he had last seen it, her features luminous with tender feeling, her dark eyes dwelling gravely on him, just as she used to look. As she stood there, the realization of his haunting dreams, he had to fight down an impulse to take her in his arms. But it was not the moment for that. Because of the graveness of their situation, love had to stand aside.

"Sisily, why did you go away?" he asked at length.

She did not immediately reply, but lowered her glance as though collecting her thoughts. His look fastened with anxious scrutiny on her downcast face. She did not raise her eyes as she answered.

"I had to go, Charles," was all she said.

"Why did you not tell me, Sisily?" he said in a tone of reproach. "Why did you not let me know, that last day on the cliffs?"

He failed to understand the glance she cast at him as he asked these questions, but it seemed to contain an element of surprise, almost astonishment. Absorbed in his own gloomy thoughts, he went on.

"Do you remember what you told me about your mother's old nurse, and our memory pictures of her name? I thought you had gone there. So I went to Charleswood to look for you."

"I did think of going there. I intended to when I left Cornwall," she hurriedly rejoined. "Then, afterwards, I thought it best not to. I stayed at a private hotel in Euston Road on my first night in London, but did not like it, and next day I went to a boarding-house near Russell Square. I meant to write to Mrs. Pursill from there, telling her my mother was dead. But that night after dinner I heard some of the boarders talking of—the murder, and I knew I couldn't go to Charleswood—then. I left that place early next morning, and came here. I had been walking about all the morning, not knowing what to do, when I saw the card in this window saying that there was a room to let. Mrs. Johns told me she wanted to let the room more for company than anything else, because she lived alone. I was glad to find it, and grateful to her."

"You have known all along that the police are looking for you?" he said gravely.

"After I heard them talking at the boarding-house," rejoined simply. "One of the women had an evening paper, and read it aloud to the others. I knew then, of course. The woman kept looking at me as she read as though she suspected that I was the missing girl. I was very nervous, but tried to pretend that I didn't notice, and left the room as soon as I dared." "What about this Mrs. Johns—does she suspect anything?" he asked anxiously.

"Oh, no. She is a very unworldly kind of woman, and thinks of nothing but spiritualism. She never reads newspapers."

"Do not talk about it," he said suddenly, as though this picture of her wanderings was too much to be borne. "Why did you go away from Cornwall without a word? You said you had reasons. What were they, Sisily?"

"I will tell you—now." The soft difference in the tone of the last word was too femininely subtle for him to understand. "That afternoon, when my father was talking to you all in the front room downstairs—do you remember?"

"Yes, yes," he said impatiently.

"I heard something—I was at the door."

"It was you, then, and not Thalassa, who looked through the door!" he said, glancing at her curiously.

"I did not mean to listen," she replied, flushing slightly. "I was going out to the cliffs—to the Moon Rock. I was very unhappy, and wanted to be alone with my thoughts. On my way past the door something my father was saying reached me. It concerned me. I did not take it in at first, or understand what it really meant. As I stood there, wondering, my eyes met my aunt's through the opening in the door, and I saw her spring to her feet. I hurried away because I did not want to see her. I wanted to think over what I had just heard, to try and understand what it meant.

"I went down to the Moon Rock, and sat there, thinking and thinking. They were so strange and terrible, those words I had overheard, but they were so few that I did not really guess then all that they meant. All I knew was that there was some dreadful secret behind them, some secret of my mother's which had something to do with me. I wished that I had heard more. As I sat there, wondering what I ought to do, you came—"

"To tell you that I loved you, that I shall love you as long as I live," he interrupted eagerly.

Again a faint flush rose to her cheeks, but she hurried on: "I could not tell you that I loved you while those dreadful words of my father were ringing in my ears. I wanted to see him first, to question him, to know if I had partly guessed the truth, or if there was any loophole of escape for me. Oh, do not think any worse of me now if I tell you that I loved you then and shall always love you. I wanted to tell you so that day by the Moon Rock, but I knew that I must not."

"Why not?" His louder voice broke in on her subdued tones impetuously. "You should not have sent me away, Sisily. That was wrong. It has brought much misery upon us both."

"It was not wrong!" she replied, with unexpected firmness and a momentary hardness of glance, which reminded him of her father's look. "It was because I was nobody—less than that, if what I thought was true. There was your position to think of. You were to come into the title—my father told me that before."

"Damn the title!" the young man burst out furiously. "I told you that day I would have nothing to do with it. Why did you think about that?"

"Because I've heard of nothing else all my life, I suppose," she rejoined with the ghost of a smile. "I couldn't tell you then that I loved you, because of it, and other things. Now, it is different. It does not matter what I say—now." She spoke these words with an underlying note of deep sadness, and went on: "When you told me that you loved me I saw my duty plainly. I knew I must go away and hide myself from you, from everybody, go somewhere where nobody knew me, where I would never be known. But I wanted to see my father first, to make sure."

"I understand," he muttered in a dull voice.

"I thought it all out on the way to the hotel with my aunt. I determined to go back and see my father that night. I felt that I could not sleep until I knew the whole truth. I left the dinner table as soon as I could, and hurried down to the station to catch the half-past seven wagonette to St. Fair.

"I got out of the wagonette at the cross-roads, and walked over the moors. When I reached Flint House I knocked at the door, and Thalassa let me in. I told him I wanted to see my father, and he said he would wait downstairs and take me back across the moors when I came down.

"I ran upstairs and knocked at the door of my father's study. He did not reply, so I opened the door and went in. He was sitting at his table writing, and when he looked up and saw me he was very angry. 'You, Sisily!' he said—'what has brought you here at this hour?' I told him I had come to hear the truth from his own lips. I asked him to tell me everything. He gave me one of his black looks, but it did not frighten me—nothing would have frightened me then. He seemed to consider for a moment, and then said that perhaps, after all, it would be better if he told me himself.

"So he told me—told me in half-a-dozen sentences which seemed to burn into my brain. I sat still for a while, almost stunned, I think; then, as the full force of what he had told me came home to my mind, I did something I had never done before. I pleaded with my father—not for my own sake, but for my mother's. I told him I would go anywhere, do anything, if he would only keep her secret safe. I might as well have pleaded with the rocks. He sat there with a stern face until I went down on my knees to him and begged him to think about it—to keep it secret for a little while at least. He grew angry, very angry, at that. I remember—I shall never be able to forget—his reply. 'A little while?' he said, 'and the claim for the title is to be heard next week. I'm to postpone my claim for the sake of your mother, a — —'"

Sisily broke off suddenly, her white face flaming scarlet, her eyes widely distended, as though that last terrible scene was again produced before her vision. Charles Turold watched her mutely, with the understanding that nothing he could say would bring comfort to her stricken soul.

She continued after a pause—

"I left him then. I knew that I should never be able to speak to him again. Downstairs, Thalassa was waiting for me. He had a letter in his hand. He looked at me, but did not speak, just opened the door, and we went out across the moors. We went silently. Thalassa was always kind to me, and I think that somehow he understood. It was not until we were nearing the cross-roads that I turned to him and said quickly, 'Thalassa, you must not tell anybody that I saw my father tonight.' I wanted to keep it secret, I wanted nobody to know—never. I knew my father would not talk, it was not of sufficient consequence to him. He thought of nothing but the title. Thalassa promised that he wouldn't. 'Nobody will ever find out from me, Miss Sisily,' he said.

"Thalassa went back, across the moors, and I waited by the cross-roads till the wagonette came. When I got back to the hotel I went up to my room and to bed. I do not know what time it was next morning when my aunt came into my room, and told me that my father was dead. She did not tell me much. There had been a terrible accident, she said, and he had been found dead in his room. I did not feel shocked, only ... indifferent. I did not even wonder what had happened—not then. Afterwards I overheard one of the maids in the corridor telling another that it was suicide.

"That made no difference to me, except that I wanted more than ever to get away. I formed my plans quickly, to go to London that day, but not by the express. I knew my aunt would not go back that morning after what had happened, but I thought her husband might have to go on business. And the express is always crowded. I did not wish to be seen and brought back. So I decided the slow midday train would be safest for me. I waited for a time, and then I was able to slip away from the hotel without being noticed, while my aunt was out. I got to London that night, feeling lonely and miserable. I knew I had done right, but I could not help thinking ... of you."

She ceased. Charles Turold got up from his seat and took a turn round the room, then came back and stood looking down at her as she sat with her hand resting on the dark polished surface of the table. His first words seemed to convey some inward doubt of the adequacy of the motive for disappearance which her story revealed.

"You should not have gone away like that, Sisily," he said soberly. "There was no reason, no real reason, I mean. Where was the necessity, after what I told you? Why should your father's death have made you more anxious to go? It seems to me that you had no reason then."

She looked at him sadly in her first experience of masculine incomprehension of woman's exaltation of sacrifice in love, but she did not speak. He continued. "But we must think of what's to be done." He walked up and down the room again, considering this question with compressed brows. He stopped, struck by a thought, and looked at her. "The police have been trying to find out from Thalassa whether you went back to Flint House that night, but he will not tell them anything. So they suspect him also."

She roused at that. "Oh, they must not!" she cried in distress. "Poor Thalassa! He must tell them the truth."

"The question is—what is the truth?" It flashed through his mind as he spoke that his interrogation was the echo of one put to him by his father before he left Cornwall.

"The truth is, that Thalassa and I left the house together that night before it happened. Oh, cannot they believe that? Cannot it be proved?"

"I could tell them when you left," he said in a low tone.

"You!" she cried, looking at him with a kind of fear. "How do you know?"

"Because I saw you. I was standing outside, close to the house."

"Why were you there?" she put in quickly.

He was slower in answering. "I had gone to see your father—about you. I was standing there, thinking ... waiting, when the front door opened, and you and Thalassa came out. I was surprised to see you, but it seemed to me an opportunity—a final chance—to speak to you again. I started after you, Sisily, once more to ask you to consider my love for you, but you and Thalassa were swallowed up in the darkness of the moors before I could reach you. I followed with the intention of overtaking you, but I got lost on the moors instead, and was wandering about in the blackness for nearly half an hour before I found my way back to Flint House again."

"Could you not tell them—the police—that?" she asked, a little wistfully.

"It would be useless," he solemnly replied.

"What do you mean?" she said breathlessly.

His rejoinder was a long time in coming. When his set lips moved the words were barely audible. "Because I would not be believed. Because I went straight up the path to the house, determined to see your father before it grew later. The front door was open, and the house seemed in complete darkness. I entered, and went upstairs. There was a light in your father's study. I found your father—dead." He fixed care-worn eyes upon her. "That story sounds incredible, even to you, doesn't it? But—"

"Oh!" That startled cry seemed wrung from her involuntarily. Then, swiftly, as if her mind had detached itself to look on her own actions that night through his eyes: "You thought, you believed that I—" She checked herself, but her look completed the thought.

"I did not know what to think, but I did not think—that," he gloomily rejoined. "Afterwards, the next night, I found out something which made me think—" He paused.

"Yes, yes, tell me what you thought," she said nervously.

"I thought it was Thalassa."

She shook her head.

"Who was it then? The latest theory of the police is that I had something to do with it. They're looking for both of us. They must have found out that I was at Flint House that night. It's too late to tell them the truth now, not that they were likely to have believed me at any time. Why, my own father believes that I did this thing." He laughed discordantly. "I tried to convince your father's lawyer of your innocence, and I might have told him the truth if he had been sympathetic. I don't know, though," he added anxiously. "I had to consider your position all along. If my story was disbelieved it only made it worse for you. If it was not Thalassa, who could it have been? Have you any idea—the faintest suspicion?"

Again she shook her head. She made an effort to look at him, but there were tears in her eyes for the first time. His hand was resting on the table, and she touched it gently with her fingers.

"We must find out." He spoke loudly, as if with the idea that a firm utterance lessened the tremendous difficulty of that performance.

"What can we do?" Her tone was hopeless enough.

"Let me think." He fiddled with the planchette on the table as though he had some notion of invoking the shade of Robert Turold to answer the question. "Had your father any enemy? Did he fear anybody?"

She raised thoughtful eyes to his in reply.

"My father feared nobody," she said, "at least, I do not think so. Nobody had any real influence over him except Thalassa."

"What sort of an influence?"

"It is difficult to describe," she hesitatingly answered. "Thalassa could take liberties which nobody else would have dared. He used to go into his room at any time. Sometimes I have awakened late at night and heard the murmur of their voices coming from my father's study."

"Anything else?" he said, looking at her keenly.

"There was never any question of Thalassa leaving us," she went on. "Wherever we went, and we were always going to some fresh part of England about the title, Thalassa went also. Perhaps it was because he had known him for so long that my father allowed Thalassa to do things which nobody else could do. Thalassa used to sneer about the title, and say no good would come of it. They had a quarrel once, long, long ago. I was a very little girl at the time, and I can just remember it," she added dreamily.

She was apparently unconscious of the significance of these revelations, but they made a deep impression upon Charles. There was something expectant and cruel in his face as he listened—the aroused instinct of the hunter. He addressed her—

"This bears out what I have believed all along. Thalassa knows about the murder. He is mixed up in it in some way."

"Oh, why do you think that?" she exclaimed, clasping her hand in distress.

"Why?" he echoed. "Because your father was not the man to stand insolence from Thalassa or anybody else unless he had to. Thalassa must have had him under his thumb in some way. Why did I not know of this before? It's clear enough now. Thalassa, even if he did not commit the murder—"

"He did not," she said quickly. "He left the house with me, so he could not have done it."

"Then he knows who did. He and your father shared some secret together—some dreadful secret which brought about your father's death. That is one reason why Thalassa will not speak—because he is implicated in this mystery, whatever it is."

"No, no. He is keeping silence because of me—I feel sure. I made him promise not to tell."

Charles Turold shook his head decidedly. "He may have more than one reason for keeping silent," he said with a swift flash of intuition. "If it is as you say, he is shielding himself as well as you. If your father was killed while Thalassa was out of the house that night, Thalassa knows who did it."

Her eyes met his in an agony of perplexity and distress. "Oh, no, I cannot think you are right," she said. "If I could only see Thalassa—for five minutes—"

"What good would that do?" he abruptly demanded.

"He would tell me the truth—if he knew."

He shook his head incredulously. "You do not know all," he murmured. He shrank from telling her of the marks on her father's arm. "I know Thalassa," she eagerly replied. "He would tell me if he thought it would help me."

"If you think that I will go down and see him—and get it all out of him."

"No, no! You must not go," she cried in affright. "It would not be safe for you."

"Would it be any more dangerous than hiding in London like a skulking rat?" he bitterly replied. "This cannot go on. We are both in a dangerous position, and might be arrested at any moment. What would happen then? Who would believe my story—or yours? They sound improbable even to ourselves. Here, at least, is a chance of discovering the truth, for I most solemnly believe that Thalassa knows it, or guesses it. What other chance have we of finding out the hideous mystery of that night? I must go, Sisily. I will be careful, for your sake."

She knew by his voice that he was not to be deterred from the hazardous enterprise, so she did not attempt to dissuade him further. But she clung to him trembling, as though she would have shielded him from the menace of capture. He was thinking rapidly.

"It may be that I shall fail," he said. "I do not think so, because I shall take every precaution, but the police will be watching for me in Cornwall as well as here. If I fail—if I do not come back ... you will understand?"

Her look answered him.

"You had better watch the papers. And be careful on your own account." He eyed her anxiously. "Do you think you will be safe here till I get back?"

"Yes—I think so," she murmured sadly.

"Very well. I will go down by to-night's train—I've just time to catch it." He glanced at his watch with an assumption of cheerfulness. "When you wake up in the morning I shall be in Cornwall."

"I shall not sleep," she said, in a miserable broken voice. "I shall lie awake, thinking of you."

He caught her swiftly in his arms, and kissed her on the lips. "If I find out the truth, nothing shall come between us then, Sisily?"

"No, nothing," she said.

He turned with a sudden swift movement as though to go, but she still held him.

"Tell Thalassa ... that I ask him to tell you the truth, if he knows it...."

She released him then, and stood looking after him as he walked from the room and out of the house.

Chapter XXVII

Flint House looked a picture of desolation in the chill grey day, wrapped in such silence that Charles's cautious knock seemed to reverberate through the stillness around. But the knocking, repeated more loudly, aroused no human response. After waiting awhile the young man pulled the bell. From within the house a cracked and jangling tinkle echoed faintly, and then quivered into silence. He rang again, but there was no sound of foot or voice; no noise but the cries of the gulls overhead and the hoarse beat of the sea at the foot of the cliffs.

A cormorant, sitting on a rock near by, twisted its thin neck to stare fearlessly at the visitor. But Charles Turold was not thinking of cormorants. Where was Thalassa? Where was his wife? He believed they were still in Cornwall, but they might have left the house. He had been in London a long while. Not so long, though—only twelve days. Twelve days! Twelve eternities of unendurable hopelessness and loneliness, such as the damned might know. Was he to fail, now, after finding Sisily? He had a responsibility, a solemn duty. He had reached Cornwall safely from London—run the gauntlet of all the watching eyes of the police—and he would not go back without seeing Thalassa. His mind was thoroughly made up. He would find him, if he had to walk every inch of Cornwall in search of him. And when he found him he would wrest the truth out of him—yes, by God, he would! When he found him, but where was he to be found? The crafty old scoundrel might be in the house at that moment, lurking there like a wolf, perhaps grinning down at him from behind some closed window.... A sudden rage surged over him at that thought, and he fell savagely on the shut door, beating it with insensate fury with his fists. Damn him, he would force his way in!

The cormorant ruffled its greenish feathers and watched him curiously. The faint cries of the gulls overhead seemed borne downward with a note of mocking derision. Charles Turold stepped back from the door with an uneasy look at the cormorant, as though fearing to detect in its unreflecting beadiness of glance some humanly cynical enjoyment at his loss of self-control. The wave of feeling had spent itself. Not thus was victory to be won. He paused to consider, then tried the knocker again. The knocker smote the wood with a hollow sound, like a stroke on the iron door of a vault, loud enough to rouse the dead. Charles Turold had a disagreeable impression of Robert Turold starting up in his grave-clothes at the summons, listening.... But no! The dead man was safe in his grave by this time. He had forgotten that.

A sudden silence fell on the house: a deep and profound stillness, as though seas and wind had hushed their wailing speech to listen for the answer to the knock. The birds, too, were silent. The house remained immutably quiet. Charles Turold bent down, and peered through the keyhole, but could see nothing within but darkness. Then, as he looked, a sound reached his ears, a sound like a thin cackle of laughter from the interior of the house. In the gathering gloom within he had a momentary impression of a stealing greyish shape—a shape which vanished from his vision as he looked.

He rose to his feet, his mind groping blindly for some tangible explanation of this spectral thing, but finding none. A ghost? He shook off that feeling roughly. God knows, that house might well be haunted, but not by a ghost that could laugh, though there was no merriment in that ghastly cackle. The reality of the thing, whatever it was, could not be worse than the sound. Had he really seen anything, after all? Was there some trap about it, some danger to himself? He would have to risk that.

The distant sight of a human figure far away on the wide space of the moors, clambering over the granite slabs of a stile, turned his thoughts to a more perceptible danger. If he could see that man more than half a mile away, his own figure must be apparent over a long distance in that clear brown expanse. Perhaps at that very moment the policeman from the churchtown was prowling about the moors in search of him. His actions at that lonely house were suspicious enough to attract anybody's attention. That was an act of imprudence which he had no right to commit. He had not evaded the keen eyes of the London police to be trapped like a rat by a rural constable. It was too dangerous for him to remain there. He determined to spend the rest of the day among the cliffs, and return to Flint House when night fell.

He walked away, briskly at first, but with a more laggard step as he plunged into the shelter of the great rocks, for he had had nothing to eat since the night before, and was beginning to be conscious of his weakness.

But he strode on, doggedly enough, for more than an hour, until he found himself at a part of the coast he had not seen before—a theatre of black rocks, with dark towering walls, and a hissing sea whitening at the base.

At the foot of these cliffs three jagged conical rocks rose bare and glistening, the spray from the broken sea dashing far up their sides. As Charles stood there, looking down, he saw a man appear from the edge of the furthest one and walk rapidly across the sloping shelf of rock which spanned the narrow bay near the surface of the sea. His heart leapt within him as he took in the figure of the man. It was Thalassa.

As Charles climbed down from the higher cliffs to intercept him, there came to his mind an imperfectly comprehended fragment of conversation which he had overheard, between waking and dozing, in the train that morning. The voices drifted to his dulled hearing from the next compartment, where some men seemed to be discussing somebody of whom they stood in dread, somebody who was forever striding along the cliffs with his eyes fixed on some distant horizon, as though seeking some one. The object of the mysterious being's quest, if it was a quest, nobody who met him cared to ask. So much he had gathered. He had heard one of the speakers say: "I've met un, ever so laate, stalkin' aloong like th' devil. Tes aw token o' a bad conscience. Tes dreadful to think about. I got owt o' his way…. I'd as soon speak to th' devil. Iss, aw'd." Charles had thought nothing of this chatter at the time, but he wondered now if they were talking of Thalassa. Did the local fisherfolk believe that he had something to do with the murder, and shunned him like Ishmael in consequence?

He looked like Ishmael at that moment, crossing that wild place, earnestly scanning every nook of those seamed and riven walls, sometimes glancing stealthily behind him. His preoccupation in this search—if it was a search—was so great that he never once glanced ahead, and he did not see Charles until the young man leaped down the last few paces of his slippery descent and stood plainly forth before him. Thalassa's brown face did not move a muscle as he looked at him.

"Thalassa," said Charles sternly, "I have been looking for you."

Thalassa went on, still scanning the secret places of the towering cliffs as he walked forward with Charles beside him. When the rugged passage was crossed, and the narrow wild bay left behind, he spoke.

"For what?"

"To have the truth out of you, you infernal scoundrel!" cried the young man fiercely, his self-control suddenly vanishing at that indifferent tone.

"You know all about the murder of your master; you're going to tell me, or I'll throw you off these cliffs into the sea."

He gripped the other's arm as he spoke, but Thalassa tore off his fingers, and leapt backward against a rock, a knife in his hand, snarling like a wild beast.

"Keep off!" he cried. "Keep off, or by Christ, I'll—" He hooked the air with his knife.

Charles eyed him across the space, affected almost to nausea by his evil glance. What a fool he had been to lose his temper! Not in that way was the truth to be reached. The man before him was not to be terrorized or intimidated. Sisily's way would have been the best. He wondered whether it was too late to attempt it.

"I was hasty, Thalassa," he said. "Come, do not let us quarrel after I have risked everything to get down here to see you. I have a message for you—from Sisily."

The face of the man crouching by the rock changed instantly. He made a step forward, as if to speak, then cast a gleaming eye of unbelief at his companion.

"It's a lie!" he said. "You haven't seen her."

"I'm speaking the truth," Charles earnestly replied. "Do you think I'd have come back to Cornwall otherwise, knowing the police are searching for me?"

"Ay, you know that, do you?" muttered the other. "They've been watching Flint House for you. You were a fool to come back here."

"I'd risk more than that to learn the truth, Thalassa. It's for Sisily's sake. I've seen her. She's in London, and I've come from her. She gave me this message to bring to you. She said: 'Tell Thalassa that I ask him to tell the truth—if he knows it.' The police are looking for her as well as me."

"I've heered so." With these words, uttered quickly, Thalassa fell into the silence of a man on his guard and pondering. Charles approached nearer.

"Thalassa," he pleaded, "if you are keeping anything back you must tell me for Sisily's sake."

"How do I know you've seen her?" retorted Thalassa, darting a dark crafty look at him.

Charles was overwhelmed by a sense of catastrophe. Here was a possibility which had been overlooked. How was he to instil belief that he spoke the truth? A moment passed. Thalassa cast another black look at him, and turned as if to walk away. "I'll keep my word," he muttered to himself.

The young man's quick ear caught the whispered sentence, and saw the way. "I'll prove it to you," he said. "You promised Sisily that you'd tell nobody she was at Flint House to see her father on the night he was killed. How could I know that unless I'd seen her?"

"What else?" said Thalassa, facing him with a strange and doubtful glance.

"You let her in," Charles rapidly continued, "and you waited downstairs for her. Afterwards you took her back across the moors to catch the wagonette. It was on the way, near the cross-roads, that Sisily made you promise not to tell anybody that she'd been there that night."

"Suppose it's true—what then?" Thalassa's voice was edged with the craftiest caution. "She's sent you to me to ask for the truth, say you. 'Twould have been safer not. What else is there to say, when she's told you everything?" He cast a look of savage jealousy at the young man.

"Much." Charles spoke rapidly, but his glance was despairing. "What happened while you were away from the house? What sent your wife mad? What did you find when you returned? You know these things, Thalassa."

"Happen I did, what good'd come of telling them?"

"To save Sisily."

"They'd not help to save her."

"Do you think she shot her father?"

Thalassa gave him another dark look, but remained silent.

"You know she didn't, you hound!" cried Charles, anger flaring up in him again. "It was you—it must have been you. Listen to me! I know almost enough to hang you. I was in the house while you were away, and found your master lying dead in his study, and the key of the door in the passage outside. Who could have dropped it there except you?"

"'Tweren't me. 'Twas done afore I got back to the house," answered Thalassa.

"What time was it when you left the house with Sisily?"

"Agone half-past eight: perhaps ten minutes after. She came running downstairs, her eyes staring and blazing. 'Thalassa, dear Thalassa, for pity's sake let me out,' she said half-sobbing. 'Oh, what did I come for?

He's wicked—wicked.' Twasn't for me to say anything between father and daughter, so I just opened the door without a word, and went out with her."

"What time did Sisily catch the wagonette?"

"That's what I don't know. She made me go back when we got to the cross-roads. She knew as well as I did that the old fool who drives it wasn't particular as to time, and she worried about my old woman getting scairt if she found herself alone, and me out. 'Go back to her, Thalassa,' she said, 'I shall be all right now.' That was just after she'd made me promise to tell nobody that she'd been to see her father that night. And, by God, I kept my word. Nobody got anything out of me, though they tried hard enough. Well, when she sent me back I went, leaving her standing, for I had my own reason for going. When I looked back after a bit I saw her standing there by the light of the dirty little lamp above the cross-roads."

"Did you see the wagonette on the road?"

"Not a sign of it. Just her—alone."

A faint hope died in Charles's breast. Even the drunken irregularity of a Cornish cabman told against Sisily. But that point was not so immediately important as Thalassa's story that the murder had been committed during his absence from Flint House. Although his own experience supported that supposition, Charles was reluctant to accept a theory which plunged the events of that night into deeper mystery than ever.

"Well, go on," he said. "What did you find when you got back?"

"The house was dark and the door open. The wind was coming in from the sea sharp enough to take your head off your shoulders, and I thought perhaps I'd jammed the door without closing it, and it had blowed open with the wind. But when I got inside I heered something like moaning. I thought that might be the wind too, for it's for ever screeching up and down the passages like a devil, specially o' nights. I—" He stopped suddenly, with a cautious sidelong look at his listener.

"Yes, yes!" cried Charles. "And what then?"

Thalassa went on, but a little moodily.

"I went along to the kitchen and found the old woman lying on the floor, in a kind of fit or faint, making the queer noise I'd just heered. When I picked her up she opened her eyes, laughing and crying and making mouths as she pointed to the ceiling. I could get nothing out of her for a while. Then she mutters something about a crash upstairs, and goes off into another fit. I carried her into her bedroom and went upstairs as fast as my legs would take me. There was a light under his door, but he didn't answer when I knocked. I tried to open it, but it was locked inside. In a bit there was a knock downstairs. You know what happened after that." He lapsed into silence again, with another look at the young man.

"That was when my aunt and her husband and Dr. Ravenshaw came to the door?" said Charles, filling in the pause. "But how was it that you told them that you feared something had happened to your master? Was that pure guesswork on your part? You hadn't been in the room, you say."

"I had to tell them something, hadn't I?" retorted the other sullenly. "If I hadn't told them that, it would a' all come out about me going out with Miss Sisily, and not into the coal cellar, as I said."

"It is astonishing that your story should have been so near the truth when you knew nothing of what had taken place."

"I did know something. The door was open, the house dark, and she in a fit on the floor, saying there'd been a crash upstairs. Then his door was locked, and I couldn't get an answer. Wasn't that enough?"

"Hardly enough to warrant your saying that you feared your master had been murdered—unless you expected him to be murdered."

"I didn't say that," replied Thalassa with unusual quickness. "All I said was that I was afeered something had happened to him. There was reason for thinking that. I had to make up my story quick—that part about just going for Dr. Ravenshaw. That was because I'd still got my hat and topcoat on, just as I'd come in from the moors, and I wasn't going to break my promise to Miss Sisily."

"Did you see the blood under the door when you went up and tried to get in?"

"I've told you all there is to tell," was the dogged response.

"What frightened your wife so much? Do you think she saw the murderer?"

"That's what I would like to know," responded Thalassa, with a swift cunning glance.

He turned his face away and looked across the sea, the brown outline of his hooked profile more than ever like an effigy carved by savage hands. Charles scanned him despairingly. The feeling was strong within him that he was still keeping something back.

"Thalassa," he said, "you should have told this story before. You have done wrong in keeping it back."

"'Twould a' been breaking of my word to Miss Sisily."

"It was of more importance to clear her. You could have done that if you had come forward and told the police, as you've just told me, that she left the house with you before nine o'clock on that night."

"'Twouldn't a' helped if I had. I found out next day that the wagonette didn't get to the cross-roads that night till nearly ten o'clock. 'Twas after half-past nine when it left the inn."

"What made you find out that?"

"Do you think I didn't put my wits to work when the damned detective was trying to put me into it as well as her? I thought it all out then—about telling the truth. But I saw 'twould a' been no good for her, but only made matters worse. Who'd a' believed me? There be times when a man can say too much, so I kept my mouth shut."

There was so much sense in this that Charles had nothing to say in reply. In silence they tramped along till they reached the dip of the sea in which the Moon Rock lay. Here they paused, as if with the mutual feeling that the time had come for the interview to end. Behind them towered the cliffs, with Flint House hanging crazily on the summit far above where they stood. The eye of Charles ranged along the shore to the spot where he had said good-bye to Sisily not so very long ago, then returned to rest doubtingly on Thalassa. The old man stood with his hand resting on a giant rock, his dark eyes fixed on the rim of the waste of grey water where a weak declining sun hung irresolutely, as though fearing the inevitable plunge.

"I'd a' given my right arm to have saved her from this," Charles heard him mutter.

Charles found himself looking down at Thalassa's brown muscular arm, corded with veins, stretched out on the rock by which he stood. It was as though it had been bared for his inspection, which was not, indeed, the case. If that arm could save Sisily, it was at her service. But what was the good of that? What was the good of his own efforts to help her? Charles had a suffocating feeling of the futility of human effort when opposed by the malignity of Fate. He asked himself with aching heart what was to be the outcome of it all? He had failed. What then? It was not until that moment that he realized how strongly he had been buoyed up by the false optimism of hope. His consciousness, as though directed by the power of a devil, was forced to look for the first time upon the hideous inevitability of the appointed end.

"No, no! Not that—not that," he shudderingly whispered to himself.

Neither moved. The minutes passed leaden-footed. It was silent and still in that wild spot, as if theirs were the only two human hearts beating in a dead world. It seemed as though neither could bring it upon himself to terminate the interview. Charles was the first to break the silence. He spoke like a man coming out of a dream.

"Did that clock upstairs keep good time?" he asked in a low voice.

Thalassa turned on him as if not understanding the purport of the question.

"It was going shipshape and Bristol fashion in the afternoon. What's that got to do with it? What does it signify if it was five minutes fast or slow?"

The logic of the answer was apparent to Charles, who knew he was only attempting to pluck something by chance out of the dark maze. But another and shrewder idea started up in his mind.

"What was your reason for hurrying back across the moors that night?"

"Miss Sisily told me to go."

"But you had another reason—a reason of your own," said Charles, turning quickly to regard him. "You said so yourself."

"If I had I've forgotten what it was," said Thalassa with a black look.

"You cannot have forgotten!" cried Charles. "What was it?" Hope sprang up in his heart again like a warm flame as he detected something confused and irresolute in the other's attitude. "Thalassa, you are keeping something back. You know, or you guess, who the murderer is!"

"I'm keeping nothing back."

"You are. I can see it in your face. What is it that you will not tell? What do you fear?"

"The gallows—for one thing."

"You'd sooner see Sisily lose her life on them?"

This bitter taunt, wrung from the depth of the young man's anguished heart, had an instantaneous and unexpected effect on his companion.

"No, no!" he hoarsely cried, "I couldn't a' bear that. But it's nothing to tell, nothing to help. It was earlier that night, before she came. I was looking out of the kitchen window, when I thought I saw a rock move. Then I looked again, and it seemed like a man—though I couldn't see his face."

"Is that all?" Bitter disappointment rang in Charles's voice. "That might have been me. I was out on the rocks that night, close to Flint House."

"'Tweren't you." Thalassa's reply was so low as to be almost inaudible. "I don't know who it was, but I'll take my Bible oath it weren't you."

"Who was it then?" Charles asked breathlessly.

"A dead man, or his spirit. I know that now, though I laughed when *he* said it. I know better now."

He stopped suddenly, like one who has said too much, and looked moodily out to sea.

"What do you mean by that?"

"Never mind what I mean. It's nothing to do with you. A man's a fool when he gets talking. The tongue trips you up."

"Thalassa," said Charles solemnly, "if you know anything which might throw the remotest light on this mystery it is your duty to reveal it."

"It's easy to talk. But I swore—I swore I would never tell."

"This is the moment to forget your oath."

"It's fine to talk—for you. But he'd come back to haunt me, if he knew." He jerked his thumb in the direction of the distant churchyard where Robert Turold lay.

Charles looked at his grim and secret face in despair. "I hope you realize what you are doing by keeping silence," he said.

"I'm keeping a still tongue in my head, for one thing."

"For one thing—yes. For another, you're injuring Sisily—you're doing more than injure her. You're letting her remain under suspicion of her father's death, in hiding in London, hunted by the police. Yet she believed in you. It was she who sent me to you, it was she who said: 'Tell Thalassa from me to tell the truth, if he knows it.' Is she mistaken in you, Thalassa? Do you think more of your own skin than her safety?"

Chapter XXVIII

It was a strange story which Charles Turold heard by that grey Cornish sea—a story touched with the glitter of adventurous fortune in the sombre setting of a trachytic island, where wine-dark breakers beat monotonously on a black beach of volcanic sand strewn with driftwood, kelp, dead shells, and the squirming forms of blindworms tossed up from the bowels of a dead sea. It was there in the spell of solitude thirty years before that Robert Turold's soul had yielded to temptation at the beck of his monstrous ambition.

That, however, was the end—or what Robert Turold imagined to be the end—of the story. The listener was first invited to contemplate a scene in human progress when men gathered from the four corners of the earth and underwent incredible hardships of hunger, thirst, disease, lived like beasts and died like vermin for the sake of precious stones in the earth. Thalassa brought up before the young man's eyes a vivid picture of an African diamond rush of that period—a corrugated iron settlement of one straggling street, knee-deep in sand, swarming with vermin and scorpions, almost waterless, crowded with a mongrel, ever-increasing lot of needy adventurers brought from all parts of the world by reports of diamonds which could be picked out with a penknife from the dunes and sandy shingle which formed the background of the villainous "town." In the great waves and ridges of sand which stretched everywhere as far as the eye could reach, runaway scoundrels of every shade of colour wormed on their bellies with the terrible pertinacity of ants, sweating and groping in that choking dust for the glittering crystals so rarely found.

Thalassa had been infected by the diamond fever like so many more. Like other young men he wanted plenty of money for women and grog— what else, he asked, could a man get for money that was worth having? In those days he was a sailor before the mast, lacking the capital for such delights. So he deserted his timber tramp when she touched at Port Elizabeth, and set out for the diamond fields with another runaway—the ship's cook, who had an ambition to have his meals cooked for him for the rest of his life, instead of cooking meals for other people.

The fields were far to the north. Thalassa reached them after a terrible journey through the stony veldt and sandy desert, broken by barren hills. His companion died of the hardships, and was buried in the desert which stretched to the wandering course of the Orange River. Thalassa secured his license and went "prospecting."

"Dost a' know anything about diamonds—digging for them?" he broke off to ask.

Charles Turold shook his head.

Thalassa lapsed into silence for some moments, his eyes fixed on the sea hissing among the black wet rocks at his feet, then said—

"A man's a fool most of his days, but sometimes he can be such a fool that the memory 'll come up to mock him when he lays dying. Here was I, deserting my ship and throwing away a year's wages and a'most my life to get to these damned fields, thinking to pick up diamonds cut and glittering like I'd seen them in London shops, when as soon as I'd clapped eyes on the first diamond I saw dug up I knew that I'd left behind me at the other end of the world as many rough diamonds as there was in the whole of that dustbin of a place—diamonds that didn't have to be dug for, either, only I didn't know them when I saw them."

His narrowed eye gleamed craftily, a mere pin's point of expression in the direction of Charles, as though expecting a question. But Charles kept silence, so he went on with his story. He let it be understood that his luck on the fields was of the worst possible description—never a solitary stone came his way. But he had no heart for digging. He was always thinking of the diamonds in that remote spot which he had ignorantly let slip from his grasp, like the dog in the fable dropping the substance for the shadow. He would have gone back to look for them, but he'd spent most of his little capital in that wild-goose chase, and the miserable remnant oozed away like water in a place where the barest necessaries of life cost fabulous prices. Soon he became stranded, practically penniless.

It was this precarious moment of his fortunes which his star (his evil star, he insisted on that) selected to bring him into juxtaposition with the man whose life was to be inexorably mingled with his own from that time henceforward. The actual meeting place was a tin-roofed grog shanty kept by a giant Kaffir woman and a sore-eyed degenerate white man, whose subjection to his black paramour had earned for him among the blacks on the field the terrible sobriquet of "White Harry." Here, one night, Thalassa sat drinking bad beer and planning impossible schemes for returning to his diamonds at the other end of the world. The place was empty of other customers. The Kaffir woman slumbered behind the flimsy planking of the bar, and "White Harry" sat on the counter scraping tunes out of a little fiddle. Thalassa remembered the tune he was playing—"Annie Laurie." Upon this scene there entered two young men, Englishmen. Thalassa discerned that at once by the cut of their jib. Besides, they ordered Bass beer. Who else but Englishmen would order Bass beer at five shillings a bottle in a God-forsaken place like that?

"*He* was one of them." Thalassa moved his hand vaguely in the direction of St. Fair churchyard. "Smart and lively he was then—not like what he was afore he died. I took a fancy to him as soon as I set my eyes on him. He was a man in those days, and I knowed a man when I saw 'un. I didn't care so much for the looks of the other 'un—Remington was his name, as I heered afterwards. Well enough for some tastes, but too much of the God Almighty Englishman about him to suit me. A handsome chap he was, this Remington, I'm bound to say—young and slim, wi' a pink face like a girl's, not a hair on it, and lookin' as though he might a' turned out of a bandbox. Him—Turold—had a moustache, and his face was a dark 'un, but I liked him for all his black looks—though not so black in those days, either. More eager like."

Charles Turold found himself trying to picture Robert Turold in the part of a smart lively young fellow, and failing utterly. But Time took the smartness out of a man in less than thirty years. It had also taken the liveliness out of Robert Turold for good and all.

Thalassa went on with his story. The young men were served with their beer at five shillings a bottle, and sat down in a corner to drink it. They talked as they sipped, and Thalassa listened. His original idea that they were young men of wealth (because of the Bass) was soon dispersed by the trend of their conversation. They had gone out from England to make their fortunes on the fields, but had come a cropper like himself, and were discussing what they'd do next. The fair-haired one, Remington, was all for getting back to England while they had any money left, but Turold was dead against it. There were plenty of diamonds to be found, and he was going to have some of them. He'd been talking to a man who was just back from the interior with a story of a river beach full of diamonds, and he was fitting up an expedition to go back and get them. Turold wanted to join in, but Remington said he'd heard too many stories of diamonds to be picked up for the asking. Had he forgotten about the cursed Jew who got a hundred pounds out of them? Turold said this was different—the man had brought back a little bottleful of diamonds. Remington replied with a sneer about "salting." They argued. "Suppose we dropped the last of our money?" Remington asked. "No worse than crawling back to England like whipped curs, poorer than we set out," said the other. Remington said he didn't want to go back to England like that, but he'd sooner face it than run the risk of being stranded in that hell of a place. Turold answered he was not going back till he'd made a fortune. He said (Thalassa remembered his exact words): "I don't care how I do it, Remington, but I will do it—mark my words." "Show me a more sensible plan than this, and I'm with you," Remington had replied.

It was at this stage that Thalassa was seized with an inclination to thrust himself into the dialogue. Striving to explain his reasons at that distance of time, he said it was Robert Turold's last remark which really decided him—did the trick, as he phrased it. Actually it must have been a prompt recognition of the kinship between two lawless souls.

He left his seat and went across to where the two young Englishmen were earnestly talking, unaware that they had been overheard. He approached them as one shipwrecked sailor might approach two other castaways marooned on the same rock. They all wanted money, and they all wanted to get away from that God-forsaken hole. Diamonds they were after? Well, he could take them to a place at the other end of the world where there were enough diamonds in the rough to make them all rich for life.

After the first surprise at his interruption they heard him in silence, and then plied him with questions. Where were these diamonds? In a volcanic island in the South Pacific. Where about? They couldn't expect him to tell them that. It was Robert Turold (Thalassa seemed to have addressed himself principally to him) who asked him how he knew that the diamonds were still there. Thalassa's reply was that they were buried in a big box, and the island was out of the run of ships. What sort of a big box? Turold had asked. Thalassa replied (perhaps reluctantly) that the box was "a kind of a coffin," and that there was a dead man inside of it as well as the diamonds, but he, at all events, was not likely to run off with them.

Remington and Turold were startled by this answer, and conferred hastily apart. They returned to ask more questions. They wanted to know how the body and the diamonds had got there in the first instance, but that was a story which Thalassa refused to reveal. That had nothing to do with it, he said. The ship which had buried the man there had gone down afterwards with all hands, so nobody knew about the diamonds except him.

After that Remington became the chief questioner, Robert Turold merely looking on, his dark eyes frequently meeting Thalassa's. It seemed as though he must have realized that these last replies concealed a story better left unprobed. But Remington wanted to know why Thalassa had come searching for diamonds in that part of the world when he knew of plenty in another, and Thalassa had replied, in all simplicity, that it was because the Almighty had endowed him with more muscles than brains, and he hadn't recognized the worth of the stones at the time. In fact, he didn't know that they were diamonds. His experience on the fields had improved his knowledge in that respect, and he now knew that he had left behind him on the lonely island enough diamonds in the rough to make them all rich — two bottlesful, and some in a leather bag, where the dead man also kept one of those digging licenses which the damned German officials sold you — what did they call it? Prospector's license — a *schurfschein*? said Remington. Yes, that was it. He knew it again as soon as he got one on the fields.

Turold and Remington again talked together in whispers, and then Turold asked Thalassa how he proposed to get the diamonds. Thalassa had his plan ready. They must get down to the Cape and get a boat to Sydney from Capetown. That was the jumping-off place. From Sydney they were to take a boat to — another place. The island was a bare two days' sail from the "other place," and Thalassa proposed to hire a cutter on the mainland and sail over to it. He was no navigator, but he could find his way back to that island again at any time.

Turold seemed inclined to agree, but Remington put in another of his sharp questions. Why did he want to bring two strangers into the business? What was to prevent him getting the diamonds on his own account, without sharing with anybody? Thalassa replied that he had no money to finance the expedition, and even if he got the diamonds they'd be no use to him. How could a rough seaman like himself, who could hardly write his own name, turn the stones into the large sum of money they represented? That was an enterprise which called for civilized qualities of education and address which he did not possess. From his standpoint it was an even deal between them. They were to supply the money and intelligence in return for his knowledge, and they would share and share alike.

It was Robert Turold who ultimately settled the decision — winning over the reluctant Remington with words which Thalassa had never forgotten. He also recognized the risk, but he thought it was well worth taking. It seemed that the two had a little more than £200 left between them — just about enough to carry the thing through. What was the use of returning to England with that paltry sum, he had asked. He spoke of a girl — some girl who was waiting in England for Remington while he made his fortune abroad. Was he going to go back to her penniless? "Even if this doesn't turn out right," he went on, "we'll have reached another part of the world, with a fresh chance of making money, instead of being poor in England, that breeding-ground for tame rabbits, where poverty is the unforgiveable sin." "I liked him for those words," said Thalassa, "for they came from a man whose thoughts were after the style of my own. 'Twas they decided the other chap, and next morning we set out for Capetown. From there we got passages in a cargo boat for Sydney."

Charles found it easier to visualize this picture than the former. The departure of the three upon such a wild romantic venture had in its elements all the audacity, greed, and splendour of youth, and he also was young.

Thalassa went on with his story.

During the voyage to Sydney, Robert Turold used to talk to him on deck at nights after Remington had gone to his bunk. It was in these solitary deck tramps under glittering stars that Thalassa first heard from the other's lips of the Turrald title: the title for which the fortune he was seeking was merely a stepping stone—the means to obtain it. "Night after night he talked of nothing else," said Thalassa, "and I knew he would do what he wanted to do." It was easy to gather from his story that his original admiration for Robert Turold soon grew into a deeper and stronger feeling. There was something in the dead man's masterful ambitious character which exercised a reluctantly conceded but undoubted fascination upon his companion's fierce spirit.

Such were their relations when they reached Sydney and set out on a further voyage to the other place which Thalassa was so reluctant to name. On arriving at the "other place" they made their way to its east coast, which was the starting point of their journey to the island. From a brown man living on the coast Thalassa hired a smart little ketch which the three of them could easily handle, and in this they embarked for the island from a beach which curved like a white tusk around a blue bay.

They did not reach the island for six days—through baffling winds, and not because they did not steer a right course. As Thalassa had said, there was no difficulty in finding it, for they had only been one day at sea when the smouldering smoke of the distant volcanic cone came into vision, making an unholy mark against the clear sky which they never lost again. Gradually they beat nearer until they made it—a circular ragged high ridge jutting abruptly from a deep sullen sea, with a red glow showing fitfully in the smoke of the summit.

There was an outer reef, but Thalassa knew the passage, and steered the ketch through a tortuous channel above sunken needle-pointed rocks to a little sheltered harbour inshore. Here they made the ketch fast, and landed on a beach of volcanic violet, where they sometimes sank knee deep into sulphuric water, and felt squirming sea things squelch beneath their tread. Above this margin of violet-black sand, deposits of volcanic rock and lava rose almost perpendicularly, enclosing the central cone in a kind of amphitheatre.

The stones they had travelled so far to obtain were there waiting for them. Thalassa hurried over that part of the story, narrating it in barest outline with suspicious glances directed at his listener's intent face. Apparently he led his companions to the spot as soon as they landed—up a path through a gap in the crater wall, across a furrowed slope all a-quake, where jets of steam issued from gurgling fissures in snaky spirals. On the other side of this dreary waste Thalassa led the way across a ledge to firmer ground and a grave. Charles gathered that the occupant of the grave had been coffined in a seaman's chest in his clothes: "There he was, with his bottles of diamonds in his coat pockets, and more in his leather bag in his breast pocket, just as I left him twelve months afore to go to the other end of the world looking for what I'd buried." A grim smile curved Thalassa's face as he uttered these words; the idea seemed to contain elements of humour for him.

"They were diamonds, then?" said Charles curiously.

"Ay; they were diamonds right enough. Him—Turold—said they were diamonds as soon as he uncorked one of the bottles and poured a few into the palm of his hand. There was some rare big ones in one of the bottles—enough to have brought all those fools tumbling out of Africa if they'd know of them. From some papers they found on the chap Turold said he'd must a-been prospecting in nigh every part of the world."

"How did he come to be buried there with his diamonds, in that lonely spot?" asked Charles wonderingly.

"He was a passenger, and died as we was passing the island. 'Twas the skipper's fancy to give him a land burial. But that doesn't matter a dump—it's outside the story." He turned his eyes away from Charles.

Dusk had fallen before they finished their search, and Thalassa would not undertake the risk of threading the boat out from the tortuous reef passage in the darkness. They decided to camp on the island for the night, preferring the sulphur-impregnated air ("A lighted match would blaze and fizzle in it like a torch," Thalassa declared) to the cramped discomfort of their little craft. They brought some food ashore, and made a flimsy sort of camp above high water, at the foot of the encircling walls of the crater. There they had their supper, and there, as they lounged smoking, Remington in an evil moment for himself suggested that they should sort the diamonds into three heaps—share and share alike. Robert Turold agreed, and they emptied the stones out of the bottles and leather bag into a single heap. Remington took one bottle and Robert Turold another; to Thalassa fell the empty bag. As the stones were sorted one was to be placed in each receptacle until the tally ran out.

It must have been a strange spectacle — so strange that it made a lasting impression on the least imaginative mind of the three, for he tried in his rude way to reproduce it on that Cornish beach after the lapse of thirty long years. He threw bits of rock on the sand to indicate the positions in which they had sat. From his description Charles pictured the scene adequately enough: the violet-black beach, exhaling sulphuric vapours, the yellow-grey volcanic rocks, the gurgling ebullitions of a geyser throwing off volumes of smoke high above them, and the faces of the three men (ruddy in the fire-glow, white in the moonlight) intent on the division of the heap of dull stones scattered on a flat rock between them. Thalassa remembered all these things; he remembered also how startled they were, the three of them, at the unexpected sound of a kind of throaty chuckle near by, and turned in affright to see a large bird regarding them from the shadow of the rocks — a sea bird with rounded wings, light-coloured plumage, and curiously staring eyes above a yellow beak. When it saw it was observed it vanished swiftly seaward in noiseless flight.

The division, commenced good-humouredly enough, soon developed the elements of a gamble between Robert Turold and Remington. They forgot Thalassa's existence as they argued and disputed over the allotment of certain stones. The foot or so of flat rock became the circumference of their thoughts, ambitions, and passions — their world for the time being. In that sordid drama of greed Thalassa seemed to have comported himself with greater dignity than his two superiors by birth and education. He even took it upon himself to reason with them on their folly. Perhaps he knew from his own seamy experience of life what such things developed into. At all events, he urged his companions to defer the division until they returned to civilization and could get the spoils appraised by eyes expert in the knowledge of precious stones. But they would not listen, so, not liking the look of things, he withdrew a little distance off and watched them, leaning against a rock. That was his tacit admission (so Charles interpreted this action) that he was on Robert Turold's side, and felt that his own interests were identical with those of the master mind. The two, left to themselves, wrangled more fiercely than ever. There were unpleasant taunts and mutual revilings. The listener by the rock learnt definitely what he had previously suspected—that there was bitter blood and bad feeling between the two men, buried for a time, but now revived with a savageness which revealed the hollowness of their supposed reconciliation. It was about a girl, some girl in England with whom they had both been in love. Thalassa gathered that Remington had left England as the favoured suitor. He had (in Thalassa's words) "cut Turold out."

Charles Turold could not forbear a faint exclamation of astonishment. His brain reeled in trying to imagine the austere figure of Robert Turold squabbling over a girl and some diamonds on a lonely island in the South Pacific. He was too amazed at the moment to see the implications of this part of the story.

"They went on snarling and showing their teeth, but not biting," continued Thalassa, "sorting out the little stones all right, but quarrelling over the bigger. There was two—the biggest in the bunch by far—which they kept putting aside because they couldn't agree about the sharing of them. At last it came about that there was only these two big 'uns left, lying like two beans on the bit o' rock, side by side. Before I could guess what was likely to happen Turold grabbed them up quick, and put them in his bottle. 'These two are mine, Thalassa's and mine,' he said. 'You've had your share, Remington.' Remington sprang from the rock quick as a snake. 'One's mine,' he said. But Turold was up as quick. 'It's not for you,' he says, with his dark smile. 'We'll put it against the girl you filched from me, and call it an even deal. What does a happy lover want with diamonds?' 'Damn you!' cries the other, and hit him in the face. They both went down, scuffling and panting in the sand. I stood where I was, for I weren't going to come between them till I saw how it was going to be. Presently I could see that Remington was stronger, and that Turold was getting the worst of it. After a bit Turold called out, 'Thalassa!'

"I ran down at that fast enough, and got out my knife as I went. They'd slipped down the sloping beach half-way to the sea, writhing like a couple of the blind-worms that I kept stepping on, going over and over so quick that I couldn't do anything at first. But one of them was sobbing in his breath as though he was pretty well finished, and I guessed it was Turold. Then I saw Remington's face on top, and before they could swing round again I got a good stroke in his neck where it gleamed white in the moonlight. The blood jumped out warm on my hand, and he rolled over so quick that I thought I had killed him. But as I stooped over him he was up like a flash, staggering up the steep beach, his feet plopping and sucking in the water underneath.

Turold was on his feet by that time, breathing hard, getting back his breath. 'After him—quick!' he says to me, his face black with rage—'he's got the diamonds.'

"I ran after him up the beach, but he heard me coming and had the start of me. He had firm ground under him by then, and was tearing along the rocks towards the path I'd taken them that afternoon, turning round now and again to look back, the blood glistening in the moonlight on his white face. There we was—him going higher and higher, me after him, and Turold standing below on the beach, staring up at the two of us.

"Run my best, I couldn't get near him. I suppose he thought he was done for if I caught him, and by that time my blood was pretty well up. I had one pull over him—I knew the island, and he didn't. The path he was taking led to the top of the island, where the crater was, with a kind of wall of rocks round it. But before you came to that there was a great hole which fell down God Almighty knows how deep, and was supposed to have been another volcano at some time or other. This hole was divided into two by a narrow ridge running right across it, and the path Remington was on took him straight to the edge. So he'd either got to go across this ridge when he come to it or turn back and be caught.

"He was a long way ahead when he come to it, but he never stopped. He just gave one glance down at me, and went on to the ridge. I watched him balancing along it like a man on a tight rope, mounting higher and higher, for the ridge went up steep on the far side. Thinks I to myself, 'You're a plucky one,' then all of a sudden I heard a shout from below, and looked down. There stood Turold, waving me out of the way. He'd been to the boat for a gun we'd brought with us, and was taking aim at Remington. The next thing I saw was Remington turning round on the ledge to come back to my side, having found out, I suppose, that the ridge would take him into the crater. Just as he turned I heard the shot. It must have winged Remington pretty bad, because he went tumbling off the ridge head first, like a man taking a dive into the water. I turned and climbed down to where I'd left Turold. His face was all aglow with rage. 'The infernal scoundrel!' he said, then—'Did you get the diamonds?' 'How was I to get them when I never caught him?' I said. 'Then we'll get them off his body in the morning,' he said in a low tone. 'You'll never do that,' says I. He asks me why not, turning on me a face as savage as a dog's. 'Because whichever side he's dropped he's safe from us,' I said. 'There's a hole that no man's ever seen the bottom of on one side of the ridge, and on the other a stinking lake of green boiling sulphur. When you shot him you sent him into one or the other, so you can say good-bye to him and the diamonds.' 'Oh!' he cries, when he heard that—just like that; then after a bit he points up the path, and asks me to go back and have a look for him. I went back as far as the ridge. The moon was clear as day, shining on that infernal green lake on the one side, and into the deep hole on the other. The lake was bubbling and stewing in the moonlight like a witchpot, and the other side of the ridge was just black emptiness, and there was no sign of Remington—I knowed there couldn't be. Back I went again, and as I was climbing down the path to where Turold was standing I saw something glinting in the black sand at his feet, and when I got there I picked up the bottle of diamonds where Remington must have dropped them when struggling with Turold. I gave them to Turold. 'And now,' says I, 'let's get out of here. The moon's bright enough to let me find my way through the reefs, and this island ain't a healthy place to stay too long on. I know it, and you don't.' He was glad enough to follow me to the boat, and we got through on a good flowing tide."

Thalassa stopped abruptly, as though to leave on his listener's mind an impression of that furtive departure on a dark whispering sea beneath a blood-red moon.

"You got back to the mainland?" queried Charles, as he remained silent.

"Ay—and to England. Afore we got there Turold had persuaded himself that Remington slipped off the ridge accidental, and that he missed him when he fired."

"Perhaps his conscience pricked him. Go on."

"There's nowt much more to tell. Turold got me my share of the money, and then we parted. He offered to invest it for me, but I wasn't going to trust no banks—not I. It took me two years to waste it on gambling and women. Then I took to sea again. That lasted another year. Then I found myself in 'Frisco, where I shipped in a four-masted barque and come home round the Horn. I was pretty sick of the sea after two bad goes of rheumatic fever, so I made up my mind to hunt up Turold. I found him after a while. He didn't seem best pleased to see me at first, but he said I could stay till he had time to think out what he could do for me. That was the beginning of it. We never parted again, him and me, until he was carried out of yon house feet first. We got used to each other's ways, and I was worth all he paid me because I saved him worry and expense. He was all for saving, in those days. Married he was too, to a little timid thing of a girl who was in fear and trembling of him. 'Twas a black day for her when she married that headstrong stubborn devil. 'Mr.' Thalassa she always called me, poor woman. I married a maid-servant they had. That was Turold's idea—he thought by that way he could get his household looked after very cheaply by the pair of us. I wasn't keen on marrying, but it didn't make much odds one way or the other, for no living woman, wife or no wife, would have kept me in England if I'd wanted to get out. As it happened, I never did. I stayed on, going from place to place where they went—where Turold took us."

"Whom did my uncle marry?" asked Charles.

"You might a' guessed that. 'Twas the girl t'other had cut him out of. I thought the masterful devil'd get her when Remington was out of the way, but I asked him once straight out, and he said yes, it was the same girl. She was a pretty timid little thing in those days, but I don't know why they was both so mad after her. However, there it was."

"And do you think that after all these years, Remington is really alive?" said Charles, looking at him earnestly. "Do you think it was he who murdered my uncle?"

"Happen maybe, happen not. The night he was killed I found him in a rare funk in his room. He rang his bell like a fury, and when I went up he swore he heard the footsteps of Remington just afore, running round the rocks outside of Flint House just as he heard him pattering along the rocks on the island that night. I didn't believe 'un then, but I'm not so sure since. If he's come back to get Turold it's for sure he's still somewhere about, waiting his chance to get me as well. I'm keeping my eye open for 'un—walked the coast for miles, I have, looking for him. He won't take me unawares, same as Turold." His eyes searched the cliffs behind them.

"You may not recognize him if you meet him. It is thirty years since you saw him. A man changes a lot in thirty years."

"That's true, 'tis a thought which never crossed my mind." Thalassa's look was troubled.

"As you've told me this story you'd better leave it in my hands, and not go looking for anybody with that knife of yours."

"What be you going to do?"

"I must go to Scotland Yard and tell them your story. It's the only chance."

"And get me into trouble?"

"There's not much fear of that. In any case, you must stand that, for Sisily's sake."

Thalassa nodded his acquiescence. "Better be careful yersel' getting back to London. The police here is watching for you. They've been a' Flint House more than once, looking for both of you."

"It's a risk I must take, nevertheless," said the young man, rising from his seat as he spoke. "It's for Sisily's sake. Good-bye, Thalassa, and thank you for what you've told me."

Thalassa did not reply or offer to accompany him. From his seat on the rocks he followed Charles's ascent up the narrow path with contemplative eyes.

Chapter XXIX

Barrant returned to London in the mental disposition of a man who sees an elaborate theory thrown into the melting-pot by an unexpected turn of events. The humbling thought was that he had allowed a second fish to glide through his hands without even suspecting that it was on his line. He had never remotely connected Charles Turold with the murder until Mr. Brimsdown had imparted Mrs. Brierly's disclosure to him. He had acted promptly enough on that piece of information, but once again he was too late.

Austin Turold might have felt reassured if he had known how little his share in the events of that night occupied Barrant's mind during their last interview. The complexion Austin's conduct bore to the detective's reflection was that of a father who had intentionally misled the power of authority in order to shield his son. The law took a serious view of that offense, but it was a matter which could be dealt with at leisure in Austin's case. By his brother's death Austin Turold had become a man of property and standing. It was the drawback of his wealth that he could not disappear like his son. He was to be found when wanted. The main thing just then was to catch the son, or the girl — or both. Barrant went back to London for that purpose.

As the days slipped away without that end being achieved he became worried and perplexed. His own position was an unenviable one, and his thoughts were far from pleasant. He felt that he had failed badly, and that his standing with his superiors in Scotland Yard was under a cloud in consequence. But he could not see where he had actually been at fault. It was such a damned amazing case. In most crimes the trouble was to find sufficient clues, but in this case there were too many. And the inferences pointed different ways. That was the trouble. He was not even sure that in this latest discovery, so annoyingly belated, he had reached the ultimate solution of the facts. It was not that the theory of these two young people committing murder for love was too cynical for belief. He had encountered more incredible things than that in his professional career. Life was a cynical business, and youth could be brutal in pursuit of its aims, especially when the aim was passion, as it usually was. In his experience youth and age were the dangerous periods—youth, because it knew nothing of life, and age because it knew too much. There were fewer surprises in middle-age. That was the period of responsibility—when humanity clung to the ordered way with the painful rectitude of a procession of laden ants toiling up a hill. Youth was not like that—nor age.

No, it was not that. His difficulty was to fit all the circumstances into any compact theory of the case. Try as he would, there were always some loose ends left over, some elements of uncertainty which left him perplexed. He fashioned a new view of the murder, with Charles Turold as the principal figure in it—the actual murderer. He assumed that Charles and Sisily had gone to Flint House that night to prevent the truth about Sisily's birth becoming known. The assertion of her illegitimacy rested upon her father's bare statement, but his lawyer was convinced he would not have made the statement without having the proofs in his possession. These proofs had not been found. Very well. What inference was to be drawn from that? Sisily knew that they were kept in the clock-case, and pointed out the hiding place to her lover. In a struggle for their possession Robert Turold was shot down, or he might have been shot first and staggered to the clock afterwards to see if they had been stolen. Either supposition accounted for the fallen clock, and fitted in with nearly all the known facts of the murder.

Nearly all, but not all! In face of Mrs. Brierly's disclosure it seemed a condition precedent to the elucidation of the mystery to substitute Charles Turold for Thalassa as the person whose undisciplined love for Sisily had led him to shoot her father to shield her name. Nor was it incredible to suppose that he had remained in Cornwall to cover her flight in the hope of diverting suspicion from her. But the loose end in the theory was Thalassa's share in that night's events, and his dogged silence since under strong suspicion.

Thalassa knew more than he had yet revealed, but what did he know? What was his share in the business? It was difficult to say. Barrant was unable to accept the assumption that three people were concerned in the murder. That idea, if not impossible, was at least contrary to reason. But if it was excluded, how was the silence of Thalassa to be explained? Was he afraid? It was as difficult to associate that quality with him as with an eagle or beast of prey.

And the theory failed to explain the reason for Robert Turold's frantic letter to his lawyer on the night of the murder. That was another loose end.

What a case! It was an abnormal and sinister mystery in any light, with no absolute or demonstrative certainty of proof by any of its circumstances, however regarded. The effect of its perplexing clues distorted the imagination, outraged the sense of possibility and experience. To reach conclusiveness in it seemed as impossible as an attempt to scale an unending staircase in a nightmare. The facts were there, but they were inexplicable, or at least they stared at him with the aspect of many faces.

As he weighed these doubts he found his thoughts reverting with increasing frequency to the hood clock in Robert Turold's study and the question of its connection with the crime. He pondered over the point with the nervous anxiety of a puzzled brain, and it seemed to him now that he had not devoted as much investigation to this peculiar clue as it deserved. He recalled Mr. Brimsdown's conversation on the matter. He remembered that he had been struck at the time by the penetration of his remarks about the clock, and while not accepting his fantastic theory, had determined to give more careful thought to the point. But Mrs. Brierly's disclosure put the idea out of his head.

It recurred to him with renewed force when he found himself in Exeter nearly a fortnight later on another case. It was a good opportunity to go on to Cornwall, and he took it. His business completed, he caught the early train, and in due time arrived at Penzance. With an obscure instinct for solitude he hastened through the town and struck out across the moors.

The afternoon was waning when he reached Flint House and pulled the old-fashioned bell-handle of the weatherbeaten door. There was no reply, and a second ring passed disregarded. That was disconcerting and unexpected. He wondered whether Thalassa and his wife had left the place. Then he noticed that the door was merely closed and not shut. He lifted the heavy iron knocker, and knocked loudly. The repeated knocking sent the door flying open, and Barrant found himself looking into an empty hall. Half-way down a pair of curtains stirred slightly and parted suddenly, revealing a narrower passage which led to the door of the kitchen. The curtains streamed horizontally, twisting and coiling like snakes. Barrant stepped quickly inside and closed the door. The curtains fell together again.

There was something so startling in this action of the wind that Barrant stood motionless, looking round him. The cold current of air he had admitted died away in the draughty passages with queer gasping noises, like a wind strangled. Then there was the most absolute silence. The curtains hung perpendicular, as thickly motionless as blankets. Barrant noticed that the hallstand and a chair beside it were thick with dust. Evidently the house was empty.

Turning first to make quite sure that the front door was securely shut, he took his way upstairs to Robert Turold's study.

A point of light, falling through the shattered panel of the closed door, pierced the vague gloom of the passage and hovered on the door of the bedroom opposite — the room into which the dead man had been carried.

Barrant entered the study and looked around him. It was intolerably dirty and neglected; everything was covered with a thick grey dust. Barrant walked over to the clock and regarded it attentively.

What a rascally fat face that moon had! It must have seen some queer sights in old houses during its two hundred years of life. Strange that those old clockmakers could make clocks to last so long, but couldn't keep their own life-springs running half the time! The moral verse was curious enough. Why should a man who spent half his lifetime putting together a clock presume to tell his fellow creatures to make the most of the passing hour?

His reflections took a more practical turn. The clock was the sole witness to the time of the murder. There were two other clocks in Flint House, but nobody had thought of looking at them when the crime was discovered. Barrant regarded that as a regrettable oversight. It was always important to know the exact time when a murder was committed. Thalassa said that the hood clock was going and kept excellent time, but the value of that secondary testimony was impaired by the fact that Thalassa might not be telling the truth. On the other hand, there was certain presumptive evidence which suggested that he was. It was a proved fact that Mr. and Mrs. Pendleton and Dr. Ravenshaw left the doctor's house in a motor-car for Flint House not later than half-past nine on the night of the murder. Assuming that they covered the journey across the moors in five or six minutes and occupied another five minutes in getting upstairs and breaking in the door, the testimony of the hood clock seemed correct, because Dr. Ravenshaw said death had just taken place, and he and the doctor who made the post-mortem examination were both agreed that Robert Turold could not have lived many minutes after he was shot. Therefore the presumptive evidence seemed to determine the time of death accurately enough.

But that was only a minor phase of the mystery. The real problem was the hidden connection between the clock and the murder. What had brought the clock down, and why had Robert Turold fallen almost on top of it, his outstretched hands resting on the dial? The complete elucidation of the mystery lay behind the obscurity in which these two points were shrouded. To find the answer to them was the surest and quickest way of reconciling all the contradictory facts of the case. But Barrant racked his brains for the reason in vain.

He examined the room. There was a leather-topped writing-table with drawers, several cabinets filled with manuscripts and papers, some walnut chairs with carved legs, and a tall deep bookcase filled with dreary-looking books. His eyes wandered over the titles of the volumes. They also belonged to a bygone period—a melancholy accumulation of works as dead as their writers. Two whole shelves were occupied with the numbers of a forgotten periodical which claimed to give "ample details of the unhappy difference between Queen Caroline of Great Britain and her consort George the Fourth." Barrant wondered idly why human nature was always so interested in the washing of dirty linen. Above these was ranged a row of published sermons. Barrant's eye roamed higher and fell on a fat sturdy volume wedged in between some slimmer books. The title of this book was "Clocks of All Periods." Clocks!

He reached for the volume and placed it on the table. A cursory glance through the pages conveyed the suggestion that it contained more information about clocks than was worth acquiring or writing down. There was a chapter on water clocks, to begin with: "Known to the Egyptians and the Holy Land." Barrant turned the leaves. "The Ancient Chinese used a smouldering wick as timekeeper." Barrant shook his head impatiently. "King Alfred's supposed device of measuring Time by Candles—a Myth." Would to heaven his invention of juries was a myth, too. Scotland Yard would get on much better without them. "A Lamp-clock was another Simple and Ingenious Design." How intolerably long-winded the writer was. What had he to say about hood clocks? "Very few of the Early Clocks had Dials. The Device was generally a Mechanical Figure which struck the Hour on a Bell." Evidently the forerunner of the devilish alarum clock. "Early clockmakers—Old English monks as Clockmakers." The pages flowed rapidly through Barrant's fingers. "Introduction of Minute Hand Marks—Period of Clocks Showing Tides—Longfaced Clocks." Ah, here it was at last—"Hood Clocks."

He began to read the chapter with interest, but as he was about to turn the first page the silence of the room was broken by a faint cackling laugh—an elfin sound which died away instantly. He looked up, startled. His surprise was not lessened at the sight of Mrs. Thalassa watching him from the open doorway. She entered on tiptoe, with a strange air of caution, examining him with restless eyes.

"I heard you," she mumbled. "I saw you go upstairs. Mr. Thalassa was out, and I was afraid to go to the door. I've been playing patience, and it won't come out."

She showed her apron full of small cards. She placed them on the table, and arranged them in rows.

A new idea came into Barrant's mind as he looked at her. If the poor creature had recovered sufficient wits to take to her cards again she might be coaxed to recall what she had seen on the night of the murder. He drew near her. "Can I help you?" he said.

She nodded sideways at him like a child—a child with withered face and grey hair.

Together they bent over the cards. A gull flashed past the window with a scream, as though it had seen them and was repelled at the strange sight.

"Only kings can go into vacant spaces," murmured Barrant's companion, intent on the game.

The result of the game was inconclusive. A king remained surrounded by small cards, like a real monarch overwhelmed by the rabble on May Day. Mrs. Thalassa's eyes strayed mournfully over the rows, then she gathered up the cards and shuffled them again.

"Do you know any other games of patience?" Barrant asked.

She shook her head.

"Then this is the game you were playing on that night?"

"What night?" she whispered.

"The night Mr. Turold was killed."

"I don't want to think of that—it frightens me."

She remembered, then! Her face went grey, but her eyes were alert, watching his.

"Listen to me"—he spoke very gently—"I want to help you get rid of your fear and terror, but to do so I must talk to you about that night. Do you understand?"

The kindness in his voice seemed to reach her feeble consciousness, and she looked at him earnestly.

"Will you try and recollect?"

She seemed to search his eyes for courage, and gave a trembling nod.

"What time was it when you heard the crash upstairs? Think well."

She seemed to make an effort to remember. "I don't know," she said at last.

"Think again. You were playing patience—the game you have just shown me?"

Her eyes turned to the cards on the table. "Yes," she said.

"What time did you commence—can you think?"

She shook her head. "I seem to remember it was half-past eight by the kitchen clock when I started my last game. I was alone in the kitchen then. The game was just coming out when I heard a crash—"

She broke off suddenly with a painful sigh and a frightened glance at the hood clock on the wall.

"One game!" Barrant glanced at his watch with an air of mistrust. "You mean two, don't you?"

Her eyes returned to his. She shook her head with a rapid tremulous motion. "No!" she exclaimed excitedly. "One, only one!"

Barrant cast another glance at his watch, which he Still held in his hand. "You are quite sure you did not play two?" he persisted, with a puzzled glance.

"No, no—one!" She sprang to her feet excitedly.

"Very well—one," acquiesced Barrant soothingly. "One. Go on."

But his effort to calm her came too late. She cast a wild and fearful glance at the wall behind her, as if there was something there which frightened her.

"How it rings—how it rings!" Her indistinct utterance grew louder. "Yes, Jasper, I hear. Yes, sir, I'm coming. Where's the supper tray?"

"Don't be afraid, Mrs. Thalassa," said Barrant, approaching her, but she backed hurriedly away towards the door.

"Coming with the supper tray—coming with the supper tray.... What's that? Ah-h-h-h-h!"

Her disjointed mutterings ended in a shrill scream which went ringing through the stillness and seemed to linger in the room after she had disappeared. Barrant heard her muttering and laughing as she descended the stairs.

The sounds died away into a silence so absolute as to suggest the impression of a universe suddenly stricken dumb. Barrant crossed the room to the window, where he stood looking out, deep in thought.

What was the meaning of it all — of this latest scene in particular? The game of patience so tempestuously concluded had occupied half-an-hour. He had noted the time. Yet Mrs. Thalassa insisted she had played only one game after half-past eight on the night of the murder. If he dared accept such a computation of time an unimagined possibility in the case stood revealed. But — a demented woman. "A parable in the mouth of a fool." Perhaps it was because she was a fool that he had stumbled on this revelation. She lacked the wit to lie about it.

If so —

His eyes, straying incuriously over the outstretched panorama of sea and cliffs beneath the window, fell upon a man's outline scaling the cliff path near the Moon Rock. Disturbed in his meditations, Barrant watched the climber. He reached the top and appeared in full view on the bare summit of the cliffs. Barrant stared down upon him, amazed beyond measure. The advancing figure was Charles Turold.

Chapter XXX

Barrant hastened from the room downstairs to the front door. From the open doorway he saw Charles Turold advancing across the rocks in the direction of the house, and he ran swiftly down the gravel path to intercept him.

Charles looked up and came on as if there was nothing to turn back for. His clear glance dwelt on the figure by the gate without fear—with seeming gratification. Barrant was amazed. He had been prepared for an attempt at flight, but not this welcoming look. Never before had he known a man show joy at the prospect of arrest. The experience was so disturbing that he went across the intervening space to meet Charles, and laid a hand upon his arm.

"I suppose you know you are wanted by the police?" he said.

"I am aware of it," was the quiet reply. "I was going to give myself up."

"Did you come back to Cornwall for that purpose?" asked the detective, shooting another puzzled glance at him.

"I came back to try and discover the truth."

"About what?"

"About my uncle's death."

"And have you discovered it?"

"I have."

Barrant did not understand the young man's attitude, or the tone of heartfelt relief in which he uttered these words, but he felt that the conversation in its present form had gone far enough.

"Do you propose to tell me the truth?" he asked, with a slight cynical emphasis on the last word.

"I do."

Barrant's surprise kept him silent for a moment, but when he spoke he was very incisive—

"In that case it is my duty to warn you—"

"There is no need to warn me," Charles quickly interrupted. "I know. Any statement I make will be taken down and used against me. That's the formula, isn't it, or something to that effect? Let us go into the house—my story will take some time in the telling."

He made this request as a right rather than a favour, and Barrant found himself turning in at the gate with him. In silence they walked to the house, and it was Charles Turold who led the way to the sitting-room.

"It was here it began," he murmured, glancing round the deserted apartment, "and it seems fitting that the truth should be brought to light in the same place."

"Provided that it is the truth," commented his companion.

Charles did not reply. They had been standing face to face, but he now drew a chair to the table and sat down. Barrant walked to the door and locked it before seating himself beside him.

"You can begin as soon as you like," he said.

"I think I had better tell you about my own actions, first of all, on that night," said Charles, after a brief silence. "It will clear the way for what follows. I was up here that night—the night of the murder."

"I know that much," was Barrant's cold comment.

"You suspected it—you did not know it," Charles quickly rejoined.

He remained profoundly silent for a moment, as if meditating his words, and then plunged into his tale.

The account of his own visit to Flint House on the night of the murder he related with details withheld from Sisily. The visit was the outcome of a quarrel between father and son over Robert Turold's announcement about his wife's previous marriage. Charles was shocked by his uncle's decision to make the story public, and had wandered about the cliffs until dark trying to decide what to do. Ultimately he returned home and asked his father to use his influence with his brother to keep the secret in the family. His father called him a fool for suggesting such a thing, declined to offend his brother or blast his own prospects by such damned quixotic nonsense. On this Charles had announced his intention of seeing his uncle and telling him he would leave England immediately and forever unless the scandal was kept quiet. That made his father angry, and they quarrelled violently. Charles cut the quarrel short by flinging out of the house in the rain, to carry out his intention of interviewing his uncle. He walked across the moors to Flint House. The front door was open, the downstairs portion of the house in darkness, and his uncle lying upstairs in his study—dead.

He hurried over all this as of small importance in the deeper significance of Thalassa's story. That was to him the great thing—the wonderful discovery which was to clear Sisily and put everything right. He believed that the plan which had brought him to Cornwall was working splendidly. The chance encounter with the detective was really providential—a speeding up, a saving of valuable time.

The possibility of disbelief did not dawn upon him. He overlooked that his listener was also his custodian and judge—the suspicious arbiter of a belated story told by one whose own actions were in the highest degree suspicious. His overburdened mind forgot these things in the excitement of hope. He talked with the candour and freedom of one young man confiding in another. When he had finished he looked at his companion expectantly, but Barrant's eyes were coldly official.

"A strange story!" he said.

"A true one," Charles eagerly rejoined. "Thalassa has been walking along the coast ever since in the expectation of finding this man. He will kill him if he meets him."

It was Barrant's lot to listen to many strange stories which were always true, according to the narrators, but generally they caused him to feel ashamed of the poverty of human invention. He was not immediately concerned to discover whether Thalassa's story was true or false, or whether it had been concocted between him and Charles with the object of deceiving the authorities. The consideration of that infamous brownfaced scoundrel's confession could be postponed—if it had ever been made. The present business was with Charles Turold. There was something infernally mysterious in his unexpected reappearance in that spot. He had gone to London when he disappeared—he admitted that. What had brought him back? To see Thalassa, as he said, in order to try and get at the truth? Nonsense! He—Barrant—was not simple enough to believe that. What then?

Barrant was not prepared to supply a ready answer to that question. But his trained ear had detected many gaps in the young man's own narrative which, filled in, might give it. Turold knew more than he had said—he was keeping things back. Again—what things? Behind him stood the shadowy figure of the girl and her unexplained flight. Barrant's instinct told him that Charles was shielding her. He turned to the task of endeavouring to reach the truth.

"Let's go back a bit," he said casually. "You've left one or two points in your own story unexplained. What about the key?"

"The key?" Charles started slightly. "You mean—"

"I mean the key of the room upstairs. You said you found the key in the passage outside. You must have locked the door after you and taken it away with you."

"I did," replied the young man, in some hesitation.

"For what reason?"

Charles realized that he was on very thin ice. In his intense preoccupation with Thalassa's story he had forgotten that his own impulsive actions on that night must be construed as proof of his own guilt or bear too literal interpretation of having been done to shield Sisily. He saw that he was in a position of extraordinary difficulty.

"I was hardly conscious of what I was doing, at the time," he said.

"You took the key away with you?"

Charles nodded with the feeling that the ice was cracking beneath him.

"And how did it get back into the room afterwards?"

Charles paused to consider his reply, but the detective supplied it.

"The inference is fairly obvious," he said. "The key was found inside the study after the locked door was burst open. It was your father who found it, on the floor. At least, he pretended to find it there. It was your father who started the suicide theory." He paused, then added in a smooth reflective voice, "Really, the whole thing was very ingenious. It reflects much credit on both of you."

Charles spoke with an air of sudden decision.

"My father did these things to shield me," he said. "I did not want to reveal that, but I see that concealment will only direct unmerited suspicion to him. When I returned from Flint House that night I let myself in with my latchkey and went straight to my bedroom. My clothes were wet through, and I lit a fire in my room to dry them. As I was spreading them out in front of the blaze the key of the study dropped out of the waistcoat pocket on to the floor. I had forgotten all about it till then. I picked it up and placed it on the mantel-piece.

"Some time after I was aroused by my father entering the room. He had come to tell me of my uncle's death—the news had just arrived from Flint House. His face was very white. 'Your uncle has been found dead—shot in his study,' he said. I had jumped up when he came in and was standing in the centre of the room. As he spoke his eyes travelled past me to my wet clothes in front of the fire, and then returned to my face with a strange expression. 'Did you go to Flint House?' he asked sharply. I could only nod. 'And did you see him—your uncle?' was his next question. On that, I told him the truth—told him what I had found. I told him about locking the door, and showed him the key on the mantel-piece. He slipped it in his pocket, then turned and gave me a terrible look. 'I am going over to Flint House,' he said, 'but you had better stay here.' And he left the room."

"What time did you reach Flint House that night?" asked Barrant.

Charles Turold realized that the critical moment had come. He had foreseen it when he saw the detective standing at the gate of Flint House. The relation of Thalassa's story to Barrant had carried with it the inevitable admission that Sisily was at Flint House on the night of her father's death. The point Charles had to decide was whether he should divulge the additional information that he had seen her leave Flint House with Thalassa on that night. As he covered the space which intervened between him and Barrant waiting at the gate, he decided that the moment had come to tell all he knew.

"I know now that it couldn't have been much after half-past eight," he said in reply to Barrant's question.

"Did you see Miss Turold there?"

"I was coming to that. I was standing outside, considering what I would say to my uncle, when the door opened and she and Thalassa came out."

"Did you not speak to them?"

"I went to do so, but they disappeared in the darkness of the moors before I could reach them. I hastened after them, but I got off the road track and wandered about the moors for nearly half an hour before I could find my way back to Flint House."

"And found the door open and your uncle lying dead upstairs?"

"Yes."

"Why have you not come forward with this story before?"

"How could I expect any one to believe a story which sounds improbable in my own ears? Even my father refused to believe it—then, or afterwards."

"Still, you might have cleared Miss Turold on the question of time. There was the stopped clock, you know. You reached Flint House shortly after half-past eight, and went upstairs thirty minutes later."

Charles Turold was subtle enough to see that this remark covered more than a trap. It suggested that Barrant discredited the whole of his story. The hood clock in the dead man's study had pointed to half-past nine on the night he was killed. Thalassa's story, as it stood, proved that Sisily must have left the house long before then. But Charles's story threw suspicion back on to Sisily by suggesting that the police had been misled about the time of the murder, which must have been committed at least half an hour earlier than they assumed. Charles did not attempt to point out this supposed flaw in the detective's reasoning. He confined himself to a reply which was a strict statement of fact, so far as it went.

"Until I heard Thalassa's story to-day I had no idea of the time of my own arrival at Flint House on that night," he said.

"The clock found lying on the floor upstairs was stopped at half-past nine," remarked Barrant with a reflective air, as though turning over all the facts in his mind. "According to the story told you by Thalassa, he and Miss Turold left the house shortly after half-past eight. Thalassa could not have returned until after half-past nine. He found the house in darkness, his wife lying unconscious in the kitchen, and his master dead upstairs. Thalassa, retracting his previous statement that he was not out of Flint House that night, for the first time tells of some mysterious avenger who, he thinks, killed Robert Turold while he was out of the house with Miss Turold. Thalassa now suggests (if I understand you rightly) that this man Remington, wronged by Robert Turold many years before, was lurking outside in the darkness, and seized the opportunity of Thalassa's absence to enter the house and murder the man who had wronged him. Have I got it right?"

"Yes," said Charles, "you have it right."

"The story rests on Thalassa's bare statement, and Thalassa is a facile liar." Barrant's tone was scornful.

"He is not lying now," returned Charles, "and there is more than his bare statement to support his story. Thalassa found his master cowering upstairs with fear in his study shortly before he met his death. He then told Thalassa he had heard Remington's footsteps outside. Thalassa laughed at him, but undoubtedly Remington was out there, waiting for his opportunity, which he took as soon as he saw Thalassa leave the house. If I had not followed Thalassa and Miss Turold I might have seen him."

"It's rather a pity you didn't." Barrant's tone was not free from irony. "For then you might have secured the proof which at present the story lacks."

"There are other proofs," Charles earnestly continued. "There were the marks on my uncle's arm, and the letter he wrote to his lawyer under the influence of the terror in which Thalassa found him—the fear caused by overhearing Remington's footsteps. Thalassa posted that letter."

"Did he tell you so?" asked Barrant quickly. Then, as Charles remained silent, he went on—

"How did you find out about the marks on your uncle's arm?"

Charles hesitated before replying in a low voice—

"I paid a visit to Flint House on the night after the murder."

"For what purpose?"

"To see if I could find out anything which might throw light on the mystery. I got in through a window and went upstairs. I saw the marks ... then."

"Did you discover anything else?"

"No; the dog started to bark, and I left as quickly as I could."

"I see."

Barrant's voice was non-committal, followed after a pause by a quick change of tone.

"I shall investigate this story later," he said coldly. "Meantime—"

"Why not investigate it immediately?" asked Charles in a disappointed voice. "Thalassa will be back directly, or I can take you down to the cliffs were I left him."

Barrant was reminded of the flight of time. It would be as well to remove Charles before Thalassa returned. Time enough for Thalassa's story later! At that moment it seemed to Barrant that the final solution of the mystery was almost in his hands. Mrs. Thalassa had been wiser than he. The single game of patience suggested the solution of the problem of the time. It did more than that. It seemed to provide the key of the greater problem of Charles Turold's actions on that night. He had endeavoured to shield Sisily by altering the hands of the clock. The rest, for the present, must remain mere conjecture. One more question he essayed—

"Can you tell me where Miss Turold is to be found?"

"I know, but I am not going to tell you."

Barrant's eye rested on Charles.

"You must come with me," he said.

Charles nodded. Despairingly he reflected that the interview had not turned out as he expected. There were other means, and he must be patient.

And Sisily? There was anguish in that thought.

Chapter XXXI

With a beating heart Sisily gained the shelter of her room and locked the door, her eyes glancing quickly around her. She did not expect to see anything there, but she had reached the stage of instinctive terror when one fears lurking shadows, unexpected noises, or an imagined alteration in the contour of familiar things. There was nothing in the room to alarm her, and her thoughts flew back to the face of the man she had seen in the street outside. The owner of the face had leered at first, and then his glance hardened into suspicion as he looked. When she hurried past him he had shifted his position to stare at her by the light of the street lamp. Had he followed her? That was the question she could not answer. She had heard footsteps behind her in the dark street, horrible stealthy footsteps which had caused terror to rush over her like a flood, and sent her flying along the street to her one haven. As she ran she had felt a touching faith in the security of her room, if she could reach it. Out there, in the open street, it had seemed impregnable, like a fortress.

Now as she sat there she had a revulsion of feeling. The room was not safe, the house was not safe. Not now. She had been very imprudent. She had run straight home to her hiding-place, her only refuge. Why had she not waited to make sure that she was followed? Then she could have slipped away in a different direction until she had evaded pursuit, and returned to her room afterwards. She had been very foolish.

She approached her window and gazed down, but could discern nothing in the darkness. She tried to shake off her fear, telling herself that it was imagination. But her mind remained full of misgivings, and her inner consciousness peopled the obscurity of the street below with lurking figures.

Weariness overcame her. She retired from the window and laid down on her bed, not to sleep, but to think. Her fright had turned her mind temporarily from the contemplation of a greater disaster. That was the arrest of Charles Turold. She had learnt the news from an evening paper which she had bought at the corner of the street. The announcement was very brief, merely stating that he had been arrested in Cornwall. The guarded significance of the information was not lost upon her. Charles had been captured on his way back to her, and her agonized heart whispered that she was responsible for his fate.

Bitterly she now blamed herself for having let him go on the quest. She hardly asked herself whether it had succeeded or failed, perhaps because she had subconsciously accepted the view that Thalassa, after all, had nothing to tell. Nor did she think of the calamity which had again overtaken her love. The effect of her original renunciation was still strong within her, and Charles's discovery of her and her promise to him had not really altered her attitude. His finding her, and their subsequent conversation in the room below, bore an air of the strangest unreality to her, as if she had been merely an actor in a stirring scene which did not actually affect her. Some subtle inward voice told her that these things did not matter to her.

It was part of a feeling which she had always within her — the sense of living under the shadow of some dark destiny which would not be mitigated or withheld. It was a strange point of view for one so young, but it had been hers ever since she remembered anything. The tragedy and the shame which had come into her life recently had found her, as it were, waiting. She regarded them merely as the partial fulfilment of the unescapable thing which had been prepared for her before she was born, and had dogged her lonely footsteps since childhood. In the isolated circumstances of her life and upbringings it was not strange, perhaps, that she had such imaginings.

She had loved Charles Turold with all the strength of a passionate solitary nature, and it was this feeling or instinct of fatality which had given her the strength to renounce him. Indeed, it seemed to her that that inseparable companion of her inmost thoughts had prompted her to linger outside the door at Flint House on this afternoon so that she should overhear her father's words — catch that sinister fragment of a sentence which compelled her to refuse the love of Charles until she had learnt the truth. She could not listen to him with that secret half-guessed. And, the full truth known, no other course was open to her save renunciation.

She had not wavered. Sometimes, in the vain way of the young heart seeking for happiness, she found herself wishing that she had not listened at the door to those few words which sent her back to Flint House that awful night to learn the truth from her father, or, at least, had not acted upon them. The words she overheard had not told her much, and she might have tried to forget them. But she thrust that thought from her like an evil thing. She would have hated herself if she had followed that course and found out the truth of her birth afterwards, deeming herself unworthy of the love of one who had been ready to sacrifice everything for her sake. No! It was better, far better, that she should know.

She had not thought of suspicion falling on herself. Her youth and inexperience, borne upward on the lofty wings of sacrifice, had not foreseen the damning significance which might gather round her secret visit to Flint House and her subsequent disappearance. Not even when she heard of her father's death had the folly of her contemplated action dawned on her. Her dreamy unpractical temperament, keyed up to the great act of abnegation, had not paused to consider what the consequences might be to herself.

Lying there in the darkness of her room, she recalled how that revelation had been made to her. It was the first night after her arrival in London, in the drawing-room of a private hotel near Russell Square, where she had intended staying for a few days while she sought for some kind of employment. There was a group of women seated round the fireplace, talking. She was seated by herself some distance away, turning over the leaves of a magazine, when a loud remark by one of the speakers startled her into an attitude of listening fear. "Have you read about this Cornwall murder?" The words, cold and distinct, had broken into her sad reflections like a stone dropped from a great height. They had gone on talking without looking at her, and she had listened intently, masking her conscious features with the open magazine. It was well that she did. They discussed the murder in animated tones. The strangest case! ... A great title ... the Turrald title ... to be heard before the House of Lords next week ... and now the claimant was murdered ... he was very wealthy, too. Thus they talked; then the first voice, which seemed to dominate all the others, broke in: "It was thought to be suicide at first, but I see by tonight's paper that his daughter is suspected. She has disappeared, and is supposed to have fled to London. What are girls coming to—always shooting somebody or somebody shooting them! It's the war, I suppose...."

The shock of that double disclosure had been almost too much to bear. Till then she had not known that her father had been murdered, much less that she was suspected of killing him. Dizziness had swept over her. Things seemed to spin round her, yet she saw them rotating with a kind of dreadful distinctness—the false smiling faces of the women, the furniture, a cat blinking on the hearthrug, an empty coffee cup on a small table. One stout lady, enthroned on a pile of red and blue cushions, sailed round and round on a sofa with the preposterous repetition and tragic reality of a fat woman on a roundabout. Then the circling faces and furniture vanished. She swayed with the sensation of growing darkness, and had the oddest fancy that the break of the waves on Cornish cliffs was sounding in her ears. She was dreamily inhaling the sea air....

She had pulled herself sharply together. She had something of her father's tenacity and courage in her composition, and that had nerved her to face the ordeal and saved her from giving herself away. The darkness lightened, the electric lights danced dizzily back into view, and the room became stationary once more. With an effort at calmness she rose from her seat and sought her room, and next morning she left the house. Henceforth her lot was one of furtive movement and concealment.

As she lay there, staring open-eyed into the darkness, her thoughts slipped back to the night of her visit to Flint House in a vain effort to recollect some overlooked incident which might throw light on her father's mysterious death. There was one thing over which she had frequently puzzled without arriving at any interpretation of it. She thought of it now. She saw herself stealing from her father's room with the sound of his last awful words ringing through her being. Beneath, near the foot of the staircase, she could see Thalassa waiting, the glow of the tiny hall light falling on his stern listening face. She was walking along the passage to go to him when some impulse impelled her to glance through a window which looked out on the moors and the rocks near the house.

Her eyes had fallen on a shape, shrouded in the obscurity of the rocks not far from the window, which seemed to have some semblance to the motionless figure of a man. She had stood there for a moment, glancing down intently, but it had not stirred. If it had human semblance, it seemed to be carved in stone. She came to the conclusion that she was mistaken. Experience had taught her what strange shapes the rocks took after nightfall. With another fleeting glance she had hurried downstairs, and from the house.

She thought about it now without arriving at any conclusion as to what it was that she had seen so indistinctly — whether man or rock. Charles had been up there that night, but it was not Charles. This figure or rock was on the other side of the house.

Stupor descended gradually on her tired brain like the coming of darkness, and she fell into sleep—the first rest that had visited her since she learnt of Charles's arrest. But her slumber was disturbed by dreams. She dreamt that she was back in Cornwall, sitting on her old perch at the foot of the cliffs, looking at the Moon Rock. The face in the Rock was watching her, as it had always watched her, but this time with a dreadful sneer which she had never seen before. It frightened her so that she moaned and tossed uneasily, and awoke with a cry, shaking with terror.

As she reached out her hand for the matches by the bedside to light the gas, the sound of the front door-bell pealed through the house. Sisily sprang up, her eyes seeking to pierce the darkness, her ears listening intently. Who could it be? She was alone in the house. Mrs. Johns had gone to one of her spiritualistic meetings, and was not likely to be home until late. Besides, she had her own key, with which she always let herself in. She crept cautiously to the window and strained her eyes downward. She was just able to catch a glimpse of two vague figures underneath in the darkness. The light of the street lamp glinted on something one of them was wearing on his head. It was a policeman's helmet.

The terror of the hunted took possession of her. She sought to remain calm; her trembling lips essayed a sentence of a prayer. But it was no use. She was too young for philosophy or Christian resignation. Terror shook her with massive jaws. She did not want to be caught, to be put in prison, to be killed. She wandered aimlessly about the room like a trapped creature. She must escape—she would escape!

With a great effort she calmed herself to reflect—to calculate if there was any chance of getting away. She esteemed it fortunate that she had not lit the gas in her room. The whole house was in darkness. The policeman might think there was nobody in, and go away. But she dared not reckon on that.

There came another and louder ring of the bell downstairs.

Again she crept to the window and looked down. The policeman and the other man were conferring in a murmur which reached her ears. The policeman stepped back into the garden path and scanned the darkened windows of the house. She shrank back from the window.

The ring was followed by the sound of knocking at the front door— knocking heavy and prolonged, which reverberated solemnly through the silent house. Then once more there was silence.

In her ignorance of the methods of the law she wondered wildly whether the next step would be to break in the door and search the house. Terror shook her again at this thought, scorched her with burning breath. She would escape—she must. But how? Her fingernails pierced the palms of her hands as she vainly tried to think out a way. Should she hide somewhere? She rejected that plan as impracticable. The back way? But there was no outlet—only a small garden abutting on other back gardens. There was a dark side street only a few houses away. If she could only reach it....

She stood quite motionless, expecting the knocking to start again. But it did not. She thought she heard the shuffle of feet and husky whispers in the garden path underneath, but she could not be sure of that. What were they doing? Why were they so silent? "Suppose they got in through the window?" she whispered to herself. Her soul died within her at that thought. She tried to assure herself that the windows were locked, but her staring eyes peopled the invisible staircase with creeping figures. The darkness grew intense and terrifying, like a rushing black torrent flowing over her head. She was alone, in an empty world ... The torrent ceased, and the darkness took the form of a great sable wing, moving, flapping, seeking to enfold her. She put up her hands to ward it off.

At that instant a sharp and decisive sound reached her. It was the click of a shut gate. As she recognized the sound a new thought came to her—a hope, when hope seemed gone. She stepped noiselessly to the window and looked down. She was just in time to catch a glimpse of two retreating figures revealed in dark contour beneath the rays of the street lamp. The next moment they passed out of sight.

They had gone! But they would return—she felt sure of that. She must get away at once before they did—run out of the door and make for the side street.

She listened for a moment longer. There was no sound anywhere now. The house was lapped in absolute quietness. She felt for her hat, and calming her nerves with a desperate effort, stole quickly from the room and downstairs. As she stood in the silent hall, facing the closed door, she again thought she heard whisperings. She recoiled in fear, wondering if they were outside, waiting. It was her worst ordeal yet. Then desperation conquered her terror. Her trembling fingers pulled back the bolt, and she issued forth.

There was no one there to check her flight. The streets seemed empty. Without turning her head she ran past the houses which intervened between her and the side street. She gained it, and turned into its friendly darkness. She was as free as a bird again, for the moment.

A kind of exultation seized her at this unexpected deliverance from her adventure, but that mood passed as she reflected upon her present position. She had left the house without her few belongings, and what was far worse, without her money, which she kept in a hand-bag locked up in her small case in the bedroom she had just left.

She had not a penny in the world, and she dared not go back.

That was not the moment to reflect upon the grimness of her situation. The sound of approaching footsteps shaped her fears of capture into renewed action. She walked rapidly away.

The time was near midnight, and the streets were almost empty. She kept her way along dark obscure streets, shunning the lighted thoroughfares. She had no settled plan in her mind, except to keep on. Hers was the instinct of the hunted creature for darkness and obscurity. Her fevered spirit hurried her along, spurring her with the menace of an imprisonment which was worse than the cramped horror of the grave. In the grave there was no consciousness of the weight of the earth above, but in prison, held like an animal, watched by horrible men, beating despairing hands against locked doors — ah, no, no! Her free young body and soul revolted with nausea at the thought. Death would be better than that. She walked still more rapidly.

With that possibility impending she shrank from any chance contact with passers-by, turning into side streets to avoid any one she saw coming. Once, a policeman, appearing unexpectedly out of the shadows, set her heart beating wildly, but he passed by without looking at her.

It grew later, and the streets became quite deserted. She had been walking for more than an hour when she noticed that the houses were scattered, with open spaces now and then, and a bracing freshness in the air which suggested that she was getting away from where the herds of London slept, into open spaces. For some obscure reason this made her nervous, and she turned back. After a while London closed in on her again, but this time in a more squalid quarter, a wilderness of dirty narrow streets, where even in the darkness the debasing marks and odours of squalid poverty were perceptible in the endless rows of houses which seemed to crowd in upon her. She came to a bridge and crossed it into an area of gaunt and darkened factories. Here, strange nocturnal noises and sights frightened her. She saw shadowy forms, and heard rough voices on a wharf in the blackness of the river beneath her, followed by a woman's scream. She ran when she heard that — ran along the riverside till she came to another bridge, which she recrossed. She found herself in a quieter and better part of London, where the streets were wide and well-kept, and she slackened her pace into a walk again.

The night wore on like eternity, with immeasurable slowness yet incredible swiftness. She had been walking for hours, and yet she had no feeling of fatigue. She seemed to move through the streets without any effort of her own. Towards the morning she was carried along with a complete absence of bodily sensation, as if she had been in very truth one of those disembodied spirits of Mrs. Johns' spirit world, driven through the solitude of the ages by the implacable decree of some incalculable malignant force called immortality. She felt as though centuries of time had rolled over her head when the murk of the lowering sky lightened, and the London dawn was born, naked and grey.

The dawn brought London to life with a speed which was in the nature of a miracle. From the appearance of the first workers to the flocking of the streets, was, as it were, but a moment. The 'buses and trams commenced running, and shops opened. Sisily found herself walking along Holborn, where the thickening crowds jostled her as she walked. But she did not care for that now, nor did she seek the comparative seclusion of the side streets. Her fear of capture had passed away, and her only feeling was impenetrable isolation and loneliness. The people who were passing had no more existence to her than if they had been a troop of ghosts. She had the sensation of belonging to another world and could not have communicated with them if she had wished. But the spirit which had sustained her during the night disappeared with the clamorous advance of the day. She became in an instant conscious of the grievous pangs of a body which seemed to have been flung back to her in a damaged state. It ached all over. Her head throbbed with a dull buzzing sound, and she was so tired that she could hardly stand. She felt as if she must lie down—in the street, anywhere. And she was tormented by thirst. But she still kept on.

She found herself, after a while, by one of those little backwaters which are the salvation of strangers to London: a green railed square, with trees and fountains, and a quiet pavement where a street artist was drawing bright pictures with crayons. An old four-wheeler was moored in the gutter by the entrance, the horse munching in the depths of a nose-bag, the elderly driver reclining against the side of the cab, smoking and watching the pavement artist.

Sisily entered the empty square to rest herself. As she sat there on one of the wooden seats the full misery of her situation came home to her, and she asked herself anxiously what she was to do. She had nowhere to go, and no money to buy food or shelter—nothing in the world that she could call her own except the clothes she was wearing. They were the coat and skirt she had put on to come to London, and she noticed with feminine concern that the dark cloth showed disreputable stains and splashes of her night's exposure. Hastily she took her handkerchief from her pocket to remove the tell tale marks. As she did so a bit of buff cardboard fluttered on to the gravel at her feet. She stooped and picked it up. It was the return half of her ticket to Cornwall.

The remembrance of her arrival at Paddington revived in her as she looked at it—the fright she had had when the ticket collector caught her by the arm to return half of the whole ticket she had given up. She had put the ticket in the pocket of her jacket and never thought of it again. Had Fate decreed her original mistake of taking a return ticket when she needed only a single one? She was at that moment inclined to think so.

The question of its use was decided as soon as she saw it. The ticket would take her back to Cornwall and Thalassa. Thalassa would help and shield her.

The gilt hands of a church clock opposite the square pointed to half-past eight. She knew that the morning express for Cornwall started shortly after ten, but she did not know what part of London she was in or the direction of Paddington. Animated by a new hope, she left her seat and asked the cabman for directions.

The cabman looked at her with a ruminating eye. That eye, with unfathomable perspicacity, seemed to pry into her empty pockets and pierce her penniless state. He did not ask her if she wanted to be driven there, but intimated with a shake of his grey head that Paddington was a goodish walk. Then he gave her directions for finding it—implicit and repeated directions, as though his all-seeing eye had also divined that she was a stranger to the ways of London.

Sisily thanked him and turned away, repeating his directions so that she should not have to ask anybody else. First to the right, second to the left, along Tottenham Court Road to Oxford Street, up Oxford Street to Edgeware Road, down Edgeware Road to Praed Street—so it ran. She followed them carefully, and found herself on Paddington station a quarter of an hour before the departure of the express.

She entered a third-class carriage, but sat in a corner seat, longing for the train to move out. The minutes dragged slowly, and passengers kept thronging in. All sorts of people seemed to have business in Cornwall at that late season of the year. They came hurrying along in groups looking for vacant compartments. Sisily kept an eager eye upon the late arrivals, hoping that they would pass by her compartment. By some miraculous chance she was left undisturbed until almost starting time, then a group of fat women dashed along the platform with the celerity of fear, and crowded ponderously in. The next moment the train began to slip away from the station, and was soon rushing into the open country at high speed.

Of the details of that journey she knew nothing at all. She sat staring out of the window, her thoughts racing faster than the train. The events of the last few days receded from her mental vision like the flying houses and fields outside the carriage window, fading into some remote distance of her mind. Relief swelled in her heart as the train rushed west and London was left farther and farther behind. Something within her seemed to sing piercingly for joy, as though she had been a strange wild bird escaping from captivity to wing her way westward to the open spaces by the sea. London had frightened her. Its crowded vastness had suffocated her, its indifference had appalled her. She had felt so hopelessly alone there; far lonelier than she had ever been in Cornwall or Norfolk. Nature could be brutal, but never indifferent. She could be friendly—sometimes. The sea and the sky had whispered loving greetings to her, but not London. There was nothing but a hideous and blank indifference there. She was glad to get away—away from the endless rows of shops and houses, from the unceasing throngs of indifferent people, back to the lonely moors of Cornwall, to look down from the rocks at the sea, and breathe the keen gusty air.

As the journey advanced and the train swept farther west she became dull, languid, almost inert. Lack of food and the previous night's exposure induced in her a feeling of giddiness which at times had in it something of the nature of delirium. In this state her mind turned persistently to Thalassa, and the object of her return to him. She was struggling towards him, up great heights, under a nightmare burden. She seemed to see him standing there with his hands outstretched, ready to lift the burden off her shoulders if she could only reach him. Then she was back in the kitchen at Flint House, watching him bending over his lamps, listening to the wicked old song he used to sing—

"The devil and me we went away to sea,
In the old brig 'Lizbeth-Jane....'"

The train caught up the refrain and thundered it into her tired head … "Went away to sea, went away to sea, In the old brig 'Lizbeth-Jane." And, listening to it, she fell into a dazed slumber.

She awoke with a start to find that it was getting dusk and the train was running smoothly through South Cornwall. As she looked out of the window a grey corpse of a hill seemed to rise out of the sea. It was Mount St. Michael. Then she caught a glimpse of Carn Brea and the purple moors. The people in the carriage began to collect light luggage and put on coats and wraps. The next moment the train came to a standstill at Penzance station.

She clung to the safety of the throng in passing through the barrier, fearing most the St. Fair wagonette which might be drawn up outside. She was not known in Penzance, but the driver of the wagonette might recognize her. But Mr. Crows, indifferent to shillings, had not yet arrived. Sisily hurried past a group scanning the distant heights for the gaunt outline of the descending cab, like shipwrecked mariners on the look-out for a sail.

She reached the moor road by a short cut through the back part of the town, and set out for Flint House in the velvety shadows of the early gloaming.

It had been raining, but the rain had ceased. The sun, hidden through a long grey day, shone with dying brilliance in a patch of horizon blue, gilding the wet road, and making the wayside puddles glitter like mirrors. A soddened little bird twittered joyfully in the hedge, casting a round black eye at her as she passed. The moors, carpeted with purple, stretched all around her, glistening, wet, beautiful.

In the train she had felt hungry and tired, with burning head and cold limbs. As she walked these feelings wore off, and were replaced by a feeling of upliftment which was magical in its change. Her misery and her burden dropped from her. The softness of the moors was beneath her feet, and a sweet wind touched her lips and cheeks with a breath which was a caress. The plaintive distant cry of a gull reached her like a greeting. The solitude of Cornwall surrounded her.

When she reached the cross-roads she struck out across the moors. Before her, at no great distance, she could see the swelling mountainous reaches of green water breaking on the rocks in a long white line of foam, and the dark outline of Flint House clinging to the dizzy summit of the black broken cliffs.

Her false strength failed her suddenly as she neared her journey's end. The house loomed dimly before her tired vision in the fast gathering darkness. She stumbled with faltering steps round the side of the house to the kitchen door, and turned the handle. It was locked. She knocked loudly.

As in a vision she saw the white furtive face of Mrs. Thalassa peering out at her from the window, and her fluttering hands pressed against the glass, as though to thrust her back. Sisily rushed to the window.

"Let me in!" she cried. "It is I—Sisily."

The window opened suddenly, and Mrs. Thalassa stood there looking out at her like a small grey ghost—a ghost with watchful glittering eyes.

"Go away—go away," she whispered with a cunning glance. "Quick! They're looking for you—they'll catch you."

Sisily's heart went cold within her. "Where is Thalassa?" she faltered. "Send him to me—tell him I have come back." Her eyes travelled vainly around the gloom of the empty kitchen in search of him.

"He's gone—gone away!"

"Gone? Oh, no, no! Don't say that. Where has he gone?"

"I don't know. He went away. He's not coming back." She shook her head angrily, with a wild gleam in her eye. "You go away, too, or they'll catch you—the police. They come every night to look for you."

She cast another cunning look at the girl, and shut down the window. Sisily could see her reaching up and fumbling with the lock. Thalassa gone! Despair clutched her with iron hands, and held her fast. She glanced up at the window of her father's study, and thought she saw the dead man there, his stern face looking coldly down upon her. She turned away shuddering. Where could she go? She had nowhere to go, and she knew her strength would not carry her much farther.

She plunged blindly into the shelter of the great rocks near the house. She found herself wandering among them like a being in a dream. Then complete unconsciousness overtook her, and she sank down.

When she came to herself again night had descended and a storm was brewing. She sat up wonderingly and looked around her, indifferent to the rain which had commenced to fall on her uncovered head. Gradually remembrance came back to her. She saw that she was lying on the great slab of basalt which overhung the Moon Rock. She could hear the beat of the sea far beneath her, but she felt no fear. She was not conscious of her body or limbs — of nothing but a burning brain, and wide-open eyes which gazed out into the darkness and stillness around her.

As she looked it seemed to her startled imagination that the masses of rocks which littered the edge of the cliff moved closer to each other, starting out of the shadows into monstrous grotesque life, then circling round her in a strange and dizzy whirl. It was as though the old Cornish giants had come back to life for a corybantic dance with the demirips of their race — dancing to the music of the sea sucking and gurgling into the caves at the base of the cliffs. With swimming eyes Sisily watched them careering and pirouetting around her. Faster and faster they went, advancing, retreating, bending clumsily, then wavering, toppling, reeling, like giants well drunk. A great stone fell into the sea with a splash, as if dislodged by a giant foot. As though that signalled the cockcrow of their glee, the dancers stopped in listening attitudes, and sank back into rocks once more.

Sisily turned her eyes weakly from the slumbering rocks to the hills. The light of a coming moon behind them showed the outline of the granite pillars and stone altars of the Druids, where they had once sought to appease their savage gods, like the Israelites of old. Sisily had often meditated by these places of sacrifice, trying to picture the scene. Now, as she looked, it was enacted before her eyes. A red light brooded on one of the hills, growing brighter and brighter. Brutish shaggy figures came out of the darkness, dragging a youth to the altar. Sisily saw him distinctly. He was naked, with a beautiful face, haggard and white, and was bound with cords. Suddenly he freed himself, and dashed down the slope into the darkness. He was pursued and brought back, and the cries of his pursuers mingled with an appalling scream for help which seemed to float down the mountain side to where she lay, filling the silent air with echoes.

This scene, too, faded away, and the beams of the rising moon, now beginning to show over the hill-tops, formed in her mind the mirage of a beautiful day — one of those exquisite days which Nature produces at long intervals. Sisily saw a blue sky, sunlight like burnished silver, green fields and clear pools in which everything was reflected … a slumbrous perfect day, with drowsy cattle knee-deep in grass, bees, and floating butterflies, and the shrill notes of happy birds.

Once more the tangled loom of her fevered brain wove a new picture. She was back in her bedroom at Flint House, looking down at the graven face of the Moon Rock. As she looked, a great hand seemed to come out of the sea and beckon to her. The summons was one she dare not disobey. She left her bed, crept downstairs in the darkness, out to the edge of the cliff, and looked down. The face of the Moon Rock was watching her intently. She thought it called her name.

Ah, what was that cry? She came to her senses, startled, and looked fearfully round her. She was alone on the cliffs, above the Moon Rock, and she could hear the sea hissing at its base. But what else had she heard? Had somebody called her name? It was still very dark. To the south the light of the Lizard stabbed the black sky with a white flaming finger as if seeking to pierce the darkness of eternity. Nearer, the red light of the Wolf rock gleamed — a warning to passing souls flying southward from England to eternal bliss to fly high above the rock where the spirit dog lay howling in wait. Had the cry come from there?

"Sisily! Sisily!"

No. It was not the howl of the Wolf dog that she had heard. That was her own name. She crept closer to the edge of the cliff and looked down into the sea — down at the Moon Rock. The old Cornish legend of the drowned love came back to her. Was Charles dead? and calling her to him? She would go to him gladly. She had loved him in life, and if he wanted her in death she would go to him.

She clutched a broken spur of rock on the brink and looked down to where the sea bored round the black sides of the Moon Rock. She could see her own pool too, lying peaceful and calm in the encircling arm of the rock. In her delirium she struggled to her feet and started to climb down the face of the cliff.

Chapter XXXII

The wind tapped angrily at the windows of Flint House, the rain fell stealthily, the sea made a droning uneasy sound. The fire which burnt on the kitchen hearth was a poor one, a sullen thing of green boughs and coal which refused to harmonize, but spluttered and fizzed angrily. The coal smouldered blackly, but sometimes cracked with a startling report. When this happened, a crooked bough sticking up in the middle of the fire, like a curved fang, would jump out on to the hearthstone as though frightened by the noise.

Thalassa sat on one side of the fire, his wife on the other. Her eyes were rapt and vacant; he sat with frowning brows, deep in thought. Robert Turold's dog crouched in the circle of the glow with amber eyes fixed on the old man's face as if he were a god, and Thalassa lived up to one of the attributes of divinity by not deigning to give his worshipper a sign. Occasionally the dog lifted a wistful supplicating paw, dropping it again in dejection when it passed unregarded.

Presently Thalassa got up and went to a cupboard in the corner. From some hidden receptacle he extracted a coil of ship's tobacco and a wooden pipe shaped into a negro's head, with little beads for eyes, such as may be bought for a few pence in shops near the London docks. He returned to his seat, filled the pipe, lit it with a burning bough, and fell to smoking with lingering whiffs, gazing into the fire with dark gleaming eyes as motionless as the glinting beads in the negro's carved head.

The clock on the mantel-piece ticked steadily away in the silence. The dog, with a brute recognition of the unsatisfactory nature of spiritual aspiration, descended to the care of his own affairs, and scratched for fleas which knew no other world than his hind-quarters.

"Go away, go away! You mustn't come in here!"

The shrill voice of Mrs. Thalassa broke the silence like a cracked bell, shattering her husband's meditations, and causing the dog to spring to his feet. Thalassa looked at her angrily. She was making mysterious motions with her hands, as if expostulating with some phantom of her thoughts, muttering and shaking her head rapidly. Her husband stared across in silence for a moment.

"By God! she doesn't improve with age," he growled; then, louder: "What's the matter with you? What are you making that noise for?"

The question went unheeded. To his astonishment she sprang to her feet with a kind of grotesque vivacity, and, darting over to the window, began gesticulating again with an angry persistency, as if to some one outside.

Thalassa left his seat and went to the window also. His wife had ceased her gestures, and stood still listening and watching. Thalassa pulled back the blind, and looked out. The moor and rocks were draped in black, and the only sounds which reached him were the disconsolate wail of the wind and the savage break of the sea on the rocks below. He looked at his wife. She had started tossing her hands again at some spectral invisible thing in the shadowy night. She was quite mad—there could be no doubt of that. He endeavoured to lead her back to her seat by the fireside, but she broke away from him with surprising strength, and again her voice rang out—

"Go away ... go away! You can't come in. I won't let you in. You're a wicked girl, Miss Sisily, and I won't let you in. You killed your father, and you'd like to kill me, but I'll keep you locked out. Go away!" Her voice rose to a screech.

The blood rushed to Thalassa's head as he listened to these words. He understood quite suddenly—this was not a demented raving. Sisily had been there—she had come back to him in her fear—and she had been driven away. He turned to his wife and caught her up in his great arms, shaking her violently, as one shakes a child. The sight was terrible and absurd, but there was no one to witness it but the dog, who circled round and round in yelping excitement, as though the scene was enacted for his benefit alone.

"Has Miss Sisily been here?"

The question thundered out in the empty silence. Mrs. Thalassa crouched like a preposterous hunched-up doll on the seat where her husband had flung her, looking up at him with stupid eyes, but not speaking. He approached her again.

"Speak, woman, speak, or I'll strangle you."

She backed away, whimpering with fear. "No, no, Jasper, leave me alone."

"Has Miss Sisily been here?"

The sight of those long outstretched hands, by their menace to her life, seemed to restore her reason. "Yes," she mumbled.

"When?"

"This evening—before dark—when you were out."

"And you wouldn't let her in?"

"No."

"How did you know it was her?"

"She knocked at the door, and I looked out of the window."

"Did you see which way she went?"

"Over by the cliffs, where she used to go."

Thalassa repeated these last words mechanically. Anger possessed him, but apprehension stirred in his heart. Sisily had trusted him, she had come back to him, and he had failed her. That had been at six o'clock, and it was now nine. Three hours, and there had been a storm. Where was she? Had she been out in the storm?

He searched in the cupboard for a lantern, lit it, and made for the door, followed by the dog. As he flung open the door the wind rushed in with such force that it beat him back, and the candle in the lantern flickered and lengthened like a naked flame. He fought his way out furiously, slamming the door behind him.

Outside, the rocks crouched in the darkness in nameless shapes. Thalassa prowled among them, struggling desperately with the wind, telling himself that she was safe—yes, by God, she was safe. Of course she wouldn't stay on the rocks in that storm. She would seek shelter. "Where?" asked something within him mockingly, "Where would she dare go, except to you?" He stood still to reflect. "She might go to Dr. Ravenshaw's," he said aloud, as though answering an unseen but real questioner. "Fool!" came the reply, "you know she would not go to Dr. Ravenshaw's. She would not dare." And fear gripped his heart coldly.

He stumbled on again, bruising and cutting his limbs among the rocks. As he went he kept calling her name—"Miss Sisily" at first, and then, as his fear grew stronger, "Sisily, Sisily!" The wind wailed back to him, but that was all.

He stopped again to reflect. It was useless looking for her in the darkness. He could do nothing until the moon was up. The sky was already beginning to brighten with the coming light. So he stood where he was, waiting.

In a quarter of an hour the moon showed above the horizon, slurred through the rain, like a great drowned face. Higher and higher it rose until the black curtain lifted off the moors, and the light shimmered on little pools left after the rain, made fretwork in the shadows of the rocks, and fell upon the surface of the sea. And as the moon rose the hideous uproar of wind and sea began to die away.

Thalassa threw down the lantern, and resumed his search. Carefully he explored in and out among the rude masses of rock, beating farther and farther away from the house, cautiously skirting the perpendicular edge of the cliffs, looking over, and backing away again. His wider cast brought him at length to where the Moon Rock rose from the turmoil of the sea. He crept on hands and knees to the bald face of the cliff, and looked down.

By the light of the moon something caught his eye far below—something white and small, showing distinctly against the black glistening base of the Moon Rock. He could not discern what it was, but a nameless terror seized him, and his jaw dropped as he crouched there, gazing. Then he scrambled to his feet with a wild cry, and made for the path down the cliffs to the pool. It was some distance from where he was, but there was no shorter way. He rushed recklessly along the cliff edge till he reached it, and climbed down.

It was there he found her.

She was lying limp and motionless on the edge of the pool, and the receding tide was still lapping over the shelf of the rock where the sea had flung her.

Thalassa dropped on his knees beside her. "Sisily, Sisily!" he cried hoarsely—"It's me—Thalassa!"

He stooped over her, calling her repeatedly, but she did not reply. Her face showed still and white in the moonlight. He unfastened the front of her dress, and put his hard hand on her soft flesh, but he could not feel her heart beating. He lifted her tenderly in his arms, and she lay against his body inert and cold, her wet head resting on his shoulder. Thus he started the ascent of the cliff.

A giant's strength still lurked in his ageing frame. It was well for him that it did. He had only his feet to depend upon in that long slippery ascent, and the wind tugged at him angrily, as if anxious to jerk him off the path into the sea. But he fought his way up with his burden, though his body was swaying and his head was dizzy when he reached the top.

He did not stop for a moment. Still holding her fast he set out, not for Flint House, but to the churchtown. Dizzy, panting, and staggering, he struggled on across the moors, and as he walked he listened anxiously for any sound from the inanimate form in his arms.

But she lay still and motionless against his breast.

On he went until he reached the churchtown, and made his way up the empty street to Dr. Ravenshaw's house. He turned in the garden gate, and beat with his heavy boot against the closed door.

Chapter XXXIII

Some one stirred within, and a ray of light in the fanlight grew bright as footsteps in the passage drew near. The door opened, and showed the figure of Dr. Ravenshaw holding in his hand a lighted lamp which shone upon Thalassa and the dripping figure in his arms. The doctor looked down from the doorstep in silent surprise, then stepped quickly back from the threshold and opened the surgery door, holding the lamp high to guide Thalassa in.

"There — on the couch," he said, placing the lamp on the table. "What has happened?"

"Miss Sisily fell over the cliffs by the Moon Rock. I found her and carried her up, and brought her straight here."

The doctor's quick glance was a professional tribute to the strength of a frame capable of performing such a feat. He turned his attention to Sisily, bending over her and feeling her pulse. With a sharp exclamation he dropped her wrist and tore open the front of her dress, placing his hand on her heart. With his other hand he took up his stethoscope from the table.

"Bring that lamp closer — quick!" he cried.

Thalassa lifted the lamp from the table and stood beside him. The yellow glow of the lamp enveloped the livid bluish features of Sisily and the stooping form with the stethoscope. The instrument of silver and rubber held miraculous possibilities of life and death to Thalassa. He watched it anxiously — directed the light upon it. The shape on the couch remained motionless.

Thalassa's gaze wandered from the stethoscope to Dr. Ravenshaw. The doctor's bent neck showed white between the top of his shirt and the grey hair above it. He was wearing no collar, so he must have been going to bed — when the knock came. Thalassa's eyes dwelt on the exposed flesh with a steady yet wondering contemplation. The lamp in his hand wavered slightly.

Dr. Ravenshaw rose to his feet, oblivious of the man who was staring at his neck from behind. His downward glance rested on Sisily's face, and his eyes were grave. He turned away and walked out of the room, but returned almost immediately with a small mirror.

"Hold the lamp higher," he said to Thalassa. "I want the light to fall right on her face. Higher still—so."

He fell on his knees by the couch and held the mirrored side of the glass to Sisily's lips. The lamp, held aloft, illumined his face as well as hers. His features were set and rigid.

Thalassa stood still, his eyes brooding on the sharp outline of the bent mask. A vague idea, startling and terrible, was magnifying itself in his mind. Once his glance wandered to Ravenshaw's neck, then returned with growing fixity to his face, seen at closer range than he had ever beheld it. In the vivid light the elemental lines beneath the changes of time took on a strange resemblance to a face he had known in the distant past. A spectral being seemed to rise from the dead and resume life in the kneeling body of Dr. Ravenshaw.

Involuntarily he stepped back, and the likeness vanished in the added distance. The veil of the past was dropped again. He could see nothing now but the commonplace whiskered face of an elderly Cornish doctor bending over the inanimate form on the couch. Again the lamp shook slightly.

"What are you doing with that light?" said Ravenshaw peevishly. "Cannot you hold it steady? Bring it closer, man—closer than that. Now, hold it there."

In the nearer vision the elemental lines of a forgotten face again confronted Thalassa beneath the flabby contours of age. It was like looking at a familiar outline covered by a mask—a transparent mask. He stood stock still with uplifted lamp, like a man in a trance, but his eyes never left Dr. Ravenshaw's face.

Some minutes passed silently before Dr. Ravenshaw withdrew the mirror from Sisily's lips. He turned it over and looked closely at the surface of the glass. The man behind him stared over his shoulder. Their eyes met in the mirror, and held for a moment fascinated. In that brief space of time the revelation and recognition were completed. Dr. Ravenshaw's glance was the first to break away. The hard brown eyes watching him followed the direction of his view to a pair of spectacles resting on the table. Thalassa understood the intention, and harshly forestalled it.

"No use to put on your glasses now," he said. "I recognize ye, and I've seen that damned scar on your neck."

He put the lamp back on the table, and his hand went towards his belt. Ravenshaw understood the motion and checked it with a gesture.

"No need for that, either, Thalassa. There are other things to think about."

Thalassa's hand dropped to his side. "You're right," he muttered. "Get on with your doctoring."

"No—not now," answered Ravenshaw sadly. "It's no use. She is dead."

"Dead!" Thalassa stood overwhelmed. Silently he surveyed the slight recumbent form on the couch, his moving lips seemed to be counting the drops which dripped from her clinging garments on to the carpet. "Dead, did ye say? Why, I carried her here—brought her across the moors to you." His voice trembled. "Can't ye do nothing?"

"No—not now. It is too late."

Thalassa's eyes rested attentively on the other's face. Ravenshaw's complete acquiescence in death as an unalterable fact stung his untutored feelings by its calmness. "Dead!" he repeated fiercely. "Then you've got that to pay for now—Remington."

"Pay? Oh, yes, I'll pay—make payment in full," was the reply, delivered with a bitter look. "But not to you."

"To think I shouldn't a' known ye!" Thalassa spoke like a man in a dream.

"After all these years? After what I suffered alone on that island—through you and Turold? You'd hardly have known me if you'd met me six months afterwards instead of thirty years. Robert Turold didn't know me. Nobody knew me."

Thalassa's eyes still dwelt upon him with the unwilling look of a man compelled to gaze upon an evocation of the dead.

"Where did you get to—that night?" he quavered. "I could a' sworn—could a' taken Bible oath—"

"That you and that other scoundrel had killed me? I've no doubt. But it so happened that I was saved—miraculously and unfortunately. I fell on to a projecting spur of stone or rock not far down, which caught and held me. By the light of the moon I saw you come along the ridge to look for me. You were almost close enough for me to push you into that infernal sulphur lake where you hoped I had gone. You turned back in time—fortunately for yourself."

Thalassa kept his gaze upon him with the meditating intentness of one trying to learn anew a face so greatly altered by the awful changes of the years. His great brown hands, hanging loosely at his sides, clenched and opened rapidly with a quickness of action which had something vaguely menacing in it.

"I know your eyes now," he mumbled. "With the glasses on, you're different. That's why ye wore them, I suppose. Turold heered ye that night you killed 'un. He knew your footstep—or thought he did. I laughed at him. A' would to God A'mighty I'd hearkened to him, and then I might a' catched you. How did ye get away from the island?"

Ravenshaw raised his head to reply, then stood mute, in a listening attitude. Outside the window the sound of footsteps crunched the gravel walk, and approached the house. Thalassa heard and listened too. The crunching ceased, and there was a knock at the door. Thalassa looked questioningly at Ravenshaw, who nodded in the direction of the door.

"Open it," he said. Thalassa hesitated. His eyes sought the couch. "Yes, in here," said Ravenshaw understandingly. "We shall want witnesses."

Thalassa went to the door and opened it.

A man's voice in the darkness asked for Dr. Ravenshaw, and the owner of the voice stepped quickly inside at Thalassa's invitation. The visitor peered at the tall figure in the unlighted passage. "Is it you, Thalassa?" he said hesitatingly, and Thalassa recognized the voice of Austin Turold. The voice went on: "Tell me—"

"In there." Thalassa jerked his head towards the gleam falling through the partly open surgery door. "He wants you." He walked ahead and pushed the door open. Austin Turold followed, but started back as he looked within. Then he entered, his eyes dwelling on the shadowy outline on the couch in the corner.

"What has happened at Flint House, Ravenshaw? Now—to-night, I mean." He spoke shakily. "There's a story abroad of Thalassa having been seen carrying a figure through the churchtown and entering your house. Has somebody fallen off the cliffs—been drowned? Is that it?" He stepped quickly across to the couch, and, looking down, as swiftly recoiled. "What does this mean?" he hoarsely cried.

Ravenshaw did not speak.

"Miss Sisily fell over the cliffs by the Moon Rock," said Thalassa. "I went down for her, but it was too late. She was drowned."

Austin's look sought Ravenshaw's, who nodded in confirmation.

"More horror—more misery," whispered Austin. A shudder ran through him. "I do not understand," he said simply. "Thalassa?"

"It's not for me to explain," said Thalassa quickly.

"You then, Ravenshaw."

Ravenshaw spoke slowly.

"They have been looking for the man who killed Robert Turold—your brother. Well, I am he."

"You!" gasped Austin, in a choking voice. "What do you mean? I do not understand you. My son has been arrested."

"He has been arrested wrongly, then. It is I—I alone am responsible."

Austin groped for his glasses like a man suddenly enveloped in darkness. His fingers closed on them and adjusted them on the bridge of his nose. Through them he surveyed the man before him with close attention.

"Ravenshaw," he said gravely, "either you are mad or I am. Did not my sister call here to see you on the night my brother was killed, and did you not go with her to Flint House and break into my brother's room? How, then, could you have killed Robert? Besides, I saw my son at Penzance to-day. He tells me he is innocent, and that the murderer is a man whom Robert and Thalassa robbed and wounded on a lonely island thirty years ago, and left there for dead, as they thought. What does it all mean?"

"These things can all be explained," replied Ravenshaw. "It is a long story. Sit down, and I will tell it to you."

"Not here—not here!" replied Austin unsteadily. His glance went to the corner of the room and the tranquil figure on the couch. He hid his face for a moment in his hands, then said: "Let us go to another room."

Ravenshaw made a sad gesture of acquiescence. "Come," he said quietly, lifting the lamp from the table. The other two followed him, and Thalassa closed the surgery door gently behind them. The doctor led them into a sitting-room opposite, where they seated themselves. After a moment's silence Ravenshaw began to speak in low controlled tones which gave no indication of the state of his feelings.

"You know all about this island part of the story," he said, inquiringly, "how your brother and Remington, seeking their fortune together, came to be there?"

Austin Turold nodded.

"I am Remington," pursued the other. "I will take up the story from that point—it will save time."

Again Austin Turold assented with a nod. There was neither anger nor resentment in his glance. The look which rested on the speaker was one of unmixed amazement.

Chapter XXXIV

"I will pass over as briefly as possible what happened after I was left behind in that horrible place. By the light of the moon I saw them go — from the ridge I saw them put out to sea. I watched them until the boat was a mere speck on the luminous waters, and finally vanished from sight. I was left alone, a desperately wounded man, on an arid sulphurous island, without food or water.

"When I was sure the boat had gone I returned to our camping place, and bound my wounds with strips torn off my shirt. Then I fell asleep. I must have developed fever in my slumber, for I have no clear recollections of the next few days. I vaguely recall roaming like a demented being among those solitudes in search of water, and finding a boiling spring. The water, when cooled, was drinkable. I suppose that saved my life. For food, there was shell-fish and mutton-bird eggs, with no lack of boiling water to cook them.

"I lived there so long that I forgot the flight of time. I became a wild man — a mere shaggy animal, living, eating, and sleeping like a beast.

"I was rescued by a passing steamer at last, rescued without any effort of my own, for I had gone past caring. From the ship they saw me leaping about the naked sides of the volcanic hills like a goat, and they put off a boat. Some lady passengers were badly scared when I was brought aboard — and no wonder. They were very kind to me on that ship. She was homeward bound, and brought me to England. I told the captain my story, but I could see that he didn't believe me, so I told nobody else. Not that anybody wanted to know — really. One's misfortunes are never interesting to other people.

"I had a little money left when I landed in England — not much, but sufficient to take me to my wife and support me until I found Robert Turold. I had left my wife living with her parents in a London suburb. Robert Turold and I had both been in love with her before we left England. She loved me, but he had some strange kind of influence over her — the dominance of a strong nature over a weak, I think. Or perhaps it was a more primitive feminine instinct. He was always the strong man — even then — ruthless, determined. It was strange that he should have loved such a gentle timid creature, though that, perhaps, was not so strange as a man like Robert Turold loving any woman. But love her he did.

"She had a great capacity for affection—she was one of those women who have to love, and be loved. Her guileless face, her appealing eyes, seemed to beseech the protection of a masculine shield in a world which has no mercy for the weak. She was born to be guided, to be led. It was my fear of her simple trustful disposition which led me to urge her to marry me secretly before I left England with Turold. Her parents did not favour me, and they wished their daughter to marry well—there was an aunt from whom she had expectations, and the aunt had a prospective husband in view for her. I feared their joint influence. She consented willingly enough; she was easy to persuade—on the eve of our parting. She clung to me weeping—her husband.

"I was to make enough money to return to England to claim her in a year or so—that was the plan. But I had been absent nearly three when I was left on the island. And another twelve months passed before I reached England again. Four years! A long time. Almost any combination of circumstances can be brought about in such a period. People die, marry, or can be forgotten as though they had never existed. It was my lot to be forgotten.

"I hastened to London, to my wife's old home, and learnt that the family no longer lived there. Where had they gone to? The maid who opened the door could not tell me—she did not know. At my request she went for her mistress. The lady of the house came down to me, a tall slender woman, indifferent, but well-bred enough to be polite. She had taken the house from the Bruntons, she said. It was too large for them after their daughter's marriage. It was dusk, and she could not see my face, but she heard my startled exclamation—'Married? To whom?' To a Mr. Turold—a very suitable match. They had been married for some months, and she was expecting a child.

"How she gathered that last piece of information I do not know. Perhaps she and Mrs. Brunton exchanged letters—women write to one another on the slightest pretexts. That thought made me cautious. Fortunately, I had not given my name. I thanked her, and rose to go. She offered to write down the Bruntons' address for me (they had gone to live in the country), but I said I could remember it. And I got away from the house in the gathering darkness without her actually seeing my face—not that it would have mattered much, if she had.

"I thought it all over that night. I visualized readily enough what had happened. Robert Turold, returning to England with some concocted story of my death, had swept her off her feet, caught her on the rebound. He had returned a prosperous man, and doubtless his love-making was reinforced by Alice's worldly parents and the match-making old aunt. The combination was a strong one, and I was supposed to be dead. So she married him, without breathing a word to anybody of her previous secret marriage to me. I realized that at once. She would be too afraid—left to herself. She would tell herself that it wasn't worth while—that nobody need ever know now. I could imagine her twisting her little hands together in apprehension as she faced the problem—our secret—then gradually becoming calmer as something whispered in her ear that it was her secret now, and need not be told. You see, I knew her nature so well. There are many such natures—gentle souls who shrink from responsibility in a world which, sooner or later, generally sees to it that we are compelled to shoulder the burden of our own acts.

"I was not long in making up my mind. I determined to do nothing. I take no special credit to myself for that decision. The marriage with Robert Turold was an accomplished fact, and my belated reappearance upon the scene would have plunged her in unhappiness. She was about to become a mother, too. That weighed with me. I loved her far too well to injure her or her child. It meant letting Robert Turold go free if I remained dead, but there are other things in life besides money and revenge. Fortunately the position from the practical point of view was simplified by the death of my only relative, my uncle, during my absence from England, who had bequeathed his small property to me—not much, but sufficient for my own simple needs.

"I took my uncle's name, the better to conceal my identity, and resumed the medical studies which had been interrupted by my departure from England four years before. When I received my degree I searched for a remote spot where I was not likely to encounter any one who had known me in my past life, and chose this lonely part of the Cornish coast. And here I have remained for thirty years.

"They have not been unhappy years. It was not my disposition to waste my life by hugging the illusions of the past. My days were occupied walking long distances to see my patients scattered at distant intervals on this desolate coast, and my nights I spent in antiquarian and archaeological studies, which were always a favourite pursuit of mine. It was a hobby which earned me some local repute in the course of the years, and was ultimately the means of bringing me face to face with Robert Turold again. That was the last thing in the world I desired to happen. In the early years I used to think of him wedded to my wife, and wonder whether he had succeeded in his great ambition. After a while the memory faded, as most memories do with the passing of the years.

"Then the meeting came—six months ago. I heard Flint House was let, though not to whom. The news did not interest me. But next evening, when I returned from my rounds, my servant met me at the door with the information that the new tenant of Flint House was in the consulting-room waiting to see me.

"I went in. The tall elderly figure sitting there rose at my entrance and said: 'Not a patient, doctor—quite another matter.' I started slightly at the familiar ring to that harsh authoritative voice, but I did not know who he was until he handed me his card. He had already commenced talking about that accursed title as he did so, and he did not notice my agitation. He had come to Cornwall in pursuit of the last pieces of evidence for his family tree, and some local busybody had told him that I was versed in Cornish antiquities and heraldry. That piece of information had brought him to me. He begged for my assistance—my valuable assistance—in elucidating the last scraps of his genealogy from the graves of the past.

"I could have cut him short by laughing aloud—though not in mirth. I had regained my self-command, for I saw that he had not the slightest suspicion to whom he was talking. That in itself was not surprising. I had not recognized him. And how much greater was the change in my own case! Time alters us all in a much less period than thirty years, and there was more than the passage of time. Those months of horrible solitude on that island had changed me into an old man in appearance, with grey hair, and bleared and weak eyes from the sulphur fumes. And Time had made the disguise impenetrable in the thirty added years. I was an old man. My hair and beard were white, and I wore thick glasses. I felt I need be under no apprehension of Robert Turold recognizing me—then, or at any time, unless I was careless.

"His request for my help had a strange fascination for me. There was an uncanny thrill in sitting there within an arm's length of him, meeting his unsuspicious glance, and listening to him with the knowledge that I could have put his plans and ambitions to flight with a single word, and had him begging for mercy. I was in the position of Providence, and withheld my hand, as Providence generally does. My desire to punish Robert Turold had long since died. At sixty, revenge is a small thing. What is human retribution to the ferocity of Time's revenge on us all? Retribution and Justice—these are human catchwords, signifying nothing. What is Justice? Who is to judge when the scales are even? It was easier to comply with his request than arouse suspicion by refusal, but that wasn't what weighed with me. I wanted to see more of him, to win his confidence, if possible. I was curious to know what kind of life he had given the woman for whose sake I had let him go free for thirty years.

"He took a liking to me. My knowledge of ancient Cornish lore proved useful in the final stages of his search—his thirty years' search for a family tree. It was not long before I discovered that he had found no happiness in life. At times his face wore a hunted look—the look of a man who walked his days in fear. His imperfect vision peered out on a darkened world with apprehension, though not of me. In my strange position with him I felt like a ghost permitted to watch, unseen and unsuspected, the travail of a gloomy solitary mind. It was apparent enough, but only to me. My quickened eyes pierced the outward husk and saw within. I thought I had outlived my desire for revenge, but it grew again at the sight of a punishment which was so much more subtle than anything I could have planned. Death would have put his restless soul to sleep, granted him eternal respite. The sufferings of the spirit were a living torment. His was a strange case. His lifelong pursuit of a single idea, his restricted consciousness of one image, had made him morbid, lonely, introspective. And so the past had revisited him, darkening and disquieting his mind. He feared shadows, he was haunted by footsteps.

"Footsteps! I learnt that when he consulted me for sleeplessness. He told me he used to lie awake at night, imagining he heard footsteps pattering on the rocks outside. I knew well enough whose footsteps he was haunted by. I imagined him lying there in that lonely house, sweating with horror, listening … listening. He asked me once, did I believe in ghosts? I told him no, but I said I'd known a case of man returning to life long after he was supposed to be dead. I related the story—one which had come under my observation as a medical man. He listened with gnawing lip and pale face, and from my window afterwards I saw him striding home across the moors, glancing backwards in the dusk.

"It was his own fault that he ever heard those footsteps in the way he feared. He did not play the game, according to our poor conception of what the game is. If he had done so he would have been quite safe from me. But there are some things too shocking to be contemplated, even in the worst of our kind. A man does not give away a woman—that is one of the rules. Robert Turold put a woman to shame in her coffin.

"I had kept out of her way, never going to Flint House because I feared her feminine eyes might be too sharp for me. But she fell ill, and Robert Turold asked me to attend her. Refusal was impossible, as there was no other doctor nearer than Penzance.

"She did not recognize me—at first, but the shock I received when I saw her left me almost stunned. I had carried her memory through the years—the image of a pretty slim girl, with brown hair and eyes, and kind of soft vivacity which was her greatest charm. In her place I found, lying there, a withered grey woman with dim eyes and broken spirit. God knows what she had gone through at his hands, but it had destroyed her.

"It was her death-bed. She was worn out in body and spirit, and had no strength to rally. She was weeks dying, but her life was steadily ebbing all that time. It was a kind of slow fever. She was delirious when I first saw her, and delirious or unconscious, with few lucid intervals, until she died. And the jargon of her wandering mind was in reality the outpouring of a tortured soul. It was the title and the family name—always that, and nothing else. She wasn't well-born enough or sufficiently educated to bear the title as his wife—it seemed that that fact had been impressed on her again and again in the long lean years of the search for the family tree. Let her go away … go away somewhere quietly with Sisily, and she would never bother him any more. That was the unceasing burden of her cry, a cry to which I was compelled to listen with a torn heart.

"The reserve, the frame of mind, which I wore like armour in Robert Turold's company I dropped altogether at her bedside. Her lucid intervals were few, but I was not afraid of her recognizing the old Cornish doctor with his muffler, his glasses, his shaggy white hair and beard. The daily sight of her shrunken ageing features reminded me that I had nothing to fear—that Time had effectually disguised us from each other's recognition. We were old, we two. Life had receded from us—what had we to do with its fever, its regrets, its passions and futile joys? The clock had ticked the time away, the fire was dying out, the hearth desolate and cold. I was resigned before, I was resigned then. I did what I could for her, which was little enough. Human progress, such as it is, has been acquired through the spirit. The body defies us—we have no control over it. So she died—mercifully unconscious most of the time—and died, as I had hoped, without the least suspicion of the truth.

"You cannot faintly imagine the shock of Turold's announcement on the day of her burial, to me, who had been so arrogantly certain that the secret was safe. If you remember what took place at Flint House on that occasion you will recall that it was a question from me which brought the truth to light. Your brother's answer awakened my suspicions, and made me determined to find out what he actually knew. He brought out the truth then, as I've no doubt now he intended to do in any case.

"The puzzle to me was the exact extent of his knowledge. He knew two things for certain. One was that I had married Alice before leaving England,

and the other was that I was still alive. But he obviously did not know that I was Remington. How had he found out the two facts? I guessed that the woman he believed to be his wife had revealed the secret of her earlier marriage on her death-bed, but the other was a problem which I could not solve. Nor did I try to. When I reached home I went mad. The calmness, the self-repression of thirty years, vanished in an instant in the monstrous infamy of that disclosure. There was something too horribly sinister in the character of a man who could be driven by ambition to make such a disclosure without regret, almost without hesitation. He sacrificed and put to shame two gentle creatures at the beck of his implacable mania. For the title he had forfeited tenderness, pity, decency—all the human attributes—with a brazen and unashamed face. That man walked the earth alone. By that act he set himself apart, defying all laws, all feeling—everything.

"As I grew calmer I reflected that he could not defy me. I could bring him tumbling from his lofty perch with a few words. He might brazen out his attitude to the whole world, but not to me. What was more, I could dictate to him—could keep his mouth shut with a threat of reviving the past, of putting him on his trial for robbery and attempted murder thirty years before.

"I determined to do it—to see him and reveal myself, and let him know that my own course of action would be decided by his. If he chose to keep silent, he would have nothing to fear from me.

"I set out across the moors in the darkness. It was raining, and I walked fast until Flint House loomed out of the blackness before me. Then I paused to consider my course of action. I was about to thwart a madman with a fixed idea, in a lonely house where he had in his service another man who could be depended on to make common cause against me when he knew the truth. I was not afraid of Robert Turold, but I was of Thalassa. I knew he was strong enough to hurl me through the window into the sea. These elements in the situation called for caution. I crept across the rocks towards the kitchen window. As I did so I thought I saw a figure move among the rocks, and I ran quickly to the narrow lip of cliff which overhangs the sea at the back of the house. There I stood for awhile, but could hear nothing but the sea raging far down beneath me. I came to the conclusion that I had been mistaken. Who was likely to be prowling round Flint House in a storm—except myself? I crept round the side of the house and looked through the kitchen window.

"Thalassa's wife was in the kitchen, alone, with some playing cards spread out on the table in front of her. But before long the door leading into the passage opened, and Thalassa came in. He sat down, but after the lapse of a few minutes he rose from his chair and approached the window. I shrank back into the shadow of a rock, watching him. He stood looking out into the darkness for perhaps five minutes, then I saw him start, turn his head, and go out of the room. I heard the front door open, followed by the sound of footsteps ascending the stairs. A moment later I heard the murmur of voices in Robert Turold's room upstairs.

"I went nearer to try and find out what had happened, but it was no use. I could see a gleam of light in the study window, and could hear Robert Turold's voice mingled with feminine tones, then—silence, followed once more by the sound of an opening door. From my place of concealment I saw two people going down the garden path—Thalassa and a female figure. They passed through the gate and vanished into the darkness of the moors.

"My opportunity had come. I went to the house and tried the front window. It was unlocked, and yielded. I got through, and went quickly upstairs. A light was shining underneath the study door. I opened it, and saw Robert Turold sitting at his table writing with his back towards me.

"At the sight of that atrocious scoundrel sitting there immersed in his shameful project against a woman I had loved, my self-control gave way utterly, completely. I had intended to be calm, to reason with him, to exact my terms with a cold logical brain. I did none of these things. Without a word of warning, before he even knew I was in the room, I sprang on him, clutching him, shaking him in a blind insensate fury till my strength suddenly failed me and left me sick and giddy.

"'I am Remington,' I said—'Jim Remington.' I leaned against the table, panting and exhausted, looking at him. His self-control was something to marvel at. He just sat still, returning my look with cold motionless eyes, no doubt trying to discern the features of the man he had wronged through the film of age. But in spite of his self-control I could see the grey pallor of fear creeping into his face, and he could not keep his lips from trembling. Twice he essayed to speak, but his mouth refused to utter the words. What he did say was strange to me, when he got it out at last. 'I was right'—I heard him whisper, almost to himself—'I knew, I knew.' He repeated those words several times. It was then I saw that his self-control arose from the fact that although he was terrified he did not appear to be so greatly surprised. Surprised he was, but not in the way I had expected. His prime difficulty seemed to be to get out of his head the identity by which he had known me. 'You are Ravenshaw—Dr. Ravenshaw,' he said. 'How can you be Remington?' He brought out this with an effort, like a man trying to shake off an unreasoning horror.

"I had expected him to face it out, to challenge me, perhaps deny all knowledge of my existence. Instead, he merely sat there staring at me with an air of terrified realization, like a person gazing upon the dreadful materialization of an expected phantom. I told him the truth in the fewest possible words, and he listened silently, never removing his eyes from me, the phantom of his past. When I had finished he lay back in his chair, but his eyes stared up at me with a kind of dead look, like half-closed eyes in a coffin. 'I knew that you were rescued from the island,' he said. 'But I thought you were long since dead.'

"That statement surprised me. I asked him how he had learned of it. He told me it was through the medium of an overheard conversation in a London hotel nearly thirty years before. He had gone up to town to see his lawyer, and one of the people at the hotel where he put up happened to be one of the passengers of the *Erechtheus*, the steamer which had rescued me. The man sat at the next table, and Turold heard him tell the story to a friend one night at dinner. It had happened just like that—quite simply, but it was a possibility I had overlooked. Not that it mattered, as it happened, but it would have—if Alice had been with him. Turold, of course, kept his knowledge to himself. He was too cautious to approach the passenger, but he instructed his lawyer to make guarded inquiries at the shipping office of the vessel in order to verify the story. Then he returned home, consumed by anxiety, no doubt, to wait for my reappearance. As the months slipped past and I did not appear, hope revived within him. It appears that he had heard the passenger say that I was a wreck—a physical wreck. That must have been a cheering item in a bad piece of news. I can imagine its growing importance in Turold's mind as the time went on and I made no sign. Finally (and thankfully) he reached the conclusion that I was indeed dead, and that he had nothing more to fear. There was an element of uncertainty about it, though, a lack of definite knowledge. I fancy that was one of the reasons which led him to take Thalassa into his service when he turned up some time later. It was a deep and subtle thing to do. Thalassa was bound to help him against me, if ever I came back.

"The years went on, and he grew quite certain, as any man in his position would, in the circumstances. He forgot all about me. That frame of mind lasted until he came to Cornwall, and then, it seemed, I came back into his life in the strangest way. I haunted him in the spirit, and he never once guessed that I might be there in the flesh. Who can explain this?

"As he spoke of it he looked as though he had a grievance against me, as, perhaps, he had—from his point of view. 'You faded from my mind for twenty years,' he said. 'But here—in Cornwall—your memory began to haunt me. It was your footsteps, principally. I used to fancy you were following me across the moors. Tonight for the first time I actually heard them—heard them above the noise of the storm. They came to my ears clear and sharp, around the house, on the rocks, under the window.' He cast on me an appalled, a hopeless glance. 'Why have you left it so long?' he cried. 'What do you want—now?'

"He positively had no glimmering of my feelings. His fixed idea, like a cancerous growth, had sucked all the healthy life out of him. Hot anger stirred within me again, but I retained control of myself this time. I asked him how he had found out about the earlier marriage, and he told me Alice had babbled something in her delirium—enough to arouse his suspicions. It seemed that he had waited for one of her lucid intervals, and wormed the truth out of her. 'The proofs—of course you've obtained them?' I asked casually. Yes, he had the proofs. He had sent to London for them immediately. I asked him where they were. 'What do you want to know for?' he asked in an agitated voice. I told him quite simply, that he must give me his proofs and tell the members of his family that he had been mistaken—that Alice's first husband had really died before she married him. If he agreed to do that he had nothing farther to fear from me—I would remain dead forever. 'You can destroy proofs, but not facts,' he muttered in reply to this. I told him the facts were never likely to come to light if he entered into a compact of silence.

"He sat for a few moments as if contemplating the alternatives I had placed before him—sat with one hand in his table-drawer, seeking for papers, I thought. He desisted from doing this, and said quite suddenly, 'The proofs are in the clock-case.'

"I had no suspicion. He had once shown me a curious receptacle in the bottom of the clock-case, where he kept papers. I went towards the clock, and was stooping over the drawer in the bottom of the case when I heard a swift footstep behind me. I turned. He was approaching with a revolver. The secret of his disclosure and the open drawer were explained. I suppose I owed my life to his dim sight, which compelled him to come so near.

"I sprang at him, and we struggled. That struggle brought down the clock with a shattering crash. Robert Turold and I were locked in one another's arms, wrestling desperately for the revolver, when I saw the great moon face of the clock flit past my vision like the face of a man taking a header off a pier. The crash startled Robert Turold. His hand loosened, and I got the revolver from him. As I tore it from his fingers it went off, and shot him.

"He backed away from me with a kind of frozen smile, then crumpled up and slid to the floor. I bent over him. He made a slight movement, but I could see that he was dying—that he had only a very few moments to live.

"Coolly and rapidly I reflected. The fall of the clock would be heard downstairs. Flight! There was a chance, if Thalassa had not returned. My other instinct was to secure the proofs first, though they were really useless then. I rummaged in the clock-case, and found a large envelope which I stuffed in my pocket. The face stared up at me; the clock had stopped at a minute to nine. I had an idea—an inspiration. I pulled the long hand down to the hour-half—to half-past nine. If I escaped from the house undiscovered, with only that half-stupid little woman downstairs, I would rush across the moors home—call my servant on some pretext as soon as I got in, and ask her the time. Then I should be quite safe—could defy everybody. Make it ten o'clock, then! No—too long to be safe. It might be discovered.

"It is strange how quickly the brain works when the instinct of self-preservation is aroused. These thoughts flashed through my mind in a kind of mental lightning. In the briefest possible space of time I was on my feet and out of the room. I locked the door on the outside, intending to take the key to defer discovery, but it slipped from my fingers in my haste, and fell in the dark passage. I dared not stop to search, for just then I heard a sound—or thought I did. Panic seized me. I feared I was trapped—my escape cut off. I flung precaution aside and went leaping downstairs to the door. I fumbled for the door-catch in the darkness, flung open the door, and ran out into the night—across the moors and home.

"I had hardly got inside before your sister came with her husband to see me—to beg me to go with her to Flint House and reason with your brother. To reason with him! He was beyond the futility of argument, the folly of retort. I did not want to go—at first. Then it dawned upon me that a kindly fate offered me a providential chance of securing my safety. No suspicion could fall on me if I went back—and found the body.

"And so it turned out. We reached Flint House just at the right moment, for me. I broke into the room and found him—dead. He was not where I had left him. In a last paroxysm he had struggled to his feet and fallen across the clock-case, with the intention, as I shall always believe, of putting back the hand of the clock. I think his dying vision saw me alter it, and his last thought—his last effort—was to thwart my intention to mislead those upon whom would devolve the duty of investigating his death. But death was too quick to allow him to carry out his intention."

The cessation of the speaker's voice was followed by silence. Thalassa had nothing to say—no need for words. Austin Turold could not trust himself to speak. It was not that his cynical philosophy of life failed him at that moment. The eternal staging of the drama was the eternal tragedy of the performers. But he was thinking of his son. He had vision enough to realize that in Sisily's death Charles had lost all. His own hardness of outlook melted at that thought. It crumbled his worldliness to ashes, flooded his heart with vain regret, found utterance at last in the whispered words—

"How am I to tell my son?"

His eyes, dwelling on the door of the inner room, revealed the direction of his thought.